"*I love the way the author developed her characters, and admire the difficult, painful themes and life choices upon which she thoughtfully, elegantly and, at times, humorously touched.*"

—Michele Caprario, Editor.

*To Yvonne Thorpe:*

*Best Wishes Always!*

*Enjoy the read!*

*Augusta G. Trimum*

*3-20-08*

# MEADOWSBROOK

# MEADOWSBROOK

When the Well Runs Dry

*Augusta Grimm*

iUniverse, Inc.
New York  Lincoln  Shanghai

**Meadowsbrook**
**When the Well Runs Dry**

Copyright © 2005, 2006 by Augusta Grimm

All rights reserved. No part of this book may be used or reproduced by any means, graphic, electronic, or mechanical, including photocopying, recording, taping or by any information storage retrieval system without the written permission of the publisher except in the case of brief quotations embodied in critical articles and reviews.

iUniverse books may be ordered through booksellers or by contacting:

iUniverse
2021 Pine Lake Road, Suite 100
Lincoln, NE 68512
www.iuniverse.com
1-800-Authors (1-800-288-4677)

augusta.grimm@comcast.net

augusta@augustagrimm.com

Website page:
www.meadowsbrook.org

ISBN-13: 978-0-595-36079-6 (pbk)
ISBN-13: 978-0-595-80587-7 (cloth)
ISBN-13: 978-0-595-80529-7 (ebk)
ISBN-10: 0-595-36079-3 (pbk)
ISBN-10: 0-595-80587-6 (cloth)
ISBN-10: 0-595-80529-9 (ebk)

Printed in the United States of America

# *Acknowledgements*

I'd like to thank my family and friends for their help. I give special thanks to my daughter LaLanya who exhibited talents I never knew she possessed. Her insight and attention to detail were invaluable. I also want to give special thanks to my editor, Michele Caprario, Freelance Writer and Editor, who shared with me her energy and good vibes, and helped me to keep the faith, throughout the process.

# Meadowsbrook Characters

The Dawson Family
Natalie Dawson—School teacher and seamstress
    Parents—Marcus Dawson, builder, Odessa, homemaker
    Brother—Alan Dawson, married Sweet Hogan, military career
    Grandparents—Conrad and Maude
    Uncle—Percy, brother to Marcus, married to Helene. Daughters Queenie and Sophia

The Mack Family
Tamara Mack—torch singer, married to Tobias Dupree
    Parents—Asha and Obie Mack
    Grandmother—Ginger

The Farrell Family—owners of town's only beauty shop
Elizabeth Farrell
    Son—Dominic
    Parents—Ernestine and Gus Farrell
    Grandmother—Bessie Mae Wanker, midwife
    Violet—married to Joe, sister to Ernestine, Elizabeth's aunt

The Pastures Family—sharecroppers
Georgia Mae Pastures—works in Pharmacy
    Grandparents—Caleb and Sadie Pastures
    Brother—Deacon

### The Lamont Family—landowners, and own the town's mortuary
Shelton Lamont—married to Natalie
    Daughter—Makela
    Parents—Thaddeus and Esther Lamont
    Brother—Greyland, Married to Jozell
    Cousin—Warren Gilliam, married to Della

### The Wade Family—owners of Michael's Market
Lydia Wade—Daughter Kornelia (KoKo)
    Parents—Jake and Tessa Wade
    Lula Hanks—Jake Wade's sister, aunt to Lydia and Tilly
    Tilly—Lydia's sister, married to Virgil Henderson

### Spuds and Jenny Joyride—owners of Spuds' Drugs
    Daughter—Melanie Joyride
    Slick Joyride—Brother to Spuds, father to Brick and Goose

### The Hopper Family—owners of the Fish Kitchen
    Cash "Fats" Hopper
    Parents—Sissy and Tex Hopper

### Billy Hardwood—owner of town Garage
    Married to Neva Pecker

### Doc Hoot Peterson—Head Doctor at Morningstar Hospital
    Wife—Ellie Peterson
    Daughter—Paige Peterson
    Doctor Ely Flack, Surgeon

### The Baraldi Family—owners of the meat packing plant in Baysville
    Vince Baraldi 'the meat man'
    Father—Pete Barali
    Brother—Frank Baraldi

### Other Notable Characters
Della Gilliam—town gossip, married to Warren Gilliam
Carrie Lucas—nurse at Morningstar Hospital, Della's friend
Delano Phillips—school teacher, married to Sunny, also a teacher

Both work at school with Natalie
Reverend Buddy McCord—good-looking, charismatic preacher

# CHAPTER 1

Meadowsbrook, Mississippi, a small picturesque community some sixty or seventy miles south of Memphis, Tennessee, stood right smack in the heart of the delta.

Located on the main artery, Highway 61, the town was surrounded by tall maples, spruces, pines, and big oak trees draped in Spanish moss. The dense foliage kept it almost hidden from the everyday traveler.

Underneath the trees grew wild mushrooms, which many picked and put on the table to compliment meals.

There was also the parasitic mistletoe plant which attached itself to many of the healthy trees and, although poisonous, it was used to cure just about anything. In the wrong hands, however, it was deadly.

A variety of grasses and wild flowers grew along the roadsides. Daisies and poppies were in profusion, and bright yellow dandelions offered their young leaves in spring as a food source. Meadows of clover and alfalfa and fields of young cotton stretched for miles around Meadowsbrook, and vines covered with the plump, juicy blackberries favored in cobblers and pies grew along the railroad tracks.

The townsfolk loved their flowering plants. The familiar white and pink bracts of the small flowering dogwoods graced several yards in springtime, and honeysuckle vines sent their treasured, sweet fragrance drifting through open doors and windows throughout the summer. A canal snaked through the countryside and the town, inviting youngsters to swim and frolic. Though the water seemed peaceful, it was at times treacherous. A nice summer day sometimes turned tragic when a life was claimed by the current.

Summers were insufferably hot, and the heat often caused sickness and sometimes death. Winters were so harsh that folk claimed, jokingly, a man might awaken in the wee hours to find his gonads all but frozen and stuck so far up his scrotum he needed a pitch fork to pull them back into their rightful place. While unknown to most travelers, Meadowsbrook was a haven to blacks who had few options at a time when inequality and discrimination were the norm and signs in every establishment window read, "No Coloreds Allowed."

🍁   🍁   🍁

The town was home to several thousand folk who ranged in color from pasty white to berry black with all shades of tans and browns in between. Most were sharecroppers who often ended up as poor after harvest as when they began. Life was a daily grind for them, and their futures seemed bleak. Yet, somehow, in spite of life's hardships, they managed to persevere.

However, some were fortunate enough to own their land and homes. Although it was not openly discussed, many were class and color conscious, and at times, as uppity and unforgiving as their own oppressors.

There was only one school in the community when two were needed, but the town boasted three churches.

Mount Zion Baptist was at one end of town, the Temple of God Pentecostal at the other, and standing in the center of town, but on the opposite side of the railroad tracks, was Saint Luke Methodist.

The three steeples were easily discernable, and the bells in each belfry, which rang out for Sunday services and in times of distress such as fires or when someone died, could be heard for miles.

Saint Luke Methodist was painted a dark grey, and the other two were white. But all three churches caught the eye with beautiful multicolored stained glass windows.

Dedicated members worked diligently to keep the grounds pristine, and they often kept the inside of the churches cleaner than they kept their own homes.

Church was the main social activity for many. Although each church had its own pastor, services were held at each church on a different Sunday to ensure full attendance at all functions.

❧   ❧   ❧

Michael's Market, a small, white front building, owned by Jake and Tessa Wade, was located on the main thoroughfare along with several other businesses. Two wooden benches secured to the wall on either side of the market's door were places where several men too old and broken to work could loiter. With nothing more to do in life but wait for death, they met and wiled away their time under the green and white striped awning. When they did leave the bench, it was just long enough to take a piss in some nearby darkened, dank corner. Later, returning to the bench, they recalled their past, and lamented their misfortunes to Jake who often came out to chat with them.

Inside the store were two counters one on each side of the room. Tessa worked one and Jake worked the other. Facing the door and near the back of the room was a big, long, glass front refrigerator, which held a variety of meats and cheeses that the locals called the "meat keeper."

As soon as fall arrived, Jake brought out the ancient potbellied stove, set it up in the center of the room and fired it up. At that time the old-timers who continued their daily ritual of warming up the benches, meandered inside. As they huddled around this relic, the warmth radiated through their bones and took the chill from their old gray balls.

On one side of Michael's was "Spuds' Drugs," the town's only pharmacy and soda fountain, which was owned by Spuds Joyride. Next door to the pharmacy was the Fish Kitchen Café, owned by the Hopper family. Their specialty was fried fish. Because of the pool table in the back of the establishment, customers were enticed to come daily and stay a while. Next door to the Café was Ernestine's. Although the shingle read "Ernestine's Beauty Salon," it was also the owner's home.

In summer, Ernestine worked on her back porch. But in winter she worked in her kitchen. Throughout the year, she washed, rolled, straightened, curled and crimped hair, and generally gave Madam Walker's hair products an extreme workout.

The post office, operated by Spuds' wife, Jenny Joyride, was across the railroad tracks. Jenny left no stone unturned. She looked at every piece of mail that came in and was able to tell recipients who had written them a letter even before they retrieved it from their box. She also sold train and Greyhound bus tickets, and knew the destination of anyone who left town.

The jail, located near the railroad tracks and across the street from the post office, was a small one-room white building with bars on all four windows. It was where Sheriff Duncan threatened to put folk who got drunker than he if they didn't toe the line. Of course, that was an empty threat since he never arrested anyone for anything. Like so many in the community, he spent many of his evenings hugging a drink.

Morningstar Hospital was located a short distance from Highway 61 and near the Lamont family's Weeping Willows Funeral Home. Staffed by two exemplary medical practitioners, Dr. Hoot Peterson and Dr. Ely Flack, the hospital was the pride and joy of the community.

Doc Peterson was a tall, thin high yellow man with grey eyes. He laughed a lot, and handled routine problems and day-to-day diagnoses. Only in an emergency did he perform surgery.

Doc Flack, a surgeon, on the other hand, was a short man, as black as a berry and thought he was just as sweet. He was the younger of the two and owned his own practice in Chicago, but came to Meadowsbrook once a month. He would stay for a week and, during that time, would cure with his scalpel what Doc Peterson's pills could not. When someone went in with a belly ache, Doc Flack immediately talked that person into getting his appendix removed. When patients complained of a sore throat, Doc Flack slapped the ether cup on the individual's face and cut out his tonsils. In fact, because of Doc Flack's extreme prevention measures, few folk in Meadowsbrook owned tonsils or appendixes.

The Lavender Lounge, called the "Joint" by most, was located some distance past the railroad tracks, but close to Highway 61. A large white, one-story building and the only reputable place folk gathered to socialize other than church, was known as a hot spot, and was the place to go.

A large elm tree stood in the spacious parking area, hedges lined the walkway, and green and white striped awnings provided gay coverage to the windows and front entrance.

The bar, covered with red imitation leather, was located near the front door. Its matching barstools were seldom empty after sundown. Across from the bar was the bandstand, and between the bar and bandstand was a sizeable dance floor. The large overhead fan, which spun continuously during summer, was a much appreciated fixture.

Farther back, overlooking the canal, was the Bayou Bowl restaurant where proprietor Charlie Fountaine and his wife, Orchid served everything from alligator to frog's legs. Though the food was delicious, the place was best known for entertainment. Well-known musicians traveled long distances to perform at the popular spot, and hordes of fans journeyed just as far to party and dance to their music.

Directly behind the Joint was the Shady Shack Hotel, a twenty-room building, which was usually filled to capacity during spring and summer. It was as important to weary travelers as an oasis to nomads in the middle of a desert.

# CHAPTER 2

Summer 1934. Natalie Dawson, Tamara Mack, Elizabeth Farrell, and Georgia Mae Pastures were best friends who attended the same school, the same church, and spent much of their leisure time together. Their plan was to go to college together, return home and pass their knowledge on to others through teaching.

As the four very young girls stood by and watched still another family climb aboard the northbound train, they renewed their vow. "We cross our hearts and hope to die," they voiced in unison. "We'll *never* leave Meadowsbrook."

They loved Meadowsbrook and they felt this was a nice place to live and, since they were born here they planned to die here, convinced they could work together and make their town an even better place in which to live.

Natalie Dawson was a vibrant young woman with large, bright, hazel eyes, a small slightly upturned nose and full sensual lips set in an angelic face. Her skin, the color of honey, was flawless. Her dark brown hair was long and curly. Her small waistline was accentuated by perfectly formed hips, and her shapely legs made her a striking individual.

She excelled in school and hoped to become a teacher one day, but she also had a passion to create beautiful clothing. At age fourteen she already made clothes for her family, friends, and anyone else interested.

🍁 🍁 🍁

Her best customer was also her best friend, Tamara Mack, who never came with a pattern but always knew what she wanted. As she explained her idea, Natalie sketched until they came up with something stunning.

Considered fast as lightning, Tamara was the buzz about town. The fact that her hair was red, her eyes green, and her skin almost white when both her parents, Asha and Obie, were as dark as hot brewed coffee had little to do with it.

Tamara fascinated most folk because she painted her lips and fingernails a bright red, sported high heel shoes and wore sinfully tight dresses at a time when other girls her age still jumped rope, engaged in hopscotch games, and rode bikes for pleasure.

She had a beautiful voice and often walked into the Lavender Lounge as if she owned it. Entering the Lounge one evening, she planned to ask Charlie Fountaine to let her sing there on weekends. As she approached the bar, he called to her.

"Hey, Tam. How'd you like to sing here on weekends?"

Tamara couldn't believe her ears and wondered if Charlie could read her mind. Turning to his son, Zeke, she asked "Does he mean it?"

"Sure, he means it. Everybody likes to hear you sing. It's business."

🍁 🍁 🍁

By the time Tamara reached puberty, she was an incorrigible tyrant whose acid tongue kept her mother, Asha, in tears, her grandmother, Ginger, voicing threats, and her daddy, Obie, wishing he had finished her off when she was just a baby.

From the time she was born, Asha thought her baby, Tamara, was the prettiest she had ever seen so she doted on the child. Picking her up at first whimper, she constantly cuddled and rocked her, and always bought the child the prettiest clothes she could find.

Regardless how much Obie complained she was spoiling the child, Asha never listened, and often got testy.

It wasn't long before Obie wondered why he let Ginger talk him into the mess. Of course, he knew the answer. He was much better off.

Not only did he have a little money in his pocket, and owned a parcel of land, but he no longer saw the moon and stars through cracks in the house rooftop when he went to bed at night. Best of all he slept next to Asha every night. Even though she treated him like a ghost, he still loved her.

Ginger knew he was sweet on Asha. That's why she came to him when Asha got herself in trouble. He knew Asha had no love for him, but he hoped. If only she'd give me half the love she gave her screaming ass baby, I'd be happy, he thought. But as time passed he thought as long as the baby lived, a fart would get more time in drawers than Asha gave him.

It wasn't until Asha and Ginger left the baby with him one day that he saw things clearly, at least from his point of view. As the child slept, he went into the room and picked up a small decorative pillow from the bed. Staring down at the child, he hesitated momentarily before placing the pretty pillow on the baby's face.

The pressure woke her. Struggling, she tried to turn her little head, but she couldn't move. He watched as she kicked her little legs and flayed her little arms.

Just as the excitement of seeing her struggle coursed through his body, he heard voices. Ginger and Asha returned. Jesus! He felt hot all over. They were on the porch. Throwing the pillow aside, he picked up the baby. Lawdy, he thought. What am I to do? The baby was red as a beet and was gasping for air. And just as Asha and Ginger entered the house, the baby began to cry hysterically.

"What's wrong with my baby?" Asha hollered rushing over and taking the child from him.

"I don't know," he lied. "I was just trying to calm her down."

As she got older, Tamara demanded Asha's undivided attention. When she failed to get it, the girl fell onto the floor where she kicked and screamed until Asha came to her aid.

Now that she was a teenager she screamed even louder and told everyone in the house what she thought about them. This caused Obie to wish he had succeeded that day years ago.

"I hate you," Tamara yelled when she didn't get her way.

"I don't give a damn who you hate, but you better not ever tell me that again," her grandmother yelled as Tamara rushed out the door.

"You might let that girl put you in your grave," Ginger told Asha. "But I swear I'll kill her before she kills me. I plan to die of natural causes. So I suggest you get control of your child. If you don't, someone in them streets will, and it won't be pretty."

Then came the day when Tamara came home, looked into the pot and saw red beans instead of the special stew she wanted.

"You said we'd have rabbit stew. I don't want any beans," she yelled slamming the pot cover down. "And I'm not eating any. I'm going to Nat's house," she bellowed causing Asha to cry.

"What is it now, Asha?" Ginger, a tall, big boned, imposing woman, asked as she entered the kitchen.

"Tam's going to Nat's house to eat. She doesn't want the food we cooked. She wants…

"I don't give a damn about what she wants." Ginger walked over to where Tamara stood near the stove.

"I don't want it, Grandma," she said just as Ginger's hand connected to her cheek.

Her grandma had never hit her before, and the slap surprised and frightened her. Rubbing her cheek, Tamara backed away. Looking up into her grandma's face, she eased into a chair and sat at the table.

"Now, you listen to me, Miss Ann. There ain't no rabbit in this house today," Ginger hissed. "And I want you to get it through your head once and for all. Just 'cause your skin is light and your hair is straight don't make you special. You're no better than your mama, Obie, or me. We're all in the same boat. Do you understand me?"

"Yes, Grandma," she said timidly. She had never seen her grandma in such an agitated state and hoped sitting quietly would calm her grandma's nerves.

"I don't understand that child," Asha cried.

"I understand her," Ginger said. "She's an ingrate. After all you've given her, she appreciates nothing. Walking around here thinking she's better than everybody else. And you're the cause of it. So stop your crying.

"And from now on young lady," Ginger said as she turned and looked at Tamara. "I want you to understand one thing. You're only a child in this house, and you don't make the rules. I do.

"So you might as well get off your high horse. And anytime you feel this house is too small for you, get to stepping. It might be best for all concerned," Ginger said.

All the while, Obie sat quietly, watching it all unfold, wishing for the umpteenth time Asha and Ginger hadn't returned home unexpectedly that day back then.

🍁 🍁 🍁

Elizabeth Farrell had chestnut brown skin. She had thick eyebrows and long lashes over pretty brown eyes, which at times she nervously squinted. Her long, thick, black hair hung loosely down her back.

No more than five feet tall she was the shortest of the group, but she had the biggest breasts, and large, pretty legs. She was a cheerful girl who enjoyed life.

Elizabeth lived with her mother, Ernestine, and her grandmother, Bessie Mae Wanker, a midwife. Her dad, Gus, died of sunstroke when she was just a little girl.

On Friday evenings and Saturday mornings she helped her mother. Using every product Madam Walker ever invented, they beautified almost every woman in town. By the time each customer walked outside, her hair looked as slick as any woman's from Detroit, Kansas City, Chicago or Harlem. Though the salon was good business, Liz had no plans or desires to continue the work.

🍁 🍁 🍁

Georgia Mae had two brothers, Benji and Deacon. Her mother died while giving birth to her younger brother, Deacon, leaving a void in Georgia Mae which was never to be filled. Her older brother, Benji, drowned while swimming in the canal.

Her dad went north, and the family never heard from him again. So, Georgia Mae and her brother, Deacon, lived with their grandparents, Sadie and Caleb Pastures.

Sadie was a cold hearted, domineering woman who demanded her family live by the Good Book. Even though she constantly quoted passages, she showed her grandchildren little warmth or love.

The Pastures were hardworking sharecroppers, but they had very little to show for their efforts. Food was scarce, and they barely eked out a living until Georgia Mae went on to work and brought her money home.

Tall and thin, Georgia Mae was a brown skinned girl who constantly worried her skin was not pretty enough. Her hair was very short and hard to manage. It didn't matter how many Madam Walker products Ernestine Farrell used on her head; her hair refused to grow.

When, at that awkward stage girls giggled uncontrollably, Georgia Mae was so self-conscious of the unusually wide gap between her upper front teeth that her right hand stayed in constant motion covering her mouth until her laughter subsided.

She used every product under the sun on her skin, but it was never clear enough and that frustrated her.

Comparing herself to her friends, she considered herself an ugly duckling. Though unhappy about her looks, Georgia Mae was pretty, but she refused to believe it. Only in the classroom did her confidence allow her to show command and that was when she worked with her favorite subject, mathematics.

Each year the school held a contest. And the year prior she competed with Nat to solve a problem within a limited time period. When Georgia Mae was announced contest winner by a split second, she was taken by surprise and almost fainted.

She could not believe it. Natalie or Tamara was usually favored because everyone thought they were very pretty and they were winners at everything.

Later when she talked about her insecurities, Natalie explained there was no need to feel that way. Everyone thought a lot of her. They knew she was quite smart, and they were proud of her too.

Georgia Mae went on to take a job at the pharmacy, an unusual position for a girl, but she was certain she had found her niche.

Now sitting silently on a grassy knoll near the water's edge with her friends, Georgia Mae stared at the weeping willow tree, nestled on the canal bank. As its droopy limbs lapped at the cool, gurgling water, the girls remembered Benji.

Though warned about the canal's danger few youngsters took heed. Eager to cool their overheated bodies during summer they jumped into the deep water.

Benji never believed the horror stories about the canal. Striding about he often bragged about what he planned to do if he ever got in trouble. So when he screamed for help one day and disappeared beneath the water no one believed he needed help. Benji drowned.

"I miss Benji so much," Georgia Mae said breaking the silence.

"We miss him too," Natalie said putting her arm around Georgia Mae's shoulder.

"When Benji drowned, I just wanted to die too, but Spuds Joyride said I was too young to think that way." She stopped short of telling her friends how Spuds held her close, kissed her, and gave her reason to live.

She listened as the other girls discussed the dangers of the canal. "I have an idea," Natalie said suddenly. "Let's raise money to get a swimming pool like in the big city." Everyone thought it was a great idea.

Tamara, always wanting to do things quickly, asked, "When do we start?"

"I'm not sure," Natalie replied. "I just know it's something that has to be done."

"Well, why don't we take the money we put in the collection plate every week and save it for the pool?" Tamara asked.

"That's a good idea," Elizabeth said.

"Let's take it to the church," Elizabeth proposed. "I'm sure Reverend Stringer will help raise money."

"You're right, Liz," Tamara said. "He's never shy about asking for whatever he wants."

"You can say that again. You heard what he said last Sunday, 'Open up them pocketbooks and be generous. And I don't want to hear any coins jingling in them baskets,' Elizabeth said jokingly. The girls whooped with laughter.

"You're right," Natalie agreed as she thought about the church with its full attendance as well as hefty collections.

"So maybe it's something we should bring up at the next meeting," Georgia Mae said.

"We'll see," Natalie said. "But in all fairness since it will be used by everybody, I think we should approach everyone in the town."

Little did they know plans such as these were fantasies and pipe dreams. Fate had decreed in times like these, in the great depression, simply getting enough to eat was a fantasy for many.

# CHAPTER 3

❈

Once a year, in late summer, the circus came to town for a week. It was something Natalie and her friends looked forward to all year.

This year, just as in the past, the girls were some of the first to arrive at the fairgrounds as the sun went down. And just like the year before, the gate was locked. Joining the crowd, they got in line, chatted noisily, while waiting impatiently.

"Nat," Shelton called just as the gate opened. Looking back, she caught a glimpse of him, as he, his brother Greyland and Greyland's girlfriend, Jozell, walked towards her. As her girlfriends moved along, Natalie stepped aside and waited.

Not only were the two boys good looking, but their parents, Thaddeus and Esther Lamont, owned the Weeping Willows Funeral Home and farmland as far as the eye could see. Folk said both boys were a real catch. So there wasn't one girl in town who wouldn't give her right arm to be in their company.

Shelton, grinning broadly, greeted Natatlie.

"Hi, Shel," she said. As he took her hand in his and pulled her along, her heart flittered. Moments later, they reached her friends who waited in line near the Ferris wheel. Eventually they climbed onto it. When the wheel reached the top, it stopped momentarily, and Natalie was amazed how far she could see in the twilight.

Spread out below was the small town of Meadowsbrook reminding her of a green and brown patchwork quilt. And for the first time in her life she wondered how the rest of the world looked.

When the wheel started again, it went faster and faster, giving her a sense of exhilaration she never had.

Afterwards, Natalie sat beside Shelton and stared in disbelief while exotic animals performed tricks she never thought possible. Most impressive were the trapeze artists who delighted the crowd with their daring performances. Natalie looked on breathlessly just as she had in the past. Then all too soon it ended, and Shelton offered them a ride home.

"What about Grey and Jozell?" Natalie looked worried. "Is there enough room for all of us?"

"Don't worry, Nat. I'm walking Jozell home," Turning to his brother, he said, "Pick me up later."

"Okay, Grey," Shelton said as Natalie got in beside him and the other girls climbed in the back. Then he drove the black sedan like a maniac, stopping and dropping each girl off at her front door.

"You're crazy, Shelton Lamont," Georgia Mae said. "You drive too fast."

"Ah, come on Georgia Mae. Was it really that bad?" he laughed.

"It was. And I'll never ride with you again," Georgia Mae said as she stepped out of the car and walked through her front gate.

"See you later, Georgia Mae," he laughed.

"Don't forget the barbeque on Saturday, Georgia Mae," Natalie reminded her.

"I'll be there," she said running up the walkway.

"Bye, Georgia Mae," Elizabeth and Tamara said in unison.

"How about inviting *me* to the barbeque?" Shelton teased Natalie as he pulled back onto the highway.

"Okay," she laughed. "How would you like to come to the barbeque Saturday, Shel?"

"I'll be there with a healthy appetite, baby," he said stopping at Elizabeth's house.

"Thanks, Shel. See you at the barbeque." Elizabeth said as she got out of the car.

"I'm getting out here, too," Tamara said. "Gonna stop at Liz's for a minute."

"See you later," Natalie said.

"Okay."

"Hey, you gonna sing tonight, Tam?" Shelton asked.

"You bet I am."

"You want to go hear Tam sing?" he asked as he drove away.

"Not tonight," Natalie said. Though she really did want to hear Tamara sing, her parents hadn't given her permission to go to the Lounge. Of course, she was not about to tell him that.

"Well, when can I see you again?" Shelton asked as they neared her house.

"When would you like to see me again?"

"Anytime you say, pretty." He stopped the car abruptly, pulled her close and gave her a long kiss.

"Well then. I'll see you on Saturday," she whispered breathlessly when he finally let her go."

"I'll be here," he said. Then getting out of the car, he walked around to the other side and opened the door for her. Putting his arm around her waist, he walked her through the gate and onto the porch.

❦ ❦ ❦

The evening before the barbeque, Marcus Dawson put a goat on the spit. The meat slowly roasted throughout the night.

Early the next day, while Marcus removed the roasted goat from the spit and replaced it with a pig, Natalie led the geese from the yard to an outside area where they would stay until late evening. Then she and her brother Alan swept the yard clean.

That afternoon as the aroma of roasting meat filled the air, Natalie placed a large bowl of green salad on the long table under the big elm tree. Just as she turned to go back into the house, Zachery, Leonard, and Isador Pearson came through the gate. She waved.

They were singers known as the Soul Healers and traveled all over the area to perform. "Hey, Nat," they harmonized causing her to smile.

"Hey, brothers," she said. That was what everyone called them. "So glad you came."

Laughingly, Zachery spread his arms and said, "You know we wouldn't miss all this. Right, boys?"

"Right, Zach," his brothers agreed.

"Good," Natalie said. "I hope you'll sing for us before the evening ends."

"You know we will. After all there's nothing we wouldn't do for such a pretty young lady," Zachery said.

"Thanks. I'll look forward to that," she said as Cash Hopper, who everyone called "Fats" came into the yard carrying a big pan of fried fish.

"Hey, Nat," he called out.

"Hey, Cash," she said calling him by his real name because she detested nicknames. "Come on in and join the party." Fats beamed. No one knew, but Fats had a longstanding crush on Natalie.

"Here comes Mr. Heartthrob himself," Helene said, jokingly.

"Humf," Odessa grunted. Looking up she caught a glimpse of Shelton and his brother, Greyland Lamont as they came into the yard.

Shelton was a good looking black boy with beautiful white teeth and a head full of curly hair. The Lamont family was well off, and from what she gathered, several women around town thought he was just what their daughters needed and deserved.

However, she was not one of those women. College was in her daughter's immediate future. So Odessa wasn't ready for Natalie to marry anyone. Glancing about, she caught Natalie's eye. Walking briskly she went over and took Natalie aside.

"Listen hon," she said. "I know you like Shelton, but I hear he's a bit wild."

"Goodness, Mama. Those are just rumors. You can't believe everything you hear."

"So you say, hon. But please be careful. I got a feeling that boy's more trouble than he's worth."

"Well, he's just my friend. I'm not marrying him," Natalie said. Though she never voiced it to anyone, that was exactly what she wanted to do.

"How're you doing, Mrs. Dawson?" Shelton asked as he approached them.

"Just fine, thank you. And how's your mama?" Odessa asked.

"Well, as you know, my mama's kind of sickly, and she's not feeling well today."

"Sorry to hear that," Odessa said just as Elizabeth, Georgia Mae, her brother Deacon, and Tamara bounced into the yard.

"Hey, Mrs. Dawson, I can't wait to eat some of your good food," Deacon yelled causing Odessa to smile. "It's always good to have you and Georgia Mae here, Deacon."

Odessa always made sure Deacon and Georgia Mae felt at home in her house because of all the tragedy in their family. The barbeque went off without a hitch.

Days later, the circus folded its tents and moved on. Even so no one forgot the inspiring performances. And months later, youngsters daringly attempted to imitate trapeze artists. Some jumped from rooftops. Others climbed trees, hooked legs over limbs and suspended themselves in midair. Still others turned and twisted their little bodies in unfamiliar positions, dreaming of the day when they too might join the circus.

One Saturday evening at dinner, Natalie looked directly at her mother and asked if she could go to the Lounge. "Tam sings there on weekends and I'd like to go see her tonight."

"No need to go to the Lounge," Marcus protested thinking the Lounge was too fast a place for his daughter. "You can hear Tam sing at church."

"Everyone else goes to the Lounge," Natalie sulked. "I don't know why I can't."

"I think..." Marcus started.

"I think Nat's talking to me, Marcus," Odessa cut in. "No need for you to get involved."

"Okay. Okay. Just thought I'd put in a..."

"No need you putting in anything. I can take care of it," Odessa said thinking it was time she let her daughter enjoy her friends. After all, she trusted Natalie.

"What do you think, Mama?"

"I think you're smart enough to take care of yourself. Just be careful."

"I'll do that. Thank you, Mama," Natalie said cheerfully while rolling her eyes at her daddy. She got up and went over and kissed her mother's cheek. Then she hurriedly ran from her house. Reaching Tamara's house, she rushed onto the porch where Ginger Lynn sat alone.

"Tam, Tam," she called out.

"Goodness, Nat. What's the problem, girl?" Ginger asked as Tam and Asha came onto the porch.

"I'm going to the Lounge, Tam," Natalie said as she and Tamara laughed happily and embraced.

"Lawdy, Nat. Is this your first time to go?" Asha asked.

"Yes, ma'am. It is."

"Good grief, girl. I don't see what's to get excited about," Ginger said.

"Oh, for heaven sakes, Mama, Nat's just beginning to live," Asha said.

"I can't stay. I gotta go tell Liz and Georgia Mae," Natalie said running down the walkway and into the street.

Shaking her head, Ginger laughed, "The devil just got another one."

Later that evening, when Natalie, Elizabeth, and Georgia Mae walked into the Lounge, they found a table near the stage. When Tamara walked onto the stage and grabbed the microphone, they were there to share the moment.

Natalie danced with Shelton until her feet hurt. Glancing about her, she saw her brother, Alan dancing with Lydia. Though Lydia Wade had a bad temper, Alan liked her.

Years earlier, when the teacher, Mrs. Oats, gave Lydia the grades she deserved rather than grades she wanted, Lydia complained to her friend Billy Hardwood. Billy, a known prankster, wasted no time filling a bag with fresh cow manure and placed it at the teacher's front door. When the teacher later stepped in the manure, she knew immediately who did it and spoke with their parents. Though neither was punished for the deed, young Billy and Lydia were the talk of the town for a month. Ever since then Natalie thought of Lydia as a real witch.

So, when Lydia and Tilly's mother, Tessa Wade, invited all the youngsters to Lydia's birthday party, Natalie didn't want to go. But, when Alan, her friends, and Shelton said they were going, although a bit apprehensive, she went, too.

When they arrived at the house, a beautiful four tier chocolate cake with "Happy Birthday, Lydia," written on it in pink icing was on the long table along with other yummy looking food.

Things went well until Melanie Joyride came into the yard wearing a new straw hat and plopped it onto Tilly's head. When Lydia in a fit of envy asked for the hat, Tilly put her hand on top of her head and held onto the hat as Lydia tried to take it.

Unable to get the hat, she became enraged and punched Tilly in the stomach. Gasping for breath, Tilly bent over, but in spite of the pain and to spite Lydia, she held onto the hat. When Lydia realized Tilly would die rather than give her the hat, she picked up a brick and threw it on Tilly's foot.

Though Tilly screamed loud enough to wake the dead, she held onto the hat. As all the youngsters looked on, Tilly hopped to her mother, Tessa, who was sitting on the porch.

"Mama, Mama," she cried. "Look what Lydia did." She pointed to her bloody foot.

"It's your own fault," Tessa said. "You should've let her have the hat."

When Tilly got no support from her mother, she ran to look for her daddy, Jake.

Because no one knew who Lydia might attack next, everyone scattered and that was the end of the party.

"Did you get the chance to eat any goodies?" Odessa asked when Natalie told the story.

"No one ate anything, Mama. Everyone was so scared of Lydia, we ran. I suppose if Lydia doesn't kill Tilly about that hat, Tilly might get the chance to eat some of that food."

"Lawdy, Nat. Is Lydia really that bad?" Odessa asked.

# CHAPTER 4

Cash "Fats" Hopper was a mild mannered and good hearted youngster who followed his daddy, Tex, to the mighty Mississippi river twice a week to get the catch of the day, which meant anything they hooked on a line.

After filling the box on the back of the black truck, they went into the countryside, sounding the horn as they approached to alert everyone they had arrived. They then sold all had from gator to gar.

Even though his mother, Sissy, taught him to cook just about everything, his specialty was fried fish and fried potatoes. And from the size of his waistline he ate more than he sold.

Whenever he took a break he went a couple doors down the street to Michael's Market where he listened to Candyman Cates and Seb Pardeau, the oldest musicians and storytellers in town. At times, he talked with Lydia and Tilly.

But he still remembered the birthday party years earlier and stayed no longer than Lydia's mood allowed. She was different, and when she turned ugly, he took off. Returning to his own territory, he sat outside on the empty Coca Cola case, and waited for his friends Billy Hardwood, Shelton and Greyland Lamont, and their cousin, Warren Gilliam who lived with the Lamonts.

"Hi, Georgia Mae," Fats yelled as she left the pharmacy late one evening.

"Hi, Fats. What's up?" she said to the chubby youngster who seemed to spend more time sitting outside the café than inside cooking.

"Nothing going on here," he said as Shelton drove up.

"Hey, Georgia Mae," Shelton yelled as he got out of the car. "You going to Nat's house?"

"Why do you want to know?" she laughed.

"'Cause I'm thinking you should tell her I'm thinking about her," he laughed.

"Okay, I'll do that. But why don't you go and tell her yourself?"

"Don't think that's a good idea, Georgia Mae. You know how Nat is. She might not let me in the house. Think I better wait 'til she invites me there."

"Okay," she said.

"Tell her I said 'hi' too," Fats yelled.

"I'll do that," she said as she walked away.

"Hey, Georgia Mae," Fats called out causing her to stop and turn around. "You seen Liz today?" he asked.

"No, but I'm sure I will. I'll tell her you asked about her." Then she happily hurried up the street.

"You do that, Georgia Mae," he yelled.

When Georgia Mae reached Natalie's house and told her Shelton asked about her, Natalie simply smiled. Then she invited Georgia Mae to Sunday dinner.

"Liz and Tam are coming," she said when Georgia Mae hesitated.

"Okay, I'll come."

Sundays were special at the Dawson home. Odessa loved beauty and set her table every day. Though she covered the table with oil cloth during the week, she made sure her place settings matched. Then when Sunday rolled around, she brought out her nice linen cloth and linen napkins.

Long before the children were born, Marcus built a table with four removable panels. When all panels were inserted, the table accommodated sixteen.

Though she never thought she would use the panels, she often did because Natalie and Alan frequently brought home other youngsters who eagerly joined the family for a meal. To see her family and friends enjoy her meals brought Odessa great satisfaction.

🍁 🍁 🍁

Georgia Mae lived with her family in a small unpainted house. The house was neat and clean, but sparsely furnished. A dogwood tree stood in the front yard, and several scented rosebushes hugged the fence, while others lined the walkway from the street to the steps. On a quiet, hot, summer evening Georgia

Mae sat on those steps with Natalie, Tamara, and Elizabeth and told them her secret. What she said was not something the girls expected to hear, and all sat momentarily in stunned silence.

"Oh, Georgia Mae," Natalie said when she was finally able to speak. "What will you do?"

"How…" She started. She wanted to ask how it happened, but decided such question would only prove her ignorance so she kept quiet. Now she knew the rumors were true. Spuds Joyride really did like young girls, and it was obvious he taught Georgia Mae something other than filling prescriptions. Just thinking about what Spuds taught her caused Natalie to gag.

Rushing down the steps and to the side of the house, she retched. Following close behind her, Elizabeth put her hand on Natalie's shoulder.

"Are you all right?" Elizabeth asked.

"Yes, I'm okay. The thought of what that old man's done to Georgia Mae makes me sick. And I'm sad because we planned to do so much together. Now Georgia Mae's future is uncertain."

"I know," Elizabeth said as both girls returned to the step.

"You all right, Nat?" Tamara asked.

"Yes, I'm okay."

"I think you better tell your grandma about this," Tamara said to Georgia Mae.

"Yeah, you need to tell your grandma about Spuds, and you need to tell Spuds about everything," Elizabeth said. "This won't just go away, you know."

"I can't do that," Georgia Mae whispered.

"You can't do what?" Natalie glared at her.

"I can't tell my grandma."

"Why can't you? I know that old man forced himself on you," Natalie pronounced, authoritatively.

"Wait now, Nat. That wasn't exactly how it happened." Georgia Mae allowed her facial expression to reveal what she could not say.

"Don't tell me you wanted that old man to…" Natalie gasped. Appalled, Natalie's mouth dropped open, and she ran to the side of the house again. When she returned she was as green as a cotton leaf. So she sat quietly.

"But what will you do? Tamara asked.

"I don't know." Georgia Mae shook her head sadly.

"Don't you have relatives up north?" Tamara wanted to solve the problem instantly and move on. This wasn't something she wanted or needed.

"I do."

"So take your money and go live with them," Tamara said.

"I give all my money to Grandma," Georgia Mae said.

"Can't you get it back?" Tamara was noticeably irritated. She was angry that Georgia Mae hadn't kicked Spuds where it hurts. The teachers said she was brilliant, but evidently she stopped thinking in the back room of Spuds' Drugs. Now she would never go to college.

"I don't think so," Georgia Mae said.

"I got it!" Natalie said feeling somewhat better now. "We'll buy you a train ticket." Natalie looked from Elizabeth to Tamara.

"Sounds great," Elizabeth said while thinking about her own situation. Lately, she thought more about a certain man than her books, but hoped she never found herself in a situation like Georgia Mae. Though no one knew, she too had a secret. She often stood at the front gate and waved to Vince, known as "the meat man," whenever he came to the market. She had done so for several years.

"I'm sorry, girls, but I don't want to go away," Georgia Mae said. "I love Spuds, and he loves me."

"For goodness sakes," Natalie said. "That old man can't marry you."

"Yeah," Elizabeth said. "He's already married."

"You know what I think," Tamara said.

"What's that?" Natalie asked.

"You heard her. She loves Spuds, and he loves her," Tamara mimicked. "So I say let Spuds take care of her problem. He's responsible for this mess. Let him buy her a ticket and put her on that train. Let's keep our noses out of it."

"Oh, Tam, how could you say that? Georgia Mae's our friend. She needs us now," Natalie assured them. "And we should do what we can to help her."

"Okay," Tamara said giving in to Natalie. "Let's see what we can do. You agree, Liz?"

"Yeah, I do."

"Good. You think about it, Georgia Mae," Tamara said. "We'll save our money because you gonna need all the help you can get."

"Okay," Georgia Mae said sadly. Then as they sat quietly watching the sun fall beyond the treetops, Natalie thought Georgia Mae not only lost her virginity, but her mind as well. And as far as she was concerned, Spuds Joyride was nothing more than a savage beast.

Customarily, the girls saw one another every day. So when several days passed, and Georgia Mae had not come to visit, Natalie worried. As she sat in the back yard on the bench under the elm tree with Tamara and Elizabeth late one evening, she voiced her concern. "Have you seen Georgia Mae, lately?"

"Not since Sunday," Elizabeth said.

"Neither have I, and today is Wednesday," Natalie said.

"You know me, Nat. I didn't give Georgia Mae much thought," Tamara replied.

"I think you should. What would you do if it happened to you?"

"Me? Come on, Nat. You know me. I'd never allow Spuds to touch me."

"That's not what I mean, Tam," Natalie said. "I'm thinking that her grandma learned her secret and locked her inside the house."

"Oh, come on," Tamara laughed.

"It's not funny. Georgia Mae might be in trouble." Natalie grimaced.

"If she is, there's nothing we can do," Elizabeth said.

"I know, but I want to see her anyway." Natalie rushed from the yard and into the street.

"Hey, wait for us, will you," Tamara called as she and Elizabeth ran after her. Running all the way to Georgia Mae's house, they were almost too winded to knock and stood on the porch momentarily before Tamara tapped lightly on the door. When Georgia Mae's grandmother, Sadie opened the door, the girls spoke in unison. "Where's Georgia Mae?"

"We haven't seen her for several days," Natalie blurted. "So we were worried about her."

"Yeah," Tamara said. "So we came to see about her."

"Is she all right?" Elizabeth asked.

"Come on in," Sadie said. Stepping aside, she let them in.

"Georgia Mae isn't feeling good." Sadie led them into the bedroom where Georgia Mae lay in bed moaning. Her knees were drawn to her chest and sweat poured from her forehead. There was no doubt Georgia Mae was sick.

"What's wrong with her?" Natalie asked as she grabbed a towel from the back of a nearby chair and went to the bed while Tamara and Elizabeth looked on.

"Oh, Georgia Mae," Natalie cried. Bending down she wiped her friend's brow. Georgia Mae opened her eyes, smiled weakly, but never spoke.

"What's happened to her?" Natalie asked when she noticed blood on the top sheet. Flipping it back, she saw that Georgia Mae lay in a pool of blood.

Sadie never gave her an answer. Instead she left the room and came back with a steaming cup of tea.

"Shouldn't we call Doc Peterson?" Natalie asked horrified by what she saw.

"No, we shouldn't." Sadie spoke sternly. Pushing Natalie aside and taking the towel from her hand, she pulled the sheet up around her granddaughter's chin. Leaning down over the bed, Sadie put her hand under Georgia Mae's head and pushed the cup to her lips.

"Swallow, girl!" she demanded. "Swallow." Still holding Georgia Mae's head, she turned to them.

"Don't you girls worry about Georgia Mae. I'll take care of her. She'll be all right."

Just as Natalie attempted to ask another question, Sadie said, "I think it's time you girls went home."

They said goodbye to Georgia Mae, but she was too sick to respond. Once outside the girls huddled and cried.

❦ ❦ ❦

"Nat, Nat, Nat," Fats Hopper yelled as he ran onto the back porch where she and her mother Odessa sat peeling peaches.

"My goodness, young man, what is it?" Odessa asked. "You act as if the house is on fire."

"Sorry, Mrs. Dawson, but Georgia Mae just died," he said trying to catch his breath. Natalie burst into tears and ran to the front porch.

"I'm sorry, Nat," he said as he ran after her and sat down next to her on the porch swing. "I know you'll miss Georgia Mae because you were as close as sisters. But I want you to know I hurt, and I'll miss her too."

"Thanks, Cash. I know you will," she sniffled.

As Fats got up to leave, he longed to tell Natalie he loved her more than Shelton ever would, but he knew she loved Shelton too much to hear him. "Well, I'll…I'll see you later," he stammered and slowly walked out the door. As he left the yard, Natalie went back into the house and took a chair at the dining table. Lowering her head onto her arms, she sobbed.

"I'm so sorry, hon," Odessa said. Wiping her own eyes, she went to the window and stared into the garden. Several moments later, she returned to the table.

"I know it's quite a shock." Odessa put her hand on Natalie's shoulder and sat down next to her. "I know you'll miss her, but so will I. You know how I feel about your friends. And Georgia Mae spent so much time here I feel I lost a daughter. I can't believe she's gone. She was such an intelligent girl with a bright future. What a waste! I trust you'll use your head, hon, and not let Shelton talk you into anything. Such things can wait. You know what I'm saying, Nat?"

"I understand, Mama." Natalie lifted her head and looked at Odessa.

"Lawdy, it seems the devil's always watching and waiting for a chance to stick his fingers in the pie. I wonder if Sadie gave the girl mistletoe tea."

"Mistletoe!" Natalie exclaimed. She knew about mistletoe tea but only as a cure.

"Yes, hon. It's good for many things, but it must be used correctly, otherwise it can cause problems. I got a feeling Sadie was afraid Georgia Mae's condition might bring her shame. So she did what she thought was best. She tried to get rid of the baby, but she lost Georgia Mae too."

"That's awful, Mama," Natalie cried.

"I know it is. If she did something, I feel sorry for her."

The day before they buried Georgia Mae, Natalie, Tamara, and Elizabeth went over to Weeping Willows Funeral Home, where Thaddeus Lamont hobbled over to them.

"I'm sorry for your loss, girls," he said offering his condolences. Then he led them to Georgia Mae's coffin. She was dressed in white.

"She looks like she's sleeping," Tamara said.

"She is sleeping," Elizabeth replied.

"Yes, she is. But she'll never wake up," Natalie whispered.

They lowered their heads and stayed there for some time before leaving.

The very next day as the bell tolled, they went to the church, and listened as Reverend Stringer said nice things about their friend and preached her soul into the pearly gates. Then they buried Georgia Mae under the tall oaks wrapped in graceful strands of Spanish moss. As the men shoveled dirt onto the box, Natalie wanted to die too. But instead of dying, she returned to school along with Elizabeth and Tamara.

Months later, Georgia Mae's brother, Deacon, told Natalie, Tamara, and Elizabeth an awful story about how Georgia Mae died.

A strange old woman he had never seen before came to the house and sent him outside. She was much older than his grandma. The old lady lowered the window shade, but because of the hole in the shade he was able to peek inside.

He watched as the old woman spread Georgia Mae's legs apart, pushed something that looked like a long wire inside Georgia Mae several times. Georgia Mae screamed like a scared animal. He said he cried too.

Afterwards, Georgia Mae never stopped crying and moaning. When he couldn't stand to hear his sister suffer anymore, he went and got Doc Peterson. Doc Peterson cursed under his breath when he saw Georgia Mae. He was mad at his Grandma Sadie who sat in a chair in the corner of the room and cried.

Doc Peterson said Georgia Mae had lost too much blood. So it was too late to help her. Doc gave Georgia Mae a shot, and she quieted down. Then just before she died, she called out for the one person she missed most, *Mama*.

# CHAPTER 5

It was 1936. The Olympic Games were in Berlin and Jesse Owens, the young black American track star performed admirably and won four gold medals. It was a historic moment for black Americans and was something they would talk about for years to come.

But Tamara was oblivious to all of this. Her concern was what she saw in the mirror. She stood studying her reflection for some time before walking into the kitchen and asking the very question her mother always dreaded she might hear. "Mama, who's my daddy?"

"Why, Obie is, honey," Asha answered nervously. "Why do you ask?"

"Because I don't look like Obie." Tamara stared at a silent Obie. "As a matter of fact I don't look like you, either."

"Goodness sakes, Tam. Don't start that. Obie is your daddy, girl." Asha was visibly shaken.

"I don't believe you, and I got a right to know." Tamara sat down at the table and stared at her mother.

"Lawdy, Tam, what difference does it make?" Ginger asked. "You gonna go to his home and say, 'Hey daddy, your little girl is here?' Well let me tell you something, missy. If that's your plan you don't deserve to know."

Suddenly Tamara felt relieved. Her grandma had confirmed her suspicions. Obie was not her daddy. She was glad because she never liked him.

"I don't want to do anything, Grandma. I just want to know."

Her grandma continued talking, unaware of what she'd just said. "I don't care what you want," her grandma yelled. "All you need to know right now is we're family. Asha is your mama, Obie is your daddy, I'm your grandma, and we love you. That's all that counts. Now get outta here before I really get mad.

By the way, I don't think it's a good idea for you to spend so much time at the Joint either. I want you to do more singing in the church."

"I don't care what you want," Tamara hissed. "I'm gonna do whatever *I* want." She rushed out the door.

Ginger, still annoyed at her granddaughter, suddenly turned her anger towards her own daughter. "I'll tell you one thing, Asha," Ginger said sternly, eyeing her daughter with contempt. "I don't care how much money that man gives you. He can never make up for taking advantage of you."

The man Ginger spoke of was Tamara's real father, a white man, who gave Asha money for Tamara's education and her daily upkeep.

Upon hearing that Obie laughed. He doubted that man or any man ever took advantage of Asha. The woman danced to her own drumbeat. Hell, he slept with her, he thought, and even he couldn't take advantage of her.

"I know, Mama," Asha said. "I take the money so Tam can get a good education."

"I know," Ginger sighed. "But she's the most ungrateful child I know. I want you to tell her everything, but only when she's old enough to understand."

"I'll do that, Mama."

As fate would have it, later that night at the Lounge, Tamara met Pete Baraldi. But it would be years before she knew exactly who he was and what part he played in her life.

❦   ❦   ❦

When Jake Wade's sister, Lula Hanks, came from Chicago to Meadowsbrook for her yearly visit, Jake and Tessa took off for a day's trip and left her in charge of Michael's Market and their daughters, Tilly and Lydia.

Jake and Tessa were to return home that evening, but had not returned when the clock struck midnight. Lula began to worry. Unable to sleep, she got out of bed, dressed, and waited.

At sunrise, she began knocking on doors to let everyone know Jake and Tessa had not come home. By midmorning everyone started to search for them. When no one found them by late afternoon, most gave up and went on about their own business.

Fats Hopper went back to the Kitchen while Warren Gilliam strolled along the canal. As he walked along the bank near the bridge, he looked down and saw a black truck underwater. Rushing back to the store, Warren, a stutterer since he began to talk, tried to tell Candyman Cates and Seb Pardeau what he found.

"Spit it out, boy," Seb yelled. However, Warren was too excited and unable to explain. So he pointed, and, with Candyman and Seb on his heels, he led them back to the canal.

"Lawdy," Candyman screamed. "Seems old Jake drove straight into the water 'cause I can't see no damage to the bridge."

"Yep. Guess you right 'bout that," Seb said. "Betcha he had one too many and never should've been behind the wheel anyhow."

By late evening Jake and Tessa were stretched out in the Weeping Willows Funeral Home where Thaddeus, Greyland, and Shelton Lamont prepared them for burial. Several days later, Ernestine did Tessa's hair, and Esther Lamont got out her kit and put makeup on Tessa's water bloated face.

Tessa and Jake were put to rest in side by side graves. Afterwards, Lula grieved and was stunned when neither Tilly nor Lydia shed a tear for their parents. It just wasn't normal, she thought. It seemed neither girl had any feelings.

Several days went by before it dawned on Lula that both girls had certain peculiarities. Lydia was completely headstrong and totally unmanageable. Tilly gave everybody the silent treatment, never saying a word unless someone talked to her first. Though Tilly was off center, she seemed sane compared to Lydia.

Now Lula realized there was something greater than the shock of losing her brother and sister-in-law. The thought that she was stuck with two crazy nieces who didn't know their asses from a hole in the ground and didn't seem to care sent her into a tizzy. "Oh my God," she whispered. "What have I done to deserve such punishment?"

# CHAPTER 6

❀

"Hey, Miss Lula," Elizabeth said to the woman behind the counter as she entered the door. She was at the store to buy a can of Spam, which her mother and grandma considered a treat.

"I'm just fine, Liz. How you doing?"

"I'm…" she started, but before she could speak the man everyone called 'the meat man' interrupted.

"Hi, Lizzy," he said standing so close their bodies almost touched. His name was Vince Baraldi. His family owned the big meat packing plant in Baysville. He made deliveries once a week to Michael's Market.

"How are you?" His friendliness surprised her. But the fact that he knew her name stunned her. She looked up cautiously. His hair was thick, wavy, and black as coal. His face was deeply tanned. His green eyes were the prettiest she ever saw and reminded her of two beautiful marbles. They held hers like a magnet.

She knew he liked her and at that moment her mind went blank. Forgetting the reason she came to the store, she ran out the door and back to her house.

"Where's the Spam, Liz?" her mother yelled when she entered the house.

"Oh," she said still shaking like a leaf on a tree. "I forgot, Mama."

"Whatta you mean you forgot? What's wrong with you, girl? Where's your head?"

"I'm sorry, Mama. I'll go back and get it," she said. Then, instead of going to the store immediately, she went into the yard and stood at the gate until Vince came out and waved to her. And only after he drove away did she return to store.

Several months later when Elizabeth went to the store, Lula stared at her angrily and pushed a small box across the counter. "Vince, the meat man, left this for you."

Not knowing what to do, Elizabeth hesitated. Vince's forwardness so disturbed her she stopped standing at the gate. Even so, he left gifts for her.

"Go on, take it. It's yours. He didn't leave it for me, you know." Lula rolled her eyes disapprovingly as Elizabeth reluctantly picked up the box. "Of course it's none of my business. But it just makes you wonder about them white folks. I mean, in daylight hours they hate you. But come nightfall them sons-of-bitches can't wait to jump in your bed. Makes you wonder what makes them buggers tick, wouldn't you say? I'll tell you one thing. They're evil people, Liz.

"So, don't you let that Vince get in your bed. You hear me, Liz? Don't let him put his mojo on you. Don't you let him stick it in you, Liz. No lawdy, don't ever let that meat man stick it in you."

Elizabeth was taught early on never to get involved with Vince or any of his kind. Her mama told her to always maintain "your distance." They lived by rules. There were certain things they were never to do. He knew it, and so did she.

She didn't trust Miss Lula and knew she would eventually tell everything to anyone who listened including her mother. So without ever looking Miss Lula in the eye, she took the box and stuck it in her grocery bag and walked out the door.

When she reached the house her mother and grandmother were on the back porch. This gave her time to hide the box. She hurriedly took it from the bag and hid it inside a bigger box under the bed.

Later that night when everyone was asleep, she opened the gift with trembling hands. It was a small bottle of perfume so strong it was intoxicating. She could never wear it because she could never explain how she got it. So she stuck it in the bottom bureau drawer under some clothes.

The gifts kept coming, and she kept taking them. He gave her fancy panties and a beautiful pearl necklace, which she could wear only when she was older. Not knowing what else to do, she continued to accept the gifts and hide them.

Then one evening Fats Hopper appeared at her door and said Vince wanted to see her. She refused to go that time and each time after until Fats told her Vince might get angry.

"If he gets mad enough," Fats explained. "He might take it out on me. You wouldn't want that to happen would you?"

"You're right, Fats," she said. Since she wanted nothing to happen to him she went to see Vince. He was waiting in his black pickup truck some distance from her house.

When she reached his truck, she got in beside him and after listening to him talk about himself for almost an hour she knew Vince loved himself. In fact, he reminded her of Shelton Lamont. But it was his age which sent her into a panic.

"Thirty," she yelled. As far as she was concerned, he was an old man. "I'm only sixteen."

"So what? I like you. You know that, don't you?"

"I guess so."

"Whatta you mean you guess so? Surely, you know I don't give gifts to just any girl. Hell, I'd like to get to know you better, Lizzy." He pulled a cigarette from the package and stuck it in his mouth, struck a match, and lit it. She watched him inhale then turn his head and blow the smoke out the window. "Don't you like me just a little bit?"

"Well...I..."

"Well, I what?" he sounded annoyed, but really wasn't. Raising his eyebrows, he said, "You either like me or you don't. What's it gonna take to get close to you?"

"I don't know." She was wondered if she should tell him how she really felt. Should she tell him she liked him from a distance for a very long time? She decided to keep that to herself. She feigned naivety. "Just how close do you want to get?"

"Whatta you mean by that? You might be just sixteen, but I bet you're going on sixty. You're not dumb. Most sixteen-year-olds in this neck of the woods are in the thick of things. So don't pull that shit with me. How close you think I wanna get?" He studied her face while she stared silently at nothing in particular. "Well, what's your problem?" he asked.

"I think you already know my problem. We're not supposed to be together. There're rules. You know that."

"Rules? Goddammit, Lizzy! Fuck the rules. Rules are made to be broken, baby. Don't you know that?" Then he grabbed her and gave her a long, warm, wet kiss. When he let her go, she trembled and obviously looked as scared as she felt because he threw back his head and laughed out loud.

"Oh, Lizzy," he said as she hastily got out of the truck. "You and I are gonna have some fun." He continued to laugh.

Even though she ran away, he continued to leave the pretty boxes with Miss Lula, and Elizabeth continued to accept them, but she avoided him.

But late one evening when she went to visit Natalie, he followed her. She tried to run away, but he got out of the truck and chased after her. When he caught her, he picked her up and threw her in the truck causing her to have mixed emotions. She was scared yet thrilled.

"I want you to get this through your head once and for all. I like you, Lizzy. I like you a lot," he yelled and slid behind the wheel. "I've been good to you. I've given you gifts and money. How else can I prove I care for you? I'm not gonna hurt you. You know that."

"I don't know what you're gonna do to me."

"Well, just so you can settle down, I'll tell you what I'm gonna do to you, Lizzy. I'm gonna fuck you," he said emphatically as he put the truck in gear and drove away.

When they reached his house, he picked her up again, carried her inside, and dumped her on his bed. Falling on the bed beside her, he took her in his arms and kissed her. He sucked her breasts as if he were a baby. He tantalized her. His fingers were all over her and inside her. He put his head between her legs and did things with his tongue she never knew possible. She thought she would die. But instead of dying, she screamed her head off.

Later, he did what Miss Lula said she shouldn't allow him to do. He slipped between her legs and plunged his big hot cock, unmercifully, into her.

"Oh, my God!" he murmured when she cried out. "You're a virgin?"

"I know," she whimpered.

"Well, I'll be damned," he whispered amazed by his discovery. "I didn't know, Lizzy." He was genuinely concerned.

Then he nuzzled his face in her neck, put a hand under each of her hips and held her. He gently thrust deep inside of her and proceeded to fuck her until their bodies were wet with sweat.

Her toes curled, she moaned loudly and held onto him tightly. Then they exploded like fire crackers on the Fourth of July. As her body shook uncontrollably, she screamed in the night. Not in pain but in unbelievable pleasure.

Then all too quickly it ended. He wanted to take her home, but she wanted more of what he just gave her. He gladly obliged.

Later that night as she lay in her own bed, the memory of what they did kept her awake.

When Fats failed to come for her the next day or the day after, she was disappointed and ashamed because she did with Vince what Miss Lula told her not to do. She let Vince put his mojo on her and in her.

It was two weeks later when Vince sent for her again. She eagerly went to him. That night he took her back to his house, and almost every night afterwards. They spent every stolen moment in his bedroom.

🍁     🍁     🍁

"Do you really like him?" Natalie asked one summer evening as they sat on the grassy knoll near the canal.

"Like him? Lawdy, Nat, I love him."

"Listen, Liz," Natalie said. "All I have to say is be careful and don't forget where you are or who you are."

"I can never forget that."

She loved Natalie because she was willing to listen, but never criticized. She guessed Natalie was that way because she loved Shelton so deeply, and he was far from perfect.

She promised Natalie she'd be careful and continued to meet Vince. The rules, which Vince refused to follow, only served to heighten their desires.

"You got no idea how much I care for you, Lizzy," he said as he drove her home late one evening. "I'll do anything for you. You tell me your wishes, and I'll grant them. I just want to make you happy." He touched her breast lightly. "What can I do to make you happy, Lizzy?" he teased.

"I don't know." She giggled. She was so much in love, she thought no farther than her nose. The future never entered her mind. She simply lived for the moment.

"What you mean you don't know, Lizzy?"

"I'll think about it," she said as he parked the truck a short distance from her house. "And I'll let you know next time I see you."

"You do that, Lizzy," he said pulling her close and kissing her. Then she got out of the truck and walked home.

It was a clear, beautiful, night. The stars twinkled, and the moon was so bright it cast deep purple shadows. Vince watched spellbound as Elizabeth walked through the yard and into the house. I love that girl, he thought. I really do love her.

Although Vince loved Elizabeth, he knew because of the times, they would always live in the shadows and the darkness of night.

Elizabeth planned to sneak into the house as always, but standing akimbo in the doorway of her bedroom was her very angry mother.

"Come on in here, girl," her mother said. "You got a lot of 'splaining to do."

She played ignorant. "What's wrong, Mama?"

"You tell me. Where you been 'til this time of night, anyway?" her mother shrieked. "Answer me, girl. And where'd you get all these things?" Ernestine pointed to the open bureau drawers.

All the gifts Vince gave her and she'd carefully hidden away were now exposed. Miss Lula finally got the word out.

Her mother walked over, stuck her hand inside a drawer, and taking out several dainty items said, "This is no cheap stuff. Who gave it to you, Liz?"

"Lawdy, Liz," she yelled loudly as she made still another discovery. "Where'd you get all this money from, girl? There must be hundreds of dollars here. You might as well tell me since everybody else in town knows."

"Everybody knows what, Mama?"

"Don't you pull that on me, girl!" she screamed hoping her daughter would tell her the truth. "Don't you mean 'who,' Miss Ann?" Her mother raised her hand and slapped her hard across the face. "Everybody in town's talking about you and the meat man. How long you been carrying on with him, Liz?"

"I'm not carrying on with anybody, Mama," she lied as her mother's hand connected with her face again, and she fell backwards. If not for the bed, she would have landed on the floor.

"I love him, Mama," she confessed covering her face with both hands. "I love him."

"What you been drinking, girl? Have you lost your mind?" Her mother, who was much taller, stared down at her. Noticing the fullness of her waist, her mother screamed, "Oh, my God, you're pregnant. He raped you, didn't he, Liz? Please tell me he raped you."

"I can't do that, Mama, because he didn't rape me." Hurt registered on her mother's face, and she seemed to shrink a couple of inches.

"Don't tell me that," she pleaded tearfully. "Don't tell me you went to bed willingly with Vince."

"I'm sorry, Mama. But that's exactly what I did."

"What am I gonna do with you, Liz Farrell?" Ernestine cried.

"But I love him, Mama."

"Dammit, girl. Shut your mouth. I don't want to hear it," she screamed. "Mama, Mama," Ernestine called out for her own mother, Bessie Mae Wanker.

The older woman came into the room wearing a long flannel gown even though it was hot enough to roast a pig. "For heaven sakes, Ernestine," Bessie Mae said. "What you making such a racket about this time of night?"

"Liz got herself pregnant, Mama."

"Oh, no! Not our Liz!" her grandmother moaned. "I never thought it'd happen to our Liz.

Though she was in trouble, Elizabeth stared at the two women and wondered how her grandmother wore the flannel and withstood the heat.

"Lawdy, what you gonna do, Ernestine?"

"I don't know, Mama. I just don't know." Ernestine wiped her eyes.

"I know it hurts, Ernestine, but it ain't the end of the world. So dry your eyes." Then turning to Elizabeth, she said. "Now, see what you done. You broke your mama's heart. Mine, too."

"I'm sorry, Grandma." She felt awful. But she was in love. She never thought about a baby or the consequences of her actions. She never wanted this to happen.

"I know you're sorry, baby. Now, I just want to know who done it to you? Who got you in all this trouble?" Her grandma looked as sad as her mother.

"Vince the meat man did it to her, Mama," Ernestine blurted angrily before Elizabeth could speak. "Everybody in town knows about him and her except us. If Lula hadn't told me, I'd still be in the dark."

"Well, what's done is done, Ernestine. No need crying over spilt milk. And don't you do anything foolish. I don't want our Liz seeing some bloody butcher or drinking no potions, either. Do you understand me? Just you remember poor Georgia Mae. God would never forgive us if Liz went the way of Georgia Mae."

"I understand, Mama," Ernestine said.

"I still can't get over that Sadie," Bessie Mae said still smarting that Sadie hadn't come to her for advice about Georgia Mae. "Some say she let some butcher in her house to cut that baby outta that child's belly."

"Lawdy, Mama. That's over and buried. Anyway, some say Sadie gave Georgia Mae mistletoe tea. But it's old and stinking. I got a problem here and now."

"Well," Bessie Mae said. "That baby Liz is carrying might belong to Vince the meat man, but our blood runs in its veins too. So I want you to think carefully before you do anything. Don't act foolishly."

"I know, Mama. Don't worry. I love Liz too much to do anything like Sadie did. I suppose it's best to send her away."

"No, no, no. You can't, Mama," Elizabeth screamed. "Please don't send me away."

"Stop your crying now, Liz. It's best for all of us," Bessie Mae said.

"I don't want to go away, Grandma." Going away meant she would never see Vince again.

"I know you don't, baby," Bessie Mae said. "But you should've thought about that before you let the meat man get you in a fix. We figured you were smarter than this. Now we'll have to send you to your Aunt Violet."

"Please, don't send me away, Grandma." She cried. When she got no response, she turned to her mother. "Please don't send me away, Mama."

"Then you tell me, what am I supposed to do, Liz?"

"I want to stay with you, Mama."

"Yeah, I know. That's why you spent so much time with Vince, I suppose. Am I right? Where was your head, Liz? Did you think Vince would marry you? Did you forget who you were? Or where you are? Did you? Talk to me, girl."

"No. I never forgot who I was, Mama."

"Good. I'm glad to hear that. Now let me tell you this. You might be in love, but it's no dream. It's a nightmare. You see Vince can do no more for you than he's already done."

"But I love him, Mama. And sending me away won't change that." Elizabeth felt defiant.

"I know that *Miss Ann*. But I'll have the satisfaction of knowing you won't see him again. By the way, did you tell him about the baby?"

"No, I didn't tell him." She started to tell him earlier that night, but decided to wait until she saw him the next time.

"Why is that? You love him and that child is as much his responsibility as yours. I swear if I saw that Vince right now I'd shoot him," her mother spat vehemently.

"You'd do no such thing," Bessie Mae said. "No need for that kind of talk. Vince is your grandchild's father. Now when you gonna send her away, Ernestine?"

"Just as soon as I can."

The very next morning Natalie sat on the front porch beside Elizabeth. While her friend offered details about herself and Vince, Natalie wondered what had gone wrong along the way. They were a team, and they planned to do things together. They were to help make their world a better place in which to live. Lawdy, she was as unprepared to hear Elizabeth's troubles as she was Georgia Mae's.

"My God!" Natalie whispered and shook her head as though to clear it. Georgia Mae's loss still weighed heavily on her heart. She'd died tragically, Natalie thought, because her grandma felt the shame was too great to bear.

Only two years later, Liz was in the same situation. She thought she knew her friends, but she had grossly miscalculated. She realized she was lucky to have a family who showered her with love. She had no need to look for it in the wrong places because she was surrounded by it.

"Nat, Nat," Elizabeth called breaking the silence and tugging at her friend's arm. "Mama's sending me away. But I don't want to go."

"Oh, I'm so sorry, Liz." Natalie felt pain in her soul, and her heart was heavy.

"Mama's sending me away," Elizabeth cried.

"I know. But I suppose it's better to go away and live with relatives than visiting a butcher or drinking mistletoe tea. Remember Georgia Mae?"

"I suppose you're right."

"I'll miss you very much, Liz. Life won't be the same without you. But I guess we had to grow up some time. I just never thought it would be so soon."

"I'm sorry it happened, Nat."

"Me, too. Remember how we said we were going to the same college and would return home to help other youngsters?"

"I remember. Even if I can't do it, you can. You're strong, Nat. You'll make it."

"I don't know about all that. But I hope I can."

"I'm sure you can. And I'll write," Elizabeth answered.

"Okay. You do that, Liz," Natalie said giving her a hug as tears flowed down her cheek.

Several days after Elizabeth boarded the train and headed for California to live with relatives, Natalie prepared to go away to college and, to everyone's surprise so did Tamara.

Just days before Natalie was to leave home, her Uncle Percy's young wife, Helene, gave birth to twin girls, Queenie and Sophia. Natalie thought they were the loveliest babies she ever saw—even with wrinkles. Though she knew it was a long time in the future, Natalie looked forward to the time when she might have her own family.

Natalie was afraid to leave Meadowsbrook, but knew she needed an education. She chose a college close to home and returned often to see her family and Shelton. Tamara, who was afraid of nothing, and would miss no one except Natalie, chose a college up north. She was happy to get away from home.

# CHAPTER 7

When Tamara went off to college, Obie, a short, stocky, black man with a short man's complex shouted with joy. He would be boss now. At last he thought he would get Asha's attention. If she gave him just half the love she gave Tamara, he'd be happy.

But it wasn't long before Obie's plans turned sour. Asha was as stubborn as a mule. And as they lay in bed late one night, she let him know she had no interest in him.

"You," she said sitting up in bed and staring down at him, "were in my Mama's plans. Not mine. I never wanted her to bring you into this house, and, as far as I'm concerned, you can leave."

"What the hell you talking 'bout?" He sat up, grabbed her by the shoulders, and shook her. "I can't understand you woman. I love you."

"That's *your* problem."

"I did everything for you and that screaming baby, Tam. You always came first," he bellowed. She struggled free, jumped from the bed, and ran to the kitchen.

"Sure, we were first," she said turning to look at him as he came through the door. "But you only did it after Mama greased your palm."

Rushing over to her, he caught her by the arm and hit her so hard her eyeballs hurt.

"Why, you son-of-a-bitch!" she hissed. She took a knife from the drawer and slashed at him, but he backed away quickly, and she sliced thin air. "You got no right to hit me. And don't you ever mention my daughter's name again. I know what you did when she was a baby. And I hate you for it," she yelled.

"What you talking 'bout?"

"I'm talking 'bout the day you tried to kill my baby. Remember the day you put that pillow over her face and tried to smother her?"

"I did no such thing," he said.

"Yes, you did. You didn't think I knew. But I knew. There was crochet on the pillow case, and the print of the trim was on her face. When I asked why she cried so hard you said you didn't know. I never told Mama because she loved you so much. But if you remember, I never left my baby with you again. I never did love you, and I never will!"

Obie stepped back, plopped down into a chair, and stared. All these years she knew but never said a word. I should've left the house long ago, he thought.

"Look, Asha. I'm sorry. But Tam started crying and wouldn't stop. I guess I lost my head."

"I guess you did," she said. "Now I'm losing mine. I want you out of this house within a week, and I never want to see you again. And until you get a place to live, you can sleep on the sofa, on the floor, or in Mama's bed, but don't you ever come to my room again."

He was unable to move. As she left the room he said, "I'm sorry, Asha." But Asha never looked back.

When Asha told Ginger what Obie did to her baby so long ago, Ginger was appalled. "But didn't he say he was sorry? He's a good man, Asha."

"He's gotta go, Mama."

On Friday, Ginger went away with her church group for the weekend. On Friday night Obie did exactly what Asha told him not to do. He went to her room and demanded sex. To his surprise, Asha made no attempt to stop him as he huffed, puffed, and humped over her. She allowed him to do whatever made him happy even though she wanted to scream. When he finished, he rolled over and went to sleep.

She realized unless she did something she was in for a hell of a ride, and it would be no fun. This was not what she wanted.

On Saturday morning, she got up, took her basket and strolled into the woods where she picked wild greens and wild mushrooms.

That afternoon, she went into the yard, and chose a chicken for her pot. After making her choice, she caught the chicken and wrung its neck like a wet towel until it went limp. Then she walked to the chopping block and hacked off its head.

Later she cooked a meal consisting of hot biscuits, rice, chicken and gravy, cornbread, wild greens, and wild mushrooms.

When Obie sat down at the table that evening, he noticed Asha smiled. He was sure his bedroom antics the night before put the smile on her face. Since she fixed such a wonderful meal, he was certain she'd changed her mind about his leaving.

"It's about time you started acting like a wife," he said as Asha placed a cup of mistletoe tea in front of him.

"You're right Obie. And I'm sorry about my actions in the past," she confessed.

"You should be. And I accept your apology," he said.

Asha took his plate and filled it with food. Then she sat and watched as he ate every morsel and drank his tea.

"Thanks, Asha. That was a very nice meal."

"My pleasure." And while she cleaned the kitchen he went to the front room and lay on the sofa.

Several hours later when she went to the front room, Obie looked up and spoke. "I don't feel so good, Asha. I think I'll go to bed."

"You do that. But don't you get in my bed," she said causing him to turn and wonder if she lost her mind. He didn't understand and wanted to talk to her about what she said, but he was just too sick.

"Why don't you get in Mama's bed since she loves you so much."

Once he disappeared into Ginger's bedroom, Asha picked up the catalogue. Sitting on the sofa until late in the night, she thumbed through it without really seeing anything because of what she had done.

"Hey, Obie," she called when she went to her mother's room. "You all right in there?"

When there was no response, she flipped on the wall light, went to the bed, and shook him. He didn't move. She felt his pulse. There was none. She had done it. Obie was dead.

Feeling free for the first time since her Mama made the deal with Obie, she laughed uncontrollably. Returning to the kitchen, she threw away the remaining noxious food and cleaned the kitchen spotless.

Still later she pondered getting Doc Peterson. But why would she do that when she really needed Thad Lamont? Hell, Obie was going to the morgue.

Tomorrow, she thought, I'll take care of things. And as rigor mortis set in Obie in the very next room, Asha undressed and put on her prettiest gown. Then climbing into her bed, she fell asleep.

It was late Sunday evening when Ginger returned home to find Obie in her bedroom as cold as stone. Feeling as though someone walked on her grave, she rushed into Asha's room. "What the hell happened here, Asha?" she yelled.

"Nothing happened, Mama." Asha stared at the ceiling. "I just helped Obie make up his mind about leaving the house. That's all. You brought him here." Asha slowly turned and gave her mother a blank stare. "That's why I made him get in your bed."

"Lawdy, Asha. I did what I thought was best for you. That's why I brought Obie here. You couldn't marry the other man. Do you remember that?"

Turning her head, once again Asha stared at the ceiling. "Yes, I remember. I also remember you did it against my wishes. So don't you come in here bossing me around ole lady, 'cause you might find yourself in the same fix as Obie."

The way Asha talked scared Ginger speechless. Something had happened to Asha and Ginger didn't know what to do. Thinking Asha might make good on her threat, Ginger never turned out the lights. She sat on the sofa with her eyes wide open all night.

She was glad to see sunrise the next morning. Still in a state of shock, she prepared to walk out the door to get Thaddeus Lamont to pick up Obie's body. But she noticed the house was unusually quiet. She became concerned, and called out her daughter's name.

"Asha," she called as she approached her daughter's bedroom. When there was no response, Ginger went inside and tried to get Asha out of the bed. But Asha never spoke or moved because during the night, she had a massive stroke.

"Lawdy," Ginger cried. "What's happened to my child?"

It was the worst day in Ginger's life. Her daughter couldn't move or speak, and Obie was dead. Standing in the middle of her daughter's bedroom, Ginger screamed and fell to her knees.

Nearby neighbors heard the screams and came to Ginger's aid.

When Tamara got the news of Obie's death, she was shocked, and took the first train back home. When it was rumored that her mother was suspected of killing Obie, she felt sick and she cried. Even though she had no love for Obie, she never wanted such a terrible thing to happen to him.

# CHAPTER 8

❀

Thea and Harry Rogers were man and wife, but looked so much alike folk swore they were sister and brother. Early one evening they took off with friends Lydia Wade and Billy Hardwood, and went to the small town of Sugar Hill to a dance.

Whenever Lydia saw a man she liked, she did whatever it took to get him. As soon as they walked into the lounge, she saw just her kind of man. He was sitting alone at the bar. Leaving her friends, she went over and started a conversation. He was friendly and laughed a lot. Before long, she snuggled up to him.

Just as he whispered in her ear, a short, buxom, woman and her two skinny girlfriends came through the door. Walking to the bar, the buxom woman approached Lydia.

"What you think you doing with my man?" she asked, standing with hands on hips, ready for a fight while her girlfriends looked on.

"I don't see a sign on him," Lydia snapped.

"Don't need no sign. I'm telling you he's mine. So keep your hands off him."

"Okay," the man said. "That's enough. Nothing's going on here."

"Sorry," Lydia said. Raising her hands in defense she backed off and joined her friends at the other end of the bar.

Later that evening when they decided to leave and walked outside, Lydia lagged behind. The woman she had words with earlier and her girlfriends followed Lydia closely.

"Hey, bitch," the woman yelled. Lydia turned and looked back.

"Who me?"

"Yeah, I'm talking to you," the woman said. "If I ever catch you talking to my man again, I'll cut your throat."

By this time Billy, Harry, and Thea were already at the car waiting for Lydia.

After the threat, Lydia put her hand in the pocket of the lightweight jacket she wore. As she continued to walk, the woman and her two pals trailed her.

"Yeah, she gonna cut your throat from ear to ear and leave you to die," one of the women threatened.

Lydia never spoke a word, but thinking they might carry out the threat now rather than later, she turned, pulled out her derringer, which she started carrying months earlier, and fired.

The bullet hit its mark. Someone screamed and instead of chasing her, the women ran in one direction and Lydia ran in the other towards the car.

"Let's get outta here," Billy yelled.

Later it was rumored the bullet grazed the accuser's ear. Lydia never went back to Sugar Hill and tried to forget the incident.

✺ ✺ ✺

Billy Hardwood, a short, skinny, black man, had four upper front teeth capped in gold. Though not always lit, a hand-rolled cigarette hung from his lips like a permanent fixture on some prominent statue.

His back yard was his garage, and several cars usually decorated his property. He and Harry Rogers worked together and were the only mechanics within miles of their town. On any given day the two men lay on their backs underneath cars soaked in grease.

But when Saturday noon rolled around they put away their tools, washed the muck from their bodies, and prepared to have a good time. As far as Billy was concerned, life should have been one big party. In spite of things, he turned up the volume of his jukebox loud enough for neighbors to hear, brought out the booze, and welcomed his friends into his home.

When Billy brought his new wife, Neva Pecker, home, Lydia, his friend since childhood, was happy Billy found a woman he liked enough to marry. Neva was friendly and outgoing. Within just a short time she and Lydia became friends. And because Lydia thought of Billy as a brother, she was at their house almost every day. The love she had for Billy extended to Neva.

Neva, on the other hand, hated Lydia from the first moment they met, but she never let Lydia know, and pretended her friendship was genuine.

Though no one knew it, Neva had a bone to pick with Lydia, and it had nothing to do with the nice clothes Lydia wore which seemed to scream, "Look at me."

It wasn't long before Billy knew Lydia's very presence rattled Neva's cage. She told Billy she didn't want Lydia visiting so much. But Billy explained he and Lydia were friends since childhood. "I call her *little sister* and she calls me *big brother*. We're friends and I think you better get used to the idea."

Fact was Billy considered Neva's complaints silly. He never realized the deep hatred she felt for Lydia nor the reason why.

# CHAPTER 9

During her college years, Natalie rushed home every chance she had to see Shelton, and, as soon as she returned to school, Shelton rushed off to see some other young lady. Her family was aware of his gadding about, and tried to discourage her interest in him. But Natalie never listened.

She was very astute academically and during the summer of 1939, she completed her studies and graduated a year ahead of most classmates. Leaving the campus behind, she returned home, and, against her family's wishes, the very headstrong Natalie married Shelton in the family home, surrounded by family members and her friend, Tamara, who came home for the special occasion.

January 1940. It was a cold day, and a light snow blanketed the ground. As Odessa Dawson set a steaming bowl of chicken and dumplings on the table, everyone took their places.

Natalie and Shelton owned a home only a half mile away, but because she shared a special bond with her mother, she insisted they join her family for dinner a couple times a week.

Sitting across from Natalie and Shelton, was her brother, Alan. He was a tall, well built, brown skinned man with black, wavy, cropped hair and a thin moustache. For the last few days, he had been contemplating his future. Not sure what his dad's response might be, he spoke quickly. "I just want you to know I'm planning to marry Sweet Hogan," he gushed.

"Why, I think that's a wonderful idea, son," Odessa said. But Marcus thought little of it and told him so.

"What is it with you, Alan? Why the rush to marry? You felt the same way about Lydia. Now, it's this girl, Sweet. You don't even know her. I wish to hell you'd take off the blinders, boy. Why are you so eager to jump from the frying pan into the fire?

"I'll tell you the same thing I told your sister. We don't get divorces in this family. Marriage is a lifetime commitment. Are you ready for that? Get to know this girl before you go off the deep end."

He watched his daddy squint, stretch his neck like one of his mama's long neck geese, then methodically take a quick puff on his cigar and then extinguish it in the ashtray.

"Or better yet, forget her," Marcus said shaking his head. "I never understood you at all."

Shoot, Alan thought as he put food on his plate. Sweet was no Lydia. She already laid down the law. She wanted a ring on her finger. No ring, no romp. He wanted to romp, so he planned to give her the ring with or without family blessings.

He was about to express that fact rather eloquently when the knock on the door interrupted them. His mother attempted to get up to answer it, but he motioned her to sit.

When he arrived at the door, he pulled back the curtain and peeked through the glass pane. He saw Lydia and immediately sensed something was wrong. Snow was falling, and most sane people were huddled inside their homes.

"Hi, Alan," she greeted cheerfully as he opened the door.

"Hey, Lydia, what can I do for you?"

"I just dropped in to see you and talk a bit."

"Why?" he asked puzzled by her sudden affable disposition.

"Well, for one thing I wanted to wish you a Happy New Year."

"It's a little late for that, don't you think? You should have come two weeks ago."

"Sorry, but I was out of town."

"Yeah, I know." He stared at her and asked, "Why did you do it, Lydia?"

"Do what?" she asked.

"Why did you go away with Slick?" Slick was Spuds Joyride's brother who lived in Chicago and came to town a couple times a year.

Leaning against the wall, she snapped, "That's none of your business."

"You're right. It's not." He dug his hands deep into his pockets. "Well, thanks for thinking about me. I wish you well too," he told her without feeling. "Now, why don't you tell me the real reason you came here." He didn't believe she had just dropped in. She never had in the past. She was always too busy doing whatever it was she did.

He could count on one hand the number of times she'd shared a meal with his family and still have three fingers to spare, he thought. He cared so much for her, but she betrayed him. Now, she acted so unlike the combative Lydia he knew. But he had known her far too long and was certain she had something up her sleeve.

"Come on, Lydia," he said arching his brow suspiciously. "It's cold as hell out there, and you want me to believe you just dropped by."

He wondered if she, like his daddy, thought he was nuts. Come to think of it, maybe he was. Everyone in town had tried to tell him about her recklessness but he hadn't listened.

Lydia was always restless and once left home with a man she barely knew. She stayed away for six months and during that time no one knew where she was or if she was alive or dead.

She could get ugly at times and had few friends other than Billy Hardwood, but that never fazed her. She was a real tyrant, and he foolishly thought he could change her. But a year into the relationship he knew something was amiss. She was as wild as a prairie horse. She was pretty but a depraved little bed-hopper who no one man could ever please. Her problems were insurmountable, and he couldn't possibly resolve them and no sane man would try.

She needed freedom. He needed stability, so he walked out. They split amicably in November and went their separate ways. He hadn't seen her since. Then she took off and went north with Slick.

In December, a young woman by the name of Sweet Hogan came into town to visit her family, and he fell in love.

"Did you hear me, Alan?" Lydia shouted jarring him back to the present.

"What's that?" It was obvious she said something, but he hadn't heard.

"I said I'd like us to be friends."

"Oh? Why is that? The last time I tried that, you showed no interest."

"Well, things are different now. I'm gonna have a baby."

"You're what?" he hissed.

"I'm gonna have a baby."

"So, why, why did you come to me?" he stammered.

"Because it's *your* baby," she said.

"What do you mean it's *my* baby?" He was stunned.

"It's like I said. It's your baby."

"How can you be sure when you jump up and down with any and every…"

"Don't you dare say it," she shouted angrily, armed to fight like the Lydia he had always known.

"Hey, keep your voice down." This wasn't something he wanted his parents to hear.

"I do not jump up and down with any and everybody." She seethed. "But I did jump with you."

"I don't care if you did." He spoke harshly. Fact was he simply wasn't ready to be a parent. "I still say you don't know who that baby belongs to."

"Now listen to me you slack ass son-of-a-bitch," she jeered. "This *is* your baby and don't you try to deny it."

"So you say," he snapped. He knew she was right. He was in no position to deny anything. He had dipped his wick in the oil, and she meant to burn his ass. He loathed ugliness. But Lydia's news brought out the worst in him, and he was about to show an ugly side he usually kept under wraps.

Like a spider, she'd spun her web and snared him as if he were some unsuspecting bug. He felt sick. Neither of them needed a baby, and he was not ready for this burden she thrust his way.

Suddenly, he wanted to jump all over her. But instead, he imagined his hands around her throat and slowly squeezing until her face contorted and she gasped her last breath. Was he capable of doing such a thing? Would this actually come to pass? He wondered.

His daddy told him she was a conniving hussy. He wasn't convinced back then, but now he was.

"You liar!" he shouted. "I knew when you walked through that door you had a problem. What the hell you gonna do with a baby?" He already felt sorry for the unborn child.

"You got no time nor the patience needed to be a mother. You're a roadrunner, Lydia." He berated her, hoping to hurt her so she would turn and run. It didn't work.

"Just who the hell do you think you are to call me names?" she hissed. "You lousy bastard."

"Whoa, girl. You better mind your manners or I'll slap your face."

"Don't you threaten me, Alan Dawson. This kid is as much your responsibility as mine. You've been a live wire all this time. You better not peter out on me now."

He crossed the room hoping the space between them might help him think more clearly. Unless he calmed down, they would celebrate a death long before the upcoming birth. Staring at the snow-covered garden he took several deep breaths.

"What do you expect me to do?" he asked after regaining his composure.

"I want you to do what a daddy is supposed to do. Take care of your baby."

"Okay, Lydia." He clenched his fists, realizing this was not a situation he could win. "I'll do that. But I'll never marry you. You'd drive me crazy."

"When did I ever ask you to marry me?" She spoke defiantly.

"It wouldn't do any good if you did," he said looking at her sneeringly. "I'd have to put you in chains to keep you home. Anyway, I plan to marry Sweet. She's…"

"She's what?" Lydia snapped.

"Well, she's…she's normal."

"Forget you, Alan," she smirked. "You just do your job when the time comes, and I'll do mine."

"Now you listen to me," he said realizing his ears burned even though there was no heat in the room. "And you listen carefully."

Turning to face her, he said, "If that's not my baby, you'll have hell to pay." He was hotter than the noonday sun and felt spewing his guts was better than killing her. "You better be telling the truth."

"I *am* telling the truth."

"I hope so. Otherwise, you'll wish you never met me."

As Lydia turned and started to leave, he followed and opened the door. She walked out without speaking a word and made her way from the porch. He waited until she went through the gate. As she disappeared up the street, the train whistle sounded in the distance, and he slowly closed the door.

"Okay, we're still waiting to hear about those big plans of yours," Marcus said as Alan returned to the room, trying to regain his composure.

"Well, as I said I'm planning to marry Sweet, and I hope you'll give me your blessings." He spoke quickly as if he thought someone might interrupt before he finished.

"Yeah, and as I said, please get to know the girl first."

"I already know her," he replied angrily.

"Sure you do," his daddy said ignoring him. "You go through with this marriage, and you'll be sorry. Mark my word. It's best you forget her."

"Damn, daddy. Get off my back."

"I'll get off your back when you get off your backside and make something of yourself."

Both were angry. He wanted to hit his dad but knew to do so would mean trouble. And he loved his family too much to let anger come between them. Giving his daddy a deadly stare, he thought of Sweet. He couldn't wait to give her a ring.

"Don't worry about a thing, son," Odessa said hoping both would calm down.

"You do whatever you think is right for *you*, and I'll be there for you."

Lydia's visit prodded Alan to marry Sweet Hogan right away against his daddy's wishes. Two weeks later he and Sweet went to Chicago putting as many miles as possible between Lydia and himself.

He went to work for the railroad, and true to his word, he sent Lydia money. Then on August 1, 1940, she gave birth to a baby girl, Kornelia.

🍁  🍁  🍁

After she finished college, Tamara came home that summer with high expectations of living the same good life she'd become accustomed to during the past four years. But her grandmother, Ginger, who had cared for Tamara's mother Asha for the past several years, had a stroke too. Then both women lay in bed unmoving and unable to speak. And Tamara, who wanted better things in life, had a real burden to bear.

# CHAPTER 10

December 7, 1941. The Japanese attacked Pearl Harbor, and a shocked nation entered the war. And while everyone in Meadowsbrook feared imminent death and destruction, Natalie Dawson Lamont lay in bed enduring such terrible labor pains she thought she would die.

While her mother held one hand and talked soothingly, her friend, Tamara, held the other. As each pain tore at her, she screamed a little louder while the midwife, Bessie Mae Wanker, wiped perspiration from her forehead.

Realizing Natalie was having unforeseen difficulty, Bessie Mae Wanker sent Shelton to get Doc Peterson.

As Shelton walked out the door into the night, he muttered to himself, "Shoot, Billy's having a party tonight and I wanted to go and have some fun." His wife was about to give birth, and bombs had fallen on Pearl Harbor, Hawaii, early that morning, but, at that moment, the seriousness of it all never fazed him.

"If it's not one damn thing, it's another," he cursed under his breath. "Now I gotta get Doc Peterson. Nat wanted this damn baby. Now she can't even have it without having some kind of problem."

As he headed to the car, he tipped toed carefully in order to avoid mud puddles. Even though he wore boots, he wanted them to stay perfectly clean.

Climbing into the car, he revved the motor, pulled off, and drove as fast as he could. Instead of being concerned about Natalie, he was worried about the young women he might miss by not being at Billy's.

If I hurry and get Doc, he thought, I just might make it to Billy's before the party's over.

Suddenly, he lost control of the car, and it slipped off the road and into the ditch.

"Goddammit!" he screamed as he gunned the motor and got back onto the road. Keeping his mind on his driving, he slowed down and reached the hospital in one piece.

Hours after Shelton and Doc's arrival back at the house, everyone stood around the bed. Natalie still suffered, and turning to Bessie Mae Wanker, Doc said, "It seems this baby doesn't want to come into this world." Finally, Natalie gave that last push giving birth to a little girl she named Makela.

Ecstatically happy that the worst was over and she had a healthy child, she cried. Even though Shelton wasn't the perfect husband, she hoped one day he might be. But this wasn't the time to worry since loving others meant sacrifices. The passion she felt for him was so deep she could easily walk to the end of the rainbow for him.

❦ ❦ ❦

Shelton Lamont was tall, still good-looking, and wore hair longer than most. His teeth were as white as expensive pearls, and his chocolate skin as smooth as satin. He was a fastidious man who liked nice clothes and, thanks to his wife's talent as a seamstress, folk said he was the snazziest dresser in town.

Though he liked the clothes she made, his most prized possessions were his shoes, which he loved almost as much as he loved himself.

In summer he carried a small cloth to brush dust from his shoes. When the rains came, he stepped carefully around puddles, but carried the same small cloth to clean any mud that happened to get on his shoes. If, by chance, someone stepped on his foot and marred his shoe, he became irate.

Whenever he went out, he looked like he'd stepped from a catalogue page. This, of course, caused heads to turn wherever he went. He was considered the perfect catch by most women, and he had everything most men wished for. He was married to Natalie who was always there for him and gave him her heart. Yet, he lusted after other women and had a hard time keeping his pants above his knees.

❦ ❦ ❦

Spring 1942, on a warm evening as Odessa prepared to take her bath, she looked around the room as if seeing it for the first time. Suddenly she thought of her parents. Though she never voiced it to anyone, she longed for their presence.

Born in New Orleans, Louisiana, she was the product of a Cherokee mother of the Carolinas and a black father of New Orleans. Both parents died when she was just a child.

Though quite young when Marcus came along and offered her marriage, she was delighted and accepted. Marcus, whose grandmother was an octoroon and granddaddy a white man, was tall, thin, and dark, with warm brown eyes and wavy hair. She thought he was the handsomest man she'd ever seen. In addition to his good looks, he was intelligent, well read, and a skilled builder by trade. He, she thought, would make certain she had a good life.

She felt fortunate to have what many others could not afford and considered it special. She prized her indoor toilet because since childhood she was afraid of any and all "creepy crawlers." And such fear caused her to suffer with stomach pains and bouts of constipation. But when Marcus installed the indoor plumbing, it changed her life.

The tub was a Godsend, but it was secondary. Still, the first time she sat in it, she stayed so long Marcus came to see if she had drowned.

Now as she stepped into the tub and slid down into the warm, soothing water, she thought about the first day she arrived in Meadowsbrook.

🍁 🍁 🍁

It was the summer of 1910. Shortly after she and Marcus married, her daddy's sister, Aunt Maggie, became ill and sent her a letter. "I'm very sick," the letter read. "Would you please come?"

She and Marcus left New Orleans a few days after receiving the letter and took the train to Meadowsbrook. The day they arrived ghastly heat waves danced across the terrain and the ground temperature was such it burned bare feet.

Even though streets had no names, and houses had no numbers, they easily found Aunt Maggie's little house because it was the only white house on the main street. The house was merely a shotgun shack, so called because the three small rooms were built one directly behind the other, and one could fire a shotgun at the front door and accurately hit a target on the back door.

A magnolia tree stood in the front yard, and a flock of long necked geese hissed and ran about the back yard. She kept the geese and to this very day she still had geese in her yard.

※　※　※

The honking of the geese brought her back to the present. Stepping out of the tub, Odessa took a towel from the rack, and dried her body. Walking into her small bedroom, she slipped into a summer dress Natalie made. Then she made her way to the dining room and took several glasses from the buffet and a pitcher of lemonade from the refrigerator. Placing the pitcher and glasses on a tray, she carried the tray onto the front porch.

"I thought you said Nat was coming," Marcus commented as she placed the tray on a small table beside her chair.

"I'm sure she is. Would you like some?" she asked as she poured lemonade into a glass.

"Not at the moment," he said preferring his homemade wine instead.

She expected Natalie and Shelton to arrive soon and looked forward to spending the evening with her daughter. Turning her head, she listened for the roar of Shelton's car engine. But to her dismay, she heard only the whir of the electric fan on the shelf in the corner.

"I thought you said Nat was coming," Marcus interrupted her thoughts again with his query.

"I thought we just talked about that." She knew the wine was taking its toll. "I suppose she'll be here soon."

"Well, I really don't know why I asked. I get a headache anytime I think of her and Alan."

"Why's that?"

"Because neither she nor Alan's done anything worthwhile that I can see."

"Then shame on you, Marcus. You can't live their lives. So you might as well stop trying. They'll be all right."

"So you say. And I know I can't live for them. I just wish things were different," he said raising his glass and taking a sip.

Growing impatient with him, Odessa changed the subject. "You know, I was just thinking how much I hated this place when we first came here."

"I know," Marcus said. "As soon as Aunt Maggie died, you wanted to go back to New Orleans. But she left those little plots of land, and I finally got it through your head the importance of staying here and working the land."

"Yes, you did," she said. "And life's not as bad as I thought it might be." She stared out at the front gate and hoped Natalie would soon arrive.

"Yeah, I still remember." He stared at Odessa. She had smooth, tan skin, and her bright brown eyes twinkled above high cheekbones. She wore her long, soft, black hair braided and pinned at the nape of her neck. She was a good looking woman, he thought, and he loved her as much now as he had when he first saw her. He chuckled loudly.

"What's so funny?" she asked.

"I was just thinking about the first time we met Bessie Mae Wanker. She was quite the talker back then." Closing his eyes he reminisced.

❧   ❧   ❧

"I'm Bessie Mae Wanker," a very small, dark, older woman announced when she opened the door and faced him and Odessa when they arrived.

Bessie Mae said she wrote the letter for Maggie. "I tried to get Maggie to the hospital, but she refused to go."

"Well, we appreciate your help, Mrs. Wanker," he said as they walked to Aunt Maggie's bedside. Looking down, they realized Aunt Maggie was frail, and her body was merely skin and bone. Leaning closer to Aunt Maggie, Odessa laid her hand on Aunt Maggie's feverish forehead. As she raised the sheet, they saw that Aunt Maggie's body was covered in blisters.

"Good Lord! I think we better get the doctor."

"I tried to get her to let the doctor come in," Mrs. Wanker said as he turned and asked where he might find the doctor.

"Well," she said. "You walk up the main street a ways. Then you cut across the railroad tracks. Go past the post office, and across the highway. Then you'll see the Weeping Willows. That's the funeral home, ya know. It's owned by the Lamonts."

"So where can I find the doctor, Mrs. Wanker?" he asked irritably. And even now he could feel that moment. He had become impatient with the woman.

"Why, in the hospital, mind ya. It's called Morningstar. And it's right next door to the funeral home."

As he rushed from the house and out into the hot, dusty street, he wondered how much longer Bessie Mae Wanker would have talked had he not stopped her. Running up the incline to the railroad, he crossed the tracks. As he rushed down the other side of the tracks, he hurried along until he saw the Weeping Willows Funeral Home. Taking a short cut, he made his way through a weed patch and up the hospital steps.

Sweat poured down his face as he hurried through the hospital door. "I'm sorry," he said as he literally bumped into the young doctor. "But I'm in a hurry. I need to see the doctor right away."

"Hold on a minute, will you. *I am* the doctor. My name is Doctor Hoot Peterson," he said, holding out his hand. "Now what can I do for you."

Marcus stared at the man in the white medical coat, which he had not been aware of previously, and reached for the doctor's hand.

"I'm Marcus Dawson. My wife and I just came to town to see about her Aunt Maggie who's much sicker than we expected. Can you come take a look at her?"

Doc Peterson left him for a minute and came back with his bag. Then they got into Doc's car and went to Aunt Maggie's house.

After examining Aunt Maggie, Doc Peterson was unable to determine her illness. He insisted she go to the hospital, but Aunt Maggie refused. When Doc tired of talking, he gave her medicine to ease her pain.

"If she gets any worse," he told Odessa. "Get her to the hospital."

"I'll do that, Doc," Odessa promised.

Since Aunt Maggie occupied the only bedroom in the house, Odessa made a quilt pallet for the floor, where they slept on the screen-enclosed back porch.

They waited for Aunt Maggie to get better. But several days later when there was no improvement, they put Aunt Maggie in the hospital where she died two days later.

He realized they had good farmland and established gardens. Standing in the center of the plot next to the house was a fig tree and growing along the garden fence were thick blackberry bushes. At the back of the house was another garden plot where two peach trees grew. In the back yard stood an elm tree and a pecan tree grew just outside the back gate.

From the time they took over the property, they worked so hard from sunrise to sundown they barely had strength to crawl into bed by nightfall.

Soon their hard work paid off. Trees produced fruit and gardens yielded vegetables in abundance. Like a squirrel preparing for winter, Odessa preserved much of the harvest in clear glass Mason jars for later use while sharing with less fortunate neighbors.

Within time, they acquired several pigs, goats, cows and horses. Before long they owned enough animals that they could afford to barbeque a goat or pig. And on weekends they invited neighbors, including Bessie Mae Wanker, to feast with them.

Everyone loved his special spicy recipe and soon there was such a demand for his barbeque from affluent folk in the nearby town of Baysville that he sold whole pigs and goats. What started out as a family feast, became a lucrative business.

After several years of living in the small house he surprised Odessa and added a room. And every year thereafter he added another until there were nine rooms with a lovely wrap-around porch. He later built a swing and suspended it from the rafters.

Later still he painted the house and the swing white. Then he trimmed the house in green and installed green awnings over the windows. When the house was finished, it was considered one of the biggest and prettiest houses in town, and most folk called it *the big house*.

As news of his skills spread, folk came from other communities to look at his home. Some promised him work in the future, but Pete Baraldi, owner of the meat packing plant in Baysville, hired him on the spot. After he built Pete's home, his business flourished.

☘ ☘ ☘

Opening his eyes, Marcus said, "Yeah, I remember it like it was yesterday. I remember I had so much work I couldn't handle it all. So I sent for my brother Percy."

"That's right," Odessa said, happy Marcus forgot about Natalie and Alan. "Percy and Helene came up for just a few months, but they never left. Then you built that little shoe shop up there on the main street for Helene and she's been smiling ever since. Then Doc asked you to build him a house 'cause his wife Ellie got tired of the country and wanted to live closer to the hospital. You know something, Marcus?"

"What's that?" he asked.

"Life hasn't been too bad for us, and I thank you," she said. Marcus smiled. As he did so, he thought about his son, Alan.

He wanted so much for his children, but they had other ideas. He never told Odessa, but Alan had so disillusioned him he felt physically revolted. He wanted Alan to study medicine. But he finally realized medicine wasn't Alan's dream, but his. As the wine warmed his body, he wondered if his son ever dreamed of anything other than a woman.

He remembered after college Alan worked with him in carpentry. But the work proved too difficult. He could hardly hold a hammer or drive a nail into wood.

"Why don't you go to medical school, son? We're prepared to pay your way. I think you'd make a good doctor. You've got the delicate hands of a surgeon." He hoped flattery would motivate Alan. "The town could use another doctor."

"I know, daddy. I'm thinking about it," Alan said. And the day he walked into the barber shop and picked up the clippers, Marcus felt heartbroken. It was evident Alan found interest, not in medicine, but cutting hair, and Marcus was devastated.

He wanted more for his son, but from the expression on Alan's face he knew the shop made a profound impression. He obviously felt the clippers better suited his hands than a scalpel. At that moment, he chided himself for owning the shop. He'd opened the doors of the one room barber shop which Aunt Maggie's husband operated until his death, hung out a sign, and on Saturday mornings charged twenty-five cents for a haircut. H had wanted to *burn* the place down.

Still he wasn't ready to admit defeat. So he kept badgering, hoping, and explaining.

"Listen, Alan, Doc Flack spends his time between Morningstar Hospital and that hospital up north. Doc Peterson is getting on in years. He'll retire one day and we'll need another doctor. You're still young. Why don't you give it a try?"

"I'm thinking about it, daddy."

"I wish you'd do more than think. You got to act. Time's a wasting. You won't be young forever. You'll wake up one morning and look in the mirror and wonder where the years went."

"Don't worry so, daddy. I'll surprise you one day."

"I bet you will." As he watched Alan clip still another head, he finally gave up.

His desires were just that. His. They weren't Alan's. Alan had to want it too in order to go after it. And for the time being he was satisfied working in the barbershop.

Then Sweet Hogan came along. Lawdy! Within no time at all she put her mojo on him and wrapped him around her finger like a rubber band. Shortly afterwards, he dropped the clippers faster than he dropped the hammer, married that short haired Sweet Hogan and went to Chicago.

He wondered about Sweet. He never saw her pull a weed from the yard. Seems all she did was sit around looking pretty. From his viewpoint she was just as cunning as Lydia. She just had longer fingernails she kept painted. He wished he could wipe his son from his memory.

Then there was Nat, a bright young woman who taught school and made beautiful clothes, but married a man who was a gold plated woman charmer. If he was to believe rumor, and he did, his son-in-law had more women than King Solomon had gold mines.

Of course, it would do no good to talk to Nat. She loved the man too much. As far as he was concerned, the only good to come from that union was that little tyke, Makela.

He wanted better things for them, but their ideas differed. Odessa was right. There was only so much a man could do. He couldn't live through his children, and it was time to let go. They, not he, were in control of their destiny.

❈   ❈   ❈

"Goddammit!" he muttered.

"What is it, Marcus?" Odessa asked annoyed that he disturbed her reverie.

"Just thinking," he answered. "I did my best for my children." "I know that, Marcus, and I'm sure they're grateful."

"But they never did anything right," he said. "Nat married a man who keeps her in tears, and I hate to think about Alan at all. The only thing he does with his head is wear a hat.

"Now, he's up there in Chicago sweating his brains out when he should be in medicine. What a waste!"

"Now, now, Marcus, don't feel that way," she replied petulantly. "He's only doing that work until he gets enough money to follow his dream."

"And what's that, pray tell?"

"He and Sweet plan to open a barbershop and beauty salon soon."

"Dammit! He needed no book learning for that. I swear I'm so disappointed in them I want to cry." He stood, shook his head in disblief, and stretched.

"For heaven sakes," she said. "It's time you stopped giving Alan a bad time. Just keep the faith. I do. Alan will be all right."

"Okay, if you say so," he replied. He looked down at this almost child-like woman and realized she spoke as a mother who loved her children in spite of things. He hoped she understood he carried on so because he wanted them to enjoy a life without so much strife and struggle.

"I think I'll take a walk. I need to do some thinking," he said ambling towards the door.

"So you say," she answered snidely. She was no idiot. She heard the rumors. "Children aren't the only disappointments around here."

"Lawdy, Odessa. Whatta you mean by that?"

"I'll tell you exactly what I mean," she started just as Shelton drove up and announced their arrival by beeping the horn several times. She clammed up, and Marcus breathed a sigh of relief. He knew Odessa sensed he was a little sweet on Jenny Joyride.

Hurriedly, he left the porch and almost ran down the walkway. It was the first time he was ever glad to see his son-in-law and to prove it he stopped to talk with him.

Odessa listened to the chatter and was surprised to hear Natalie's laughter. When they came onto the porch, she obviously looked worried because Shelton jolted her with his unusual concern.

"Is everything all right, Mama?"

"Why, yes, Shel. Everything's just fine. Thank you," she answered taking the baby from Natalie's arms. "Come on in and sit a spell."

To her surprise, Shelton sat in the swing beside Natalie and picked up the Chicago Defender, a newspaper owned and published by blacks in Chicago, and subscribed to by almost every family in town.

Because whites still believed blacks were incapable of flying planes, Shelton found special interest in the article about the black pilots. The article stated that despite all the noise made against black pilots by the Army Air Corps and the War Department, legislation passed earlier on in '41 made it possible for the activation of the all-black 99th Fighter Squadron.

Tuskegee Army Air Field, located at the Institute in Alabama, became the training center for black fighter pilots during the war. And blacks all over the nation felt a certain pride that so many interested in flying continued to follow their dreams in spite of numerous obstacles thrown in their paths.

Though he already knew about the pilots, for some reason this article started Shelton thinking. In fact, he was so inspired by the pilots he felt he too should contribute in some way to the war.

"I'll see you later, Nat," he said. Laying the paper aside, he kissed Natalie's cheek. "You too, Mama," he told Odessa.

As Natalie watched him drive away, she turned to Odessa and asked, "Will you keep the baby, Mama? I just finished a dress for Thea, and I'd like to take it to her."

"Of course, I will, hon. Just hurry back so we can chat." Odessa looked down at the baby in her arms and chuckled.

"I'll do that, Mama," Natalie said tucking the bag with the dress in it under her arm and walking out the door.

Driving like a maniac, Shelton headed for Billy's house. When he arrived, Harry Rogers, Fats Hopper, and his cousin, Warren Gilliam, were already there. He was excited and immediately told them he planned to join the army and thought they should too. "It's our obligation," he said.

"I ain't so convinced about that. Think about it. What's this country ever done for us?" Harry asked.

"I know how you feel, Harry, and I'm sure the cadets feel that way at times, too. But that's not stopping them. They plan to do something worthwhile. They intend to make a difference."

"Jeez, I don't know. We ain't cadets. We can't fly planes, you know," Billy said. "And I don't care what you say. I ain't ready to be cannon fodder for any reason."

"I understand that, Billy. But we need to do something," Shelton said.

"You do what you think you gotta do," Harry told him. "Me? I'm going to De-troit."

But then Shelton started talking as if he was in the pulpit and by the time he finished, he convinced Warren and Billy that Uncle Sam desperately needed their talents. Harry wasn't convinced, but decided to go along just for the ride.

"What about you, Fats?" Shelton asked when they piled into the car.

"Whatta you mean, what about me?" Fats asked laughingly while sticking his head inside the car window. "I tell you what. You go fight the war while I stay here and do what I do best." Then speaking seriously, he asked, "What about Nat and your baby, Shel? Did you really give this thing serious thought?"

"Sure. I gave it serious thought. Nat and the baby can stay with her mama until I get back."

"What if you don't come back?" Fats asked.

"Then you'll have to take care of them, Fats," he yelled as he put the car in gear and drove away.

When they arrived at the induction center, Shelton learned Uncle Sam had no use for him because as a young boy, a heavy piece of equipment fell on his foot and cut off his little toe.

Billy was rejected too. When he was just a boy, he'd pulled a horse's tail. The horse kicked him in the ass. Not only did the horse leave an imprint on his ass, it gave him a limp for life, and he rocked like a disabled ship bobbing on high seas.

Warren, who stuttered since childhood, was physically fit, but was too unnerved to utter his name.

Harry, the fittest of the bunch, decided this was no time to offer his services to anyone. He waited in the car until they returned.

"Well, boys," he said when they told him what happened. "I suppose you're already done fighting the war."

# CHAPTER 11

"Hi, Thea," Natalie called to the young woman sitting on the porch as she neared the house.

"Hey, how you doing, Nat?" Thea asked, but before Natalie could answer, she continued. "There was no need for you to bring it. I was coming to get it."

"I know you were, but I don't mind. I enjoy walking."

"Well, come on in, and sit a while," Thea invited.

"Jeez, it's just now spring and already hot as hell, ain't it?" Thea complained. Natalie started to speak, but Thea interrupted.

"I'm so sick and tired of this place I don't know what to do. It's just like living in hell. And it's not just the heat I'm talking about either. You know what I mean?" She glanced at Natalie who decided she had nothing to add. And even if she did, Thea would never allow her to voice it.

"Nothing ever gets better around here. And these backward ass people get crazier every day. I mean look at all the shit they pull, Nat. You never know when somebody might stab or shoot you for something somebody thought you said or did."

"My God! I had no idea you felt so out of sorts about things," Natalie retorted, surprised Thea allowed her to speak. Though she wasn't about to reveal it, she had a few gripes, too.

The fact that Della Gilliam and everyone in town knew more about her business than their own angered her. Of course, she blamed Shel and his 'I don't a give damn' attitude.

"Well, you know now. I just don't like the idea of constantly watching my back. That's the reason we're planning on leaving."

"Oh!" Natalie exclaimed.

"Surprised are you?"

"It's just that I thought you and Harry were happy here. Of course, in addition to those things you mentioned there're so few things to do and places to go, especially, for those who want to spread their wings." Natalie waited for Thea to say something but, surprisingly, she was silent.

"I suppose you want to walk on paved streets and live in a house with a number on the door," Natalie laughed.

"You got that right."

"In the meantime, why don't you try on this dress?" Natalie thrust the bag at her. Thea took the bag and walked inside the house to put on the new dress. As she did so Natalie mused. Though Thea's perception of things was closer to truth than not, she loved her life here.

"So where do you plan to go?" She asked when Thea returned to the porch.

"Detroit. I got family there."

"Not much difference in the weather up there."

"I guess not. But I want to live in the city."

"It's a perfect fit," Natalie referred to the dress. Standing, she went over to Thea. "Yes, indeed. It's a very good fit." She nudged Thea's arm, to indicate she should turn.

"Well, I never expected less," Thea laughed turning slowly. "You know your stuff, lady. But tell me something, will you?" Thea looked serious. "Don't you ever think about leaving?"

"Of course, not. My family lives here. I can't leave them."

"Hum. I know how you feel about family. But I can't believe you never get the urge to just pick up and run away at times."

"I see no reason for that," Natalie said.

"How's your friend, Tamara Mack?"

"She's fine. She's married now, and her name's…"

"Can you believe what happened in that house? Wish I'd been a fly on the wall that one night."

"Well…" Natalie started but Thea interrupted.

"I hear Asha poisoned Obie with wild greens and wild mushrooms."

"I can't believe…" Natalie started, but decided Thea wanted a one-sided conversation, and so gave up and listened.

"Ginger told me all about it herself before she got sick. Seems Asha never wanted Obie in the house, and he tried to kill Tam when she was a baby. Obie never thought Asha knew, but she did, and she bided her time.

"Seems Asha got in her prettiest gown and went to bed. Can you believe that? I mean Obie was dead in her mother's bed, and she gets in her own bed, and goes to sleep in the very next room. Wouldn't you say something was wrong with Asha's head?"

"I..." Natalie started.

"I would. You know God don't like ugly. Asha killed Obie, and she never got outta that bed again. She stroked out during the night. When Ginger found her the next morning, she was staring at the ceiling. She never spoke another word. And, as you know, later Ginger had a stroke too.

"From what I hear, Tam put them in one room so they can eyeball each other. And I bet them two's just a seething 'cause they can't talk. Whatta you think?"

"I can't say what they..."

"I got a feeling that whole damn family's nuts, and that includes Tam. Strutting around here in them high heel shoes like she's going to church, or putting on a show," Thea said enviously.

"Mercy, speak of the devil, and here she comes. Hey, Tam, how you doing? What's up, girl?" Thea yelled before Tamara was close enough to talk. Then turning to Natalie she asked, "You ever stop by and see them two ole ladies?"

"Yes, I visit them often."

"From what I hear, Tam was pretty mean to her mother when she was growing up. Is that so?"

"So I hear. But that was something they kept in the family. I knew nothing about that. Tam was always the perfect..." Natalie said.

"What's her name now that she's married?"

"Tamara Dupree."

"Hey, Tamara Dupree," Thea called out. "What's up? You singing at the Lounge tonight?"

"Yeah, I am," she said. "You coming over?"

"I might. I could use a little excitement." Then turning to Natalie, Thea asked, "Who takes care of them two ole ladies while Tam's out there good-timing?"

"God," Natalie said bluntly.

"Get outta here," Thea said laughingly.

"Wait up, Tam," Natalie yelled as Thea pressed several dollars into her hand.

"Thanks Thea. I'll see you later." Rushing down the steps and onto the streets Natalie joined Tamara. "Where're you going?" Natalie asked.

"I was looking for you. Wanted to visit. I had to get away for a while."

"Good. Come on. Mama will be glad to see you," Natalie said as they started walking down the tree lined street.

"How are the ladies?" Natalie inquired of Asha and Ginger.

"Well," Tam paused. "They ain't living, but they ain't dying either. They're just in limbo. And I don't know how much more I can take."

"I know it's difficult, and I wish I had the answer, but I'll do whatever I can to help you," Natalie said.

"I know you will," Tamara sighed. "I guess I'd really feel bad if I had a loving relationship with them. But that's not the way it was. When I was a kid we fought all the time."

"So I heard. But surely they were your best friends."

"Perhaps, but I didn't see it that way," Tamara said.

"Why's that?"

"Because they never told me who my daddy was, and we always fought. Now they can't tell me."

"I'm so sorry," Natalie replied, not sure what else to say since she thought Tamara accepted Obie as her daddy though everyone knew he wasn't. Suddenly Natalie wanted to ask Tamara about the rumor and her mother Asha. Instead, she said, "From what I hear, your mother really loved you." Tamara stared at Natalie then said, "Do you know who finally told me what I wanted to know?"

"No, I don't. Don't tell me Della…"

Della Gilliam was married to Shelton Lamont's cousin, Warren Gilliam, and had the biggest mouth in town. She snooped and found out secrets while other folk slept.

She never missed church services unless she was sick. She was usually one of the first to arrive at church and the last to leave. She prayed the longest and sang the loudest. But her main mission was to make sure she got the latest gossip from anyone gullible enough to talk to her.

Most folk knew Della well, but there was always some guileless sister who allowed Della to pump her for all she was worth. Then Della proceeded to talk about everyone in the congregation except the listener.

During the conversation, the well-meaning sister gave Della secrets she pledged never to divulge. And days later the sister realized her error in judgment. But it was too late. She learned what everyone else already knew. Della had no sense of loyalty and she was known as one who not only disturbed the shit, but the shinola as well.

"No it wasn't Della. It was old man Seb Pardeau."

"I suppose he knows," Natalie said. "He's been around since the beginning of time. He's as old as Methuselah." Both chuckled.

"You can say that again," Tamara paused though she knew Natalie was dying to hear.

"Come on, Tam. How did it come about? What did he tell you?"

"Well, I went to Michael's Market one day. You know Vince Baraldi usually makes deliveries. But Frank made deliveries that day. Told me he comes to the Lounge once in a while and had heard me sing. Said he enjoyed it. I thanked him. He got in the truck and drove away. Then Seb called me over. "And the conversation went like this:

'What you doing with that man?' Seb asked.

'Oh, he just said he admires my singing,' I told him.

'Well, I hope that's all he's admiring 'bout you,' he said.

'What's that supposed to mean?' I asked.

'Lawdy, girl, don't you know who he is?'

'Sure. He's Vince the meat man's brother,' I said.

'He sho' is,' Seb said. 'And he's *yo*' brother too.'

'What? You mean Pete Baraldi is my daddy? I don't believe it,' I said.

'Stars above, girl. Didn't your mama ever tell you?'

'No, she didn't and unless we witness a miracle, she'll carry that one to her grave.'"

"Gracious!" Natalie exclaimed. "This means you're Liz's child's aunt."

"I know. I already wrote her about it. The world is very small."

"Now that you know who you are, what do you plan to do?"

"I'm not sure. All I ever wanted was to know who my people were. After I talked to Seb, most of my questions were answered and things fell into place. Now I know Pete Baraldi gave Mama the money to buy my clothes, and he paid for college, too. I met the man years ago before I went away to school, but he never told me who he was."

"Now that his wife is dead, perhaps it's time you talked to him. But regardless of what you do, I think you should be grateful for what he and your mother did for you. I believe your mother did what she could to make sure things were right for you."

"I know she did. But I just wish we talked."

"I know, but you must move on now. How do you like married life?"

"Well, marriage isn't all it's cracked up to be. You know me, Nat. I like a little excitement," she whispered as if sharing a secret. They both laughed.

"I know you do and so do I. That's the reason I married Shel, remember? But…" Natalie said as they entered the yard.

"But what, Nat? Aren't you happy?"

"For the most part, I am."

"You want to talk about it?"

"No. Not now. But I'm surprised to hear it isn't working out for you."

"I was happy for a while. But that little something that once put a smile on my face is gone, honey."

"You've been married only a year."

"I don't care if it's only a month. It feels like ten years, girl."

"For heaven sakes, Tam, you should be ashamed," Natalie replied. As they neared the steps, she turned and studied her friend's face for a moment. "Marriage is a lifetime commitment you know," Natalie said seriously.

"For me it's not," Tamara replied looking her square in the face. "And one day you might find it's not for you either. Girl, time brings about changes.

"People change, you know, and not always for the better. I don't intend to stay in any situation for appearances. You know me better than that. Come to think of it you shouldn't either.

"You gotta think for yourself, Nat. Only you can live your life, girl. Don't let mama, papa, or Shel tell you what to do. Are you listening to me?"

"I'm listening. We'll talk later," Natalie whispered as they walked onto the porch. "Mama," Natalie called inside to Odessa. "Look who's here."

"Lawdy, look what the wind blew in," Odessa said. She joined them and acted as if she hadn't seen Tamara in weeks when Tamara had visited only several days ago. But that's how folk acted in these parts.

"Come on in here and give me a hug," she said throwing her arms around Tamara. "It's so good to see you, hon."

"It's good to see you too," Tamara said.

"How're the ladies today?"

"Well, I'll tell you the same thing I told Nat. They're not living and God knows they're not dying, though I sometimes think death would be a blessing for them and me too. They don't know they're still in this world. They're just in limbo."

"I guess it's quite a task taking care of them. Who's with them now?"

"Carrie Lucas."

"Now there's a kind spirit. You couldn't get better help being she's a nurse and all," Odessa said.

"You're right about that. And Paige drops in to see them, too," she said speaking of Doc Peterson's daughter who was also a nurse.

"You might not know it, Tamara, but you're blessed that so many people care."

"I know."

"Now you let me know if I can do more for you."

"I appreciate that. But you already do enough. Sending over all that food saves me a lot of work. I'm thankful for your hospitality."

"I don't mind, hon. I love you like my own daughter, and it wouldn't be Christian to do otherwise. Wish I had some answers. No one knows why things happen. Don't know why your mama and grandma are suffering so," Odessa said thoughtfully.

"So much happens around here. Seems the devil's lurking in every corner. Seems he's got his hooks in most and trying to get his hooks into the rest of us. There're more ugly things happening here than in hell. You think Satan's got his hooks in the two ladies, Tam?"

"For goodness sake, Mama, you should be ashamed to say such thing. Nobody believes that."

"I do," Tamara said. "I think about it often. Neither one's an angel you know. I got a feeling he had his hooks into them long before they got sick."

"Now see what you did, Mama. You got Tam talking crazy too. Where's my baby?" Natalie asked abruptly changing the subject.

"She's sleeping," Odessa said. Natalie went inside to check on the child causing Odessa to smile. Then turning to Tamara, Odessa asked, "How's married life, hon?"

"I'll tell you the same thing I told Nat. It ain't all it's cracked up to be."

Odessa laughed. "I know what you mean, hon." Then after a moment of silence, she asked, "Is Tobias any help to you with the ladies?"

"At times he is. But when he gets mad at me I see something in Tobias's eyes that gives me the chills. He wants me to give up singing, you know. But I can't do that. Singing keeps me alive."

"I understand you're committed to your career. But you must remember marriage is a commitment too," Odessa said.

"Is it now?" Tamara laughed.

"Yes, it is young lady," Odessa smiled. "Seriously, it is."

Natalie, returning to the porch, gazed into Tamara's face. She was a talented, natural born singer, Natalie thought, with a powerful voice who had a feeling for blues and jazz.

She took lyrics, wrapped her arms around them and caressed them as she would a lover. By the time she stopped singing a song, everybody in the audience felt she'd sung to each of them specifically.

Natalie loved Tamara like a sister and knew her well. She was unbendable. Married or not she did whatever she wanted. If she had to choose between singing and marriage, Tobias would be the loser. Tamara was pretty, but as stubborn as a mule and wasn't about to give it up for anyone.

She loved her fancy clothes and high heel shoes, which she wore at that very moment. Though the evening was young, she was ready to paint the town as red as her hair. "I hope everything works out for you," Natalie said.

"Thanks. So do I. Where's Shel?" Tamara asked.

"At Billy's, I suppose," Natalie said.

"I wonder what he's gonna do if Billy ever drops dead?"

"Perhaps he'll learn to spend more time with his family," Odessa said.

"Or find another juke house," Natalie retorted.

"Perhaps," Tamara said. "Well, it's been nice chatting. But I think I'd better go."

"Okay, hon. You singing over there tonight?" Odessa asked.

"I sure am. Why don't you stop by," Tamara laughed.

"Don't be surprised if I do that sometime," Odessa chuckled.

"Good. I'll keep an eye out for you."

"You do that. If you're not busy on Sunday, we'd love to have you join us for dinner. Wouldn't we, Nat?"

"Of course, we would."

"Oh, I'd like that." Tamara glanced down at her pretty high heel shoes. "Why don't you come to the Lounge later, Nat?"

"Oh, that sounds good. But I'm spending the evening with Mama. Perhaps I'll join you some other time."

"You do that. I'll see you later. I got to look in on the ladies." Tamara was already at the door. "Bye now."

"Goodbye, Tam," they chorused as she rushed down the walkway and to the gate.

"Lawdy, that girl hasn't changed one bit," Odessa said. "She can't wait to get to that Lounge. But I suppose she should follow her dreams and hope they come true."

"Oh, Mama, I hope something good happens for her because no one will change her. She dances to her own tune."

"I sure hope she's not burdened with them two the rest of her life," Odessa said. "They've lived their lives, now they're taking Tam's because such a burden sometimes takes its toll on the healthier one. Tam could keel over first."

"I know, but what can she do?"

"Well, hon. There're still a lot of them wild greens and mushrooms out there," Odessa laughed.

"Oh, Mama, I never thought you'd ever say a thing like that."

"It's just a thought, Nat. It crossed my mind because Ginger told everybody in town Asha killed Obie by feeding him wild greens and wild mushrooms. Asha knew what she cooked was bad. Now I suppose Asha is being punished for what she did. That's why she's suffering so. And I suppose Ginger thinks she has to live to look over Asha.

"You know them two might live in limbo forever and burden Tam down for years. I don't want to go on in such state. And we sometimes must do things even though we don't like it. Are you listening, Nat?"

"I hear you, Mama." Natalie stared at her mother in silence as she thought about Tamara and wondered what she might do if she wore Tamara's shoes.

# CHAPTER 12

On Saturday evening Tilly felt compelled to talk to Lydia. So she went down the hall to Lydia's room. Though the door was partially open, she dared not enter without first being invited because she feared Lydia's anger. Knocking on the door lightly, she waited. When she got no response, she knocked again.

"Hey, Lydia," she called. Sticking her head inside the door, she peeked in. Wearing only a brassiere and panties, Lydia sat at the dresser and gazed into the mirror as she prepared for a night out on the town. Stepping inside the door, Tilly waited for Lydia to acknowledge her.

"Whatta you want, Tilly?" Lydia asked grumpily as she picked up a brush and pulled it through her shoulder length hair.

"Can we talk?" Tilly asked somberly as she took a chance and sat on the bed. Lydia had a volatile temper, and Tilly hoped her calm attitude proved she came in peace.

Lydia pulled her hair back, twisted it, and clamped it at the nape of her neck with bobby pins. Turning her head from side to side, she smiled, obviously pleased with the reflection in the mirror.

"Well, what you waiting for? You said you wanted to talk."

Tilly knew by the look on Lydia's face and the tone of voice she was already annoyed. Tilly cringed at her sister's unwarranted anger. It had been that way since they were children. Lydia spoke, and she jumped. Nothing changed. Though Lydia was the youngest, she was the meanest and the toughest.

They were as distant as strangers. The sisterly love she hoped for never came. Lydia was born angry and stayed that way. Her goal in life was to get "them" before "they" got her. Of course it was anyone's guess who "they" were.

"Where you going?" Tilly asked though she already knew her sister would go to Billy's house and party all night.

"Why you wanna know?" Lydia asked vehemently.

"Lawdy, Lydia. Why are you so bitter? We're family."

"So what?"

"So there's no need to be nasty every day of your life." She wondered what, if anything, went on inside Lydia's head. "Listen, I got a feeling you should stay home tonight."

"Yeah, I know." Lydia cut her short. "You always got a feeling. Now you give me one good reason why I should do that."

"Well, we could talk for one thing. I'd like that."

"I suppose you would."

"Listen, I know what you're doing, and I'm here to tell you he's no good for you."

"I don't know what you're talking about."

"No need to pretend with me, girl. I know what's happening, and Shelton Lamont will never marry you."

"Humpf, and when did you start telling fortunes?" Lydia asked.

"There's no need to tell fortunes. Nothing's secret in this town. What's done in the dark always comes to light, especially, if Della gets wind of it. So why don't you wake up? You're just another toy to him. You're not the first, and you sure won't be the last. When he gets tired of you, he'll just throw you away.

"Don't you know Shel loves his wife? That's why he's never left home. So get it through you head, he'll never leave Nat for you. I wish you had married Alan. He was nice, and he really cared for you. I liked him too. Now, he's gone and married that slick ass Sweet."

"If you liked him so much," Lydia retorted. "*You* should've married him yourself. Shoot! Alan was a mama's boy, and I got sick of him. I'm glad he married Sweet. So get it through your head once and for all, Alan ain't the only fish in the sea."

"That maybe true, but he was the only fish for you. He was crazy 'bout you."

"Forget it, will you, Tilly? I'm glad he's gone."

"I suppose you are. But tell me this, have you forgotten you have a baby?"

"How can I forget? You remind me every minute of the day."

"Yes I do, you nitwit," she shouted. "She's *your* responsibility. Not mine."

"I never asked you to take care of her." Lydia twisted her face into an ugly mask.

"No, you didn't. But who do you think looks after her when you walk out that door?"

"I don't know. And truthfully speaking I don't…"

"Don't say it, Lydia. You see. That's your problem. You don't give a damn about anything or anybody but yourself, but she is your baby."

Suddenly, it occurred to Tilly that there was obviously an armor plate inside Lydia's head, which she was unable to penetrate. There was just no use trying. Tilly stood and walked toward the door.

"I know you don't want to hear this. But this feeling won't go away, and it worries me. I don't want you to get hurt."

"Nobody wants to hurt me unless it's you. Do you want to hurt me, Tilly?"

"No, I don't, Lydia. I never did."

"I'm glad to hear that. Now, why don't you just shut up 'cause I'm in no mood to hear any more of your shit." Lydia flung her arms wildly and went to the small clothes closet. "And since when did you ever care 'bout me anyway?"

"I always cared, Lydia." Unexpectedly, Tilly felt hopeful. "At least I tried ever since we were kids." Feeling confident she turned around, went back, and sat on the edge of the bed again. If she and Lydia could have an intelligent conversation, she would believe in miracles.

"But you always pushed me away. You were so mean I sometimes wondered if we really were sisters.

"I still remember all the times you got me in trouble." Tilly shifted and pulled her legs up on the bed, leaned on her elbow, and placed her chin in her hand. All the while Lydia rummaged through the closet in silence. "Mama beat me many a time because of you."

Lydia brought out a white dress covered in red polka dots with little red bows on puffy sleeves. Tilly recognized it as one Natalie Lamont made and thought it ironic that Lydia chose to wear it tonight.

Lydia threw the dress on the bed. Acting as if she were alone, she returned to the closet and brought out a pair of red shoes, then started to dress.

"I remember the day the teacher gave you the bad grades. Billy was crazy about you. So when you complained to him about the grades, he wasted no time filling a bag with fresh cow manure. Do you remember that, Lydia?" She waited patiently for a response. "I wish you'd talk to me. But I guess it's okay. I'm sure you remember. Anyway, somebody saw the two of you and told Mama what you did. Billy was always crazy. He put the shit in a bag with his name scrawled in red crayon.

"When someone told Mama you were with Billy, she said I should've stopped you. I told her I didn't know anything about it. But that didn't matter to Mama. She did what she always did. She beat the daylights out of me.

"But she loved you. I never understood why she showed such a difference between us. There were times when you were so mean. You didn't have a loving bone in your body.

"I never caused trouble. I tried to do everything right so Mama would love me, too. But it wasn't to be. Mama just didn't care for me. But she would've died for you. Everybody said there was something wrong with you, but that never bothered Mama. If it did, she never let anyone know.

"The way I see it, Lydia, you were born crazy. And Mama should've sent you to the nut house a long time ago." The more Tilly talked the angrier she became.

"I am not crazy, Tilly," Lydia said.

"So you say. But you'll have to convince me otherwise." Tilly sighed as she remembered Lydia's birthday party and the hat incident.

"You almost broke my foot." Tilly leaned down and touched her foot.

"What're you talking about?" Lydia looked puzzled.

"I was thinking about what happened on your birthday. You know, the day you threw the brick on my foot. You do remember that don't you?" Keeping an eye on Lydia, Tilly moved to the end of the bed and placed her arm on the high frame.

"The pain was almost unbearable, you know. I screamed and hopped to Mama because that's what children do. I wanted Mama to hold me close. I wanted her to kiss my foot. I wanted her to rub spit on it so I'd feel better. But she did no such thing.

"It happened years ago, but I still remember. And every time I think about it I get mad as a bull with his nuts in a vise.

"Instead of Mama holding me, she said it was my fault that you threw the brick. She said I should've given you the hat. She wanted to beat me, but Daddy was there that evening and better yet, he was sober. Can you believe that? Daddy was sober. He told Mama if she touched me she'd be sorry.

"He was the only reason I escaped her anger that day. It wasn't Mama, but Daddy who took care of me that evening. He put salve on my foot and held me close. Then he rubbed my foot until I fell asleep.

"Yeah, you caused me a lot of pain, and every time I think about that day, I hurt. I was finally convinced I couldn't possibly be Mama's child. I mean look at me," Tilly said. "I don't look like Mama." She pointed to her fair skin and freckles.

"Yeah, I see you. So you look a little different. You know what they say, 'Mama's baby. Papa's maybe.' Lydia laughed and stared at her. "You don't look like Mama, but you do look like Daddy. But regardless of your birthright, you can't fix it."

"Well, I just feel somebody left me on the porch. Mama let me know she didn't care about me. But I soon pushed my feelings for you and Mama into a corner of my heart and tried to leave you there. You see. It wasn't just my foot that hurt that day, Lydia. Mama hurt me so bad when all I ever wanted was her love.

"I still have problems with my foot. For a while, I limped around like Billy." She laughed loudly and gazed down at her foot.

"You know something, Lydia. That was the day I realized Mama was just as crazy as you." She paused thoughtfully as Lydia, who was completely dressed now, sat down at the bureau to apply makeup to her face. "Now that I think about it I suppose Daddy was crazy too. Otherwise, he would've put you and Mama away."

Looking down, she touched the crazy quilt on the bed and wondered why, in such warm weather, it was not in the closet on the shelf. But then she remembered this was Lydia's room where anything but the norm might occur.

"I remember the day they found Mama and Daddy in the canal." Tilly spoke as Lydia transformed herself into a picture of perfection.

"Aunt Lula came down from Chicago to take care of us. She cried and carried on, but I didn't see you cry. And, lawdy, I couldn't shed one tear. You know something?" Tilly lowered her voice to a whisper. "I never told anyone this, but that was the happiest day of my life."

"What are you talking about, girl?" Lydia asked loudly. Tilly was surprised to see a flicker of disbelief in Lydia's face which meant she felt something.

"Didn't you miss them, just a little bit?" Lydia frowned.

"Yeah, I missed them then and miss them now, too. But at that time I didn't. Death wasn't on my mind. I was just glad Mama wouldn't be able to beat my ass again."

"Good grief, Tilly. You'll be punished for sure. Why, you're as nutty as a pecan pie."

"That makes two of us, sis, and there's nothing we can do about it either." Tilly paused momentarily. "Listen, Lydia. Like I said. I got this awful feeling and I wish you'd stay home."

"For gosh sake, Tilly. I'm in no mood for your moaning. I can't live by your feelings. Shoot, I want to see my friends."

"Lawdy, girl. How many times I got to tell you. You got no friends except that addlebrained Billy."

"Billy ain't addled," Lydia emphasized.

"No?" Tilly chuckled. "You could fool me. He did use a bag with his name on it when he put the cow shit at the teacher's door. I'll never forget that one."

"But Billy's not my worry now. You are. I wish you'd listen to me. When you gonna learn Neva is no friend of yours. I don't understand why you spend so much time over there." She rose from the bed and walked towards the door.

"Neva is okay," remarked Lydia. "And Billy's like a brother to me. You know that. I have a good time there. Anyway, the house belongs to Billy. Not Neva."

"I know. But Neva is Billy's wife and she lives there too." Tilly felt exhausted. "Why not stay home tonight and work the counter with me. It's time you pulled your weight around here. Without this store, you'd be penniless."

"Nothing doing. The way I see it, you're jealous." Lydia laughed.

"Jealous about what?"

"Me! Shoot, I do whatever I want. But you're stuck here with Virg who's 'bout as interesting as a fly buzzing day old shit." Lydia turned up her nose as if the foul odor actually penetrated her nostrils.

"Why you ungrateful cow! Who do you think takes care of that kid while you're out there trying so hard to make another? Virg, that's who. He cares more about that kid than you ever did."

"Good! I'm glad. 'Cause I got a life to live."

"I know. But I worry about you." Tilly softened her tone. "And Mama would be heartbroken if she knew how you acted now."

"Yeah? Well, Mama's dead."

"I know. And if you ain't careful you gonna be just as dead as she is."

"Goddammit, Tilly. Just you shut your mouth." Lydia picked up a brush from the bureau and hurled it through the air. Tilly ducked. It narrowly missed her head, and she moved closer to the door.

"I just wish you'd learn to respect yourself and try to do something worthwhile for a change."

"And just what would you suggest I do?" Lydia took a small red beaded clutch bag from the bureau drawer and threw several items inside. Then she checked her image in the mirror for the umpteenth time.

"I suggest you do anything other than stroking some man's dick." For the moment the room was quiet.

"Forget you, Tilly," Lydia shouted shattering the silence. She shoved Tilly back towards the bed. "You can just kiss my sweet ass," she yelled. Then she walked out the door slamming it so hard the window rattled, and a lone picture of some long forgotten relative fell from the wall to the floor.

"Drop dead, Lydia," Tilly said to the closed door. She couldn't remember hating both her sister and mother more than she did at that moment.

※ ※ ※

On Sunday morning Natalie sat silently at the small kitchen table and stared intently at her mother's face. As she chatted and planned the day's meal her bright brown eyes twinkled mischievously above her high cheekbones.

Trying hard to show interest as her thoughts ran amok she smiled weakly, but heard little. Her brain seemed as scrambled as an early morning breakfast egg and the awful emptiness she felt in the pit of her stomach had little to do with lack of food.

Only hours earlier her husband came home at an ungodly hour that would embarrass any decent man, but Shelton was undaunted and his cool lack of concern infuriated her.

For some time, she closed her ears to the rumors and denied what she knew was true. But this morning Shelton rubbed his dirt in her face. He had slept in another woman's bed and the fact that she knew hurt terribly. She loathed him and wanted to lash out viciously. But she neither acted out her emotions nor voiced her displeasure.

When he attempted to kiss her, she turned her head. He said nothing. He simply shrugged his shoulders and walked away. Upon leaving the bedroom, he started to whistle a familiar tune as clearly as a pretty bird would on a beautiful spring morning.

In the past she enjoyed his shrill, but this was not one of those times. The bastard toyed with her feelings and crushed her spirits flat as a hot fried hoecake.

Even though she felt sick, she later prepared breakfast. She was unable to indulge herself, but Shelton ate like a starved wolf.

Afterwards, she dressed the baby and herself. Then he drove them into town to her parents' home, the big house. Once there, he left them within minutes without explanation.

His actions enraged her, but she dared not question him. Since she married him against family wishes, she suffered in silence.

Reflecting, Natalie remembered. Their choice for a husband had been an old family friend, Jacoby Rose, who at the time was close to sixty years old.

"'He'd be good to you, Nat,' her mother explained.

'I have no doubt about that, Mama' she replied laughingly. 'But he already has one foot in the grave. Shoot, if he were my choice, I'd probably die of boredom. Anyway, I want to live a little. I want to feel alive.'"

Just several weeks later her daddy paid Jacoby Rose a visit and found him in his favorite chair on the front porch with his Bible in hand. The old man stared into space. Jacoby Rose was dead. She was glad she ignored family wishes.

"Shoot," she mumbled. As her stomach churned she wondered what she was to do.

"What is it, hon?" Odessa asked. "Can I do something for you?"

"No. Not really. It's nothing, Mama." Of course, that was a lie. She not only wanted her mother's comfort, she needed it.

"You sure, hon?" Odessa frowned.

"Yes. I'm sure," she sighed, determined not to make mention she knew Shelton cheated. After all, she was not ready to hear, "We told you so."

When her Uncle Percy learned nothing would stop her from marrying Shelton, he wasted no time letting her know how he felt.

"I know you don't want to hear this," Uncle Percy had said. "But I think you can do better. Hell, that boy never finished school." He paused momentarily. "He's as wild as an untamed horse,' he continued. "And no need thinking you can change him because you can't.

"Of course, I know you'll do whatever you want, but frankly, I don't think he's worth a good goddamn. Anyway, he's different from us."

She knew what he meant, and the comment angered her. Shelton's skin was quite dark and her uncle was color and class conscious, too.

"You know what I mean," he continued. "And just you mark my word. The day will come when you'll regret you ever laid eyes on him."

"Lawdy, uncle," she sighed, hoping the distain she felt for him didn't show on her face. "Why would you say such awful things?"

"Because I believe they're true. I can't understand why you refuse to give other young men a chance."

They were standing in the yard at the time. A slight breeze brushed her cheeks, and she hoped it would blow his unwanted advice out of her head. Smacking her lips angrily, she turned and walked away.

She loved Shelton deeply, and it wasn't something her family understood. She doubted they ever would, but she felt life without him was meaningless.

Sure he had a reputation. She heard it all. He was fast and wild. But his wildness was the attraction. She wanted him. He enjoyed his very existence, and she wanted to share it with him. So she made the choice. She married him.

Now she wondered if she had the strength to meet the challenge. Of course, she could blame no one but herself for her heartache. She had gotten herself into this mess, and only she could get herself out.

Though she was usually soft-spoken and seldom raised her voice, at the moment she wanted to scream, but spoke instead.

"I think I'd better go now, Mama. The Brothers will sing today and I'd like to hear them. Will you join us later?"

"Don't think so, hon. I have too much to do before dinner. Do you think I'll go to hell if I miss services today?" Odessa chuckled teasingly, but the worried look on Natalie's face concerned her. "What is it, Nat? Let's talk about it."

"No. I can't. Not now, Mama. I just wish you'd come with me. I'd love to spend time with you."

"If you feel that way, hon, why not stay with me now? The world won't come to an end if you miss Sunday services, you know."

"I know. And that's not my real concern right now."

"Well, dear. I don't know what your real concern is, but you're mine."

"I know. But don't you worry about me. I'll be okay."

"I sure hope so. Since you won't talk with me, why don't you talk to Helene? I'm sure she'll be there."

"Perhaps, I will." Natalie studied her mother briefly. Then, changing the subject, she teased, "Tell me, Odessa Dawson, why do you feel obliged to make such big meals every Sunday?"

"Oh, hon," her mother smiled broadly. "You know how much I enjoy putting a decent meal on my table."

"Of course, I know. It's just that I worry about you. I think you work too hard."

"So you say, hon."

Still gazing at her mother Natalie realized she never knew her mama's real inner feelings because Odessa was such a private person and seldom showed emotions. She couldn't recall a time when her mother showed anger. She simply shrugged her shoulders or let a smile speak for her in many situations. She supposed her mother showed anger only behind closed doors.

Suddenly, the room became too warm. She had to get some air. Standing, she quickly left the kitchen and went to the bedroom where the baby was sleeping. Odessa followed.

"Why is this tyke sleeping so much?" Odessa bent down and kissed the baby's cheek.

"She's teething, and she didn't get much sleep during the night." Natalie picked up the large diaper bag and hooked it over her shoulder.

"I hope it's nothing more serious." Odessa lifted the baby from the bed and put her in Natalie's arms.

"I'm sure it's not," Natalie took the child then reached for the parasol standing in the corner near the bed.

"I wish you'd stay with me, hon," Odessa said again as they walked towards the door.

"I know you do. I'll see you when I get back." Natalie stepped into the yard and walked toward the gate. Once outside the gate she turned and waved to her mother just as a squadron of planes droned overhead.

Shifting the baby's weight in her arms, she opened her parasol and raised it over their heads to shield them from the already too hot sun. Once again, she thought of Shelton and once again she wanted to scream. But while the thought persisted, she strongly resisted the urge.

# CHAPTER 13

As laughter drifted from the front of Billy's house into the bedroom, Lydia Wade lay in bed and mused about erotic pleasures she enjoyed with her lover, Shelton, the previous night. Smiling broadly, she yawned, and stretched languidly. Realizing she felt different, she mulled momentarily, but was unable to put a name to this new emotion. Frowning, she raised her arm, placed the back of her hand against her forehead as if doing so would provide her an answer.

Then it hit her. The pain and deep-seated anger, which consumed her like some demon as long as she could remember, were gone. Those feelings were now replaced by an absolute calm, and she immediately thought about her sister, Tilly. They had quarreled bitterly the night before just as they had done so often since childhood. But unlike other times, when she later felt resentment, warmth now flowed through her body. She felt love and sadness.

Suddenly, she wanted to see Tilly and make things right. Shoot! She had to get home. Pushing herself upright, she looked out the window. It was a beautiful day. She had things to do. But instead of climbing out of bed, she fell back onto the pillow, and let the newly found peace engulf her.

When it came to Lydia's attention that the sporadic laughter and pleasant voices she heard earlier had turned ugly, the smile quickly faded from her face. Sensing something was wrong, she sat up, and swung her feet to the floor just as Billy entered the room. Neva, who followed him closely, charged him with such force he almost fell to the floor.

"Get outta here, Lydia," he yelled. "Get outta here, now!"

Unable to move, Lydia looked on as Billy struggled with Neva. He grabbed her leg, but Neva wrested from his grasp and glared at Lydia. The expression on Neva's face terrified Lydia. Lydia was confused. Neva was her friend so she didn't understand the anger.

She tried frantically to retrieve her clothes from the chair in the corner of the room. But Neva rushed toward her wielding a gun. She expected Neva to shoot, but instead, Neva raised the weapon and brought it down hard on her shoulder.

She shrieked in pain and stepped back. Neva lunged at her. Crouching like a frightened, wounded animal, she pushed Neva hard against the bed. Neva lost her balance and Lydia rushed to the front of the house. Just as she dashed through the door, a thunderous roar exploded in her ears. She cried out like a wild banshee and ran into the street.

🍁 🍁 🍁

The bloodcurdling wails interrupted Natalie's thoughts and goose pimples prickled her skin. Startled, she stopped. Looking up, she watched as people poured into the street. Her eyes followed the frenzied crowd. Then she glanced up and saw her.

There for the whole world to see was Lydia Wade as naked as a newborn baby running down the middle of the railroad tracks and screaming as if she envisioned her last moments on earth. Following her closely was a crazed Neva Hardwood who held a gun in her hand while she sprinted like an Olympic champion.

Running behind Neva was her husband Billy who pleaded with her to stop. But Neva seemed energized by some unseen entity and was oblivious to his pleas. Sadly, his efforts to stop her proved in vain.

Living his childhood dream, the engineer—a handsome man with deep blue eyes and dark brown hair—gazed ahead. He had loved trains since he was a small boy. And the very first time his daddy took him to the train yard, he stood and stared at them for a long time. Even at that young age, he wanted to climb inside and start up the gigantic engine.

Now, he was standing inside one of the magnificent giants, and doing so gave him more pleasure than bedding a woman. Trains were in his blood. His granddaddy was a railroad man. So was his daddy until his train derailed and almost killed him. Now the old man could barely walk and lived only with past memories, some of which he tried hard to forget.

He glanced over at the brakeman and smiled. They worked well together. Both men knew their good fortune since through the years they heard the horror stories, and his daddy was living proof of what could happen. It was the reason he routinely said a prayer when he started work and again when his feet hit the ground.

While keeping a steady eye on the tracks ahead, he pulled from his fob a big gold watch that dangled at the end of a large gold chain. He briefly glanced at the treasure. Satisfied that they were on time, he slipped the timepiece back into its place.

The watch had once belonged to a granddaddy he never knew, but wished he had. Fact was, he never knew his grandmother, either. Rumor was she simply walked away from the house one day and never returned. When she failed to come home after a year, his granddaddy killed himself.

🍁 🍁 🍁

Lydia remembered her sister's warning: "Neva is not your friend." At the time she had not believed anything her sister said, but she did now. And if she made it home she would be nicer to Tilly and make changes in her life.

She was exhausted and each time she gasped for air a burning sensation cut deep into her lungs. Her legs felt like rubber. Looking over her shoulder, she saw Neva in the distance. Fearing Neva would kill her, she continued to run while folk in the crowd pleaded for her to get off the track. She never heard those pleas.

🍁 🍁 🍁

Suddenly, the engineer saw movement on the track. It was too late to stop the train so he sounded the whistle repeatedly. Then he glanced over at the brakeman and both knew they were faced with the inevitable, which they had heard about, but never experienced.

Stumbling, Lydia fell to the ground. She attempted to stand, but her foot was caught in a hole underneath a tie. She struggled to free herself.

When Tobias Dupree realized she was in trouble, he ran onto the track. Bending down he tugged at her leg but it was no use. Her eyes pleaded but he couldn't help her. Then the train was dangerously close and he leapt from its path.

It all seemed so unreal to Natalie. She watched in horror as the sinister looking wheels crushed Lydia into a mere sanguine mass. Minutes later the train stopped and several men stepped down into the crowd as the steam engine hissed like some venomous serpent hidden in tall grass making ready to strike.

Natalie felt stifled by fear and nausea. Someone screamed. A hammer pounded inside her head as still another painful howl like that of a wounded animal pierced her ears. Glancing about the crowd, she searched for its source only to learn it was she who had produced the agonizing cry. But no one seemed to notice because all eyes were transfixed on the train and the tracks.

She made her way to a nearby building and sat on the steps.

Though the heat was intense, Natalie felt strangely chilled as the tragedy etched itself into her memory like the carving on stone.

Looking up, she saw Seb Pardeau and Candyman Cates, standing near the tracks. Within minutes they started to play a solemn tune. Though it was a sad moment, in some way the music soothed. Her head cleared and she thought of Lydia and Tilly, and wondered if anyone would ever know what caused Neva to act so violently.

When the engineer stepped from the train, his mouth was dry, and his heart pounded. Feeling as if every drop of blood had drained from his body, he stared at the crowd.

"Who is it?" someone inquired from the crowd. Natalie immediately recognized the voice. Looking up, she saw Della standing at the edge of the crowd and only a few feet away. She was winded and struggled to catch her breath. It was obvious she had run all the way from her house.

Her hair was disheveled. She looked as if she had been caught in a twister. Her dress was no more than a rag. Her short, stubby feet were jammed into old blue scuffs that were too small and needed a good wash.

Shaking her head in disgust, Natalie wondered if the woman ever felt embarrassment about anything. Della was the only woman in town nervy enough to leave home looking like a vagabond.

Della, of course, would make certain those who had not witnessed this tragedy would get every grisly detail. She spread news faster than a telegram if not as concisely, and what she hadn't seen or heard she would fabricate.

Turning her head, Natalie shifted her thoughts to Neva. There was no need to wonder about the woman's sanity. She proved what most already knew. Neva *was crazy*.

There was simply no other explanation for the chase. Lydia never slept with Billy. They were merely friends. Rumor was Lydia slept with Shel.

"Why did I allow it to happen? Why didn't I confront Shel? Why didn't I chase Lydia?" she muttered. Instantly, feeling ashamed, she chided herself. Such savagery would only prove she was no better than they.

"Calm yourself," she whispered. "You'll work it out."

"Who is it?" Della's voice again caught Natalie's attention.

"It's Lydia," Natalie said wondering what part Della played in the sad event, since she and Neva were best friends.

Della glanced over at Natalie dressed neatly in a pretty, light blue, bolero dress and slinky high heels. Natalie looked her squarely in the face. Casting her own eyes downward, Della realized she was a mess. Shoot, she thought. She hadn't planned it, and there was nothing she could do now.

When she first heard the commotion, she'd jumped out of bed and raced to the window. When someone told her the train had struck someone, she grabbed the old dress and slipped it on. The fact that the dress had only four buttons instead of its original ten never fazed her. She simply took two large safety pins from the dresser and hooked one near the neck of the dress and the other just above her knee. Then she crammed her feet in her old scuffs and hurried out the door.

"What happened?" she asked already feeling foolish that she allowed the words to escape her lips.

The question irritated Natalie. "What do you mean? Can't you see she's dead?"

"Yeah, I see that. But I want to know what caused it to happen?" Della asked as she approached Natalie.

"I don't know that, Della. But I do know Neva chased Lydia onto the tracks." Natalie moved over so Della could sit.

"What?" Della screeched as she sat down beside Natalie. "Lawdy, I wonder what's gonna happen next. Billy loved Lydia more than anyone around here."

"That might be so. But everyone knows Billy loved Lydia as he would a sister."

"I know that and Neva too. So something must have happened between them. Otherwise, why would Neva…?" Della hoped she sounded calmer than she felt.

"She just went crazy, Della." Thea Rogers spoke as she came over to them. "I was at the house when Neva came home. She had been drinking. I don't know what went wrong." Guilt tore at Thea. She had left the house when she first sensed trouble. Now she wished she had stayed. Perhaps she could have helped Lydia. "If that train hadn't hit her, I suppose Neva would've shot her."

"Hey, Della, ain't Neva your friend?" Tobias Dupree asked as he neared them.

"Sure she is."

"Then you ought to know why she did it." Tobias came closer and stood in front of her.

"Well! For your information, Tobias, I know no such thing."

"That's surprising. You know everything else," Tobias said. He was so close now she could feel his hot, not so sweet, breath on her face.

"I'll tell you one thing. I think they ought to hang Neva by her heels." Tobias snorted.

"What an awful thing to say!" Della grimaced. Then she realized Tobias wanted to kick her ass. So she decided to put some distance between them. While keeping her eyes on Tobias, she stood up and eased back into the crowd.

❧   ❧   ❧

Carrie Lucas worked at Morningstar hospital, but would not go to work until late afternoon. Though she heard what happened, she stayed at the house because it wasn't something she wanted to see.

Standing on her porch which, like most porches in the area, was screened, Carrie watched Della as she came into the yard. As Della neared the house, Carrie pushed open the screen door.

"What happened, Della?" she asked as both sat in the two chairs on the porch.

"The train hit Lydia. They say Neva chased her onto the tracks."

"Good gawd! I suppose Neva lost it completely with her jealous ass," Carrie shrieked.

"That's the only way to explain it."

"Lawdy, I wonder what's to happen next. I'm sure that girl lost her life over some senseless matter."

"I don't know what happened. But it's no surprise to me. Lydia was a *whore*."

"Heaven help us. I suppose Neva felt that way too. But that's no justification for her actions. And I don't like to hear you talk that way. You seem disrespectful."

"I don't mean to be. I just mean shit's always happening around here," Della said.

"Humf! I don't recall any shit like this happening. If so, jog my memory," Carrie said.

"I can't say that I recollect anything like this either. And you won't believe this, but Tobias acted like I had something to do with it."

"Well, did you?" Carrie glanced over in Della's direction.

"No, I did not. And I can't believe you asked that." Then changing the subject, she said, "Everybody was there, and you should've been there too."

"I don't care if Jesus Christ himself was there. I didn't want to see it."

"I suppose you're right. I mean it made me sick."

"If that's the case, how come you stayed so long?" Carrie asked.

"I...I..." Della sputtered.

"You can't answer that one can ya? And I don't believe you got sick. So quit your lying before lightning strikes you dead." Carrie knew Della wanted to talk, and nothing short of death would stop her, but she would only listen to so much. "Where's Neva, now?"

"I don't know," Della said.

"That surprises me since you seem to know everything else," Carrie said.

"Lawdy, Carrie. You got a bone to pick with me?" Della asked. 'Cause if you do, let me know now."

"Well, Neva is your friend," Carrie said.

"So what? Don't mean I sleep with her."

"Maybe not, but you'd better hope they find her and put her away before some of Lydia's friends catch her. I got a feeling they'll skin her alive," Carrie replied. The fact that Della looked a little green around the gills had no affect on Carrie. "Billy wasn't Lydia's only friend, you know," Carrie said. "And you can bet they'll be out for revenge."

Though Fats Hopper sat near the fan, sweat still poured down his face. He felt sick and guilty too. Instead of helping Lydia, he ran. And earlier on he was thinking only of the food Billy prepared rather than the danger Lydia faced.

His house was across the street, facing Carrie's house. From his doorway, he saw Della on the porch with Carrie, and he knew she was burning Carrie's ears with details.

Della and Neva were thick as thieves, and he suspected Della was partly to blame for Neva going off the deep end. He was not in the mood for Della and hoped she would not stop at his house.

Only a short time later though, Della did exactly that.

"Ain't it awful, Fats?" Della spoke as she came up his steps.

"Yeah, it is." He came out of the house and joined her on the porch.

"You were there, Fats. What happened?"

Groaning, he decided telling Della what happened might be easier than sending her away. So he invited her to sit in one of the two chairs on the porch. He sat in the other and recalled the morning.

"Neva's always been a little goofy. So I ignored her. It wasn't until she came into the room that I suspected she had more than her hand jammed in her pocket.

"I asked if she was packing. When Neva didn't answer, Harry said she wasn't. But then she pulled the small gun from her pocket and waved it about. Harry couldn't believe it, and neither could I. Harry called Billy. Billy rushed into the room and screamed for Neva to put the gun away.

"At that moment, I stood up and hurried towards the door as quickly as I could. You know Cousin Joe. He was there and started screaming. Then he rushed towards the door. But Joe was so scared he couldn't open the door. You know how skinny Joe is. Hell, he climbed through the nearby window.

"I wanted to follow him but I knew that was impossible. So I threw myself against the door until it opened. Then Harry and I rushed outside. It took only a few seconds to open the door, but Cousin Joe was already out of sight.

"We ran, and I felt awful when I heard the gunshot 'cause I knew I should've done something. But I thought only of myself, and my failure to help Lydia will torment me the rest of my life."

"Good Lord," Della gasped. Yet, to Fats she seemed to beam. Fats stared at her. "How about letting me in on the joke?" he asked.

"What do you mean?"

"I want to know what you got to smile about," he said as his eyes watered. He wanted to knock the beam off her face. But he lacked the courage to hit a woman even if her name was Della.

"Good grief, man. Have you lost your marbles too? I'm not smiling. I'm sorry it happened."

"Oh, I thought…" What he needed, he thought, was to be alone with his demons. Standing and turning slowly, he went back into the house without another word and closed the door. Then he peeked out the window.

A surprised Della stood with her mouth agape and stared at the door. She shrugged her shoulders. Then she walked down the steps and back onto the street. As she disappeared from sight, he went to the kitchen. Though his heart was heavy with grief, he was still hungry.

Thoroughly shaken by the experience, Della went home. The clock on the mantel told her it was late.

Walking into the kitchen, she realized she was thirsty. Taking a glass from the shelf, she opened the icebox. Then, grabbing the ice pick from the sideboard, she plunged it violently into the block of ice Fats placed there the day before.

"That evil son-of-a-bitch," she hissed recalling what just happened. "I don't know what's eating Fats." Stabbing the ice again, she picked up several pieces, dropped them into the glass, and slammed the icebox door. Walking over to the small sink, she filled the glass with water from her water bucket and lifted it to her lips. Later, she went onto the porch where she sat quietly and pondered Neva's fate.

# CHAPTER 14

After tending to her mother, Tamara went over and stood at her Grandma Ginger's bed, and watched Paige Peterson push another spoon of pureed food into her grandma's mouth.

Paige was Doc Peterson's daughter, about the same age as Tamara, and, like her mother Ellie Peterson, Paige was a nurse. She stopped by a couple times a week to check on the ladies and give Tamara a hand.

"How long you think she'll hang on?" Tamara asked.

"I don't know, Tam. So don't ask me such questions."

She could tell Paige was annoyed, but no one knew how tired she was. Her mother and grandma had been in the same condition so long she was afraid she might have a stroke, too. Then they all would become dependent on her husband, Tobias. Tobias, a hospital worker, knew as much about medicine as Doc Peterson. And Tamara suspected if the burden fell to him, Tobias would use a needle and shoot a bubble into their veins, and they'd all end up dead.

"Well, you're a nurse. Seems you could look at her and tell if she's gonna die soon."

"Shame on you, Tam," Paige gasped.

"Yeah, right," Tamara said. "I don't want you to think I don't love them. I do. But I'm so tired."

"I know you are, but I can't tell you any such thing. Did you finish feeding your mama?"

"Yes, I did," Tamara sighed.

"Listen. I know you get tired, but I have no answers. I'm only a nurse, not God. Even Doc can't tell you exactly when someone will die. Now come on. Help me turn your grandma."

After making the ladies comfortable, Tamara and Paige left them, went to the front room, and dropped onto the sofa.

"What an awful day," Tamara said. "No one should die like Lydia." She shook her head.

"I agree," Paige said. "I don't know what happened, but it's so sad."

"Yes, it is. And I'll tell you this. I think it was jealousy. Neva isn't as good looking as Lydia, and she didn't wear the clothes Lydia wore. Neva couldn't stand Lydia because men liked her even though she acted like a wild woman. And according to rumor, Neva didn't like Lydia being so close to Billy."

"What a shame. Lydia and Billy have been friends since we were kids," Paige said. For a moment they were silent.

"Well, I'm still living," Tamara said changing the subject. "And I got two sick women on my hands that refuse to get well or die. Neither can talk, and it's like living with the dead. I'll tell you one thing. It's no picnic."

"I know that, and I'm sorry. But no one's got the answer," Paige said as Tobias came into the house from work.

"Hey, Paige," he said as he sat in the easy chair.

"What's happening, Tobias?" Paige asked.

"Well, you know that crazy ass Neva chased Lydia onto the tracks. Lydia got her foot caught in some way. I tried to help her. Pulled on her leg, but it wouldn't budge. The train couldn't stop. So it hit her."

"I'm sorry you saw something like that," Paige said. "Sounds like you might need to see Doc yourself."

"No, I'm okay. But just thinking about it makes me sick."

"I'm sure it does." Paige stood to leave. Turning to face Tam, she said. "I've done all I can for your ladies today. I'll see you in a few days."

Tamara followed Paige to the door. "Thanks a lot," she said softly and watched Paige walk down the steps and onto the street.

"Nobody deserves to die like Lydia did," Tobias said as Tamara left the door and returned to the sofa.

"Della stopped by here when it first happened and told me all about it," Tamara said.

"That's no surprise. She's like a talking machine."

"That's for sure. But let's forget Della. Nat and her mother invited us over to eat," Tamara said.

"I'm not going."

"Why not? You might feel better. Mrs. Wanker will stay with the ladies."

"Are you kidding? After what I saw this morning, I don't want to. You go. And tell Nat I'll see her next time."

"I'll do that," Tamara said. She knew he was not only upset about the tragedy he witnessed, but he was also upset with her. He didn't like her working at the Lounge, but she refused to stop.

He wanted her to stay home and cater to his whims. But she couldn't do that. She was a singer. Singing kept her alive, and she dreamed of stardom.

Stardom! What am I thinking about? I got two sick old ladies here, she thought, and I don't know which way to turn.

"I'm sorry you don't feel good, Tobias, but I'm going. You know Odessa Dawson's food is good. And no one eats from a tin pan, a broken plate, or drinks from a cracked glass at her house."

"I know all that, Tam."

"Okay. Just wanted to remind you what you'll miss. Today is Sunday, she'll put linen on her table, and we'll use real linen napkins. It's not something I want to miss."

Though it was a tragic day, Tamara hoped to enjoy good company, tasty food, and finery at its best, which she wouldn't see until Natalie invited them again. This was a real occasion. It was a family ritual, and she wasn't about to miss it. She didn't care if Tobias was dying.

❧ ❧ ❧

After leaving Natalie earlier that morning, Shelton went to see his parents who told him in no uncertain terms they wanted to hear no more about his shenanigans.

They reminded him that he was married to Natalie, and it was time he acted the part. Otherwise, they planned to take the car he so enjoyed and give him a horse to ride instead.

"Think what your lady friends will say about that," his mother, Esther, remarked.

Neither of them gave him a chance to defend himself, but, then too, Shelton had no defense. Therefore, when he tired of their threats and promises, he got up to leave. Just as he reached the door Greyland, his brother, pulled into the yard in the Weeping Willows Funeral Home wagon.

"Lydia is dead," he announced as he stepped from the vehicle everyone feared. He now owned Weeping Willows Funeral Home since their daddy, Thaddeus, retired.

"What did you say?" Thaddeus asked.

Shelton hoped this was one of Greyland's morbid jokes. But the look on his brother's face told a sad story. He wanted to ask questions, but was unable to speak. His gut wrenched with pain. So he grappled for the nearest chair and sat down.

"I said Lydia is dead." Greyland repeated.

"Lawdy!" exclaimed Esther. "What happened, Grey?"

"I don't really know, Ma. I didn't see it. But I heard Neva shot at her and chased her onto the tracks. They say some yelled to Lydia that the train was coming, but she just kept on running. They say she got her foot caught. Tobias tried to pull her free, but he couldn't."

"But why would Neva do such terrible thing?" Esther shook her head in disbelief.

"I don't know, Ma. I suppose she snapped," Greyland offered. "She was never quite right in the head. You know that." Shelton stood and walked out the door.

Thaddeus continued to bombard Greyland with questions, and Greyland, hoping to hold his dad's attention so Shelton could get away without further torment, tried to appease the old man.

Thaddeus, aware of the ploy, shouted, "Don't forget what we told you, Shel. Remember, them women won't love you as much when you straddle them legs cross the back of a horse."

Ignoring his father, Shelton got into the car, turned the key in the ignition, and drove slowly from the yard. When he reached the fork in the road, he pressed his foot down on the accelerator, and the big, black Buick surged forward.

❦   ❦   ❦

"Hey, Nat," Tamara said as she came onto the porch and sat down beside Natalie at the big house.

"Hey, Tam. It's a sad day, huh?"

"I'll say it is. But Lydia was so outrageous and ugly I'm surprised it didn't happen sooner. In fact, I don't understand why you didn't shoot *her* and *Shel*."

"I agree they were ugly and for the past year they were like thorns in my side. But I couldn't solve the problem that way. I love Shel too much."

"Don't I know it? But you know me, I would've cut Shel's nuts off."

"Oh, Tam. That's so ugly. I just want Shel to be a good husband. I want him to act like he's married to *me*. I'm so upset I don't know what to do."

"You don't need to do anything. Shel owes you an apology, and he should ask your forgiveness."

"You might be right about that."

"I know I'm right, Nat. And it's time you stood up to him."

🍁    🍁    🍁

Though it was closer to two than twelve noon when Shelton arrived at the big house, Odessa had just put the mid-day meal on the table. The succotash, candied yams, golden brown fried chicken, sage and red hot pepper sausages, rice, gravy, and piping hot rolls looked good.

The bacon bit cornbread was as pretty as a pound cake. The large bowl of greens was loaded with ham. Chowchow, a pickled garnish which Odessa considered essential with all meals, was in the middle of the table, and a cold pitcher of butter milk invited the hungry to indulge.

They would later enjoy a cake or blackberry pie or maybe both. At any other time, such a meal would make Shelton's mouth water, but today was different. He had no appetite.

He studied the faces. Natalie's Uncle Percy, his wife, Helene, and their two little girls, Queenie and Sophia, were there. Delano Phillips and his wife, Sunny, two teachers who worked with Natalie, were there, too. Shelton couldn't stand Delano. He thought Delano was sweet on Natalie.

Shelton and Natalie's baby, Makela, sat in the high chair, and Tamara stood with Natalie at the window overlooking the garden.

"Hey, Tam," Shelton said as he neared them. "Where's Tobias?"

"Hey, Shel," she said as she turned and stared at him. "He's home. He's not feeling well. I'm sure you heard he tried to save Lydia, but couldn't. I think the whole thing made him sick."

"Yeah, I heard," Shelton said suddenly feeling sick under Tamara's stare.

Tamara had green eyes and very light skin like Natalie's Uncle Percy and a few others in town. However, there was one difference. She was the only one who had flaming red hair. Even though she could pass for white, she never tried to.

Hell, he couldn't stand her, he thought. She wore pants longer than his, and was as bossy as any man. He wondered how Tobias put up with her. She had a mind of her own, but that wasn't his business. He was married to Nat.

He knew she'd heard rumors and was upset. So he had to right the wrongs he'd done. As his eyes met hers, he smiled. Leaving Tamara's side, he went over to Natalie and kissed her cheek. Then he gave her behind a quick pat, and hoped she understood that he wanted to make things good between them.

Natalie's knees suddenly felt weak, and she hastily sat in the chair next to her baby. She loved Shelton too much and at the same time despised him.

"Come and get it," Odessa called out proudly. As everyone chose a chair, she took her place at one end of the table and Marcus the other.

Looking at Shelton, she pointed to a chair. He took it, and found himself sandwiched between Helene and Delano while he desperately tried to swallow food he couldn't taste. He thought of Lydia. He never loved her, but there was something about her that excited him.

Glancing out the window, he stared at the fig tree in the garden and tried to think of the good times, but his head wouldn't allow him to think and his heart wasn't in it.

Turning, he looked at Natalie and smiled, but her eyes were angry. Suddenly, he wanted to crawl under the table but couldn't. He just hoped his face didn't show the guilt he felt.

While everyone discussed Lydia, Natalie suffered mixed emotions. She stared at Shelton and decided he was a selfish man who thought only of himself. When he did try to ingratiate her with his presence, he often became irritated at the slightest annoyance. Now she watched him squirm because the conversation was about Lydia. For a brief moment she enjoyed his discomfort and hoped he hurt as much as she did.

She had no idea why the tragedy occurred. But she, like everyone else, was saddened by the turn of events even though Lydia was carrying on with Shelton. Of course, she blamed Shelton. This was not his first indiscretion, but she certainly hoped it was his last.

Glancing around the table, she realized no one was actually eating except the girls, Queenie and Sophia. The tragedy dulled their usual voracious appetites, and they toyed with their food.

Looking down at her own plate with sadness, she plunged her fork into the food. Just as she brought the fork to her mouth, Odessa spoke.

"I think that poor little tyke of Lydia's will need lots of love. Since Alan's not around, I think we should do what we can for her."

Flabbergasted, Natalie wondered about her mother's sanity. Dropping her fork onto the plate, she pushed it aside. She was sorry Lydia came to such a tragic end, but she would not miss Lydia. Lydia and Shelton had caused her too much pain, and she didn't give a damn about Lydia's baby. That baby was her brother's responsibility.

Suddenly, Natalie felt overwhelmed by the turn of events. Excusing herself, she took the baby from the high chair, left the room, and went to the front porch. Later, Tamara joined her, and they sat quietly in the swing just as they did as youngsters.

"Isn't it strange not to hear Billy Hardwood's music?" Natalie strained her ears for the familiar sound but heard nothing.

"Yeah, it is. I guess he's pretty broken up. He and Lydia were friends for years," Tamara spoke softly. "And even in death she left her mark."

"You're right. Now it seems the whole town died with her. It's as quiet as a graveyard, and the silence is deafening," Natalie said as Shelton came onto the porch.

As he sat next to Natalie, neither she nor Tamara spoke, and he wondered just what went wrong at Billy's after he left that morning. But he knew there was only one way to find out. He had to talk to Billy.

"I'm going to Billy's house, Nat. I'll be back soon," he said standing abruptly. Looking down at a silent Natatlie, he quietly walked out the door.

🍁 🍁 🍁

Billy Hardwood, Shelton, his brother Greyland Lamont, and their cousin Warren Gilliam, had been friends since childhood. So as boys they were all there when Billy had an experience that marred him for life. On a warm Saturday afternoon, Billy and his family got in their small black car, and drove to the farm to visit the Lamonts.

While the older folk talked, Shelton, Greyland, and Warren took Billy out to explore. Only moments into their adventure, he found a nearby, grazing horse to be more interesting to him than his companions.

Taking leave from his pals, Billy walked cautiously towards the horse. Fascinated, he watched the horse for some time before he got courage enough to move closer.

"Hey, Billy," Shelton called. "Don't get too close to him."

"Be careful, Billy," Greyland yelled. "Ole Blue is pretty mean."

"I don't believe you. He ain't that mean," Billy said giving the horse a few strokes.

"Oh…oh…yeah…yeah…he is," Warren laughed.

But when the horse continued to graze, Billy slapped the animal's flank hard. The horse stepped back, but otherwise kept his head down and ignored the unwanted visitor.

"Come on, Billy. Leave him alone. Let's go," Greyland pleaded, but Billy ignored the warnings.

The animal's inattention ticked him off and he, mischievously, eased behind the horse and jerked the animal's tail and then attempted to run.

Though the animal never raised his head, instinctively, he kicked the hell out of Billy. The young boy opened his mouth to scream, but he passed out just seconds before his head hit a chopping block.

Shelton, Greyland, and Warren ran over to him, but Billy was out cold, and they thought he was dead. While Greyland and Warren stayed with Billy, Shelton rushed into the house to tell what happened. "The horse kicked Billy," he yelled.

"Is he dead?" Billy's daddy asked while thinking maybe God had answered at least one prayer and took the boy on in. After all, Billy was difficult and gave him too many headaches.

"No," Shelton said. "But almost."

"Lawdy," Billy's mother cried. "Don't take my boy from me. How'd it happen, Shel?" Billy's mother asked as Shelton led them down the path to the the corral where Billy lay.

"I think he pulled the horse's tail," Shelton answered.

"Boy, what you doing pulling Ole Blue's tail?" Thaddeus asked looking down at the unconscious Billy as if the boy would instantly give him a sensible answer. "You can't play with Ole Blue. He'll come out winner every time."

"He's out cold, Daddy. He can't hear you," Greyland said.

"Maybe he can, Grey. You never know," Thaddeus said looking at Warren who was his dead sister's child, and who stood by silently. "Whatta you think, Warren?" he asked as Shelton and Greyland picked Billy up and carried him to his family's jalopy.

"I...I..." Warren stuttered unable to complete the sentence. Thaddeus laughed. "Boy, when you gonna learn to talk?"

As the Hardwoods rushed Billy to the hospital, Thaddeus, Shelton, Greyland, and Warren climbed into their car and followed them.

For several days Billy drifted in and out of consciousness. When he finally awoke, he learned his front teeth were broken, and would be that way for years to come. Doc Flack had put a silver plate in his head, and, to add insult to injury, the horse's hoof print was deeply embedded in his ass.

Shortly afterwards, Doc said he'd have a distinct limp for life. It was at that moment Billy realized the horse almost killed him and only by some miracle had he survived.

Within a short time, Billy left the hospital. But his encounter with the horse was the talk of the town, and it wasn't long before every young boy in the community stopped by the house to see him.

The boys cared little about Billy's misfortune and not one of them asked how he felt. They were simply curious and wanted to see the horses' hoof print on his ass.

🍁 🍁 🍁

"Hey Billy," Shelton yelled as he entered the house. He walked over to the table where Billy sat alone, staring into space. He pulled out a chair. "What the hell happened over here this morning? What made Neva so mad?"

"I don't know, man. But I intend to find out," he said shaking his head. "The day started out like most Sundays.

"You know how it is. After you left, Fats, Harry and Thea stayed here. I got ready to make breakfast. They partied with me all night and Lydia, like so many times in the past, slept in the back room.

"When I went in the kitchen to cook, Harry offered to help. Just as I handed Harry the apron, I heard the key turn in the lock. I knew right then Neva had come home, and it made me mad. I wanted her to stay up there with her family. 'Course I knew someone drove her back. It was too early for the train.

'Hey, Billy,' she said when she came through the door. 'Cousin Joe drove me home. He's gonna stay a few days.'

'Hey,' I hollered and peeked out at her and Cousin Joe. She had a small bag in her hand. It was her bottle. She looked at me and laughed, and I wondered if I was the joke.

"Neva annoyed me so lately she almost pushed me to the brink. And I was pissed that Cousin Joe would stay longer than a day. I got no more love for him than I do a horse."

"So you told me," Shelton laughed.

"You know why I feel that way?"

"Nope."

"He's cheap. Never pays one red cent for all the liquor he puts away."

"Is that right?"

"Shit, he can drink all of us under the table and keep standing while everybody else falls out. He squeezes money so tight the presidents cry."

"Damn, Billy," Shelton shook his head. "That's pretty tight. Is he that bad?"

"Worse. That bastard's got the first dollar he ever made 'cause he never spent a penny. He's just a frigging freeloader."

"Okay, Billy," Shelton said. "Let's forget Cousin Joe. I want to know what happened between Neva and Lydia."

"Just be patient, Shel. I'm gonna get to that. Neva said she was ready to have fun. That meant she was ready to get soused. Shoot, she clamors for a liquor bottle like a baby fighting for a tit. Boy, oh, boy. She and Cousin Joe drink more booze than I sell.

"She spent the week up north helping take care of her uncle, old man Pecker. He's real sick and expected to die any minute. 'Course the doctor had him at death's door many a time for the last ten years, but that old man refused to die. I expect he'll outlive the doctor."

Shelton sighed, but decided to let Billy talk. He needed to let it all out.

"You know the Peckers, don't you?"

"Yeah, I know them," Shelton said. "They're God fearing teetotalers. Look down their noses on anyone takes a drink."

"That's right. Don't allow alcohol in their home," Billy said. "And don't take too kindly to anyone using it for medicine, either.

"Neva's only ally in that family is her Cousin Joe. And he brought her home where she could quench her thirst in peace.

"You know me, Shel. I never wanted a drunk for a wife, but I got one," he paused momentarily. "When she came into the kitchen, I said, 'Hey baby. We're making breakfast. Go on in the room and talk to Thea. Put your feet up and lay back until it's ready.

"Then I went over to the door, glanced at Cousin Joe. He'd already pulled off his shoes and slung his feet upon the small coffee table in front of the sofa.

"He was laid back and his eyes closed. He looked as pleased as a well fed baby. That irked me. And I got a strong urge to put my fist down his throat. I actually took a few steps in his direction before I realized what I was doing.

"Then I came to my senses, stepped back into the kitchen, willed myself to calm down, and focused on the food I wanted to cook.

"Course, instead of putting her feet up like I asked her to do, Neva looked down the hallway at the closed bedroom door and started screaming.

'Who's in the room?' She looked at me and pointed back over her shoulder. 'Anybody I know?'

'You know everybody in town, don't you? Nobody's back there except Lydia,' I told her. "Then she went off the deep end, man."

'Lydia,' she screamed. 'What's she doing in there?'

'Sleeping, I suppose,' I said.

'Well, you better get her out of here.'

"Oh she was nasty, Shel. I stared at her. I could see she was upset, but I didn't know why. She knew nobody stayed in that room unless they first put money in my hand. And you already did that."

"You bet I did."

"You know Lydia was no stranger. She was my friend, and this wasn't the first time she slept over. I smiled hoping to change Neva's attitude."

'I told you I didn't want her staying over anymore,' Neva snapped.

'So what if you did? It means nothing to me. You never gave a reason for feeling that way. And just in case you forgot this is my house and Lydia is *my* friend.'

'I don't care if she is *your friend*. I want her out of here. Now, Billy. Do you understand?'

"Then she fixed me with a stare. Seems she wanted to push me to the brink. But you know me, Shel. I didn't do anything 'cause I'm not a violent man."

"I know that, Billy."

"But a man can take just so much. I figured if she kept it up, I wouldn't be responsible for my actions. 'Cause I didn't appreciate her yelling at me in front of my friends."

"So what did you do?" Shelton asked.

"I told her I wanted her to keep her mouth shut. Man, I was mad. But she paid no attention because she did the one thing I hate."

"What was that?" Shelton asked.

"She wagged her finger in my face, and I grabbed her hand and squeezed her fingers hard. I wanted to break her fucking fingers off.

"But she yelled. Then I let go. You see I saw something in her eyes, man, and it scared me. I knew then something was wrong with her. I lost my appetite and hurried to the bedroom. I figured the first thing I would do was get Lydia out of the house then I would deal with Neva. But it didn't happen that way at all."

"Well, what the hell did happen, Billy?" Shelton was frustrated.

"I went into the bedroom to get Lydia out of the house, but Neva was right on my heels. We struggled. I screamed for Lydia to run. For a moment she didn't move. When she finally realized something was wrong, she ran.

"I'll tell you one thing. I saw the train hit Lydia, and I wanted to die. But before I gave it another thought I caught Neva, slapped her face hard. Then someone pulled me off her. 'I hope you can live with it,' I told her.

"When I got back to the house I sat down, and I haven't moved since. I don't know what went wrong, Shel.

"But I been sitting here thinking about something Neva told me a while back. She said she didn't like Lydia coming around so much. I never paid much attention to her gripes or thought much about it. I just brushed it off.

"I told her Lydia was my friend. I never thought she was so jealous she would go off the deep end. Lawdy, I wish I had listened. Maybe Lydia would still be alive. I'll tell you something, Shel. I'm gonna miss Lydia."

"I know. I'll miss her too. I don't know what it was, but there was something about her that made me crazy," Shelton said.

"I called her *little sister* and she considered me the brother she always wanted but never had," Billy said.

"I know. And thanks for talking with me, man," Shelton said.

"Hey, Shel."

"Yeah?"

"I'm gonna kill Neva. I don't know how, but I'm gonna kill that bitch."

"Whoa, Billy. Hold on there. As much as I want Neva punished in some way, I don't want to get mixed up in any killing." Shelton stood, walked over to where Billy sat, and touched his shoulder. "Be careful what you say, man. You don't know who's listening to you. You're just hurt and mad right now. I feel the same way you do, but we gotta think before we act. We'll talk later. You take care. I gotta get back and talk to Nat. I got a feeling she's mad enough to *kill* me."

❦    ❦    ❦

"Lawdy, Lydia, what a terrible way to die. But it's better you than me. For sure Billy is mad as hell. He was crazy about you," Della spoke as if Lydia was sitting on the porch beside her.

Sitting alone, Della wondered if Neva would go to jail or the nut house.

Then as Shelton left Billy's and walked up the street, Della waved to him. And at that very moment, it occurred to her that Neva might be dead. Bolting from her chair she ran out the door and up the street to Billy's house. Upon arrival, she trudged inside unannounced just as she had in the past. The house was quiet, and Billy sat alone at the table.

"Where's Neva?" Della demanded looking about the room suspiciously. "What did you do to her?"

"What's it to you?" Billy asked leaping from his chair and lunging forward.

"Oh, shit!" Della shrieked loudly turning to flee. But as she did so Billy caught the back of her dress and spun her around. She cringed and threw up her hands.

"Don't be mad at me, Billy," she pleaded. "I…I had nothing to do with it." She squirmed.

"I'm gonna kill ya." Billy raised his hand to strike her. She pivoted. The intended blow missed its mark, and his hand sliced thin air as she pulled away and dashed out the door.

🍁   🍁   🍁

Greyland, a handsome, no nonsense man, loved his wife and his business. He loved making money and keeping it. His interest in women other than his wife was nonplus.

His wife, Jozell, who worked with him at the mortuary, was about five feet tall with a very small body.

Her hands were tiny and her feet so small her shoes looked like those of a young child. In fact, she was so tiny some called her 'Little Bit.' She hated the tag, but was gracious enough that no one knew.

When Greyland left his parents' home, he drove the funeral wagon slowly through the countryside. He was just a little different from most folk. He saw beauty where others saw none. And at this very minute he was driving a vehicle most folk never wanted to see. He saw beauty in the wagon because it was used for a most important function, the last ride.

Reflecting, he remembered his friends who had already left the area, but he loved Meadowsbrook. He saw a certain beauty in all of it. Life was rather pleasant for him, and he was not ready to take off for some strange place up north he knew little about.

He thought of his brother Shelton who had a beautiful wife and baby and a nice home. He wished Shelton would settle down and act like a real man instead of the whore he was.

While Shelton checked out every pretty skirt in town, Greyland kept tabs on the sick folk in the community. Just in case.

As he passed the houses, he waved to those who sat on porches. Even though they called him names, he smiled.

"Sticks and stones may break my bones, but names will never harm me," he mumbled. Over the years, he adjusted to it all. They needed him. So nothing they said bothered him, but their attitude about the inevitable did.

It took all his efforts to get some of them to join a plan. In fact, when he told old man Pardeau his policy was about to lapse, the old man laughed.

'So what Grey? I don't worry. When time comes you'll do what's right. Anyway, I'm gonna live forever.'

"Like hell you are," he said joining the old man in laughter. "We all gotta go sometime."

Of course, the old man did eventually take care of business. But persuading some of these people to prepare for the end was like digging a ditch with a twig.

As he continued driving down the hot, dusty road, the car tire hit a deep rut. It jarred him. He couldn't say why but at that instance he thought about his wife Jozell who was just as bad as everyone else. She never wanted to discuss the subject even though she worked with him.

"There's no need to discuss it, Grey," she once told him. "You'll do the right thing when time comes."

She also refused to ride in the wagon. "How many times I got to tell you, Grey. I'll ride in it when that time comes. I don't know why you're so content to drive that thing."

"Lawdy, Jozell. I don't know what upsets you so about it. That thing, as you call it, is our bread and butter."

"I know that. But you know how it is. You scare people. They hate to see you coming."

"Whoa! Hold on, Jozell. I never heard any customers complain about me. Coming or going. You know the reason I drive the wagon. During the heat of summer some folk often work too hard, and some die from heat stroke. So when I go into the countryside I'm prepared. Just in case. That's all."

"I know. But do you know some of them call you the vulture?" Jozell laughed.

"Yeah. But they never say it to my face. Anyway, Della Gilliam started that. But it's no skin off my nose, baby. You know how it is. She's got a mouth like a clatter bone in a goose's asshole." They both whooped with laughter.

"Bite your tongue," Jozell said once she was able to speak.

"Mark my word, Jozell. The time will come when somebody…"

"When somebody will do what?"

"One day somebody will teach Della a lesson. She'll get hers."

"Don't you go wishing bad things on Della now," Jozell chuckled again.

"I'll do no such thing. She puts herself in such precarious positions bad things will just seek her out."

As Greyland neared Billy's house, he decided to stop by and see him. Just as he drove around the corner, he was taken aback by the sight of a scantily clad Della Gilliam rushing from Billy's house and into the street.

"Damn," he chortled. Parking hastily, he leaped from the wagon and hurried towards the house. Had Billy done what so many others wanted to do? He wondered. Had he kicked Della's ass and killed Neva too? If that was the case, he thought, he might bury two bodies instead of one.

# CHAPTER 15

❀

Frantic, Della hurried up the street. Looking back, she saw that vulture, Greyland. "Lawdy," she whispered. As he got out of the wagon, she wondered if he had come for Neva's body. She felt sick.

Looking down, she realized she left her old scuffs in Billy's house and portions of her dress in his hand.

She called out for Warren as she entered the house. She got no answer but pondered his whereabouts only briefly. Suddenly, she remembered Carrie said Lydia's friends would want revenge and wondered if it wasn't true.

First, Tobias threatened her. Not with words, but if looks could kill she'd already be as dead as Lydia. Fats slammed the door in her face, and Billy actually attacked her. They blamed her for what Neva did.

As nausea overwhelmed her and she retched on her front room rug, she looked down, but was too sick to do anything about it. Rushing to the bedroom, she hurled herself onto the bed.

"Shit!" she shouted a short while later when it occurred to her she might become the next casualty in the war. Leaping from the bed, she rushed about shutting windows and locking doors. At that time of day, the temperature in the shade was close to a hundred degrees, and she almost suffocated.

Later that evening as Della opened the door for Neva, she screeched, "Girl, am I glad you to see you. Where you been? I thought Billy killed you."

"Well, as you can see, I'm very much alive." Neva was a skinny, small, brown skinned woman who sported a scar on the left side of her face, which extended from the top of her ear down to her chin. It was the result of a brawl in a bar when an angry man cut her after she tried to steal his change from the bar.

"You look like shit," Della said looking her up and down. Her hair stood in spikes on one side of her head. Her eyes were bloodshot and swollen where Billy punched her earlier, and the knot on her forehead was as big as an egg.

"Where you been, Neva, hiding?"

"I guess you can say that."

"But where you been?" Della asked.

Ignoring Della, Neva asked, "Why you locked up in here? You scared Billy's coming after you, too?"

"What are you talking about? Why would Billy come after me?" Della felt anxious as she opened the last window.

"Well, it was your idea," Neva said.

"What do you mean it was my idea?" Della asked shakily.

"Just what I said. It was your idea. I mean you told me I should do something about Lydia."

"I never told you to…I don't remember…"

"I remember, Della," she said calmly. "You said…"

"Now just you wait a minute. I never told you to hurt Lydia," Della shrieked. Then as images flashed before her eyes of her earlier encounters with Tobias, Fats, and Billy, she wondered if she would be punished for something Neva did.

Neva studied Della before she decided to tell Della the reason she chased Lydia.

"I'll tell you why I did it," Neva laughed.

"Lawdy," Della whispered suddenly feeling woozy after Neva finished speaking. Neva wasn't really crazy, Della thought, and if Billy ever found out he would surely kill her.

As sweat formed on her top lip, a fly buzzed her head. She waved it away. And just as someone rapped on the door, her knees buckled, and she fell to the floor in a dead faint.

Moments later Della looked up from the sofa and stared into Sheriff Duncan's face. Looking around the room she saw Marcus and Percy Dawson.

"You all right, Della?" Duncan asked.

"Yeah, I think so. What's going on?"

"You fainted," Marcus answered.

"I guess you know Duncan came to get Neva," Percy said.

"I know. But what you gonna do with her?" Della stared at Neva who had just told her something she dared not reveal.

"I'm taking her to see Doc Peterson so he can examine her," Duncan said. "Then we'll do whatever needs to be done." Then Della watched silently as they took Neva by the hand and led her outside to Duncan's truck.

❧   ❧   ❧

Once at the hospital, Carrie Lucas and Ellie Peterson looked on while Doc Peterson, who knew more about bellies than brains, examined Neva and declared her insane. Then Sheriff Duncan took her to Whitman where she would remain for several years.

❧   ❧   ❧

That same day, in late evening, Tilly lay on the bed. The bedroom door was ajar, and she watched as Virgil sat at the kitchen table feeding Lydia's child.

Virgil was a good, decent man with dark brown skin, and big droopy eyes. He wore a thin, stylish mustache and usually spoke softly until someone angered him. He smoked a pipe, and as he fed the baby, he kept it in his mouth.

Lydia said some unfair things about him on Saturday evening, but he cared more about the child than Lydia ever did. As he wiped the baby's face, Tilly remembered Lydia and was sorry she yelled those hateful words when Lydia slammed the door.

They were words she never really meant and would take to her grave. Still, she felt angry that Lydia left her with a child Lydia hadn't wanted. She supposed in some ways she was like Lydia. She never wanted children, either. Suddenly tears clouded her vision, and then the pain came as she wondered if she could find it in her heart to love this child.

❧   ❧   ❧

When Lula Hanks got word of Lydia's tragic death, she cried for Lydia's soul which was lost long before she died. Then she took the train and went back to Meadowsbrook.

❦ ❦ ❦

Still numb from the tragedy, Thea Rogers, a short thin bodied woman with pretty, smooth black skin and a gold tooth in the upper right side of her mouth, sat on the porch with her husband Harry. They had married only two years prior, and Harry now pondered his reason for doing so. Thea was a domestic who spent five days a week cleaning house and cooking for the Baraldi family. She was a talkative, but pleasant and likeable person.

If a person liked to listen to a one-sided conversation, then Thea was the person to visit because she seldom gave others the chance to voice their opinion.

"I told you Neva was nuts," she said. Neva had not been home when they visited Billy on Saturday, but as usual, they stayed playing cards, dancing, talking and drinking until Sunday morning. "I knew Neva was upset as soon as she walked through the door."

"I know you did, baby."

"I begged you to leave when you came over to the card table. What did I say to you Harry?"

"You said, 'Let's get out of here, Harry.'"

"I sure did. Fats pretended he wasn't scared, but I could tell he was scared. Yes indeed, Harry. That big ass Fats was scared."

"You shouldn't say that about him, baby."

"Yeah. I hear ya. What about you, Harry? Was you scared?"

"Not right then, baby. That's why I told you to take it easy."

"You said, 'Don't get all panicky now. Billy can handle things.' That's what you told me, Harry. But did Billy handle things, Harry?"

"No, he didn't, baby. Things kinda got outta hand." He wished to God she would shut up. He would welcome some quiet time. But he supposed if she kept quiet for one minute, she'd die. He immediately started to pray for a miracle, but then decided he was asking too much. To get Thea quieted down would be a task too big even for God.

"No need wasting God's time," he said aloud.

"What's that, Harry?"

"Oh, it's nothing, Thea."

"As I was saying, you bet it got outta hand. And when that brainless Joe put his two cents in I had enough."

'Don't worry 'bout it chickadee. Everything's copacetic,' Joe said. "You 'blieve everything was copacetic, Harry?"

"No, can't say that I did, baby."

"Did you know a truck hit Joe some time ago?"

"So I heard, baby."

"I hear most of his brains were scattered over the road. There's a wonder he ain't dead. 'Course as crazy as he is, it might be better off if he was. Would you say, Harry?"

"Could be, baby."

"You screamed at me, Harry. 'Ah, shut up,' you said. I decided right then and there you were as boneheaded as Joe, 'cause you didn't see danger signs. I did. I was so mad at you I didn't know what to do. That's why I left Billy's running. Then just as I got outside, Neva got louder. As they say in the music world, she raised her voice another octave."

"What do you know about octaves, baby?"

"I sing in the church choir, don't I? I'm not as dumb as you think I am."

"I never said you were dumb, baby."

"No, but you've hinted too many times to count."

He decided not to touch that one, and suddenly Thea was quiet. He was stunned, but thankful she finally shut her mouth.

"You know something, Harry?" she started again.

"What's that, baby?" he said standing up.

"I wish I had stayed," Thea said sadly. "Maybe I could have helped Lydia in some way. But I never thought Neva would go over the edge."

"I know, baby. None of us did," Harry said stretching and yawning like a cat.

"Where you going?" she asked as he sauntered into the house.

"Gonna get dressed and go to the Lounge for a while."

"That's a good idea, Harry. Think I'll tag along."

"Lawdy," he mumbled. "What have I ever done to deserve this?" Then he imagined God saying, "You married her, son."

🍁 🍁 🍁

The following week, Tilly, Virgil and Lula Hanks sat quietly on a front pew at Lydia's funeral, while Della and Thea talked so much and so loud that the Reverend Stringer actually asked if they wanted to preach the sermon.

Lydia's funeral was so rowdy, some folk said Lydia went out the way she lived: with a bang. Then they buried her under the tall, beautiful trees.

A few days later, a stranger came to town and went directly to Michael's Market and everyone in town speculated about his identity and his relationship to Tilly and Virgil.

But there was no way anyone could find out anything because Tilly hardly talked to Virgil, and she had no close friends. Not even Della had the nerve to ask Tilly about her guest, and Tilly's Aunt Lula dared not speak.

Within a short time, the man started working with Greyland Lamont. Though he called himself Handsome Jim, some said he was ugly enough to bring the dead to life.

# CHAPTER 16

Several days after Lydia was buried, Alan sat on the sofa, turned on the radio, and recalled his trip back to Meadowsbrook.

As soon as he learned of Lydia's death, he had taken the train back to Meadowsbrook and had gone to see Tilly immediately to discuss Lydia's child's future.

Of course, he felt like an ass. Aside from his putting the money in the mail for the child's upkeep, he never gave her much thought nor had he seen her until after Lydia's death.

Though he was supposed to be the little girl's daddy, he saw nothing of himself in her features. Still he agreed to continue to support her financially, because he made Lydia a promise. However, he asked Tilly to keep Koko until he sorted things out with his wife. Before leaving Tilly's house, he played with the little girl briefly.

Afterwards, he felt satisfied that things were settled. But when he returned to the big house his daddy ripped into him, asking questions, and spoiling his day.

"What're you doing up there in the big windy city?" his dad asked.

"For the time being I'm working for the railroad."

"Big deal." His dad spoke in a way to show the disappointment he felt. "Why?" he asked. "Why do you waste your time when you have the brain to do other things?

"Anybody can do that kind of work. Dammit! You should be a doctor." Shaking his head, his dad muttered, "I don't know. I just don't know. I never understood you, Alan."

"I know, daddy. And I never understood you either," he said angrily wanting to lash out even more. But before that emotion fully emerged, another came to the forefront. He wanted to knock the old man on his backside, but that too was but a brief notion.

He knew if he ever hit his daddy, the family would shun him, and he loved his mother too much to never see her again. Therefore, he walked away.

Now he was glad to be back in Chicago. Though he lived in a tenement and had to take four flights of stairs to get to his door, it was the place he called home. It was where he, not his daddy, paid rent.

Later, when his wife, Sweet, came into the room and sat beside him, he explained the situation about the child to her.

"So, what do you think, Sweet?" he asked. "Should I bring Koko home?"

"Whatta you mean should you bring her home?" Sweet asked mockingly. "She's with her mother's sister. So she's already home."

"But I'm her daddy. She's my responsibility."

"I'm not sure about that, and neither are you. So get that notion of bringing her home outta your head. And I said that to say this. "I'm not raising your *whore's* kid," she barked.

Alan was stunned. Staring at her, he thought about what his daddy said about Lydia. Now he wondered if his daddy was right about Sweet, too.

"Don't you get vulgar with me," he yelled. "You didn't even know Lydia so don't you dare call her names."

"So what's the big deal? Everybody else called her lots of names. Hell, she slept with every man in town. In fact, I heard more about Lydia when I was in Meadowsbrook than I did about Jesus Christ. And you know how much them so called Christians call on Him."

"Dammit, Sweet, you better shut your mouth before I shut it for you. I don't want to hear about any rumors you heard. Do you understand?"

"Whatever you say, Alan," Sweet replied meekly.

"I admit Lydia was wild and mixed up, but I never thought of her as a whore." Of course, he knew everyone else did, including his dad.

"Well, that ain't no surprise," Sweet voiced authoritatively. "You're so naïve you wouldn't know a whore unless she confessed her sins and signed a paper."

"You could be right about that." He refused to take the bait she threw at him. He was in no mood to argue. Perhaps he was naïve. He married her against his dad's advice. He learned a little too late that she was no innocent. She taught him more things in the bedroom in six months than he expected to learn in a lifetime.

Now he suspected she was probably one of the biggest whores in Chicago. She did things to him with her mouth he had never experienced before. One thing for sure, she was good at what she did. He wanted to share his thoughts with her, but thought better of it. Just thinking about the things she did to him in bed made his dick hard.

"Hey, Sweet!" he called. "Where did you learn all of that stuff?"

"All of what stuff?"

"You know." He smiled cockily. "The bedroom moves. Lydia never did all that. I mean you seem to know as much about diddling as any whore."

"I don't know what you're talking about," she said. Suddenly, she stood and looked down at him.

"Yeah, I bet you don't." He laughed.

"Now looka here, Alan. I'm no whore, and don't you call me one."

"Whatever you say, but Lydia needed help."

"I don't give a damn what Lydia needed. One thing for sure she ain't in need no more. Is she? I wish you'd forget her. And I don't appreciate you comparing me to her either," she yelled.

"I did no such thing." He grinned widely. "How could I? I mean you're in a class all by yourself." He chuckled catching her wrist and pulling her down onto his lap.

"I'm not complaining. I just want to make sure you keep all that talent right here for me," he whispered, wrapping his arms about her.

"You know something, Alan," she squinted nervously. "I don't care what you say. I'm not raising Lydia's kid."

"I got news for you, baby. You'll do whatever I tell you to." His voice was stern with no hint of a smile. She wiggled from his embrace and stood over him again.

"I doubt that baby's yours anyhow," she said as she flounced into the kitchen.

He stared after her speechless. Reaching over, he fumbled with the radio dial and turned up the volume. Her outburst angered him, but she only voiced what lurked in the back of his mind.

Yet, neither of them could deny there was a real flesh and blood baby in Meadowsbrook. Whose blood coursed through her veins was anybody's guess. Lydia spent time with Slick Joyride and God only knew who else. He had no idea whether the child was his or not, and it was his guess Lydia hadn't known, either.

❖ ❖ ❖

Just one week later Alan came home unexpected and found, of all people, Slick Joyride in his bed with his loving wife. He was so mad he wanted to kill them both.

As soon as he opened the door, Slick jumped out of bed and grabbed at his clothes. There was only one way out unless he jumped out the window. So Alan waited at the door.

When Slick attempted to pass, Alan hit him so hard his jaw cracked, his teeth rattled, and he fell, dropping his clothes. Alan waited for him to get up. Then they fought viciously until he knocked Slick out the door and down the flight of stairs.

"Damn, man. You broke my arm," Slick cried out. As Alan picked up Slick's clothes and started down the stairs, Slick yelled, "Please don't kill me man. Sweet invited me over."

Alan stopped and threw Slick's clothes down the stairs and watched as the naked man picked them up and ran.

Then he went back into the apartment. When he closed the door, it was obvious Sweet was scared and thought he was coming back to kick her ass, too. Standing naked on the opposite side of the bed, she screamed like a trapped animal. "Please don't hit me, Alan."

"Shut up, you bitch," he yelled. "You're not worth the effort."

"I'm sorry, Alan, but Slick made me do it."

Alan never spoke another word. He simply packed his bags and walked away from the woman he thought was the love of his life. But it became clear to him that women were not the answer to his needs. At least not those he chose.

After giving his plight some thought, he wished he had listened to his daddy and attended medical school. It couldn't have been any more difficult or complex as women. He knew it was time to do something worthwhile with his life. He left his wife and went to a roominghouse where he spent the remainder of the night. The next morning he went to the induction center.

❖ ❖ ❖

Summer arrived, and amidst all the ado Natalie forgave Shelton for his philandering after he promised to be faithful. Believing he understood marriage was a lifetime commitment, his promise gave her hope that better things were to come, and she smiled again.

It was late Saturday evening when Helene, who owned the small shoe store, "Simply Helene's" on the main street, closed the store. Then she and her girls, Queenie and Sophia, walked down the tree lined street to the big house where they would spend time with Odessa and Natalie. Even though Helene and Percy now had their own home, they still spent a lot of time at the big house.

"Hey, Helene," Shelton greeted, cheerfully, as she and her young girls came onto the porch. He was sitting in the swing next to Natalie.

"I'm okay, Shel. How about you?" Helene asked, surprised he was in such a good mood, and that he had taken time to actually sit a while. She turned to look at him.

"Couldn't be better," he answered.

"Glad to hear that," Helene said. As the girls made a dash for the swing, Shelton got up and sat in a nearby chair.

"Oh, Nat, you look so radiant," Helene remarked. "I guess Shel's doing something right." She laughed and winked at Shelton causing him to smile.

Natalie's mouth dropped open at her aunt's frankness and unusual joviality. Her aunt was right though. She was happy. Lately, Shelton spent time with her and the baby, and he often took them out for a drive throughout the countryside.

He even promised to take her dancing at the Lounge next weekend when one of the big bands would perform. She was not certain how long the happiness would last, but she planned to enjoy what they shared one day at a time.

"You're right, Helene. She does look happy." Odessa was amazed that Helene came to the same conclusion as she. She was even more astonished that Helene voiced it since she was usually a quiet listener who had little to say.

Pleased at family observations, Shelton stood, walked over and kissed Natalie's cheek. "See you later, Nat, Mama. You too, Aunt Helene," he said. Then he walked down the steps and into the yard. As he neared the gate, he whistled, causing Helene to glance over her shoulder.

Lydia's death dealt him a blow, she thought, and everyone knew it, including Nat. But now he seemed himself again and from the looks of Nat, their marriage was back on track.

# CHAPTER 17

❀

Summer of 1944. On a Saturday morning Elizabeth Farrell stepped back onto Meadowsbrook soil. Her arrival surprised everyone including her mother Ernestine because Elizabeth had been angry for years about her mother sending her to live with her Aunt Violet and Uncle Joe. And it had taken seven years for Elizabeth's anger towards her mother to subside.

Stepping from the train, the first person she saw was Fats Hopper who had gained even more weight, but otherwise, looked the same as he had when they were youngsters.

Though Elizabeth had blossomed, Fats recognized her instantly. For a moment, they stared at each other. "Liz, is that you?" He called.

"Yes. It's me," she replied, gaily, as he hurried towards her. Putting his arms around her, he said, "Welcome home, my friend."

"Thanks, Fats," she said as he stared at the child beside her.

"Oh, this is my son, Dominic," she said.

"How are you, Dominic?" Fats asked as the smile on Elizabeth's face told him she loved her son. Dominic looked at him, but said nothing.

"Come on, Dominic. It's okay. This is my childhood friend, Mr. Hopper."

"Hello, Mr. Hopper," the little green eyed boy said softly.

"Lawdy," Fats said. "He's got eyes just like…"

"It's okay. You can say it," Elizabeth laughed. "He's got eyes just like his daddy."

"Well, yes. That's what I was gonna say. By the way, did Nat or Tam know you were coming home?"

"No. No one knows. I didn't even tell Mama."

"Well, then. Let me help you with your bags." He had just come from the post office and held several letters in his hand. Sticking the envelopes in his shirt pocket, he picked up the larger suitcase, and she took the smaller one.

Then they walked across the tracks. Just before they reached Michael's Market, Candyman Cates, who sat on the bench in front of the store along with Seb Pardeau, looked up and screamed. "Lawdy, look what the wind blowed in!"

"Good gawd almighty," Seb yelled. "Hey, Tilly, come on out here. Look who's here," Seb called to a rather somber Tilly who still grieved for her sister, Lydia.

"Hey, Liz," Tilly said. "Welcome home. Guess you heard what happened to Lydia?"

"I did. And I'm so sorry, Tilly."

"Thanks." Tilly immediately called her husband Virgil who came and stood on the steps beside her. "This is my husband, Virgil. We call him Virg. You don't know him because he didn't grow up here. He lived over in Sugar Hill. Then he came to Meadowsbrook, and we got married. Didn't we, Virg?"

"Yeah, we did," Virg answered.

"Yeah, he's Tilly's husband," Candyman said.

"Hey, Liz," Virgil greeted. "It's good to meet ya."

"Same here," she said, eyeing Tilly as Lula Hanks stuck her head out the door and spoke.

"How you doing, Liz?" she inquired.

"I'm fine, Miss Lula," she said.

"Is that your little boy?" she asked though she wanted to ask if he was 'little Vince' the little meat man. But she didn't dare say too much. She was sure Elizabeth was still angry enough to put a foot in her ass. So she thought it was best she treaded lightly in that territory.

"Yes, it is," Elizabeth said.

Then they all started to talk at once, and the loud commotion caused Ernestine to come out to see what was going on.

Reaching the front gate, she looked towards Michael's. When she saw her daughter, she wondered if she was dreaming. "Liz, Liz. Is that you, baby?" she called loudly.

"Yes, Mama, it's me," Elizabeth shouted as she ran to Ernestine and threw her arms around her mama's neck. As the two women embraced, they cried.

"Goodness, Liz," Ernestine said. "Is this little Vince? Is this my grandson?"

Elizabeth laughed. His name is Dominic, Mama. I told you that in my letters."

"Come on over here, Dominic, and give your grandma a hug." Dominic went over and, Ernestine bent down. Kissing the boy's cheek, she hugged him. "Well, come on. Let's get your bags and go home."

As the two women went over to pick up the bags, Seb and Candyman started to sing, causing the women to smile.

"Welcome home, Liz," the older men said.

"Thanks gentlemen. It's good to be back," Liz responded while thinking some things never seem to change. She watched as Tilly quietly walked back inside the store, and wondered if Lydia had driven Tilly completely nuts before her death. Both of them were different, even as youngsters.

Her mother, Ernestine, bent down to get the larger bag, but Fats pushed her aside. "I'll take it for you."

"I'll help, too. Hey, Seb, keep an eye on things, will you?" Virgil said picking up the smaller bag.

"No problem, Virg," Seb said. As Virg and Fats walked away with Elizabeth and Ernestine, Candyman spoke.

"Wonder why Virg didn't ask me to look after the store?"

"Listen," Seb said. You might be younger, but your eyes are no good. I can still see."

"All right, Seb. No need to rub it in," Candyman replied.

❦ ❦ ❦

When Fats left Ernestine's, it was a little after noon. He drove directly over to Billy's.

Marcus had built Billy a garage a year earlier, and cars no longer stood on Billy's lawn, but were parked inside the building. Billy always closed the garage around noon on Saturday. Now, he and Harry were just putting away tools.

"Hey, Billy, Harry."

"Hey, Fats," the men spoke in unison.

"Guess who just came back home?" Fats stepped from the truck.

"Don't know, man, but I'm listening. So why don't you tell me?"

"Remember Nat and Tam's friend, Liz?"

"Yeah," Billy said. "Don't tell me she finally came back."

"Yeah she did. She just got off the train. I helped her with her bags."

"How long she staying?"

"Don't know yet," Fats replied. "But come on over to the Kitchen later this evening. I'm gonna have a fish fry to celebrate her homecoming."

"Sounds good," Billy said.

"I gotta go. See you later," Fats said.

As he walked back to his new red truck, Billy turned to Harry. "You don't know Liz, but you'll meet her. When we were kids, there were four girls. They were best friends. Did everything together. Then Georgia Mae died when she was about fourteen or fifteen. Liz's mother sent her away. She messed around with Vince the meat man and got herself pregnant."

"But what happened to Georgia Mae? How did she die?" Harry asked.

"That's a long story, man," Billy said. Then they continued to putter around in silence.

Within minutes, Fats was at Natalie and Shelton's house. "Nat, Nat," he called out rushing from the truck and onto the porch.

"What's the excitement about, Fats?" Shelton asked as he came onto the porch. "Sit down, man and stay a while. How you like the new truck?"

"Hey, Shel. I like it a lot, man. How's it going?" he asked, but before Shelton could answer, Fats continued as he sat down. "I just came to tell Nat that Liz is home."

"Nat, Nat. Come here," Shelton called. "Fats got something to tell you."

"Hi, Cash," Natalie said.

"Hey, Nat. Liz is home. She just got off the train. She said you and Tam didn't know she was coming so I thought I'd tell you."

"Oh, my word," Natalie put her hand over her mouth as if to stop the joy she felt about her friend's return. "I can't believe it. I never thought she'd come back. How does she look?"

"She's pretty, and her little boy, Dominic got eyes just like you-know-who. You'll see."

"You bet I will. I'm gonna get ready right now." Then she turned to Shelton. "Can we go to town a bit early, Shel?"

"Sure can, baby."

"Thanks so much, Cash," she told Fats. "We'll get ready. Tell Liz I'm on my way. I'll see her soon. I'm so happy she's come back."

"Yeah, me too," Fats beamed as he left the porch and got back into his truck. "I'm going to the Kitchen now. I got work to do. I'm gonna have a Saturday night fish fry to celebrate her homecoming. I'll see you there."

"Sounds good, man," Shelton said. "We'll be there."

"Thanks again," Natalie said.

"It's no problem. I knew you'd want to know." Fats spoke as he left the porch and got back into his red pickup truck.

🍁   🍁   🍁

Leaving Natalie and Shelton, Fats went to Tamara's house. Tamara and Paige were tending Tamara's mama and her grandma. But as soon as Fats told Tamara about Elizabeth's arrival, Tamara ran out the house, and all the way to Elizabeth's. Rushing inside the house, she found Elizabeth sitting on the back porch with her, mama, Ernestine, and her grandma, Bessie Mae Wanker.

"Liz, Liz," Tamara called, loudly. "I'm so glad you're home."

"Hey, Tam," Elizabeth stood and rushed into Tamara's arms. "It's good to be back." Then both women cried.

"Fats said he already told Nat you're here. She'll be here shortly. Girl, we got a lot of catching up to do."

"I know," Elizabeth said.

"Hey, Tam," Ernestine said. "Have a seat and stay a while." As Tamara sat down, Ernestine pointed to the little boy who played under the tree in the back yard. "That's my grandson, Dominic. You got to meet him. He got eyes just like Vince the meat..."

"For heaven sakes, Ernestine, don't you start that," her mother, Bessie Mae Wanker, thundered.

"Yes, please don't say that, Mama," Elizabeth pleaded. It was obvious her mother still harbored hard feelings.

"I'm sorry," Ernestine apologized. "It won't happen again."

"I hope it won't," Bessie Mae said. "Vince is that child's daddy, and there's no need to cause hard feelings where there ain't none."

"You're right, Mama. I said I was sorry." Then she looked at her daughter. "I love you and the boy too much to cause friction."

"I hope you do, Mama."

"Hey, where *is* everybody?" Natalie inquired as she, Shelton, and Makela rushed through the house and onto the back porch.

"Hey, Nat," Ernestine yelled. "Come on back."

"Hey, everybody," Natalie said as Makela held her hand tightly.

"Welcome home, Liz," Nat said as they hugged.

"Thanks, Nat. I missed you and Tam so much."

"Well, you won't miss us anymore. Will she, Tam?" Nat dabbed her eyes.

"Not unless she runs off," Tamara laughed. Then, standing back, Natalie looked Elizabeth up and down.

"You look good, Liz. I think life's been good to you."

"Thanks, Nat. I'm okay. It's good to be home, though," Elizabeth said as she glanced down at Makela. "So, this is your little girl. She's beautiful."

"Why, thank you, Liz," Natalie beamed.

"Yeah, but she's scared of everything," Shelton said. "It's good to see you, Liz," Shelton said as he kissed her cheek. Then turning his attention to Tamara, he asked, "How's it going, Tam? You gonna sing tonight?"

"Why you ask Tam a question like that?" Ernestine asked. "You know she's gonna sing."

"I just thought she might go to the fish fry tonight," Shelton said.

"I'll be there," Tamara responded. "I'll sing later."

"What fish fry?" Bessie Mae Wanker asked.

"Fats is giving a fish fry to celebrate Liz's homecoming," Natalie said.

"Oh," Ernestine said.

"He didn't tell me he was doing anything," Elizabeth said. "But it sounds good to me."

"Well, he told me all about it," Tamara said. "And I was to tell you. Just hadn't got around to it yet. I wouldn't miss it for any reason. I'm looking to have a good time, too."

"I can't believe we're back together again," Natalie said. "There's so much to talk about. Is that your Dominic in the yard?"

"It sure is," Elizabeth said. Turning she looked at the little boy and called out, "Come here, Dominic. I got somebody I want you to meet."

When Dominic came onto the porch, Elizabeth caught his hand and said, "This is your daddy's sister. She's your Aunt Tam, and this is Nat. Tam and Nat are my best friends. This is Nat's husband, Shel, and this is their little girl, Makela. They're like family."

"But if they're family and your best friends," Dominic said, "Why didn't they come to see us, Mama?"

"Well, honey I'll explain that some other time.

🍁    🍁    🍁

Later that evening, Fat's mother, Sissy, and his daddy, Tex Hopper, stood at the Fish Kitchen Café door to greet the guests. The juke box music played softly. And the first to arrive were Elizabeth, Ernestine, Bessie Mae Wanker, and Dominic.

"Come on in here, Liz, and give me a hug," Sissy said throwing her arms around Elizabeth.

"Glad to have you back in the fold, young lady," Tex said as he kissed her cheek.

"Thanks, Mr. Hopper. It's good to be back."

"Hey, Sissy, Tex. This here is Dominic," Bessie Mae Wanker said calling attention to the young boy at her side. "He's my great-grandson, you know."

"Glad to meet you, Dominic," Tex said as Shelton and Natalie came through the door together.

"Well, I'll be darned. He sure is handsome," Sissy said before excusing herself to greet Natalie and Shelton.

"Evening, Mr. and Mrs. Hopper," Natalie said.

"How you doing, young lady? And what a surprise to see ya," Tex said. "It's good to see you out and about."

"Thank you, Mr. Hopper."

"How's your mama?" Sissy asked.

"Mama's just fine."

"And where's that pretty little girl, Makela?" Sissy asked as if she actually expected Natalie to bring Makela to such a gathering.

"She's at the house with Mama," Natalie answered.

"Hey, Shel," Tex said. "You behave yourself now, you hear."

"You betcha," Shelton replied.

"You better," Sissy said rolling her eyes. Taking a step closer, she whispered, "I got my eyes on you. I heard all about your shenanigans. If I see any crap going on tonight, I'm telling your mama and daddy. You know I wouldn't mind if they did put your butt on horseback. You heard Tex. I suggest you behave yourself tonight."

"Come on, Nat," Shelton said ignoring Sissy and pulling Natalie away. "Let's go find us a table."

"What did she say to you, Shel?" Natalie asked.

"Nothing worth repeating, baby. Don't worry about it." As he glanced back over his shoulder he saw Melanie Joyride come through the door with her uncle, Slick Joyride.

Melanie was a very striking young woman with sculptured features. She had full lips, almond eyes, high cheekbones, a straight nose, and long wavy hair. And everything about her reminded Shelton of Natalie. However, in bed, Shelton found her to be almost as wild as Lydia.

By keeping close to Natalie, Shelton not only surprised Sissy, he, in fact, shocked everyone. Even though Shelton acted civil, Bessie Mae Wanker wasted no time telling Ernestine how she really felt about him.

"He ain't fooling me. That Shelton is nothing but the devil in the flesh. If I was married to him, he wouldn't be able to use them things hanging between his legs."

"For heaven sakes, Mama. That's awful. Of course, I suppose you're right. You never know. I might cut'em off too," Ernestine said as both women laughed loudly.

Looking around as they entered the door, Greyland and Jozell saw Natalie and Shelton. They waved then went over and sat with them at the table.

"Good to see you, Nat," Greyland said, pleased that his brother Shelton seemed to be having a good time with his wife.

"Yeah," Jozell said. "It's about time you started coming out, Nat. There's more to life than keeping house, you know."

"Perhaps, you're right," Natalie chuckled.

Tamara came with Tobias even though he smarted that Tamara continually talked about going north to become a star. All of Elizabeth's other friends came to celebrate, including Georgia Mae's brother, Deacon Pastures.

Deacon lived in Chicago with relatives now, but returned often to see his grandparents.

Folk very seldom saw Sadie anymore. She became a recluse after Georgia Mae died.

When Fats turned up the volume on the juke box, Bessie Mae Wanker and Dominic ate the last of their food, said goodbye, and returned home. Then they sat on the back porch where Dominic fell asleep trying to count the stars.

While his mother and daddy cooked fish and other delicacies, Fats danced with every woman in the place. But he danced with Elizabeth first.

"Hope you're having a good time," he said. "'Cause if you're not, I want to know why."

"I'm having a great time. And I thank you for the party."

"It's all my pleasure." Looking up, Fats saw Vince enter the door. Vince was not supposed to be there, but just like in the past the man broke every rule in the book. Vince did whatever the hell he wanted.

Now, we've all come full circle, Fats thought, as he danced Elizabeth closer to the door and closer to the person they all knew as Vince the meat man.

❦ ❦ ❦

Sitting in the swing on the porch at the big house, with Natalie and Tamara several days after she came back to Meadowsbrook, Elizabeth recalled the past seven years, while Natalie and Tamara listened attentively.

"As soon as I arrived in San Francisco, I fell in love with Uncle Joe and Aunt Violet because they were very good to me. We lived in the Fillmore. I loved the City, and I loved the folk in our neighborhood. Everyone had such pride.

"Within days I met the Bowmans. Mrs. Kitty Bowman was a tiny black woman, who kept one hand in her apron pocket at all times. I often wondered if she carried a weapon, but she was a friendly woman, and Aunt Vi liked her. So I liked her too.

"After Dominic was born, Aunt Vi encouraged me to go back to school. I did. Mrs. Bowman took care of small children for working parents. She also took care of Dominic."

"Geez, Liz. You were lucky to have help. By the way, what was school like there?" Natalie asked.

"School is school no matter where you go. So it was okay, but I missed home, and I missed you and Tam."

"We missed you too, girl," Tamara interjected.

"Mrs. Bowman's daughter, Maxine, and I were classmates and soon became friends. We spent lots of time together. We attended parties and went to Friday night dances at the youth center."

"Shoot, sounds like you had fun," Tamara said.

"I did, but there were times I was so homesick I cried."

"Well, no need to be homesick anymore. You're home now. I hear San Francisco is one beautiful city," Natalie said wondering just how long Elizabeth would stay in Meadowsbrook after living in a real city with bright lights.

"It *is* very pretty, and I hope you'll get to see it one day," Elizabeth said.

"Sounds good, doesn't it, Nat?" Tamara said.

"That it does."

"Anyway," Elizabeth continued, "when we graduated we both went to work. Maxine took a job working nights at a nearby club, and I went to work at a neighborhood grocery. Maxine and I continued to do things together until I met Jackie.

"Jackie came into the store almost every day. She drove a nice car and wore beautiful clothes. She lived in the Bay View area and worked nights at a bar.

She said I could work there too. So we hit it off right away. I was very impressed with Jackie, but explained I liked my present job."

"Wow," Natalie remarked. "I'm impressed too. Sounds like Jackie had it made."

"Wait until you hear the rest."

"Jackie invited Maxine and me to several parties, but Maxine never really liked Jackie. So Maxine went with us only a couple of times. After that, Maxine went her way, and I became so involved with Jackie I didn't see Maxine much. Even so, Mrs. Bowman continued to care for Dominic while I worked and whenever I partied on weekends.

"After just two months, Jackie invited me to share her apartment. Aunt Vi had a fit, but I thought it was my chance for independence. So being naïve, I jumped at the chance. Everything was fine until Jackie asked me for a favor. That was when I started to feel uneasy.

"Jackie wanted me to meet her friend, Freddy King. Jackie said Freddy wanted to take me out. And I wondered how he could like me when I didn't know him. Then Jackie said he'd seen me around, and she'd talked about me.

"I told her I didn't like her talking about me to a stranger. 'I can speak for myself, you know,' I told her, 'and I'm not interested in your friend.'

'There's no need to get all bent outta shape,' she said, 'Freddy's a nice guy, and he's got a few bucks too.'

'If that's the case,' I said. 'It seems you'd keep him for yourself since you're always broke.'"

"You see, Jackie borrowed money from me several times, but she always forgot when it was time to pay up. So I took the opportunity to jog her memory.

'Now, don't you get sidity on me, Liz Farrell,' Jackie said. 'I'm gonna pay you back as soon as I get the money. But that money's got nothing to do with Freddy. He won't bite, you know. Who knows? He just might marry you.'

'Dammit, Jackie,' I screamed. 'I never said I needed help to get married. So I'd appreciate you keeping your nose out of my personal business.'

'There's no need to get loud, Jackie said.'"

"Then I wanted to know what was in the date for her? You see, I'm not dumb, and I'd watched Jackie in action. That woman would snatch candy from a baby."

"From what you say, I don't think Jackie is a very nice person," Natalie said.

"Yeah, she sounds like she's a pain in the ass," Tamara said."

"Now you're beginning to get the true picture of my friend, Jackie."

"Jackie acted as if she was above such a thing, and yelled, 'Whatta you mean what's in it for me? Nothing's in it for me. Freddy's just my friend. That's it. Period.'"

"I needed a friend so much at that time, I guess I would have done anything for friendship. So I agreed to go out with Freddy, just once.

"So on Friday evening Freddy picked me up. Freddy was clean and smelled good, but he was much older than I expected. He drove a car with a busted muffler, and the gas tank was almost empty."

"Lawdy, you got to be kidding. He doesn't sound like a man with money to me," Tamara said.

"Wait a minute, girl. You ain't heard nothing yet. Freddy seemed nice. So I relaxed, and looked forward to having a good time.

"But instead of Freddy taking me to one of the nicer places Jackie and I frequented, he took me to a greasy spoon café. And the stale beer and piss hit my nose before we reached the door. But I didn't let it bother me because I was doing Jackie a favor.

"When the waitress placed the greasy hamburger in front of me, I accepted it graciously. Then I gulped down the beer, when I preferred a chocolate malt.

"I meant to see Freddy only once, but Freddy didn't try to talk me into his bed, and I liked him for that. He said he liked me too.

"At the time, I was lonely and needed someone to like me. So I kept seeing Freddy. We had dated almost two months, when he invited me to party at his place. I thought other people would be there, but when we arrived, I was surprised. No one was there. It was just the two of us.

"His place, a one room apartment, was a disappointment. It contained a wall bed, a rickety chair and a rickety table. One chair leg was weak, and when I sat in it, I tumbled back, but Freddy caught me and held me for a minute. Then he went over, pulled the bed from the wall and invited me to sit on it. I refused.

"The only other piece of furniture in the room was an old dresser in the corner, a small table, and two chairs. The radio, which was on the table, was new. Freddy turned it on, and soft music flowed into the room."

"Lawdy, Liz. Your Freddy seems as poor as a church mouse in winter," Tamara chuckled.

"You got to hear the rest."

"I hope it's no worse than what you've already told us," Natalie said.

"Wait. There's more. When I asked about the bathroom, Freddy said he shared with other tenants, and it was located down the hall. I excused myself and went to the bathroom.

"When I returned to the room, Freddy took a bottle from the shelf and poured us a drink in two cloudy glasses that looked like they needed washing.

"We drank rotgut. I hate rotgut. I wished I had a smooth brandy. After about ten minutes of conversation, Freddy demanded sex. I refused, and he became ugly. 'You lousy bitch,' he screamed, as he took off his clothes."

"Good Lord, Liz. What did you do?" Natalie asked.

"Wait and I'll tell you," Elizabeth replied. "He yelled, 'Who the hell do you think you are? I been spending my money on you all this time, and if you think you ain't gonna give it up, you must be crazy, girl. Get real.'"

"At that moment, I looked around and knew I was in trouble. There was only one way out of the apartment, and Freddy stood naked in the doorway.

"When I made no effort to take off my clothes, Freddy came over and slapped my face so hard I thought my eyeball would fall out. I started to cry and fight back, but that made him angrier. So he beat me until I gave up. Then he threw me onto the bed and fell on top of me.

"He pressed his arm against my chest and pressed his hand against my throat. I just knew he would kill me. With the other hand he tore off my panties. Then Freddy viciously pushed himself inside of me as I screamed in pain. I cried for help, but there was no one to help me.

"Oh, Liz, I wish I had been there to help you." Natalie looked sad.

"I know you do."

"Me too," Tamara said. "I would've kicked Freddy's you-know-what."

"I believe that, Tam." Elizabeth paused. "Within minutes of satisfying himself, Freddy fell asleep, and I got dressed and went home.

"I was so disappointed that Freddy thought those hamburgers he fed me gave him uncontested rights to my body. Jackie said he had money, but he had nothing. If so, he saved it for a rainy day. The very next morning I told Jackie I wouldn't see Freddy again.

"Then Jackie confessed to me that Freddy promised her fifty dollars if she got me to go out with him. It hurt me so much to know my so called friend, Jackie, had sold me up the river. I cried. She didn't know it, but our friendship ended then and there. I went into the bedroom and threw our belongings into a bag, and Dominic and I left Jackie's apartment.

"Though my body hurt for several days, I told no one what really happened. Not even Jackie."

"I don't blame you for leaving Jackie. You should've left long before," Tamara said. "She was no friend."

"I know," Elizabeth sighed as a tear rolled down her cheek.

"Oh, Liz," Natalie said, "I'm so sorry that happened to you."

"I know you are. But I learned a hard lesson from that experience."

"What's that?" Tamara asked.

"I should've listened to Aunt Vi."

# CHAPTER 18

Tamara met Tobias Dupree one night in a club while she was working up north one weekend. He invited himself to sit at her table. He bought drinks and immediately expressed his feelings. He not only admired her singing, he admired her. "You're the most beautiful woman I ever saw," Tobias told her. "To be truthful, I think I'm in love with you."

Tamara laughed as Tobias' shaven bald head glowed like the silvery moon in the countryside. He wore expensive clothes and shoes. He was a tall, well built man, and she stared into the most gentle brown eyes she had ever seen. His dark brown face was pleasant and his smile enchanting.

Thereafter, each time she worked the club Tobias was there. Front row. He gave her flowers, took her to expensive restaurants, and bought her nice perfume. In fact, Tobias spent so much money on her, she asked about his employment. He told her he was in business for himself. But he never told her what that business was, and she decided it was best not to ask.

When she asked about his home, he said he lived quite a distance away. When she said she wanted to see it and meet his family, he promised to take her there in the near future. He never did.

She sensed something was wrong, but she still believed in him because he was different. He never tried to talk her into bed.

In the past, most men only wanted to jump in bed with her. When she made a fuss most simply went on their way. But there were some who got real ugly, and she knew she was lucky to have survived such encounters.

She always liked men to a certain extent, but she trusted few. While growing up she watched the relationship between her mother and her mother's husband, Obie. She didn't like what she saw. Then her best friend's husband, Shelton, disappointed her when he propositioned her.

"I'll do anything for you, Tam. All I want is to fuck you one time," he told her. Tamara wanted to cry because Natalie was her best friend. However, instead of crying she set him straight.

"You know something, Shel. I always thought of you as a brother because Nat's my best friend. I respect her and love her like a sister. She loves you though I can't say why. So if you ever talk to me that way again, I'll cut off your nuts and feed them to the hogs. Then I'll tell Nat why I did it."

"Damn," Shelton whispered, "I'm sorry. There's no need to get so stirred up. It won't happen again."

"It better not. Otherwise, I'm talking to Nat about you. And she just might start thinking with her head instead of her heart."

They never spoke of the incident again, and Shelton treated her like family, but she never trusted him again.

When she learned about him and Lydia, there was nothing she could do. He was Natalie's problem, but she knew Natalie wouldn't leave him, because Natalie and her family believed marriage was a lifetime commitment. She just hoped Natalie would do something and straighten Shelton out.

Things seemed good between him and Natalie now, and Tamara hoped their marriage would continue to improve.

Tobias did something no other man did. He made Tamara feel wanted and loved. She even did something unusual. She envisioned their being married.

When Tobias finally took her home it was to his two room apartment, which surprised her because he seemed to have lots of money. Then he told her once again he had another home.

"When am I gonna see it?" she asked.

"Soon," he said. The answer pleased her, and when he asked her to marry him, she didn't hesitate one moment. She said yes and fantasized about living in a big, pretty house in the big city under bright lights.

After they married, she demanded she meet his family and see the other home. She didn't want to live in the small apartment. But Tobias made every excuse he could. Then it occurred to her that Tobias was a liar, and she had bitten off a hunk of something too big to swallow.

Realizing her mistake, she decided to make the best of things. So she invited him to live with her, and he happily accepted. In fact, Tobias was so eager to live with her she concluded he was nothing more than a boll weevil looking for a home, and she was stupid enough to fall for his game. She wanted to cry.

She was so mad she didn't even want him to touch her. But he did, and she pretended everything was great. Natalie was the only person in town who knew the truth.

She had no one to blame other than herself because she was looking for the same thing from Tobias he found in her. So she ended up married to someone she hardly knew and getting the wrong end of the stick.

As soon as they arrived in Meadowsbrook, he got a job at the hospital. When she learned Tobias knew as much about medicine as Doc Peterson, she wanted to know more about him, but Tobias gave up no secrets.

At first he was that loving man she met, but only months after their marriage, his personality changed, and he started to lash out.

"Are you coming with me to the Lounge tonight?" Tamara asked one night.

"Hell, no. I'm not going, and you ain't going either," he told her.

"What're you talking about? I'm a singer. I was singing in a club when we met. This is how I make my living, and I love it."

"I don't give a damn what you love. I don't want you singing anymore," Tobias yelled.

"That's too bad, buster. I'll do whatever the hell I want. Take it or leave it," she said just as he slammed his fist hard into her side. She doubled over. Then he punched her in her back, and beat her about her shoulders, but he never touched her face.

"You're my wife now, and you'll do what I tell you to," he screamed. Though Tamara was in pain, she realized Tobias was crazy. Within moments she regained her composure, went into the bedroom, and when she came out, she held a Saturday night special.

"If you ever touch me again, I'll kill you," Tamara told him. As he stared down the barrel of a gun he never knew Tam owned, he realized his wife was no patsy. If he got out of this alive, he thought, he would watch his step and bide his time. Then show her who was really boss.

"I'm sorry Tam. I didn't mean it. Now put that thing away. Let's talk. Let's be civil about this thing."

"Sounds good to me." That was the first time Tamara didn't go the Lounge or the Dawson home.

❦   ❦   ❦

When no one saw her for two days, Natalie and Elizabeth went to her house.

"We've fought in the past," Tamara told them. "But he never hit me before."

"My God, Tam. He really hurt you," Natalie said as Tam showed them the bruises.

"Yes, he did."

"Oh, Tam," Elizabeth sounded sad. "What will you do now?"

"I'm not sure yet," Tamara said pensively. "But don't you worry. That was the first and last time Tobias will ever hit me and live to tell about it."

❦ ❦ ❦

Autumn arrived, and as the leaves turned an array of brilliant colors, death came to Tamara's house late in the night and took her grandma, Ginger, away.

Some folk said it was about time because Ginger had suffered too long. Then just one week after Greyland and Handsome Jim lowered Ginger into the ground, Asha died too.

Their deaths affected Tamara deeply. She was in great pain as she remembered how much she fought with her mama and grandma when she was a young girl. Now she realized just how much she loved them both, but it was too late to tell them so. And she would suffer in silence for her behavior the rest of her life.

"Oh, my God," she whispered. "Please forgive me."

❦ ❦ ❦

"I wonder what really went on in that house," Natalie pondered. "Tobias is a little strange, you know. In fact, he's downright scary. I got a feeling he might have done something. Tam said he knows as much about medicine as Doc Peterson does."

"Lawdy, Nat. I can't believe you. Tobias is the kindest and sweetest man I know," said Odessa.

"Obviously, you see something I don't see in him, Mama." The two women were silent, momentarily. "You just never know though. Maybe Tam…"

"Get that notion out of your head right now," Odessa scolded.

"But she was so tired of tending them, Mama. Remember what Asha did with wild greens, mushrooms, and mistletoe tea?"

"I know."

"And even you once said maybe Tam should do something."

"Did I? I don't remember that one," Odessa feigned forgetfulness.

"Don't you remember, Mama? You said sometimes we did things we had to…"

"Lawdy, Nat. I don't want to hear it. So get such thoughts out of your head. Will you?"

Natalie wanted to forget it, but she remembered the bruises Tamara showed Elizabeth and her. Tobias beat her black and blue all because she wanted to go to the Lounge in defiance of his will.

🍁  🍁  🍁

Several days after the funerals, Tamara and Elizabeth visited Natalie at the big house. Tamara said she suspected Tobias had done something to her mother and grandma.

"Now listen, Tam. If you think Tobias did something to your family, you can't allow him to go unpunished. You should tell Duncan." Natalie was speaking of their sheriff.

"Damn! What can Duncan do? Let's face it. Duncan's a drunk. Duncan should be locked up himself. Had he not been drunk when Neva chased Lydia, she would be in that empty ass jailhouse instead of over at Whitman playing crazy.

"I got a feeling she meant to get rid of Lydia all along. If the train hadn't killed her, Neva would've shot her. I had no love for Lydia, but I hope Neva gets her due when she gets out."

"I suppose Billy will see to that," Natalie said. "By the way, Duncan is all we have as far as the law goes."

"I know that. But he's not up to the job. You know who I think would be a good sheriff?" Tamara said.

"Who?"

"Your Uncle Percy."

"Damn, Tam. He'd drive everyone nuts," Elizabeth interjected. "You know how he is."

"Liz is right. He'd put us in jail just for spitting in the dust. How could you wish that on the poor folk of this town?" Natalie said causing them to laugh.

"I wouldn't give a damn about what he did. Duncan's a disgrace. If folk ever got serious, Duncan would be in jail I tell you."

🍁   🍁   🍁

On a cold night in December, just before Christmas, rains fell and froze, turning the town into a phenomenal glassy ice world. Contrary to some folk's thinking, this area could and did get very, very, cold in winter. Sheriff Duncan, who figured so insignificantly in the scheme of things, froze to death and no one missed him for several days. When the ice thawed, Duncan lay face down at the front steps of the jail. His death meant Tamara finally got her wish. The townsfolk had a meeting and voted Percy Dawson in as sheriff and he strutted about town like a peacock.

# CHAPTER 19

Though Elizabeth once loved Vince, things happened in the seven years she was away. When she saw him the night she returned home, everything had changed. She realized they were both older and that giddy feeling she had for him was gone. There was no need to try to recapture the past. Vince would never be her lover again, and all they had in common was Dominic. Vince was simply her son's daddy.

These were the things she told Natalie and Tamara late one evening after enjoying an evening with Natalie's family.

"I don't mean to be nosy, Liz. But what's Vince doing about Dominic?" Tamara asked.

"Don't worry, Tam. He's good to my son. He wants Dominic to get a good education, and has put money aside for that."

"I'm so glad to hear that," Tamara said. "You know Papa did that for me, and I'll do what I can to help you. After all, Dominic is family."

"Liz, tell us what happened to your boyfriend, George," Natalie said. "Remember you wrote and said you were getting married?"

"Yeah," Tam said. "You never shared the breakup with us."

"Honey, I was too hurt to share that with anyone. The only reason Uncle Joe and Aunt Vi knew was because they were there.

"George was in the army. I fell in love with him and thought he loved me too. He gave me a beautiful ring. Then just before we were to get married, he was sent overseas. "He never told me about his orders, he simply walked away."

"You're kidding," Tamara said.

"No. It's no joke. And I was too hurt to talk about it with anyone.

"It all started about a year after my friendship ended with Jackie. Maxine Bowman and I became close again. We, like most youngsters, enjoyed dancing. So we hung out at clubs on weekends. Our favorite place was Jimmy's Blue Bird Club on Fillmore Street. And that's where we met the two soldiers, John Greenhouse and George Plummer.

"They looked so good in those uniforms, I just about went over the edge," Elizabeth laughed. "Of course, now that I think about it, we probably swooned more about the uniforms than the men in them. Anyway, it's a long story.

"We want to hear it anyway," Tamara said. "We got time."

"Well, within hours of meeting George, I was in love. After our first meeting, he came to see me on weekends whenever he was free.

"Six weeks after our first meeting, he gave me an engagement ring. Naturally, I thought he was in love too. Two months after he gave me the ring, he gave me a sealed envelope just before he returned to camp. He said it was a little something special for me. He asked that I not open it until the next day.

"I put the envelope on the dresser. But I was so intrigued I hardly slept. I got out of bed several times during the night to make sure that envelope hadn't somehow grown legs and walked away. Lawdy, was I ever stupid?" Elizabeth shook her head from side to side.

"Early the next morning, I leaped from bed and tore open the envelope. There was a note inside and a check for five hundred dollars. According to the note, I could spend the money any way I wanted."

"Jesus!" Natalie exclaimed. "What a generous man. That's a lot of money."

"Yeah, you struck it rich with that guy," Tamara said. "I could use that kind of money."

"I know. I couldn't believe it. I could hardly contain myself. I ran downstairs and showed the check to Aunt Vi who said, 'My gawd. That George has outdone himself this time.'

"But instead of going on a spending spree, I decided to wait for George and we would spend the money together. After all, we were getting married.

"The weekend came and went, but George neither showed up nor called. I worried something terrible happened. So I called him. He wasn't in, and the person who answered the phone couldn't tell me anything about him.

"I was an absolute wreck by Monday morning. So, instead of going to work I stayed home and phoned everybody I thought might know George. But I got no answers. Finally, after spending half day on the phone, I was able to talk to someone.

'Listen, lady,' said the voice of authority. 'I'm telling you what I know. Sergeant Plummer has been shipped overseas.'

'But we're getting married, I said.'

'Sorry, young lady. Perhaps *you're* getting married,' bellowed the voice on the other end. 'But I assure you Sergeant Plummer is *already* married, and he's been shipped out. I'm sorry.'"

"Good Lord, Elizabeth. I can't believe it," Tamara said.

"What an awful man," Natalie whispered as if George would hear her if she spoke louder.

"I'm telling you when that man hung up that phone it sounded as loud as a clap of thunder. I held the phone for a while and cried. I felt like I was caught in a bad dream. Then I remembered the check. I was happy. At least I had the money. I supposed George knew he was leaving and gave me the money out of guilt.

"The next day when I got ready for work, I decided to take the check with me and cash it during my lunch break. Imagine my surprise when the teller looked me in the eye and said, 'I'm sorry, but this account is closed.'

"I froze and couldn't move until the person behind me said, 'Lady, could you please step aside.' "I was so heartbroken I was sick. When I returned to work, my boss sent me home."

Unable to comment, Natalie and Tamara stared silently, and shook their heads. Then moments later, Natalie asked, "Did you ever hear from him again?"

"No, I never did. And since George turned out to be such a disappointment, Aunt Vi got up one morning, took the ring from my finger and had it appraised. "Guess what?"

"Don't tell us it was glass," Tamara said.

"That's exactly what it was," Elizabeth said. "And I almost died for the second time over George."

Elizabeth sat across the table from Natalie but next to Tamara. Tamara pushed her chair back and stared at Elizabeth while Natalie got up and went over and put her arm around Elizabeth's shoulders.

"So now you know what happened to George. I can also tell you one more thing. Since that happened, I've not met a man I can trust."

"Do you think you'll ever marry?" Natalie asked.

"I don't know. After talking with you and Tam, I wonder if it's worth it."

"I'll tell you this. Marriage isn't all I thought it would be. I don't know what happened to Tobias along the way. He has so much anger stored up, I swear he scares me at times," Tamara said. "What do you think about, marriage Nat?"

"Shel and I have problems, but we're trying to get it right."

# CHAPTER 20

Spring 1945. After the congregation built him a beautiful home, the young, good looking, charismatic preacher, Reverend Buddy McCord, moved to Meadowsbrook from the small town of Sugar Hill in order to be closer to his flock. However, Natalie and Elizabeth noticed the good Reverend McCord spent a lot of his time with their friend, Tamara.

The Reverend was a tall man with curly hair, olive skin, hazel eyes, and a square jaw. And every woman in town wished she could get a piece of him, which meant he was competition, and Shelton Lamont simply wished he would go back wherever he came from.

Though every woman wanted him, Buddy saw only one woman he wanted and that was Tamara Dupree. Because their way of life was so different, he was doubtful about a relationship with her. He was a preacher and she a married night club singer, but he was unable to get Tamara out of his head.

He heard a lot about her and learned she was passionate about her singing. He wasn't one to frequent places like the Lavender Lounge, but once he'd heard her sing, he sometimes went there and sat in the back of the club just so he could look at her.

When he finally got the nerve to introduce himself, she laughed and said, "I know who you are." Then they talked, and he was surprised when she agreed to attend church services and sing in the choir. But she let him know then and there, she would never give up the night clubs. Even so, their friendship grew.

When Tobias became aware of their blossoming friendship, he began to question Tamara.

"What's going on between you and the Reverend?" he asked one evening as Buddy drove up in front of the house in his big Cadillac and waited for Tamara.

"Nothing's going on, Tobias. We're just friends, and we're going to Bible study."

"You better make sure it's Bible study. Otherwise, you gonna be sorry."

❦ ❦ ❦

As the days passed, the Reverend Buddy McCord found it hard to concentrate on his work. Tamara constantly danced in his head. He tried to stay away from her, but the temptation was too great.

He knew it wasn't the right thing to do, but he drove to Tamara's house one evening while Tobias was working the night shift. As he got out of the car, visions of Tamara were overwhelming. Several red rose bushes grew along the walkway and the fragrance did something to him.

When he knocked, Tamara, who had just gotten out of the bath tub and was dressed only in a sheer negligee, opened the door. Without ever speaking a word, he grabbed her, already feeling aroused. As he slammed the door behind him, he picked her up and carried her to the bedroom. He had to have her, and she loved it.

Though Tobias worked at the hospital that night, it was his mind that worked overtime. It still bothered him that Tamara had pulled a gun on him and he had done nothing about it. Even so he still planned to make her forget about singing at the Lounge. Hell, he didn't want his wife around all those men.

Now he felt there was something going on. And his feelings didn't often lie to him, he thought. Tam denied it, but he was sure the Reverend Buddy McCord had his eye on her. But he had news for the good Reverend. If he ever got outta line, he was gonna kick his ass. Then run him outta of town.

"Hey," Carrie called out interrupting his thoughts. "How you doing, Tobias?"

"I'm just dandy," he said. He was lying, of course. At that very moment he was so preoccupied with the thought of Tamara, he wanted to go home.

"Hey, Carrie. Wait up will ya?" he called as she went around the corner.

"Yeah, what is it?"

"I need to run home for a few minutes. Will you cover for me?"

"Sure, I will."

"Make sure you keep an eye on this one," he said referring to Lula Hanks who came down from Chicago. "She's not feeling well. She stuck a nail in her foot and didn't come in to see the doctor until she was almost dead."

"So I heard," Carrie said. "Go on. We'll be okay here."

❦   ❦   ❦

With that, a suspicious Tobias went home, and just as he suspected, he found Buddy and Tamara in bed.

"Why you lousy son-of-a-bitch," Tobias said as he angrily grabbed the poker near the fireplace.

"Wait, wait." Tamara jumped from the bed. "I'm sorry, please don't hurt him," she pleaded just as Tobias slapped her face.

"I'm gonna kill ya," Tobias yelled. As Buddy leaped from the bed, Tobias struck him repeatedly with the poker. Throwing his hands up in defense, Buddy tried, unsuccessfully, to shield himself.

As Tobias continued to strike him, Buddy cried out in agony. "Please, don't kill me, man."

"Fuck you, man. You trying to take my wife," Tobias hissed.

"Stop it, Tobias," Tamara begged as she struggled to pull Tobias away from Buddy. When she was unable to separate them, she ran to the kitchen and grabbed the skillet from the top of the stove. Rushing back into the bedroom, she hit Tobias hard on the head knocking him out cold.

Buddy was in such pain, he groaned. As he sat down on the side of the bed, he realized he was only minutes from certain death. Tobias meant to kill him. Had it not been for Tamara, he would have done the job.

Of course, he thought. If it wasn't for her, he wouldn't be in such a mess in the first place.

When he finally regained his composure, he thanked Tamara for saving his life, and those were the only words he spoke for some time.

"My God, what have I done?" he cried out while he hoped Tamara hadn't killed Tobias. He did not want that kind of trouble.

"What do we do now?" Tamara asked nervously.

"I don't know," Buddy said. Then he stood up, walked over to Tobias, and checked him. "Thank God. He's still breathing, but he's out cold."

"You sure he's all right?" Tamara asked.

"Yeah, I'm sure. But he's mad as hell, you know. And he's got every right to be. I have coveted his wife and beyond." Buddy spoke as the pain began to subside. "So, the first thing I'm gonna do is tie him up. You got some rope?"

Tamara rushed out to the back porch and came back with a lengthy rope. "You won't hurt him will you?"

"No, Tam. I won't hurt him. But come tomorrow I'm putting him on the northbound train. But before I do, I should give the mean son-of-a-bitch a taste of his own medicine and beat him within an inch of his life," Buddy said already forgetting he was in Tobias's house with Tobias's wife.

"Please don't do that," Tamara said. "We don't want trouble."

"You're right. But you'll have to help me put him in the car, baby." Tobias lay face down on the floor. Ignoring Tamara's pleas, Buddy kicked Tobias right square in the ass before tying Tobias's hands behind his back. Then he and Tamara put Tobias in Buddy's car, and Buddy drove off into the night.

Tamara was on edge and worried. She was unable to sleep throughout the night. The next day when she heard nothing from Buddy by noon, she feared the worst. After getting dressed, she rushed to Buddy's home.

He opened the door when she arrived and before he could speak, she bombarded him with questions.

"Where've you been? Why didn't you come by the house? Did you put Tobias on the train?" she asked all in one breath as she dropped down onto the sofa.

"Hey, hold on a minute. I'm trying to get over that beating Tobias gave me. My body still aches, and I think I'll carry scars for the rest of my life."

"I'm so sorry it happened. But I want to know what happened to Tobias."

"Isn't he home?" Buddy asked as he went over and sat beside her. Taking her in his arms, he kissed her. She twisted from his embrace and pushed him away. "You mean you turned him loose?"

"Of course, I did. Tobias moaned and groaned until I made a deal with him. I told him to promise he would never touch you again. But Tobias said you were his wife and he could do anything he wanted. "I told him if that was the case, I'd come after him. Then I suggested he leave town because I would not stand by quietly while he harmed you."

Then he said, 'You can have the *bitch*, man. Just untie me.'

"I untied him, but before I did so, I kicked him."

"You did? And you said all that to Tobias, too?" Tamara was astonished that Tobias walked away without finishing what he started with Buddy. Now she wondered if Tobias waited in some dark corner to rush out and cut her throat. She didn't think any love was worth that though she didn't dare tell Buddy.

"I sure did. After all I love you, baby. So when Tobias left my house, I thought he went home to pack."

❦    ❦    ❦

Days later after almost dying from an infection caused by a nail that punctured her foot, Doc Peterson released Lula Hanks from the hospital.

"Hope you don't wait so long to come in the next time you stick a nail in your foot, Lula," Doc Peterson chuckled. "Otherwise, you might end up in the morgue."

"I hear you, Doc," she said as she limped out the room and towards the waiting area where Tilly waited to take her back home.

"I hear Tobias left town without his car," Lula said to Tilly as she climbed in the car beside her.

"That's what they say," Tilly said.

"I wouldn't be surprised if Tam and Reverend McCord did something to him," Lula said. "Everybody knows the Reverend is sweet on her."

"Now, now, Aunt Lula. Don't you go jumping the gun," Tilly said as she hoped Aunt Lula would take the next train out of town. Several days later when Lula and Tilly got into a spat, that's exactly what Lula did. She caught the train and returned to Chicago.

# CHAPTER 21

On a warm Saturday, around noon, Jenny Joyride who lived with her husband Spuds, their daughter Melanie and their two nephews, Brick and Goose, prepared to close the post office just as Sheriff Percy Dawson walked through the door.

"Hey, how you doing, Percy?" Jenny inquired. "I hear Tobias left and went north," she said before Percy could respond to her greeting.

"Yeah, that's what they say."

"Well, I wonder how he got there. He's got no car, 'cause it's still at Billy's shop. Funny thing, wouldn't you say? You know he's got money to buy a ticket, but I never sold him one, you know. I can't see him hitching a ride or walking. Now you tell me if the rumors make sense."

"Damn, Jenny. You sure you didn't sell Tobias a ticket?"

"Course, I'm sure. You think I'm dingy? That story Tam's spreading 'round here sounds mighty fishy to me," Jenny said handing Percy several letters.

"Looks like you got a letter from Alan," she said.

"So it seems," Percy said. "Odessa will be glad to get it. She worries about him, you know."

"I suppose she does," Jenny said. She continued talking about Tobias. "Now you and I know Tobias can't ride the train without a ticket and nobody's giving colored folk free rides anywhere. So what you think about that?"

"I don't know the answer yet, Jenny, but if you find out let me know. In the meantime, I hope to find answers somewhere. I suppose I better look into it. Tobias might become a real puzzle."

"I just thought I'd tell you what I know. It's something to think about, you know."

"Thanks, Jenny. See you later," he said walking out the door.

When Percy arrived at his brother Marcus's house, Natalie, Elizabeth, and Dominic were there along with his wife Helene, and their girls, Queenie and Sophia.

It amazed him that he provided a beautiful home for his wife and girls, but they would rather spend time at his brother's home than their own. Of course, he couldn't blame them. There was more love in that house than in the whole town. He enjoyed it himself.

"Hi, everybody," he said when he walked onto the porch. "Odessa, you got a letter from Alan." As he handed her the letter, the girls and Dominic ran outside to see the squadron of planes flying overhead.

"Where's Shel?" Percy asked noticing his absence.

"He's at Billy's," everyone answered in unison.

"Damn shame, that boy can't spend more time with the family," Percy said. Percy, who couldn't stand Shelton, never stopped thinking of inventive ways to put him behind bars for life.

"He was here, uncle," Natalie said.

"Right," Marcus said. "But he stayed only a hot minute, and he was gone."

"Leave it alone, Marcus," Odessa said. Then they, momentarily, sat in silence.

"I just talked to Jenny," Percy said. "And she said she never sold Tobias a ticket."

"Well, I'll be damned," Marcus said.

"Something is amiss," Natalie said. "But I can't say what it is. What do you think, Liz?"

"I don't know, Nat. You think Tam knows something?"

"She might. You know she spends a lot of time with the Reverend. Maybe he knows something," Nat said.

"I never heard about that," Odessa said. "And even if they do spend a lot of time together, I'm sure they're just friends."

"Who knows, Mama? It just worries me because Tam and Tobias fought a lot."

"Is that a fact?" Marcus asked as he puffed on his cigar and picked up his glass of wine.

"Yes, it is, Daddy."

"That means nothing. You and Shel fight too, and everybody in town knows it," Marcus said sarcastically.

"I know that, Daddy." Natalie felt testy. "But we're talking about Tam and Tobias. I love Tam, but Tobias was unhappy. He didn't want her singing in the Lounge or any other night club."

"Well, I can't see why he married her," Helene said. "She was singing when he met her. Surely, he didn't expect her to change. Not our Tam," Helene chuckled.

"Some people think they can change others. That's why he married her," Odessa said. "Am I right Nat?"

"I'm not trying to change Shel, Mama, if that's what you mean. And I'd like to speak if you don't mind."

"Go ahead, Nat. What worries you so?" Percy asked.

"Tam got a job up north. From what she tells me, that didn't set too well with Tobias. But she planned to go anyway."

"Well, Tam's your friend. What do you think happened?" Percy asked.

"Lawdy, Percy. I don't know why you asked that. All Nat does is read them mystery books and let her imagination run wild," Odessa laughed.

"I love Tam, too," Elizabeth said. "I hope she's not involved in anything ugly. But I still say someone should talk to the Reverend."

"Goodness, Liz. You're as bad as Nat. The Reverend's got nothing to do with Tobias's disappearance. I'll bet any amount of money on that. He's just too smart for that," Odessa remarked.

"But Tobias was not the type of man to simply walk away without telling someone, Mama."

"I don't know Tobias that well, but I agree with Nat. It does seem odd," Elizabeth interjected.

"You're right. It is odd. You know most folk talk about their trips before taking off because talking about their vacation is part of their excitement. They want every poor soul in town to know they can afford to do it," Natalie said while hoping her friend hadn't committed a crime.

"Forget it, Nat," Helene said. "Stop jumping the gun about everything."

"Yeah, Nat, I agree with Helene," Marcus said.

"We may never know what's happened to Tobias, but Reverend McCord is crazy about Tam," Elizabeth spouted. "I say talk to him." Elizabeth hated the fact that the Reverend had almost taken over Tamara's life.

"Okay, Liz. I get the picture," Percy said. "There might be something to what you say."

"Lawdy," Helene said. "Him being a preacher and all, he ought to be ashamed of himself."

"I don't believe a word of it," Odessa said trying to keep the faith.

"Well, what do you think they did with the body?" Marcus asked.

"Who knows, Mr. Dawson? Only time will tell," Elizabeth said.

"I don't know the answer either," Natalie said. "But Tam's invited everyone to a barbeque at the Lounge next weekend to celebrate her new job up north. And who knows what kind of meat she's gonna serve."

"Come on, Nat," Elizabeth chuckled. "You really think Tam's gonna barbeque him?"

"You never know, Liz. Wouldn't it be something if she fed him to us?"

"Ah, come on, Nat," Odessa said. "Tam would never do any such thing."

"Listen, young lady. Your imagination is just working overtime," Helene laughed. "You read too many of them mystery books."

Perhaps, you're right, auntie, but Tam's been our friend since childhood," Natalie said as if she enlightened strangers. "We know her well. Don't we, Liz?"

"Yeah, we do," Liz answered. "Nobody walks over Tam. She's a lot like her mother, and you know what they say her mother did."

"I never told you that Tam believes Tobias might have done something to her mama and grandma," Natalie said. "I'm the only person she told. Since Tobias is no longer around, I'm telling you." Then Natalie paused. "Now I wonder if Tam got revenge."

"Lawdy, you never told me that," Odessa said.

"No, I didn't," Nat said. "And I never told you that Doc Peterson said he was quite impressed with Tobias's knowledge in medicine. He said Tobias kept quiet about his past, but Doc had a feeling Morningstar wasn't the first hospital Tobias worked in."

"You really think somebody's killed Tobias?" Helene asked.

"Yes, I do," Natalie said. "I just hope it's not Tam."

"I swear Nat. Perhaps you should write a book. You'd probably outdo your friend Poe," Odessa chuckled.

"Laugh if you want, Mama. But you never know."

"Lawdy, Nat. Please let it rest?" Helene said.

"Okay. Okay, but don't say I didn't warn you," Natalie laughed. "You know Tam's daddy, Pete Baraldi, owns that meat packing plant. And I wouldn't be a bit surprised if poor old Tobias is hanging in the freezer like a slab of ham."

"Good Lord." Marcus slapped his leg and laughed. "You could be right. Hell, if he's dead we can't lay it all on Tam, not with her daddy and the meat packing gang running around here."

"I know you think it's funny, but if Tam serves anything other than chicken at that barbeque, I won't eat it. I don't care how good you tell me it tastes," Natalie shot back causing everyone to whoop with laughter.

❦   ❦   ❦

The next weekend everyone went to the barbeque, and most ate and drank themselves under the table. While Candyman and Seb played with the band and Tamara sang, Orchid, Charlie, and Zeke Fountaine kept the liquor flowing and glasses filled.

As the party went into full swing, Percy snooped around hoping to find a Tobias thigh on the spit, while Natalie kept true to her word. To make certain she didn't eat the wrong kind of meat, she accepted only chicken drumsticks, missing the chance to savor the meats she really liked; goat, lamb, and pig.

❦   ❦   ❦

That summer Shelton, Fats, Warren, and Billy sat listening to Harry talk about his plans to leave Meadowsbrook.

"You mean you goin' to De-troit to stay," Billy slurred. "But why, Harry?"

"Thea's mama and daddy live there, and it's time to make a change, man. Thea's never felt the same since the Lydia thing."

"Nobody's been the same, Harry," Shelton said feeling queasy.

"We'll never forget you, man," Fats said.

"Same here," Harry sighed. "What happened to Lydia was awful. We feel bad, but we can't change it."

Billy looked gloomy. Harry saw the sadness in his eyes. "You gotta stop lookin' back, Billy. Maybe it's time you made a change too. It might do you good."

"You might be right. But I can't. Not just yet anyway. So when are you leavin'?" Billy felt empty. "Bout two weeks."

"That soon, huh?"

"Yeah, that soon," answered Harry.

"I'm gonna miss you." Billy said shaking his head as if to clear it.

"I know. We go back a long way," Harry said gazing into their faces. "I can't forget you either. You're my pals. You know that. And from time to time, I'll come back to see you too." Harry picked up the bottle of whiskey and read the label. Holding it up, he laughed, "Damn, we been drinking this shit for years."

"That's for sho. Come…come on…on, man," Warren stuttered. "Pour some for…for us, too."

As soon as he poured some in Billy's glass, Billy gulped it down. Then holding his glass up, he said, "Hit me again, will you?"

Harry knew Billy still missed Lydia and hoped the fiery drink would dull the emptiness that still lingered within.

🍁 🍁 🍁

Two weeks later Thea's daddy died, and her mama brought him back to Meadowsbrook to bury him. After the funeral, Thea's mother said she didn't want to go back to Detroit without her husband. Thea and Harry put their travel plans on hold.

🍁 🍁 🍁

Percy finally decided to question Tamara and Buddy. As soon as Tamara returned to town, Percy went to see her.

"Come in, sheriff," she said as she opened the door, feeling nervous. "What can I do for you," she asked, though she already knew the answer.

"Well, I suppose you know why I'm here, Tam," Percy said as his shoulders sagged. He hated having to ask her questions about Tobias because Tamara was like family.

"Yes, I do," she sighed. "I've expected this visit for some time now."

"Then you know what I'm gonna ask," Percy said.

"I suppose so," she sighed. "You want to sit a while?"

"No thanks. I just want you to tell me if you had anything to do with Tobias's disappearance."

"No, I didn't. And I think you'd better sit," she said pointing to the easy chair. He sat down in the chair as she sat on the sofa. "I'll tell you the whole story."

After she told Percy what happened between Tobias, Buddy and herself, Percy asked, "Why didn't you tell me that earlier on?"

"I wasn't sure what to do because I suspected Buddy had killed Tobias."

"What makes you think he didn't have something to do with it now?" Percy asked.

"Because he keeps telling me he freed Tobias, and I believe him."

"I wish you'd told the truth at first. You would've saved everybody concerned a lot of worry. Liz and Nat worry that you did something to Tobias and the thought breaks their hearts."

"I'm sorry," Tamara said feeling relief and more comfortable than she had in a long time. "I'll talk to them." As Percy stood and walked to the door, she followed. "What you gonna do now?"

"I'm gonna talk to Buddy. I want to hear what he has to say," Percy said. "Perhaps we better start looking in every nook and cranny. That poor fellow might be in the canal." Percy walked out and Tamara stood at the door until he got in his truck and drove away.

🍁   🍁   🍁

After the good Reverend McCord told Percy what happened between Tobias and himself with such remorse, Percy decided it was time they searched for Tobias.

That very same evening he called a meeting at the church and just about everybody attended. He told them he had reason to believe Tobias had run into trouble the night he went missing, and they should look everywhere for him.

"And be sure to look into those neglected and sunken graves. Some are in pretty bad shape. Tobias might have lost his footing somewhere. By the way, the first to find him gets twenty dollars."

That night Brick and Goose planned to get up early the next morning and start their search. They, like everyone else, hoped to be the first to find Tobias. It wasn't that they cared about him, they simply wanted the money.

However, Goose became ill during the night and was unable to go out the next day. Brick thought about taking Dominic with him, but realized if he found Tobias, he would have to share the money. At the same time Brick, already counting the money Percy promised, went out alone to find Tobias, and so did little eight year old Dominic.

That same afternoon, Elizabeth and her family looked frantically for Dominic, but no one, including Brick knew his whereabouts.

When Della took her dog, Lockjaw, and went to visit Sadie Pastures, Della decided to take a short cut through a wooded area. On either side of the path grew thick underbrush and trees. Lockjaw trotted ahead of her. With pointed ears, the dog sniffed the ground, and started to bark.

"What is it, boy?" Della asked as Lockjaw started to run in a different direction. Running after the dog, Della called for him to stop.

"Come back here, Lockjaw. What's wrong with you?" she yelled. Lockjaw finally stopped. He looked down but continued to bark. When Della reached the spot, she was surprised to hear a faint cry.

"Lawdy, Lockjaw. I think we found something." Then she called out. "Who's down there?"

"It's me. Dominic," a weak voice replied. He had fallen into the old dry abandoned well, which everyone had forgotten. The boy had called for help so long he could barely speak.

"Hold on," Della said. "I'll go get help."

When Della returned, she brought Elizabeth and a horde of other folk. "Don't cry," Elizabeth said. "This is your mama. Help is on the way."

Soon Percy, Marcus, and several other men arrived with a horse, extended ropes down the well, and pulled Dominic out.

Though he was happy to have lived through the ordeal, he worried about the reward, which got him into trouble in the first place. "Tobias is down there, and he smells" he said shaking when he finally saw daylight again.

"Are you sure?" Percy asked.

"Yeah, I'm sure," a frightened Dominic said. Then as an afterthought, he asked, "Do I get the money, Mr. Percy?"

"You will if Tobias is down there," Percy smiled while others nearby chuckled.

As Della spread the news that Lockjaw found Dominic and Dominic had found Tobias, folk who hated Lockjaw looked at the dog in a different light. Lockjaw was now their hero.

Natalie and Elizabeth were relieved, but Tamara and the Reverend Buddy McCord were elated, not because Tobias was dead, but because the mystery of his disappearance was solved.

The night he left Buddy McCord's house, Tobias was mad enough to kill somebody. Namely, Buddy McCord, but he first planned to go home and beat the living hell out of Tamara. Then he would later deal with the good Reverend. He was tired of Tam's shit. He had to show her who was boss once and for all, he thought just as he slipped and fell. Tobias never made it home.

# CHAPTER 22

During summer of 1945 the weather was extremely hot. Little Makela lay on a quilt pallet on the floor, her braids splayed. One leg lay prone while the other was tucked underneath. One arm lay at her side while the other rested on her chest. Even though the day was uncomfortably hot, she slept soundly.

Though still asleep, she suddenly pulled one leg up towards her chest, reached down, and scratched the spot a mosquito bit the night before. Moments later, she turned on her side and rubbed her eyes with the back of her hands then opened them slowly.

Staring up, she watched a spider crawl across the ceiling. She hated spiders. Her mother said only a few were harmful, but Makela believed they all were and was certain if one bit her, she would die. She cringed at the thought.

She kept her eyes on the spider as it made its way down the wall towards the floor. When it got closer, she jumped up and ran to the back porch. Grabbing the swat from the wall, she returned to the room then waited patiently for its descent.

When it was within her reach, she swung the swat, smashing it dead. Then she carefully examined the swat. Once she was sure it was dead, she flicked it from the swat onto the floor, and left it there for her mother to dispose of it.

Turning, she went back to the porch and hung the swat on the wall. Then she went and stood at the door. While staring out at the horses, she pushed open the door and a fly rushed past her head and into the house. She knew flies were filthy pests and the porch was screened to keep them out.

Momentarily, she watched the fly soar overhead before she remembered to shut the door. Her mother had scolded her many times about holding open the door. But it was a habit she found hard to break. She hoped she wouldn't get her hide tanned. She wanted her mother, but her mother was nowhere in sight.

"Mama!" she called weakly. When she got no response, she called louder. She stared through the screen hoping for some sign of her mother's presence. The house was quiet and she hated it, but her mother said this was the most peaceful place she knew. But all she wanted to do was visit her Gramma so she could play with other children.

"Mama," she called and nervously pulled at one of her long braids as her hazel eyes stared out at the dancing heat waves. Suddenly, loneliness engulfed her, and at times like these, she pinched herself to make sure she was real. She pinched her arm now and winced as tears clouded her eyes. She started to cry, but then her mother came into view carrying a pan full of vegetables from the garden.

A broad smile lit up her small face. Pushing open the door, she clutched her mother's leg and held it tightly as her mother came onto the porch.

"Goodness, Makela. What is it?" Natalie frowned and unclasped the small hands from her leg. "What's wrong, baby?"

"I'm just glad to see you, Mama."

Natalie put the pan on the floor. She removed her gloves and wide brim straw hat, and put them on the table in the corner of the porch. As she wiped sweat from her brow, she pulled Makela into her arms.

"I'm glad to see you too, baby," she cooed holding Makela close, momentarily, before picking up items she discarded earlier. After stuffing a glove into each pocket of the old shirt she wore, she took off the shirt, and hung it along with her hat on the wall peg near the door.

She kicked off her work shoes and slung them underneath the table. Then she picked up the pan and put it onto the table.

"I thought you left me, Mama." Makela waited for Natalie to sit in the old rocking chair.

"Oh, baby," Natalie whispered pulling Makela onto her lap. "Why do you think such things? Have I ever left you?"

"No, but I sometimes think you might."

"I'll never do that, baby." Sighing, she got up and put Makela in the chair, then went into the house to get a book. She went to the bookcase and ran her fingers over the books. As she took a book of poems by Paul Laurence Dunbar from a lower shelf, she saw the dead spider on the floor and smiled.

She was surprised Makela killed it rather than run from the house. Taking a piece of old newspaper, she picked up the spider, took it to the door, and threw it into the yard.

Afterwards, she went back to the rocker. Pulling Makela onto her lap again, she opened the book and began to read while Makela listened intently.

Sometime later, the horse whinny at the side of the house caught their attention. Natalie looked up just as Shelton's dad, Thaddeus, dismounted his favorite white tail Golden Palomino. Makela squealed with delight and ran to the door. Natalie followed and waited while he tied the reins to the rail under the big pear tree.

Suddenly, Natalie's imagination got the best of her, and she wondered if there was any truth to the rumor that he disposed of bad acting relatives and took their property. She decided she had, indeed, read one Poe story too many, which caused her to have macabre thoughts. There was no truth to that, and she knew it.

"How you doing, Nat?" Thaddeus asked as he hopped onto the porch. Like Shelton, years ago, farm equipment had fallen on his leg and almost cut it off. But unlike Shelton, it crippled him, Natalie thought, as she stepped back to let him pass.

"I'm fine, Papa and you?"

"Oh, just so," he said looking down at Makela. "How's my baby girl today?"

"I'm fine, Papa." Makela grinned.

"Hot enough for you, Nat?"

"It's too hot, Papa. I sure hope the rains will come soon and cool things off a bit." She sat down at the table.

"No doubt it will come," Thaddeus said. Taking Makela's hand he hobbled to the rocker, sat down then pulled Makela onto his lap.

"What's wrong with her, Nat?" he asked studying Makela's tear-streaked face.

"It's nothing of concern. She just tends to get teary at times. She'll be just fine." He had a special bond with Makela, and she hoped to allay his concern. Greyland and Jozell had no children. So Makela was his only grandchild.

"Oh, I see," he said. Giving Makela a squeeze, he asked, "What's wrong with my baby girl?" Baby girl was his pet name for her. However, Makela refused to speak, but she gently laid her head on his chest.

"How's Mrs. Lamont, doing?" Natalie inquired of her mother-in-law.

"She's not feeling well today," he said looking annoyed. "Why, after all these years do you call her, Mrs. Lamont? Why can't you call her mama?"

"I don't know, Papa. I wish I had an answer for that."

"Can't you even try, Nat?"

"Yes, I can try," she lied. She wanted to tell him she already had a mama and she didn't need another. "What brings you over today, Papa?"

"Lawdy, why do you always ask that question?" he sighed and gazed into her face. "When will you ever feel you're part of my family? I came over to see about you because you're family," he said causing her to smile.

He gave her a warm feeling because he cared so much for her baby, she thought. But she was cautious. She never wanted to get too close to Shelton's family. Papa was nice, but she felt Shelton's mother, Esther, was self-centered. She seldom associated with others. Said she was always too sick to leave the house.

"You know Esther really likes you, and she would be pleased if you'd stop by sometime to see her. You might not know it, Nat, but she's really sick. Doctors gave her a year to live, but she's lived two."

"Oh, I didn't know," she said, feeling awful for her actions. "Does Shel know?"

"He knows."

"He never told me," she said.

"You know how Shel is. He probably forgot the seriousness of it as soon as he heard. Did you ever think of having another child?" he asked. "I think this tyke needs company."

She grimaced remembering her awful pregnancy. The morning sickness was awful and lasted almost the full nine months. That was when she needed Shel most, but he was never there. In fact, he all but deserted her then.

Luckily, he was home when her labor pains started and rushed into town and brought back her mother, Tam, and the midwife. Later, Shel went and got Doc Peterson because she had problems. The misery lasted for two whole days.

When it was over, she cried because she had taken a ride through hell. Though she loved her child, she decided to leave childbirth for those who loved pain. This was a chapter of her life she never wanted to repeat even if her marriage was made in heaven.

"Do you ever think about it, Nat?" Thaddeus asked when he got no response.

"No, I don't, Papa," she answered. "This is not the time to have another child."

Thaddeus gathered, from the tone of her voice, this wasn't a subject she wanted to discuss. He also knew his son. So he understood and respected Natalie's decision.

In fact, he admired her. She was strong, and it took a strong woman to deal with Shelton. It was best, he decided, to change the subject. Otherwise, she might tell him where to stick his bright idea, and it wouldn't be in his hat. "Where is Shel, anyway?"

"Your guess is as good as mine."

"Why can't you do something to keep him home?" he asked though he knew only an act of God could hold Shelton down.

"No one tells Shel what to do," she snapped testily. "You know that. Could you ever keep him home? Did he ever listen to you?"

"No, he didn't. Fact is he never did anything I asked. I'm sorry. I guess it's best I mind my own business."

"It's okay." She spoke softer now. "But you know how things are. I never know where he spends his time."

"Damn him. I tried to get him interested in working with Grey, but he refuses. He should have his butt here overseeing some of this work. I shouldn't have to pay someone to do what he should do. And I'll tell him when I see him too."

"I suggest you do that, Papa."

"I don't know," he drawled. "I talk to him, but he never listens. I wish he was more like Greyland."

"You don't wish that half as much as I do," she said.

"I pray he changes before it's too late."

"I doubt if prayer will help him, Papa."

"I don't know what he wants out of life, but I'd like to see a change, and soon."

"So would I, Papa," she muttered softly. "So would I." She was pleased to know he was as unhappy with Shelton's behavior as she was.

"I'd hate to see him lose you, Nat."

"That's kind of you, Papa. But I have no plans to do that yet."

"I know. But the time will come when you might." He studied her for a moment. She was beautiful and his son so foolish. "Well, I'd better go." He stood up and sat Makela in the chair. Then, digging his hand into his pocket, he prepared to play Makela's favorite game.

"Guess what I got?" He teased holding his fist just out of reach.

"Oh, Papa, you know what it is," she laughed.

"Of course, I know what it is. But do *you* know what it is?" He grinned broadly.

"Yes, yes. I know, Papa." She jumped from the chair and reached her small hand up towards his.

"You don't know," he teased.

"But I do, Papa. I do," she shouted.

"Well, you better hurry and tell me."

"It's a silver dollar, Papa."

"By gawd, it is. And who do you think it's for?"

"It's for me, Papa. It's for me," she squealed as she placed her small hand into his and took the shiny piece.

"Yeah, it is. Now, you put that away you hear."

"Okay, Papa," she said. He bent down, and lifted her up and kissed her cheek.

"I love you, Papa." She put her arms around his neck.

"And I love you, too." He went over and put Makela on Natalie's lap.

"You take care, you hear, Nat."

"I hear, Papa. I'll do that," she assured him.

"When Shel comes home, you tell him to come over to the house. I'm gonna give him a piece of my mind. If it wasn't for you and this tyke I'd take that car and put his ass on a mule."

"Okay, Papa."

"Bye, Papa." Makela jumped from Natalie's lap, and followed him to the door. Natalie followed, too.

"Bye, baby girl." He pinched her cheek lightly, then made his way down the steps and over to the pear tree where his horse waited.

Both watched as he climbed onto the horse and rode away. Then Natalie studied her daughter and asked if she enjoyed her granddad.

"Yeah. I like Papa a lot, Mama," Makela said leaving the door only when Thaddeus was out of sight. Returning to the chair, Makela began to rock.

"Don't forget to put your money in the piggy bank now," Natalie reminded. Makela leapt from the chair. Running into the house, she brought back the piggy bank and gave it to Natalie. It was almost full of coins, and Natalie made note to take it with them the next time they went into town.

She would give the coins to her daddy, Marcus. Then he would record the amount, and put it in the safe. This was a practice Natalie hoped would instill in her daughter the importance of saving money.

"By the way, Makela, did you know big girls don't cry about everything?"

"Yes, I know, Mama. But I sometimes feel lonely."

"I know, but I'm here. Just try not to cry so much. Can you remember that?"

"Okay," she said. "Mama, Mama," she called excitedly. "Can you see the dancing heat waves? Can you?"

"Of course, I see them, baby."

"Mama?"

"Yes, dear?"

"Am I real?"

"Of course, you are. How many times must I tell you so?"

"I don't know. But I sometimes pinch myself to make sure. Why don't I have a sister, Mama?" Makela asked, abruptly changing the subject.

"I suppose God's not ready for you to have one." Natalie hoped that was a satisfactory answer.

"Maybe you could ask Him to give me one."

"Maybe I could."

"You promise?"

"Yes. Yes. I promise." She kissed Makela's forehead then sat down at the sewing machine and got lost in her work.

"Are you thinking about it, Mama?" Makela asked later that evening.

"Thinking about what, dear?"

"Talking to God, Mama?"

"What?"

"You promised to talk to God about sending me a sister."

"Hum, I suppose I did. Guess I forgot. But don't worry, I will talk to Him," she promised kissing Makela's cheek at the same time peeking out the window just as Shelton raced up the driveway like a bat out of hell braking only a few feet from the house.

She was amazed that his antics hadn't already brought down the house. She just hoped the day the brakes failed, she and Makela would be elsewhere.

After America dropped the atomic bomb on Nagasaki and Hiroshima, the Japanese surrendered. World War II ended, and the nation breathed easier. And while the world celebrated a new beginning, Natalie, Tamara and Elizabeth celebrated a friendship which they hoped would continue to endure long into the future.

Folk now thought more about living than dying. The radio, which held everyone captive so long with war tragedies, was once again tuned to more pleasant programs, and each morning they awoke to Eddie Arnold's yodeling.

Folk turned their attention to Ebony Magazine and the beautiful Lena Horne was the talk of the town. Not only was she an accomplished singer, she'd made two movies, "Cabin in the Sky" and "Stormy Weather." And everyone in town wanted to see them.

During those times, folk who wanted to see the movies went to Baysville Theater where they sat in the balcony, which was for "Colored Only."

But once Lena made those movies, the people of Meadowsbrook decided it was time they had their own theater. But they knew it would take time to make that dream come true. In the meantime, they enjoyed Lena's films in the church, and every woman, man, and child saw those films.

At that time, few folk dreamed. But after viewing Lena and a host of other black actors on the screen, many were inspired and realized they too could reach for the stars.

Charlie Fountaine, owner of the Lavender Lounge, better known as the "Joint," along with other business owners brought the people together, and after many meetings, Marcus and his crew laid the foundation for the Meadowsbrook Movie Theater. The folk of Meadowsbrook began to catch up with the outside world. No longer were they subjected to insults and harassment. No longer were they shuffled to the balcony. There was no sign directing them to some dark corner, and Natalie, Tamara, and Elizabeth held their heads just a little higher.

Late one evening Shelton came home and brought Natalie a letter. It was from her brother, Alan, who was now a pilot. Alan was convinced he found his niche. Military life suited him just fine, and he planned to make it a career. He was well, and hoped to come home soon for a visit.

Even though the war ended, plane squadrons continued to fly overhead day and night, and Natalie often wondered if Alan was flying one and silently wished him well.

# CHAPTER 23

❀

She was born Kornelia Wade Dawson. Though no one knew why, Makela called her Koko, and since everyone in town liked nicknames, Koko fit like a kidskin glove.

She was a lonely little girl who learned early on her Aunt Tilly had little patience or love for her. To compensate, she sucked her thumb and pulled her short curly hair.

While sitting at the breakfast table with Tilly and Virgil one morning, she belched. "Oops," she said. She quickly put her hand to her mouth. Virgil smiled.

"Excuse me," she said. But Tilly, feeling Koko had not put her hand over her mouth quickly enough, reached across the table and smacked Koko's face. "Don't you know how to cover your mouth?"

Her cheek felt like a bee stung her, but she gave no indication she felt pain. She simply stared at Tilly.

"Don't hit her again, Tilly." Virgil caught Tilly's wrist and held it. "She just belched. That's no sin. She did nothing wrong."

"She's got to learn. I never know what she'll do next."

"So? I don't know how many times I gotta tell you. She's just a baby."

"She's no baby. She's five years old, and I wonder who she really is anyway. I wonder if Alan…"

"Don't say it. No one cares. She's a baby. And just like you, she's not responsible for her bloodline. The one thing you do know is she's your sister's child, and you should love her."

As they argued, Koko stood in the chair and started to sing.

"Sit down, girl" Tilly yelled. "Don't stand in my nice chair."

"Good Lord," Virgil yelled. "Have you lost your mind? It's just a chair."

"Dammit, Virg. If it was left up to you, she could jump on the table, and you wouldn't care."

"You're right. I wouldn't. Leave her alone, will you?" Then after a short pause, he leaned over and whispered, "You don't treat her right, Tilly."

"I don't know what you're talking about. She's Lydia's child. You know how Lydia was. She had no respect for herself or anybody else."

"I don't care about any of that. Lydia's gone. You need to show the child kindness. Show her you have a heart. You're too cold." Virgil scraped the last bit of jam from his plate with a biscuit. "There's something else I want you to understand." He bit into the biscuit and chewed.

"If you ever touch her again, you'll deal with me. So you better watch your step. I don't think you want to get me mad 'cause I won't be responsible for my actions."

"Is that a fact?" she yelled. "Well, now. Maybe Alan's not her daddy. Maybe it's you."

"You know better than that. So, don't get in my face with that shit. Lydia didn't care, and from what I see, you don't either. That's a shame," he shook his head. "Somebody's gotta care. So, I guess I'm the one."

"Maybe you're right. I don't care," she yelled as she bolted from her chair.

He watched her leave the room and realized something happened to Tilly after Lydia died. That same anger and meanness Lydia possessed now seemed manifested inside her. And unless she pulled herself together, he supposed he would send her to Whitman, the crazy house, where she might get the chance to settle the score with Neva.

The child was Tilly's kin. The same blood was in her veins, but Tilly didn't seem to care. He wondered if she was capable of loving her sister's child.

Long before Lydia's death, he took responsibility. He fed the child and kept her clean. He held her close in the middle of the night and stopped her cries because Lydia couldn't be found. And each morning, he brought the baby and the bassinet into the store, but Tilly did little to help.

For the care he gave her, Koko rewarded him with her love. She was Tilly's niece, but his baby and most days she sat on his counter near him. She was five years old and was smart as a whip. She already knew things about the business Lydia never took time to learn.

When they weren't inside the store, they spent time in the small house in back. Even though the yard was enclosed by a fence, Koko seldom spent time there, and the playmates she wanted, never came.

Although Alan sent money for her upkeep, he never came to see her. It had been long time since anyone from the Dawson family other than Odessa and Makela stopped by. Of course, he could understand Natalie's absence because Shelton was sweet on Lydia. Still, he felt it was time he did something. He supposed he should talk to Natalie. Koko needed to know her family.

He got up from his chair and went over to the child. Taking her small face in his hand, he studied it briefly. She was just like Lydia and already hard as nails. She never made a sound when Tilly slapped her.

Yes, indeed. She was Lydia's child all right. But there was some difference between the two of them. Koko wanted someone to love her while Lydia never accepted anyone's love.

"Poor Koko," he soothed as he caressed the same cheek Tilly smacked. "Don't you worry, baby, Uncle Virg loves you."

As Natalie and Makela approached the store, Natalie waved to Seb Pardeau and Candyman Cates who sat on the bench with several other old statue-like men. Natalie thought they looked more dead than alive. But just to prove they still breathed the same air as she, one yelled out enthusiastically, "Hey, pretty."

"Hubba, hubba," another yelled. Makela clutched Natalie's hand a little tighter. Embarrassed by their teasing, Natalie started to go inside, but Candyman started to puff into his harmonica, and Seb picked up his guitar and joined him. When the two men started to play, she and Makela stopped and listened.

They had entertained since Natalie was a child and were often an attraction at the Lounge. She enjoyed their music, so it was impossible to walk away. When they sang about their hotcha mamas, lost loves, and life's struggles, she was touched.

Virgil came outside and stood on the steps. Soon others gathered. When they stopped playing, everyone applauded. She put a coin in the hat on the ground. Then she followed Virgil inside.

She greeted Tilly, but it was obvious Tilly was in a bad mood because she never responded. Rumor was Tilly changed since Lydia's death and turned as mean as Lydia. So rather than risk her foul mood, Natalie spoke directly to Virgil. At the same time, Koko, who sat near him on the counter top, caught Natalie's attention.

"Well, now. Look who we found, Makela. How are you, Kornelia?" she asked while pulling Makela closer to the counter.

"For your information, she was never lost." Surprisingly, Tilly found her tongue.

"She's Koko, Mama. She's Koko." Makela grinned broadly.

"Oh, all right," Natalie chuckled ignoring Tilly. "How are you, Koko?" The child was amused by the attention but remained mute.

"What's wrong, honey? Cat got your tongue?" she teased the little girl.

"This is your Aunt Nat and your cousin, Makela. It's all right to talk to them," Virgil coaxed, but she sat quietly with crossed legs and stared at them some time before she smiled revealing small white teeth like those of a rabbit in her favorite story, Peter Cottontail.

The weather was hot, and, like most children, she wore no shoes. As the little girl pulled her bare foot towards her face and effortlessly put her foot behind her head, Natalie looked on in amazement. Then when she did the other as easily as the first, Natalie thought she would faint.

The child was really a circus act and with both legs behind her head she put her hands on the counter and walked on them. Koko laughed while Makela screamed with delight. "Look at her, Mama. Look at her."

"I see her, honey," Natalie said in disbelief. It seemed the child was double jointed or whatever it was that allowed her to be able to work her body in such manner. "My goodness, how did you ever learn to do that? You're as limber as a rubber band. Did you know that?"

"Yes," Koko answered.

"I swear. This baby is as cute as a ladybug. Why don't you bring her to visit us sometime?" Natalie felt annoyed that Tilly hadn't kept in touch.

"We're too busy," scoffed Tilly. "We got no time to visit. Nothing stops you from coming here."

"Yes, I..." Taken aback, Natalie took a deep breath and paused. There was nothing to say because Tilly was right. She shouldn't blame anyone when she too was responsible. She had done nothing to develop a relationship with the child. In fact, this was the first time she spoke to her in some time.

"I'm sorry. You're right. It's partly my fault. I should've come sooner." She spoke to Tilly but looked at Virgil.

Several customers came in and tried to talk to her. Natalie acknowledged them, but was rather cool almost to the point of rudeness. Realizing she was preoccupied, she apologized, but Koko held her interest. Then she decided it might be good for the girls to spend time together. But the fact that Koko was Lydia's child nagged at her.

She studied the child's face for a moment, and her heart grew heavy. The sadness in Koko's eyes helped her make a decision. Lydia was dead, and to punish the child was wrong. Koko needed family, she thought, and she dared not walk away from that need. She instantly let go of the past.

"You okay, Nat?" Virgil asked concerned.

"I'm fine, Virg. I'd like to take Koko home with me if you don't mind. Just for a couple of days."

"Are you sure?" Virgil asked, surprised by her decision.

"Yes, I'm sure. I'll bring her back in a few days." She spoke and looked directly at Tilly.

"Well, I don't know," Tilly said haltingly.

"That would be just fine," Virgil interjected.

Within a few moments, Tilly brought out hurachas and several outfits, which she put in a bag and placed on the counter.

"Am I going home with you, Nat?" Koko suddenly proved she could form a sentence.

"Yes, you are sweetheart," Natalie said. Lifting her from the counter she helped Koko slip her small feet into hurachas just like those Makela wore. Then Natalie took the bag from the counter. As she turned to leave, Tilly tried to kiss Koko who wanted no part of her.

"Keep her as long as you want." Tilly sounded angry, and Natalie wondered if Tilly ever wanted the child back.

"Come on, Koko," Natalie said. "We're taking you to see your Gramma."

❦ ❦ ❦

Reaching the big house, Natalie and the girls walked onto the porch, and Koko ran to Odessa who picked her up and held her close.

The family instantly fell in love with Koko and she with them. Several days later Natalie tried to take her back to Tilly, but Koko screamed louder than ever, and Odessa decided to keep her a few more days, which turned first into months then into years.

# CHAPTER 24

Spring 1947. Easter week arrived and as usual everyone prepared to celebrate the Resurrection. Most folk baked and cooked enough food so that if Christ did return from the dead, He could eat until his belly burst.

Elizabeth, who once said she never wanted to work as a beautician, did just that now. Working with her mother as she had years ago, she washed, straightened, brushed, and curled hair. Once again she was back using every product Madam Walker ever produced, making every woman of Meadowsbrook look picture perfect.

"Hey, Dominic," Thea said as she entered the house. "I know you're on the Easter Sunday program. What you gonna do?" Thea had come to get her hair done.

"I'm going to…" he started. He wanted to tell her he would sing and play piano, but she wouldn't let him talk.

"Boy you sure enough look like your daddy," Thea interrupted. "Do you ever see him these days?"

"Yeah, I see him about…" Domnic said.

"Boy, you growed a lot since you been here," Thea again interrupted. "Guess you 'bout ten years old now, huh?"

Just as he was about to speak, his grandmother, Ernestine called out. "Hey, Thea, is that you?"

"Yeah, it's me," she answered.

"Well, come on out here. Liz is ready for you," Ernestine said, rescuing Dominic from the inquisitive woman.

As Thea went to the back porch, Dominic went to the front yard where Brick and Goose were waiting to go out and explore.

❦ ❦ ❦

Natalie's grandparents, Conrad and Maude, came up from New Orleans for their yearly visit. Natalie planned to spend time with her family before the holiday arrived. However, she found that impossible to do.

With Easter around the corner, every woman in town expected to drape herself in some fashionable replica she had seen in some catalogue or magazine. So Natalie was swamped with orders. She was expected to turn their dreams into reality.

Though not the only seamstress in town, she was the favorite and considered it an honor that so many wanted to wear her creations. Therefore, she felt obligated so rarely refused work, and ended up with too much work and too little time in which to do it. It was the same every year. But, in the end, she got the job done. Just a few days prior, she finished dresses for Tamara, Elizabeth and her mother, Odessa, as well as her Aunt Helene and her girls, Queenie and Sophia.

Now as her family slept, Natalie stood over the ironing board and applied finishing touches to one of the outfits she had made for Makela and Koko. Makela's dress was pink and Koko's light blue. Both had white pinafores.

Placing the iron on the board, she inspected each little dress for defects. Finding none, she put them on hangers, which she hooked onto the clothes tree in the corner.

After she cleared scrap material from the floor and worktable, she went to the bedroom where the girls slept. Standing in the doorway momentarily she peeked in before tipping over to the bed, and watched the steady rhythm of their breathing.

It had been almost two years since she took Koko from the store. Tilly had no objections, and no one expected Koko would ever go back. When Koko wasn't with Odessa, she spent time on the farm with Natalie and Makela.

Natalie felt good about the decision she made that day. Koko and Makela were now best friends and as close as peas in a pod. They loved one another. Koko was the perfect companion, and Makela no longer insisted she needed a sister. Leaning over, Natalie kissed both girls.

Then she quietly left the room and went into the bathroom, which was a new addition to the house and Shelton's way of making amends. She turned on the spigot, undressed, and stepped into the warm, soothing water.

Early the next morning on Easter Sunday Natalie helped the girls dress. Like most children they wore new hats, dresses, gloves, socks and shoes.

Natalie anticipated a full day of activities. Makela had memorized a poem, which she would recite. Koko would sing a duet with their little friend, Theodore.

The Pearson brothers, known as the Soul Healers, would also sing. The brothers were good looking and charismatic young men who were loved to the point of being pampered by everyone.

In addition, the Temple of God members would perform. Rumor was their music sounded so good it made you want to dance. Natalie looked forward to an enjoyable day.

Even though the Temple of God Church was just at the other end of town, she never took time to visit.

"Shame on you, Natalie Dawson Lamont," she whispered while promising to do better in future. When the girls heard about the program, they too were excited about things to come.

Later that morning, they piled into the car, and Shelton drove them to the church. Upon their arrival the girls excitedly joined the other children for the annual Easter egg hunt.

Tipping through the grass stealthily, each hoped to find the greatest number of eggs and win the coveted prize, which was more of the same multicolored eggs they already had.

While the children searched for eggs, Natalie, Elizabeth, and Tamara offered raffle tickets to congregation members in hopes of raising enough money to get the swimming pool started they dreamed about long ago. In addition to their efforts, most business owners sold tickets, too, and they had almost reached their goal.

When the Easter egg hunt was over, neither girl won the prize, but their little friend did.

"Mama, Mama," Makela yelled when it all ended, and they joined the family again. "Rabbit won the prize."

"I know, honey," Natalie winced.

Of course, she was the only person to address him as Theodore. She supposed once school was out even he forgot his real name. She liked the boy. He was a sweet child who had the voice of an angel. Though he never took lessons, he played the piano flawlessly. He was simply gifted.

When they filed into the church, she was surprised that Shelton, who believed in nothing other than himself, followed them inside and sat with the family men.

Natalie wanted the girls to enjoy what she considered a special experience and led them to a front pew. To her surprise, the people from the Temple of God had brought a complete band with them prompting the girls to ask questions.

While everyone laughed at their curiosity, Sophia used her hands to demonstrate each instrument's function.

"When they gonna do something, Mama?" Makela asked.

"Soon, baby." Natalie spoke calmly.

"But I want them do something now, Mama."

"What's the rush, Makela? You got to go somewhere?"

"No. I got no place to go."

"Good. Then sit back and keep quiet. Otherwise, I just might *do* something."

Makela looked into Natalie's face and eased back in the seat. At the same time, a restless Koko got up and began exploring. Natalie called out to her, shook her finger, but the little girl simply laughed.

"Sophia, would you please bring Koko back here?" Natalie asked as Koko picked up another child's Easter basket, and ripped off the cellophane cover, causing candy to spill onto the floor.

"Natalie's gonna tan your hide." Sophia looked around for the owner of the basket. But when no one claimed it, she picked up the candy. Putting it back into the basket, she placed the basket back on the seat. Then she took a laughing Koko by the hand, and led her back to her seat.

"When they gonna make some music, Sophia?" Koko asked.

"I don't know. But you'd better behave."

"Look!" Koko exclaimed as a tall thin man with gold teeth stood and started to speak. "He's got teeth just like Billy Hardwood."

While those within earshot laughed, Sophia tugged at Koko's arm encouraging her silence. When the man stopped speaking, he picked up his guitar, then motioned to his group, and they began to play.

"It sounds like Billy Hardwood's music," Koko yelled excitedly causing those close to her to chuckle.

When Koko stood and clapped her hands in time with the music, Makela stood too. Stomping her feet and clapping her hands, she tried to enjoy as much as Koko did, but as people danced in the aisle, the music got louder and the drums sounded like thunder. Because she never heard or saw such live performances before, Makela was scared.

It was a new experience for both girls, but Koko took it in stride while Makela's throat felt funny and her lips quivered.

"Don't cry, Makela." Koko sensed her fright. "It's okay. They won't hurt you."

But Makela's bladder felt full so she crossed her legs, but that didn't help. She peed in her new panties. And as the warm water trickled down her legs, into her new socks and her new shoes, she cried.

"Oh, Makela," Natalie cooed. "I wish you'd try to enjoy. This is so inspirational." Natalie put her arm around Makela's shoulders and pulled her close. Looking down, she saw a terrified expression on her daughter's face. "What is it, baby?"

Then casting her eyes downward, she whispered "Oh, Makela. What am I to do with you?"

She was not prepared for the problem Makela presented, which meant returning to the big house. She grabbed Makela by the hand and guided her to the door. As the music grew even louder, so did Makela. By the time they were outside, the girl's whimper had grown into a pitch Natalie never thought humanly possible.

She was peeved with the child. She wanted to enjoy the program. Now she had to hurry. Luckily, Shelton saw them leave and followed them outside. After she explained, he drove them back to the house in silence.

Shelton came specifically to see Makela recite her poem. Now he was angry and Natalie hoped he held it in check. She did not want him to ruin her day.

When they later returned to the church, Makela refused to participate.

🍁 🍁 🍁

Still later that same day on Easter Sunday, Helene and Natalie finished setting the table, Odessa called everyone to eat, and Natalie took a chair next to her granddaddy, Conrad.

Conrad Dawson studied his granddaughter's face, and wondered about her. "Are you happy, Nat?" he whispered.

"Yes, I am, Granddaddy." She spoke softly.

"I asked because what works for some doesn't always work for others, and life is too short to live in misery. There's no reason to do that. You have a loving family and we're here for you. Just you remember that."

"Thanks, Granddaddy. I'll do that."

At that very moment, Shelton tried to sit in the chair beside Natalie, but Delano Phillips slid into it and pretended not to notice the offense.

Angered, Shelton went to the opposite side of the table and sat next to Natalie's grandmother, Maude. Natalie knew she would later pay for Delano's bad behavior.

Delano and Sunny Phillips were teachers and friends of Natalie's. They all worked together. They felt so close to Natalie they considered themselves family, and Natalie often invited them to share meals.

Delano piled his plate high with food, which seemed to embarrass Sunny. So Natalie decided to engage her in small talk. "Did you enjoy your trip to Chicago, Sunny?"

"Yes, I did. And I'm trying to talk Delano into moving there."

"Oh, you like it that much?"

"Yes, I do. Don't you ever think about leaving here, Nat?"

"Not really. My family is here."

"I know that. But don't you ever dream about other places?"

Natalie paused before she spoke. "Well, I guess I do at times. Liz invited me to visit her many times when she lived in San Francisco. I always refused, but lately, I've given it some thought. I think taking a trip one day might be a good change of pace."

"Well, listen to who's talking about change," Tamara chuckled, devilishly.

"It simply proves she's human, Tam," Elizabeth said.

"You never said anything to me about any dreams of going away." Shelton was surprised that Natalie thought of anything other than family matters.

"I've never spoken to anyone about it, Shel. It's just a thought, but you must remember you're not the only one with secrets."

"Tell him about it, Nat," Tamara said clapping her hands as Elizabeth smiled.

Natalie glanced over at Reverend Stringer sitting across from her. He'd seen many a moonrise. He was feeble now, but he kept on going.

Earlier he had preached a long-winded Easter sermon, putting half the congregation to sleep long before he finished. It was that sermon that caused the program to run even longer and was one reason her mother served the meal much later than usual.

🍁　　🍁　　🍁

After they found Tobias in the well, Tamara felt as free as a bird for the first time in a long time.

Although she loved Reverend McCord, the love she felt was not strong enough to make another commitment to marriage. And she told him so. After she buried Tobias, the first thing she did was take a trip north.

When she returned home, to everyone's surprise, she brought back another man, Jay Kinkaid. It was rumored he was a gambler.

Natalie and Elizabeth were curious about Jay and wanted to know exactly who he was. But when Tamara was unable to answer their modest questions, they wondered about Tamara's sanity.

"Gosh, Tam," Elizabeth said. "Are you crazy? Seems like Jay's as much a stranger to you as he is to us."

"What's wrong with you, Tam?" Natalie asked. "You just don't pick up a strange man and bring him home."

"He's not really a stranger," Tamara replied. "He and Tobias were friends. I've seen him around."

"He's almost moved into your home," Elizabeth said.

"But he's so nice to me."

"Sure he is. But for what reason?" Elizabeth asked.

"I just don't have a good feeling about this man," Nat said. Then deciding to say no more, she simply shook her head. After all, Tamara had lost her mama, grandma, and Tobias all within a short time. Even though she and Elizabeth were Tamara's friends, Tamara was very lonely and obviously searching for something deeper.

Now Natalie glanced over at Jay who sat beside Tamara, grinning so everyone could see his gold tooth in the upper right side of his mouth.

Jay Kinkaid was a tall, thin, dark skinned man. His beady hair was close cropped. He wore a fedora hat and nice clothes, and he grinned a lot.

He wore gold rings on almost every finger of each hand, and a small gold earring in each ear, which led folk to believe he was a little odd.

Turning her head, Natalie tried to forget about Tamara and Jay, as she watched Reverend Stringer who suddenly jerked his head and opened his eyes. It was Natalie's guess that the aroma of some piquant dish tickled his nose and jarred him awake.

The array of food on the table included a spicy glazed ham, hot rolls, rice, gravy, potato salad, mustards greens, bacon bit cornbread, a pitcher of butter milk, and the garnish, chowchow, which was pickled cabbage or some other pickled vegetable. Desert was peach cobbler, pound cake, and homemade ice cream.

"Lawdy, Sister Dawson, your table is beautiful and set for a king and it sure smells good," the Reverend marveled as he put food on his plate. "And I'd bet it tastes as good as it smells."

"Why, thank you, Reverend. I hope it does," Odessa said.

"I think I'm gonna hurt myself today."

"You do that, Reverend. I hope it pleases your palate."

"I'm sure it will, sister," he said. "I'm sure it will."

Natalie looked at her mother and winked. Both knew that was the extent of his conversation. This had been a long day, and he would now give the food his undivided attention.

Natalie relished the compliment as much as Odessa. She loved her mother dearly and agreed with the Reverend. The table was set for a king, but then too, she was partial. It was her opinion that all her mother's meals were fit for royalty.

"I'm so glad you came, Tam," Natalie said.

"So am I." Tamara spoke to her, but she, fleetingly, made eye contact with Jay.

Natalie turned her thoughts to Delano because she was still upset that he took Shelton's chair. But when Delano turned and smiled at her, she put on her best face.

"Listen up, everyone." Natalie hoped talking about her project would calm her nerves. "As you know, we're selling tickets to raise money for a swimming pool. And we want you to ask everyone you know to buy one."

"That's right," Elizabeth said. "I've already sold several to Vince and his family."

"That's great, Liz," Helene said.

"Anybody here wants to buy one?" Elizabeth asked.

"I already bought a couple. I hear you gonna raffle off a couple of Sister Dawson's geese. Is any truth to that, Nat?" Reverend Stringer teased.

"Now wait just a minute, Reverend. No one's touching my geese," Odessa said.

"No need to get all riled up, Odessa. No one wants those noisy geese," Helene said causing everyone to chuckle.

"I just want to make sure they don't," Odessa said.

"Odessa loves those geese," Maude interjected.

"That she does," Percy said.

"I'm just so happy the pool project is finally underway. It's something you've wanted to do since you were young girls," Odessa said. "It seems your dreams might soon come true."

"I hope so, Mama."

"Well, now, ladies. Guess I'd better do my part to help those dreams come true. What you offering as a prize?" Jay asked.

"A train ticket to a city up north," Tam said.

"Well, since I'm a gambling man, guess I'd better dig deep in my pocket. This sounds too good to pass up," Jay replied.

"What you gonna do after all the tickets are sold, Nat?" Sunny asked.

"Well, I'd..." she started, but to her dismay, Delano took off like rolling thunder, and while she sat dumbfounded, he suggested they have a barbecue.

She glanced over at Shelton. He knew that was exactly what she wanted to do. She could tell he was none too pleased that Delano showed interest in her project. Now, she was afraid Shelton would think she discussed her plans with Delano.

Delano talked incessantly. And at that moment, it occurred to her he should have married Thea. Then neither would ever know what the other said.

Delano was so wound up, Natalie wondered if he would ever slow down or if she should ask permission to speak. But just when she thought she could take no more, he turned his attention to her mother.

"This food is great, Mrs. Dawson."

"Why, thank you, Delano," she said.

Turning her attention to the children, Natalie said, "I enjoyed your presentation today, Queenie."

"Thanks, Nat."

"So did I," Elizabeth said.

"Count me in on that," Tamara said. "By the way, Sophia, why didn't you participate?"

"I just didn't want to," Sophia said shrugging her shoulders.

"Sophia does what she wants to do, Tam," Helene said shaking her head.

"Your poetry is enchanting, Queenie," Sunny told her as Queenie beamed.

Dominic sat quietly and wondered if anyone paid any attention to him. Would anyone compliment him on a job well done?

"You did a good job too, Dominic," Marcus said.

"Thank you, Mr. Dawson."

"Maybe you'll sing like your Aunt Tam when you grow up," Marcus said.

"I'm not sure about that. But I *do* like it now," he replied.

"It's something to think about," Helene said. "She travels and she's been on stage with the best of them. She enjoys that life." Helene studied Tamara's face and said, Right Tam?"

Tamara laughed. "I guess you can say that."

"Come on, Tam. Tell us about it." Sunny said.

"Not now, Sunny. Let's talk about it later," Tamara winked. "This day belongs to the kids."

"If you say so," Sunny said shrugging her shoulders. She looked at Tamara and wondered why she always returned to Meadowsbrook.

"Why do you always come back, Tam?" Sunny asked. "You have no family here."

"Oh, but I do," Tamara said thinking of the Baraldi family of Baysville. "Nat and Liz are my best friends, and it seems Nat's family is my family too. I just can't seem to leave them."

"Those are lovely words, Tam," Odessa said. "You girls have been Nat's friends so long I feel you're all my daughters. And that includes Georgia Mae." Then they were silent.

Coughing, Marcus broke the spell. "You did a good job singing with that little Rabbit today, Koko," he said. "We're real proud of you."

"Thanks, Grampa," Koko grinned feeling loved.

"I gather Miss Makela didn't feel like doing anything," Marcus said.

"I guess not," Natalie said. "But I'm sure she'll do so next time. Right, Makela?"

"Yes, I will, Mama."

The fact that so many things frightened Makela, including her great-grandparents, worried Natalie. When her great-grandmother, Maude, kissed Makela, she hastily wiped her cheek and started to cry.

Makela made quite a fuss when her great-granddaddy, Conrad, reached for her hand in affection. It was three days before she felt comfortable with them.

Natalie secretly wished Makela was more like Koko who was feisty and had enough spunk for three little girls. She watched Makela hook her small teeth into a piece of meat much too big for her to handle. As her great-granddaddy took it and cut it in smaller pieces, Makela looked at him and smiled.

Her earlier fear of him was forgotten. Only the moment at hand was important, and she and Koko attacked their food as though they were starved. And Natalie knew both girls would later complain that their bellies hurt.

# CHAPTER 25

As the sun fell below the horizon, Natalie said goodnight to family and friends. Outside, Shelton revved the engine to let her know he was ready to go.

Dragging an exhausted Makela behind her, she hurried to the car and helped her crawl onto the back seat where she immediately fell asleep.

For a while they drove in silence, and she hoped Shelton had forgotten Delano. But he had not, and when they were only a short distance from their house, he pulled the car to the side of the road and stopped.

"Why are you stopping?" she asked fearfully.

"I wanna talk," he snapped.

"But can't it wait until we're home?"

"No, it can't." He spoke loudly.

"I wish you wouldn't scream. You'll frighten Makela." She squirmed because he frightened her too.

"So what? Everything frightens Makela."

"Lawdy, Shel, I can't understand what could be so urgent it can't wait." She spoke simply to delay the inevitable. She knew what was about to happen.

"I want to talk about Delano Phillips," he yelled. "He likes you. You know it, and I know it, too. And I'm sick and tired of seeing him at the dinner table every week."

"Oh, please, Shel. He's not there every week. He doesn't like me the way you think. We just work together."

"I know you work together. But I wanna know what else you do together," he yelled.

"Don't be ridiculous. He's just a friend."

"Right, that's why he was all over you today."

"That's not so."

"It is, too. And that sneaky son-of-a-bitch even stole my chair right from under me."

"If that's your problem, perhaps you should've spoken to him at the time it occurred."

"You are my wife," he emphasized. "He makes me sick. Perhaps I should've kicked his ass. I'm a man. I know what he's got up his sleeve." He spoke heatedly.

It was too dark for her to see his face, but she knew the prominent vein in the middle of his forehead appeared larger than usual. It always did when he was angry. If it burst, they would all be in trouble.

She and Makela would have to walk back to town to get his brother, Greyland. And the dark roadway frightened her as much as a dark room frightened Makela. Damn, she thought.

"I'll tell you one thing. If Delano pulls that shit again, I'm gonna crack his nuts like a holiday *pe-can*."

"That's an awful thing to say."

"I mean it. Now I want you to come clean. Tell me what's going on."

"Nothing's going on, Shel. But I do know Delano would never treat me the way you do. He's a gentleman."

Her voice dripped with sarcasm, and she knew she was in trouble, but she couldn't stop. "Too bad some of his morals haven't rubbed off on you."

"Why, you little sidity bitch," he yelled as the back of his hand connected with her face. Even so, she felt compelled to keep talking.

"You got your nerves. You lousy alley cat! How many times have you brought home the scent of some other woman? We both know who's guilty."

"Shut your mouth," he yelled smacking her again and splitting open her lower lip. She could taste blood in her mouth.

"Stop it. Stop it, Shel," she screamed. She threw up her arm to shield her face. "Please, don't hit me again," she cried. But he hit her again and again on the side of her head.

"Get your *ass* outta the car," he bellowed. "I'm gonna *teach* you a lesson." He got out of the car and waited for her to do the same. "I said get your ass outta the car." He ran around to the passenger side and pulled at the door. But she held tight, determined not to open the door or get out of the car.

"No! I won't." She gripped the door handle tightly as her face swelled.

"We won't go home 'til you do," he shouted.

"Well, we'll spend the night here."

"I said get your ass outta the car."

"Leave me alone," she cried just as a very sleepy Makela woke up and screamed. "Mama, Mama, what's wrong, Mama?"

"It's nothing, baby. Don't worry." She spoke calmly, but was so afraid she shook and her face hurt.

"I'm scared, Mama," Makela whimpered.

"I know you are, baby. But it's all right," she said when she really wanted to say, "I'm scared too." But she knew doing so would upset her daughter even more.

"I'm scared," Makela cried again.

"Goddammit, Makela." Shelton swung open the back door. Makela screamed louder and moved to the opposite side of the car.

"Shut your mouth girl, stop your whining, and sit down before I beat your ass."

Makela scooted back onto the seat and muffled her cries because she knew her daddy might hit her, too.

Once again Shelton demanded Natalie get out of the car.

"I'm gonna beat your ass *real* good so you can always remember Delano." He continued to stand outside the car.

"Mama, Mama," Makela whispered moments later when she tired of their bickering. "Why don't you get out and let daddy beat you just a little bit so we can go home?"

Surprised and hurt, Natalie let the tears flow silently down her cheeks. "Oh, no, I can't do that, Makela. I've done nothing to deserve this. I don't want Shel hurting me anymore than you want him to hurt you."

She loved this man so much, but his anger terrified her. This wasn't their first battle, and she wondered how much more she could take. Was marriage really worth it?

"But Mama, you always let him hurt you. You never fight back. You never fight back, Mama," Makela whimpered.

"I try, but it's not easy," Natalie sniffled.

"I'm so sorry, Mama. I love you so much. I don't really want him to hurt you. I'm just sleepy." Makela got up and wrapped her arms about Natalie's neck. "Why can't we leave him, Mama?" she asked innocently. "I don't think he loves us anymore."

🍁　　　🍁　　　🍁

The next day while Shelton worked with his dad Natalie got up, looked in the mirror, and was appalled at what she saw. The left side of her face was black and blue. Her lips were swollen, her left eye was bruised and almost shut. Deciding she had enough, she packed a small bag for herself and one for Makela. Then she left the house with the bags and Makela walking beside her.

"Mama," Makela said. "Do we have to come back?"

Looking down at her daughter, she said, "Only if your dad makes an effort to change." Then they walked in silence.

🍁　　　🍁　　　🍁

At the same time Natalie was on her way to her mother's house, Shelton thought about the spat he had with her the night before.

Natalie never answered Makela's question. Now he wondered if she ever thought about leaving him. Surely, he had given her enough reasons. He did bring home the scent of other women.

One scent in particular was Lydia's. He never knew anyone like Lydia. She was pretty and had a great body, which she eagerly gave to him. He didn't love her, but he loved fucking her. He never promised her marriage 'cause he was already married, and from his vantage point, that was a mistake.

Women were all over him wherever he went. Though he loved none of them, they always fell in love with him, and he enjoyed each as if she were his first conquest. His motto was feed'em, fuck'em, and forget'em fast.

The last night he saw Lydia, they were partying at Billy's. Much later, they left their friends, went down the hall where they locked themselves in the room, and climbed into bed.

"I love you, Shelton," Lydia whispered as she reached for him.

"I know you do, honey." Then he proceeded to shank her until they both were overwrought. Her death shocked and knocked the wind out of him.

When the rumors started about him and Lydia, he denied everything. Then he lied to Natalie again about his feelings for Melanie Joyride.

🍁   🍁   🍁

"My God!" Odessa screamed when Natalie and Makela walked into the house. "What happened to you?"

"Did Shel do this to you?" Odessa asked as Koko shouted, "Makela, Makela."

"Yes, he did, Mama."

"I was so scared when daddy hit Mama in the car last night, Gramma," Makela whined.

"I'm sure you were, honey. All that ruckus would've scared me too." Odessa wanted to cry.

"Does it hurt, Nat?" a very curious Koko asked.

"A little bit."

"Come on Makela, let's play."

As Makela and Koko ran into the yard slamming the screen door behind them, tears rolled down Natalie's cheeks, and Odessa hugged her.

"I'm so sorry, Nat. Come on. Let's sit down, have a lemonade, and talk."

A while later, Natalie's granddaddy, Conrad, and her grandy, Maude, joined them to console Natalie.

In the evening when the family gathered for dinner, Helene and Percy were shocked that Shelton had left such marks on Natalie's face.

"It's a damn shame. What kind of man would do this to his woman?" Percy was extremely angry. "I oughta lock him up and throw away the key. Better yet I oughta shoot him."

"*You* should've shot him, Natalie." Helene emphasized.

"Damn, Helene! No need you and Percy talking that way," Marcus said. "Natalie knows how Shel is. We warned her, but she didn't listen. She had to marry him. Now, as far as I'm concerned marriage is a lifetime commitment. Listen to her. You can see where her heart is even after this beating. So, I think Natalie should go home, stay there, and stick it out."

"Okay, Marcus. Leave it be," Odessa said.

"Yeah, Marcus. You've had your say. Now let me have mine," Conrad said.

"Sometimes marriages just don't work. You got to follow your own mind, Nat. Remember, only you can solve your own problems."

❧ ❧ ❧

That same evening, Shelton returned home to an empty house. As soon as he reached the yard, he sensed something was wrong. He smelled no food cooking. Looking about the bedroom, he knew Natalie had packed her bags and left him.

By that time, Greyland had driven out to the farm and told Thaddeus and Esther what he heard.

"What did I tell you I'd do if you didn't treat your family right?" Thaddeus said when Shelton came back to the house for dinner that evening. As Shelton started to speak, Thaddeus threw up his hands, and said, "Leave them keys on the table."

After dinner, a deflated Shelton left the keys on the table, and rode a horse back to his own house.

❧ ❧ ❧

The news of Natalie's leaving Shelton traveled fast, and the very next day Elizabeth and Tamara rushed to the house to console their friend.

"I'm so sorry, Nat," Tamara said. "What happened?"

"Shel hit me several times with his fist and accused me of having an affair with Delano Phillips."

"He's crazy. How could he think that? If he'd open his eyes, he'd know you love him," Tamara said.

"All I can say is Shel is lucky he's married to *you* and not *me*," Elizabeth said.

During the next few days Natalie enjoyed the time she spent with her grandparents.

"Just remember, you got a loving family," Maude told her. "And we're here for you."

"I know that, Grandy."

Two weeks later Conrad and Maude returned to New Orleans and so did the comfort they provided.

After Natalie left Shelton, she saw more of him than when she lived with him. He came by the house every day. He pleaded with her to return home, but she refused.

# CHAPTER 26

The summer 1947 arrived, the telephone lines came to Meadowsbrook, and those who could afford a phone got one.

Slick Joyride, a slim, good looking black man, came from Chicago to Meadowsbrook on a very hot weekend. Slick was the father of Brick and Goose.

Driving a pretty new car, he wore a white straw hat, and a yellow zoot suit. He sported spit shine shoes and smoked a big cigar.

Clinging to his arm like a morning-glory vine was a very pretty young woman. Her name was Zenna. She didn't talk much. She just happened to be pretty and fit in the scheme of things.

Though he thought of himself as a dresser and was able to carry on a good conversation, Slick was nothing more than a simple minded, sentimental pimp.

Of course, pimping was not a word in his vocabulary. He was simply a "keeper of women," which was his secret. His family never knew how he made money. But he never dirtied his hands with an honest day's work.

An observant man, he learned early on that a smart man never hit a woman. There was no need for violence when all a man needed to do was use his cock and his tongue the right way.

Therefore, he worked hard in bed to please women. And after a week of loving, buying little trinkets, nice clothes, fake furs, and feeding them well, they were putty in his hands. They were hooked, and there was nothing they wouldn't do to keep him happy.

When Slick first arrived in Chicago, he was hungry, and the first person he met was Sylvester Braxton, a tall, brown-skinned man who lived nearby. Sylvester talked fast, drove fast, and rumor was he fucked hard and fast. He had girl friends of all shapes and colors. They smothered him with love and sometimes left him with infections. He considered it an annoyance, but felt it came with the territory.

Sylvester wore expensive clothes and drove a sleek car. Although he had a reputation for fast living and loving fast women, he was well liked by most in the neighborhood.

Sylvester and Slick became fast friends, and folk in the nearby church who knew what Sylvester did for a living finally coaxed him and Slick to attend church. They did and soon reluctantly became members.

Before long, the good sisters talked Sylvester into preaching. He did, and the rest was history. Instead of Sylvester conforming to the church, Sylvester turned many church members into whores, and half the men in the church paid for services his women provided. Not only was Sylvester a good preacher, he was the biggest pimp in town, and no one was the wiser.

Slick attended church often and demanded all his women become members. None of the women objected, and when big dignitaries came to town they needed only to speak to Sylvester, who put his finger in the dial, called Slick, and put in an order. Slick promptly provided a woman of choice for that specific man. Business was booming and success assured. It was the dirty little secret of the congregation.

Soon Sylvester built a bigger church, bought a bigger car, a bigger house, and just to keep up appearances, he finally married. And she was a big woman.

Slick liked Sylvester as a friend and business partner and as the money kept rolling in, he enjoyed life more than he ever dared dream.

On Sunday morning Slick took Zenna to church in Meadowsbrook. As they stood in the church yard, he introduced her to a curious Della. "This is Zenna," he said.

"Hey, Zenna," Della said. Turning to Slick, she asked, "When you getting married, Slick? Them two boys of yours need a mama."

"I'll marry when the time's right, Della," he laughed just as Sunny Phillips came out of the church. He and Sunny had been friends a long time. She was an attractive short, brown skinned woman, with a small waistline, small feet, and shoulder length black hair. She was very pleased to see him. He, as he liked to call it, "cemented" the relationship when she last visited Chicago. He took her to bed, licked her all over, and made her forget about Delano. In fact, she didn't want to return to Meadowsbrook.

"I don't want to go back, Slick," she said. "I want to stay here with you."

"I know you do, baby, but the time ain't right," he explained. He had a business to run and wasn't sure if Sunny was ready to work with him.

But looking at Sunny walk towards him now, he felt there would never be a better time. But first he had to find Zenna a home. Zenna had become sickly, and a woman with health problems was useless to him. Still, he was not a heartless man, and he would not leave her on the streets.

That very evening he took Zenna to the Lavender Lounge to see Tamara perform and introduce her to everyone there.

"This is Zenna," he announced hoping some eager young man liked her enough to take her home.

The following Saturday night he took her to party at Billy's house. Billy, drink in hand, opened the door.

"Hey, man," he said. "Come on in. And who's this pretty little thing with ya?"

"This is Zenna," Slick said.

"Hey, Zenna. We already heard about you. It's good to meet you," Billy said. But Zenna barely spoke.

Fats, Harry, Shelton, and Warren, who were playing a friendly game of cards, looked up.

"Hey, everybody," Slick greeted the men as he and Zenna approached the table.

"Hey, man," they chorused, laying the cards face down on the table.

"This is Zenna. Ain't she pretty?" Slick said causing them to laugh and look at the young woman. Then the men introduced themselves.

"Hey, Zenna," Fats said. Then, staring at the young woman, he realized she was quite pretty.

"Sorry, man. I got no time for pretty women right now," Fats said though he couldn't think of a reason not to have the time. Looking at Zenna again, he wondered if she would find interest in him.

He loved Elizabeth, Natalie and Tamara, but they were friends. He never had a real girl friend. Now he wondered what it would be like to have a woman of his own.

"How long you staying in town, Zenna?" he asked.

"I'm not sure," she said looking into Slick's face.

"She can stay as long as you want her to, man," Slick said crossing his fingers for good luck. As far as he knew, Fats had no love interest. He hoped the man liked Zenna enough to keep her in Meadowsbrook.

Slick could tell Fats was giving Zenna some thought, so he turned to Shelton.

"What's going on, Shel?" Slick asked.

"Oh, man. I'm sure you heard. Nat left me. I'm trying to get her back home."

"Oh, that's too bad man," Slick said thinking no better for him since everybody knew Shel didn't treat Nat right.

Two weeks later, when Fats still hadn't made up his mind about Zenna, Slick decided to return to Chicago. After promising Zenna he would return for her in a couple of weeks, he left the young woman with his sister-in-law, Jenny Joyride, and his brother, Spuds. He took Delano Phillip's wife, Sunny, back with him instead.

❦    ❦    ❦

Not long after Slick's departure, Jenny caught Spuds red-handed having an intense romp with Zenna in the back room of the drugstore. According to rumor, Jenny asked no questions. She simply pulled her gun from her purse and started shooting.

The young woman was not harmed, but she ran for her life. Some said she ran so fast she probably reached Chicago that very same night. Of course, that wasn't true. Zenna ran over to the Fish Kitchen where several customers were waiting to be served and the juke box blared.

"Jenny came into the back room just as Spuds forced himself on me. Then she shot at me," Zenna explained to Fats and his mother Sissy.

"You don't have to tell me what happened," Sissy said. "I've known about Spuds and his problem with young girls a long time. But don't you worry, you'll be all right. You can stay here with us."

"Ain't that right, Tex?" Sissy shouted across the room to her husband who worked over the grill.

"Whatever you say, baby," Tex said.

Sissy felt God had answered her prayers. Her son never had a girl friend, but it was time he thought about marriage. Shoot, from what she saw, Zenna might make him a good wife.

🍁 🍁 🍁

Jenny was tired of Spuds and his bull. Long ago she had heard about him and Georgia Mae. But she did nothing, and when Georgia Mae died, Jenny just let it go.

Of course, she thought she killed Spuds and immediately telephoned for Greyland. "I want you to pack him off, dress him down, and bury him," Jenny cold bloodedly told Greyland.

However, when he and Handsome Jim went to pick him up, Spuds was still breathing. Instead of taking Spuds to the funeral parlor, they took him to the hospital where Doc Peterson patched him up.

"What happened, Spuds," Doc Peterson chuckled.

"Jenny tried to kill me," Spuds groaned.

"And I wonder why?" Doc Peterson cackled loudly. Shaking his head, he called Ellie, "Come on in here, will you. We got another one."

🍁 🍁 🍁

After Spuds left the hospital, he went to the Shady Shack where he stayed for three quiet days. Giving his plight some serious thought, he remembered Georgia Mae. Georgia Mae had died because of him. Had he taken his responsibility like a man, Georgia Mae might have blossomed into a pretty young woman like her girlfriends.

When Georgia Mae came to him and told him she was pregnant, and put her arms around his neck in the back room of the store, he pushed her away.

"Stop that, girl. You know I'm married?"

"I know. But I love you. I'm gonna have your baby. What're *we* supposed to do? You said you loved me," she cried.

"*We?* What do you mean, *we?* I don't know what you're talking about, girl. Anyway, it's your own fault," he told her. "You should've taken better care of yourself."

Georgia Mae had left the store in tears. He should've gone after her, but he was so glad to see her go he almost shouted. He didn't want her kind of problems, and, sadly, it was the last time he saw Georgia Mae alive.

When she died, he felt ashamed. He hurt because he knew he was to blame. He should've given Georgia Mae the help she needed. He could've done so much, but he shirked his manly duties.

She was only a young girl. He knew better. He had no right to take advantage of her. And because he turned his back on her when she needed him most, Georgia Mae died. Suddenly, his heart felt heavy. But this wasn't something he could talk about.

It was too late to tell Georgia Mae he was sorry. But it wasn't too late to save his marriage. So Spuds went home to Jenny.

The evening he returned, Jenny sat alone on the porch thinking what she should do about Melanie's fixation with Shelton Lamont. It disturbed her that Melanie spent more time trying to take Shelton from Natalie than she did breathing. Looking up Jenny was surprised to see Spuds coming up the walkway.

"I want to come home, Jenny," Spuds said as he burst through the door.

"Why should I let you come home when all you ever did was to hurt and embarrass me?" Jenny asked, coldly.

"I...I..."

"Well, what you trying to say, Spuds? You want to apologize? You get down on your knees and tell me how sorry you are for the years of hurt you caused me. That's the only way you gonna get back in *this* house."

"I'm so sorry, Jenny," he said kneeling in front of her. "I didn't mean to hurt you. I just didn't think about what I was doing."

"I got a feeling you didn't care, Spuds."

"I promise to change. Please give me the chance to do right, Jenny. Will you please forgive me?"

"Yes, I'll forgive you." Jenny could only whisper as the hurt she felt resurfaced. "But I got a feeling you better ask God to forgive you, too."

That night before getting into bed beside Jenny, Spuds knelt down, and he talked to The Man Upstairs.

While sitting on the bench under the elm tree the three young women laughed and chatted gaily among themselves.

"Did you hear the latest?" Elizabeth asked.

"What's that?" Natalie asked.

"That clown Spuds begged Jenny to take him back," Elizabeth answered.

"That's no surprise. Nobody wants Spuds and he got no other place to go. So he should straighten up and act right," Tamara said. "And speaking of clowns, it's about time for the circus to come to town. So Spuds came back just in the nick of time," Tamara said as they whooped with laughter.

"I remember how we looked forward to the circus when we were youngsters," Elizabeth said.

"Me too," replied Tam.

"Oh, yes. It was the most excitement I experienced back then," Natalie said.

"I know," Elizabeth said. "Guess we'd better take the kids. What do you think, Nat?"

"Sounds great," Natalie said feeling as eager as a child again about its arrival. She was ready to go.

Later, as they prepared for that special night of bright lights under the big top, they told Makela and Koko stories of the past, and the two little girls could hardly wait for the special day to arrive when they too would experience their first visit to the circus.

Even though the older girls, Queenie and Sophia had seen it all before, they too waited anxiously, and Natalie hoped Makela would find it an enjoyable experience instead of a scary one.

When the day arrived, just as in the past, Natalie and her family were some of the first to arrive at the gates, which were locked. Tamara, Elizabeth, and Dominic met them there. Then they all got in line, and chatted just as noisily and waited just as impatiently as they'd done in the past.

After the gates opened and they went inside, to Natalie's dismay, Shelton was the first person she saw.

"Hey, Nat," he said. "How you doing?"

"I'm fine, Shel," she said coolly as they approached a tent where a large bear peered at them from a cage.

"Mama, Mama," Makela shouted as the bear opened his mouth wide. "Look at the bear. Will he bite me?"

"Of course not, Makela, he's locked up."

"Don't worry, Makela. He won't hurt you," a very grownup Koko assured.

"Hell, yes, he'll bite," Shelton grinned. "He's got a mouth."

Staring up into Shelton's face, Makela held Natalie's hand a little tighter.

"Don't talk to her that way, Shel. You'll frighten her," Natalie remarked.

"Okay. Okay. But from what I see Makela is always frightened."

While Makela worried about being eaten by the bear, Dominic stuck out his tongue at the bear and dared the bear to come out of the cage.

"Hey, how come you so scared, Makela?" Dominic teased.

"Don't ask such a crazy question, honey," Elizabeth admonished. "Makela's still young."

Queenie spoke in Makela's defense. "Yeah. She's just a baby, Dominic. That's why. And it's her first circus, too," Sophia told him.

"Oh, all right," Dominic answered as Brick and Goose rushed up to him, which got him to think of something other than the little scared girl.

"Hey, remember back when Georgia Mae was with us? Those were innocent times." Tamara spoke softly.

"Yeah, they were," Elizabeth said. "And I get goose pimples and want to cry when I think of the past."

"Me, too," Natalie answered. "I think everyone misses her."

Later, the older children took rides on the swings and the Ferris wheel. While Koko enjoyed the bumper cars, Makela refused to get in one.

"Come on, girl. Get in the car. They won't bite you," Shelton coaxed.

"But I don't want to, Daddy," Makela whined and stayed close to Natalie, but she did enjoy the Merry-go-Round.

Laughing and clapping her hands later, Makela enjoyed the antics of the clowns. She stared in disblief, completely fascinated. But it was Natalie, Elizabeth and Tamara who enjoyed the trapeze artists. They sat mesmerized just as they had when they were kids.

"I never get tired of this part of the circus," Elizabeth said.

"I know what you mean," Tamara agreed.

"They're simply amazing," Natalie said looking down at Makela on her lap. "I think Makela likes it too."

"I do, Mama. I do. I like to see the man fly."

"Me too," Koko said.

"Hey, Koko," Dominic teased. "You think you can do that?"

"Yeah, I can. Can you smarty pants?" she grinned.

"Sure I can," he answered.

"We'll see 'bout that later, Dominic. I know I can do it," Brick snapped. "What about you, Goose?"

"Yeah, I can."

"Sure you can," Queenie said. "I can't wait to see you break your neck."

"Right," said Sophia. "Hey, Goose, the only thing you can do is act like a clown. And you didn't need to come to the circus to do that. That comes naturally."

"Shame on you, Sophia," Helene said. "I want you to stop it right now." Sophia shrugged her shoulders and laughed.

When it was over, Natalie felt like a kid again. Then Shelton broke the spell when he asked her to return to the farm.

That same week Natalie, Elizabeth, and Tamara were thrilled when all the raffle tickets were sold. In addition, all three churches and most businesses gave sizeable donations. But it was the owners of the Lounge, Charlie and Orchid Fountaine, who gave the biggest gift of all. Meadowsbrook would finally get its swimming pool.

# CHAPTER 27

The Dawsons were close knit, sentimental, and an emotional family. The day Natalie's brother, Alan, came home on leave and surprised everyone, their exuberant shouts were heard a block away.

On a quiet Saturday afternoon Alan brought his new green car to an abrupt stop in front of the house.

"Hey, everybody!" He grinned as he came up the walkway. Realizing it was Alan, everyone rushed from the porch and into the yard to greet him.

"Welcome home, son," Marcus said as he embraced him. "Welcome home."

"Thanks, Daddy. It's good to be back," he said thinking he never thought he would live to see the day his daddy was actually glad to see him.

"I'm real proud of you," Marcus said.

"We're all proud of you. And we're so glad you came home in one piece," Percy said as he too gave Alan a quick hug. In the meantime, Natalie, Queenie, and Sophia cried unabashedly while Makela and Koko ran inside the house to tell Odessa.

"Gramma, Gramma," they called out in unison. "Uncle Alan is home."

"Lawdy, lawdy," whispered Odessa. "My prayers have been answered." Then turning to Koko, she said, "Alan is your daddy, Koko. He's Makela's uncle." Then she rushed out to the front porch.

"Oh, my," she shouted. "Is it really you, son?"

"Yes, Mama. It's me," Alan smiled. "How you doing?" he asked and threw his arms around Odessa. "I love you, Mama."

"And I love you, too, son. Come on in. This calls for a celebration. "How long you staying?"

"Just two weeks," he said.

"Good. It's good to have you home at last," Odessa told him.

"Thanks, Mama." Turning he embraced Natalie and teased, "I swear you get prettier each time I see you, sis."

"Of course, I do," she chuckled as she wiped away tears of happiness. "We thank God for keeping you safe, Alan. Welcome home."

By this time, Makela and Koko stood and stared silently at the man in uniform.

"Are you my daddy?" Koko asked feeling apprehensive.

"Yeah, I am," Alan said. He was tempted to say, well that's what your mama said. But instead he took the little girl's hand in his, momentarily. Looking down, he searched for some resemblance of himself. He saw none. But he claimed her as his child long before she was born. He was in this for the long haul.

As the family looked on, he bent down, picked her up, and held her close. She hesitantly put her arms around his neck and smiled down at Makela because she had a daddy, too.

"Where's Aunt Helene?" he asked.

"She's at the shoe store. She'll be here after closing time. In fact," Percy said, "guess I better go tell her you're home."

As Percy stood to leave, Alan put Koko down. Both she and Makela followed Percy out the door.

Neighbors within earshot rushed to the house to see what the commotion was all about. When they saw Alan, they joined the family and loudly welcomed him home, too. When Elizabeth and Tamara heard the news, they rushed to the house to see Alan.

"Good grief is that our little Lizzy?" Alan inquired.

"It sure is," Elizabeth laughed. "How are you Alan?"

"I'm just fine. It's so good to see you," he said kissing her cheek. He suddenly remembered rumors of her and Vince the meat man. Vince had called her "Lizzy." Turning from Elizabeth, he embraced Tamara. "How are you, Tam? Long time no see."

"I know. And I'm okay," she said thinking he was more handsome now than ever.

"I hear you're still singing," he said.

"You bet your sweet patootie I am," Tamara laughed.

"So what's keeping you here?" he asked. "Why don't you take that talent up north or where it might be appreciated and get paid for it?"

"Don't get started on that one now. I do get paid."

"I know you do. But you could get better pay if you'd let go of Meadowsbrook," Alan said.

"I know, but you know that's hard to do. But just for your information, I am thinking about making changes."

"Oh, Tam," Natalie sighed. "You never told me. Things will be completely dead around here without you. In fact, we won't know what to do. Will we, Liz?"

"You're right. It'll be very lonely," Elizabeth said thoughtfully. "Of course, I've been thinking about leaving too."

"Oh, no. You can't, Liz. What will I do if you both go away?" Natalie asked.

"I'm not leaving right away, Nat," Tamara said. "I haven't made any plans yet. I'll be here a while."

"What about you, Liz?" Natalie asked.

"Well, we just got a phone call from Uncle Joe and Aunt Vi this morning. They're coming to visit in a few days. They'll be staying three weeks, and I'm seriously thinking about returning with them."

"Why didn't you tell me?" Natalie asked. As she stared at her friends, tears welled up in her eyes, and she did all she could to keep them from rolling down her cheeks. If they left town, she thought, she would just die.

"Oh, come on, sis. Don't you start crying now," Alan said looking at her closely. "From what I hear, it might be time for you to see some other parts of the country, too."

"Oh, I don't know Alan," Natalie said.

"Well, it's something for you to seriously think about," Alan said. "There's a lot of world outside of Meadowsbrook."

"You're just the one to tell her, Alan. She needs to get away from Shel, if only for a while," Tamara said.

"I agree with that," Elizabeth said. Just as Odessa returned to the porch carrying a tray with two bottles of wine and glasses, Percy returned with Helene.

"My word," Helene shouted as she rushed onto the porch. "Look what the wind blew in. Come on and give me a hug, boy."

"I love you, auntie," Alan grinned as he put his arms around her.

"It's good to have you home, Alan."

"It's good to be home. How you doing?"

"I'm well, honey," she said. "Give me a glass, Odessa. This calls for a toast."

"I agree with that," Odessa said. After she filled everyone's glass, they all stood in a close circle. Clinking their glasses, they said, "Here's to Alan. Welcome home."

"Come on, son," Marcus pointed to the chair near him and Percy. "Tell us about your war experiences."

"Yeah," Percy said just as Shelton came into the yard. "We can't wait to hear what it's like to fly them big ass planes."

Natalie decided while celebrating the groundbreaking for the swimming pool, they would also celebrate Alan's homecoming, and everyone agreed.

🍁 🍁 🍁

Because Morningstar was the only hospital in the area for black folk, they came from some distance for medical care, which kept Paige and her parents quite busy.

Odessa knew where to find her and wasted no time. The day after Alan's arrival, she went to the hospital to see Paige. Lucky for her, Paige was sitting alone at a desk on the ward and was the first person she saw.

"Hey, Paige," Odessa greeted.

"Hi, Mrs. Dawson. How are you? And what brings you here? Are you okay?"

"Oh, I'm fine, honey. I just stopped by to talk to you for a minute."

"Oh, what about?"

"Well, you know Alan just came home, don't you?"

"So I heard," Paige said. Although no one knew, she secretly admired Alan, but always from a distance.

"Well, honey. You know Nat and her friends raised enough money for that swimming pool. It's something they wanted to do for years. We'll have a barbeque next weekend to celebrate that occasion and Alan's homecoming, too. I'd like you to come."

"I'd love to come. And thanks for making a special trip to invite me," Paige smiled.

"Good," Odessa smiled too. "I expect to see you next Saturday. It will make me very happy."

On Friday morning the Dawson men slaughtered a goat and a pig, then put them on the spit to slow roast.

That evening, Paige spoke with her mother. "I'd like to take off tomorrow, Mama," she said surprising Doc and Ellie.

"I'm glad to hear that, Paige," Ellie sighed.

"It's about time," Doc Peterson told her.

"Mrs. Dawson came over last week and personally invited me to the barbeque on Saturday."

"Why, that's great, Paige," Ellie said smiling at Doc who raised his eyebrow. She hoped this might be the start of something special between Paige and Alan.

That same evening the upcoming event generated so much excitement among the four girls, Queenie, Sophia, Koko, and Makela that they eagerly pitched in and helped Odessa clean the large back yard.

On Saturday morning, everyone gathered at the center of town where the groundbreaking for the swimming pool took place.

The Reverend Buddy McCord led a prayer and spoke briefly. Then standing beside her friends, Elizabeth and Tamara, Natalie told the crowd how as youngsters they wanted to raise money for the pool, but circumstances prevented their doing so. Though this day was a long time coming, they were happy because this accomplishment could be instrumental in saving those who might otherwise drown in the canal.

While Natalie spoke, Dominic stood proudly with his grandmother, Ernestine and his great-grandmother, Bessie Mae Wanker.

It seemed all those able to do so came to witness the phenomenon. And when the man climbed upon the backhoe and scraped the ground for the first time, they all cheered.

When it ended, Natalie invited everyone to join them in her family's backyard to feast. They almost stampeded.

There was more than enough food and while Marcus and Percy carved meat, Helene, Odessa, and Natalie prepared other foods. As folk came into the yard, Natalie hoped Shelton would not come. However, he was one of the first to arrive. She refused to talk to him.

Then looking around Natalie realized just about everybody in town had come in hopes of winning the raffle.

"Okay," Elizabeth said rushing over to Natalie and Tamara. "What can I do to help?" As Ernestine and Bessie Mae Wanker went into the house to talk with Odessa and Helene, Dominic went in a different direction in search of his pals Brick and Goose.

When he found the two boys, they stood under the big elm tree talking to Queenie and Sophia while Koko and Makela played with several other youngsters nearby. Rabbit, was the only boy to join the girls.

The fact that Rabbit preferred playing with girls fascinated Dominic. But even more intriguing, were sisters, Birdie and Bonnie. They were different, he thought, because neither spoke English. They spoke their own language. No one understood them, but they understood each other. Yet, Dominic, like all the other youngsters, liked them. So he stood and watched as Rabbit chanted along with the girls and acted out the game.

"Little Sally Walker, sitting in a saucer,
Weeping and a crying for a cool drink of water,
Rise, Sally rise. Wipe your weeping eyes.
Put your hands on your hips, let your backbone slip.
Shake it to the east, shake it to the west.
Shake it to the very one you love the best.
Mama says so, Papa says so.
That's the way to shake it when you wanna catch a beau."

Later, turning his attention to his pals, Dominic went over to the bench and joined them under the elm, where a very pretty Queenie held their attention.

"Gracious, Harry," Thea said. "You ever see so much food?"

"Well I…"

"You think we gonna eat all this?"

"I don't know…"

"Hey, Tamara Dupree," Thea called out ignoring Harry, and rushing over to Tamara. "How you doing, girl?"

"I'm…"

"And where's that gambling man, Jay? How do you know him anyhow? When you gonna marry him?"

"You tell me," Tamara responded laughingly.

# CHAPTER 28

Jay Kinkaid was a gambler who loved the life he lived. Gambling was the way he made his living. He never moved in with Tamara because he wanted no real ties with the woman. Instead, he rented a room at the Shady Shack Hotel behind the Lavender Lounge.

He and Tobias had once been good friends. In fact, while friends saw them as thick as thieves no one knew this was more than just appearance. They actually had pulled off several jobs together. That was Jay's reason for latching onto Tamara. When they pulled the last job, Tobias took most of the money with a promise to give Jay his share later.

Jay fought Tobias about the decision, but decided to trust Tobias since they never had problems before.

So Tobias took most of the money with him and Tobias, conveniently, got lost. It wasn't until after Tobias's death that Jay finally knew where Tobias lived. And the next time Tamara breezed into Chicago to sing her little heart out, he latched onto her. He told her he loved her, and she believed it.

Of course, he didn't really love Tamara. He simply wanted his share of the money. He was certain Tobias had not spent it all. He was too smart to let anyone know what he did in the past. So Jay followed Tamara home, and everyone in town thought they would marry.

But marriage was not for him. He liked going it alone. When Tamara invited him to the barbeque, he declined. "Sorry, baby," he said. "I got other fish to fry."

He waited a short distance away from Tamara's house the day of the barbeque. No one locked their doors. When Tamara walked out, he walked in.

He intended to find that money even if he had to *strangle* Tamara to get it. What really pissed him off was that Tamara had a piece of old heavy furniture in every goddamn corner of the six room house. Furthermore, the walls were covered with tapestry, and in every corner hung little "What Not" shelves.

It would be a lot of work, he decided, but it was worth it. Jay went through every drawer in the house. He looked under the beds and under the mattresses. He searched throughout the kitchen. He pulled the tapestry off the walls, and almost broke his back pulling the china cabinet from the wall.

What Jay didn't know was Tamara had hung new wallpaper before she met him. She had found Tobias's secret stash. She mulled over the situation for exactly two minutes before she concluded since Tobias was dead, all that money belonged to her.

However, it took her a little longer to decide where to put it. Sometime later it came to her. Natalie's daddy, Marcus Dawson, had a big safe in his house because there was no bank in town, and few folk trusted banks. Therefore, Marcus kept money in that safe for his family and other folk.

If she played her cards right, Mr. Dawson would think she made a bundle from her work. So each time Tamara went up north to work and returned home, she took a certain amount of Tobias's money and gave it to Marcus Dawson. He put it in the safe, and he gave her a receipt.

She put some of the money in a bucket and buried it in her back yard under the Chinaberry tree. In order to protect it from dampness, when clouds formed overhead, she dug it up and brought it into the house. If careful, Tamara thought, she would hold on to every red cent, and she would never tell a soul.

When Jay realized there was no money in the house, he was mad enough to dig Tobias up from the grave and strangle *him*. He was also mad at himself for spending so much time pretending he *loved* Tamara only to learn he wasted his time. And after all that pulling on that heavy furniture, his back hurt.

He realized he would never know what the hell Tobias did with the money. That afternoon, Jay left Tamara's house in shambles and went to find a game.

❦ ❦ ❦

The yard was crowded when Esther Lamont tugged at Natalie's arm and pulled her aside.

"From what I hear, Nat, you don't plan to come back to the farm," Esther said when they were some distance from the crowd.

"I suppose you heard right."

"Lawdy, Nat. Why don't you give this thing some serious thought? Shel is miserable."

"That's too bad! He never thought about that when he made *me* miserable. He made his bed. So let him lie in it."

"Lordy. You don't sound like the Nat we know." Esther looked puzzled.

"I'm sure I don't," Natalie said. "I'm learning to use my head."

"Don't you think I know what you been through with him?"

"No! I don't think you or anyone else knows."

"Shel knows he acted a fool. But he loves you, and he wants you back. He promises to be a better person."

*Fool*, is right, Natalie thought. "Listen, Mrs. Lamont," she said while thinking they were like strangers. Neither knew much about the other, and she was a little miffed that the woman took it upon herself to do battle for her son. "He's made promises before, but never kept one."

"I know you and I never talked much, and I don't visit you like Thad does. But I'm not in the best of health. I seldom leave the house. Of course, you're always welcome to my home," Esther said. "You do believe that, don't you, Nat?"

"Yes, I do."

"Well, now. I want you to know I'm in your corner, dear. I've talked to Shel, but he never listened in the past. However, he is listening now. So I'm begging you to take time and think it over."

Natalie looked at the older woman. This was their longest conversation ever. They only saw one another on holidays, such as Christmas and Easter. Or like now, at a barbecue, usually in her mother Odessa's back yard.

Natalie noticed Esther's furrowed forehead and wondered if the furrows came from too much squinting, or old age. Then, too, Natalie thought, perhaps Esther worried that Shel's way of life might one day get him killed by some irate man or woman.

"Okay. I'll think about it," Natalie said. "But I have to go now and help serve the food."

"I know you do, honey. By the way, I think you did a great job in raising all that money for the pool. It's a worthwhile cause."

"Thank you, Mrs. Lamont. But I didn't do it alone. Some credit goes to Tam and many others helped, too. We just don't want to see another youngster lose his life to the canal."

"Neither do I, dear."

"By the way, I appreciate your donation," Natalie remarked.

"I know you do. And I'm happy to give, dear," Esther said as Natalie walked away and joined Helene at the table.

Natalie spent the remainder of the day making sure everyone had a good time.

She scouted the crowd for Jay, but she never saw him and wondered what important event kept him from joining them on such an ocassion.

Natalie worried about Tamara because in her eyes Jay was just as scary as Tobias had been. He kept a close watch over Tamara. And Natalie, like Elizabeth, felt something was not quite right with the man. They just hadn't figured out what it was.

Glancing across the yard, she saw Alan talking with Paige. She smiled.

❦ ❦ ❦

"It's good to see you, Paige," Alan said. "How you been? I hear you work around the clock."

"Not really, but I do work a lot. There're a lot of sick people in the world."

"I know, and a lot of it's in their heads," Alan laughed.

"You can say that again. Just look around you. Listen to all the terrible things happening. You know and I know the world has gone nuts," she said.

"You ever go out, Paige?"

"I seldom do anything other than work."

"Hum. How would you like to go to the Lounge tonight?"

"I'd like that. I'd like to see Tam on stage," Paige said.

"You mean you never heard her?"

"Not for some time."

"Well, my lovely. You're in for a treat. Come on inside. Let's have a drink of mama's homemade wine."

As they worked their way through the crowded yard and onto the back porch, Paige hoped this was just the beginning of something with a future.

Alan wondered if he was still so naïve he expected more than Paige was willing to give. He needed a woman to love him as much as he loved her. So far he had lost that battle. Catching himself, he thought. Forget it, man. All you need is plain, simple friendship.

❦   ❦   ❦

"When you going back home, Nat?" Jozell asked.

"I'm not," she blurted.

"I don't believe that," Jozell told her.

"Believe what you want," Natalie said. Then, after a pregnant pause, a puzzled Jozell spoke.

"But what will you do if you don't go back to Shel?"

"For heaven sakes," Natalie snapped testily. Jozell, like everyone else in town, expected her to go back to Shel. "I don't want to talk about it."

"I'm sorry," Jozell said. Raising her hands defensively, she stepped back, and looked hurt. "I didn't mean to upset you."

"I'm sorry, too. I didn't mean to snap at you, but I'm a little edgy."

"I suppose you are." Jozell took the plate Natalie handed her.

"Forget it, Jozell," Helene interjected. "This too shall pass, and Nat's gonna be just fine."

"Hey, Nat. Can I help you do something?" Elizabeth asked as she approached the women.

"Yeah, you can help her do something," Greyland grinned. "How about getting me a plate?"

"You got it," Elizabeth said as they went over to the table.

"Thanks, Liz," Natalie said. As Candyman Cates and Seb Pardeau started to perform, they paused to listen. Natalie saw the Reverend Buddy McCord who seemed tethered to Tamara, and again she smiled.

Delano Phillips won the raffle, which was a trip to Chicago. As Natalie listened to the music, she hoped Delano would find his wife, Sunny, while there and bring her back home. Or better yet, perhaps he would stay there, too.

By late evening, as the crowd dispersed, Shelton approached Natalie.

"Can we talk, Nat?" he pleaded.

"Okay," she sighed. It wasn't something she wanted to do, but she was still Shelton's wife, and it was something she had to do.

Shelton took her by the hand and led her to the bench under the big elm tree where they sat.

"I love you, Nat. And I'm sorry I hit you. I promise it won't happen again."

"We both know you've made promises before."

"I know I have," he said. "But please believe me. It won't happen again."

"Okay," she said looking into his handsome face. "Let me think about it."

"Fair enough," he said. "I'll see you tomorrow."

"Bye, Daddy," Makela said as Shelton prepared to leave the yard. She only stared at him when she really wanted to hug him. But she was afraid to rush to him because she wasn't sure if he was in a good mood or if he was mad.

"Goodbye, Makela. I'll see you tomorrow." Then he let the gate slam behind him.

The festivities ended and a tired Natalie decided to sit on the bench under the elm and rest.

"I sure had a good time today," Tamara said as she and Elizabeth approached her.

"Hum, I bet you did. Seems like you spent a lot of time with Reverend McCord, and you laughed a lot, too." Natalie studied Tamara for a moment.

"That I did, my friend," Tamara laughed. "What about you, Nat? Did you enjoy the day?"

"Under the circumstances, it was rather pleasant."

"We know what you mean," Elizabeth said. "I wish there was something we could do to make things better. What's happening with Shel? He trying to get you back?"

"You know he is," Natalie said.

"And I suppose you're going?" Tamara said.

"I haven't made up my mind yet. What do you plan to do about Reverend McCord and Jay Kinkaid?"

"There's little I can do about the Reverend, Nat. He's in one world, and I'm in another. I like what I do. From where I stand, we can never be more than friends. You know me. I'm not giving an inch. And as far as Jay goes, I'm simply having fun."

"Oops," Elizabeth laughed. "Guess she don't love either of them enough to give up anything. Am I right, Tam?"

"You got the picture. Hey, I gotta go home and get ready for the Lounge." Tamara shook her hips and popped her fingers. They laughed.

"Okay. We'll see you later," Natalie said.

"I think I'd better go, too," Elizabeth said. "Where's Dominic?"

"I don't know, but I think you and Nat should come over to the Lounge later tonight," Tamara coaxed.

"You know, you might be right," Elizabeth said. "What do you think, Nat?"

"Why not? I need an evening out. It might help me feel better."

"I'm coming too," Helene said as she joined them.

"Good," Tamara said. "The more the merrier." Then Tamara walked out the gate, and Elizabeth, Natalie and Helene went over where Queenie was still the center of attention reciting poetry she'd composed. The three women stopped and listened then applauded when Queenie finished. "That was lovely," Natalie told her. "Keep it up."

"Thanks, Nat."

"Where's Domnic?" Elizabeth asked.

"He left a while ago with Brick and Goose," Sophia said. "Okay. I'd better go find my son. I'll see you and Helene later when you stop by the house, Nat," Elizabeth said.

"You bet," Natalie said.

"Can we take a walk up the street, Mama?" Queenie asked Helene.

"Sure you can, but don't stay too long. It's getting late, so keep your eye on Makela and Koko."

"Don't worry," Queenie replied sweetly. "I can handle it."

"I hope so. Hey, Sophia," Helene called. "Help your sister watch out for the little girls." When Helene got no response, she yelled. "Did you hear me, Sophia?"

"Good grief, Mama. Where do you think my ears are?" Sophia snapped.

"I hope they're on your head, girl. And if you don't watch your tongue, I'll box them," Helene threatened. As Sophia stuck out her tongue, Helene struck at her, but she laughed and moved out of reach.

"I sometimes wonder what I'll do with Sophia. She was born sassy."

"I know," Natalie chuckled. "She and Koko are real live wires."

When Tamara reached home, she was surprised and frightened to find her house ransacked. Walking through the house, she realized every piece of furniture had been pulled from the walls. She dropped to the sofa, puzzled.

After giving it some thought, she put it all the together. Jay Kinkaid had searched her house, and she knew why. She laughed.

Later that night, Natalie, Elizabeth, and Helene joined Alan and Paige at the Lounge. While Tamara performed, they listened and cheered her on. When she later joined them, they all had a ball.

On Sunday, when Paige Peterson joined Odessa and her family for dinner, everyone knew Paige and Alan hit it off, and the family approved.

Late that same Sunday evening they heard Jay Kinkaid had gone to Sugar Hill to gamble and *almost* got himself killed when he cheated while playing cards.

On Monday, Elizabeth's Aunt Violet and her husband Joe arrived in town. The following weekend, Elizabeth and Ernestine invited Natalie to their home to meet them. Leaving Makela with Odessa and Koko, Natalie went alone. When she arrived at Elizabeth's house, Tamara was already there.

"This is my friend, Nat," Elizabeth said. "Nat, Tam and I have been friends since we were children."

"They had another friend," Bessie Mae Wanker said, "but she died."

"For heaven sakes, Mama, don't start on that," Ernestine said.

"Well, I got a feeling she would be alive if Sadie had sent for me," Bessie Mae said. "I still can't believe Sadie brought a butcher into her house. I never got over what happened to Georgia Mae."

"Neither have we," Tam interjected.

"Please, Mama," Violet said. "We want to have a good time. So let's talk about something pleasant."

"Oh, all right," Bessie Mae sighed.

"Please do because talking about Georgia Mae makes us cry," Elizabeth remarked.

"We understand," Violet said.

"Well, first I'd like to introduce myself," Violet laughed. "I'm Vi. And he is Joe." Violet pointed to her husband.

Violet was a good-looking, dark skinned woman. Her teeth were pretty and white. Her short hair was curled and swooped to the side. She had large breasts, big hips and muscular legs. She wore big, gold, hoop earrings in her ears and a wide, yellow, gold wedding band on her finger. Her painted fingernails were short and neat.

"You can call me 'Aunt Vi' and him 'Uncle Joe,'" Violet said. Everyone laughed. Natalie liked her instantly.

Uncle Joe was a short, chubby man with smooth, dark brown skin. He wore his hair close cropped. His brows were thick. His teeth were unusually small compared to most folk. He was friendly and quite talkative.

Ernestine and Elizabeth prepared a nice meal which Natalie and Tamara raved about. They later listened as Aunt Vi and Uncle Joe talked.

"Did you tell Nat and Tam about George?" Violet directed her question at Elizabeth.

"Some of it," Elizabeth said.

"Liz had some nasty knocks, you know. That's the reason she's so suspicious of men. Can't say I blame her either. Not after what she went through with mellow-yellow George. That's what we called him. He was one of them high yellows and as mellow as an over-ripe peach," Violet said looking at Joe. "Why don't you tell them about George, Joe?"

"Now, look'a here, Vi. You know how I feel about that lowlife. I get mad just thinking about him. Hell, I'd still like to ring his neck."

"We thought George was the perfect young man for Liz," Violet shook her head. "Right, Joe?"

"We sure did. You got some brandy, Ernestine?" he asked.

"Sure do." Ernestine got up and got the bottle from the shelf. "Here you go," she said setting the bottle on the table along with several glasses. When everyone took a glass, including her mother, Bessie Mae Wanker, Ernestine poured herself a drink, too.

"I still remember our first meeting," Joe said after the sip of brandy eased its way down. "George was so nice. I was sure he was the one for Liz. I told her so, too. Yes, siree! George was as smooth as silk." Then he looked over at Elizabeth.

"I'll never forget that engagement ring. After George ran off, I told Liz all she had to do was sell it, and she'd be ahead of the game."

"So we thought," Violet said. "But several days later, I took it for an appraisal. When the jeweler said the ring was a fake, I felt so mad I wanted to jump the jeweler. But, I decided that was a dumb idea. So I came home to give Liz the bad news. I was surprised when she took the news so calmly.

"Anyway, to make a long story short, I put the ring on the dresser. But it didn't stay there too long because Joe came home and took care of it. Tell them what you did with the ring, Joe."

"Please do. I'm dying to know," Tamara said.

"So am I," said Ernestine.

"Me, too," voiced Bessie Mae Wanker while Natalie waited quietly.

"Are you sure you want to know?"

"Of course, we do," Ernestine said.

"Well, I flushed it," he laughed never taking his eyes from Natalie's face. "I actually threw it in the toilet, did my business, and flushed it down."

"Good Lord. You didn't," Natalie gasped as she stared at him.

"You better believe I did." He threw his hands in the air. "Now no need to tell me how awful I am, Ernestine. Like I told Vi, I'm not the awful one. George is."

"He's right about that," Violet chimed.

"Even I agree with that one, Joe," Bessie Mae Wanker said.

"Too bad you didn't flush George down the toilet, too." Ernestine said. "I can't understand what possessed him to treat our Liz that way."

"I can't either. I said it then. And I say it now. The no good son-of-a-bitch probably asked to be shipped out to keep me from pulverizing him," Joe said. "I hope you ladies will excuse my language. But I'd still like to ram my fist down that lowlife's throat and put my foot up his ass." Joe's lips curled into a smile. "Of course, if ever I see him again, I might do more than that."

"Darn!" Natalie said feeling no pain as the brandy totally relaxed her. "What more would you want to do?"

"I'd like to crack his nuts." Joe looked serious and expressed himself demonstratively by placing one hand in the other and cracking his knuckles. While Natalie looked incredulous everyone else howled with laughter.

"Now, stop that, Joe," Violet said when she was able to speak again. "You're scaring Nat."

"Sorry, Nat!"

"No, no. It's all right," Natalie said thinking Joe talked a lot like Shel when it came to cracking nuts.

Joe studied Natalie's face briefly and thought she was gonna jump out of her chair and run. But when she didn't, he continued.

"Yes, siree. I'm gonna pulverize that mellow-yellow son-of-a-bitch like he was a hamburger patty." Joe laughed loudly as he left the room and went into the back yard.

Natalie stared after him and wondered if he was always so fierce about getting things done. She wanted to ask Elizabeth and Violet about him, but they were laughing so hard tears rolled down their cheeks.

She noticed Ernestine, Tamara, and Bessie Mae Wanker were laughing as hard as Elizabeth and Violet. Then for some crazy reason she started to laugh too, and once her laughter stopped, she realized she felt good. It was good for her soul.

"Listen, Nat. Uncle Joe's just putting you on," Elizabeth said. "He wants you to loosen up. That's all."

"Don't let him scare you," Violet told her. "But you gotta admit that would be good punishment for George." Then Violet started to laugh again.

"You once mentioned your friend Maxine. What happened to her and that other soldier she met when you met George?" Tamara asked.

"Oh, his name was John Greenhouse. He and Maxine married. They live near Monterey, California now. He's still in the military. John was the nice one."

"Oh, well. You survived, Liz. And I got a feeling good things will come your way soon," Bessie Mae Wanker said.

"I hope you're right, Grandma."

"Where's Domnic?" Tamara asked.

"He's spending the night with Brick and Goose," Ernestine said.

"Hum," Tamara mused momentarily. "Be careful, Liz. There are two good reasons to take Dominic back to San Francisco. Those boys never pick up a book. They have no idea what's going on in the world, and you don't want Dominic to grow up dumb."

"Perhaps you're right," Elizabeth said.

A few days later, Alan prepared to return to the military base, and decided to leave his car with his daddy. He took the train back to the base, and the whole family went to the station to see him off. As the train approached, he gave everyone a hug. Then he spoke directly to Koko. "I want you to be a good girl and don't give Mama any trouble."

"Okay, Daddy," Koko said making use of the word for the first time.

"I'll be seeing you soon, Paige," he said. He held her close and promised to write often.

The train stopped, and he climbed aboard. As the train pulled out of the station, he stood in the doorway and waved.

The very next day, when Shelton told his parents Natalie was coming home, Thaddeus gave him the car keys, and Shelton gave Thaddeus the horse.

Shelton promised to change, and Natalie promised to give him another chance. Natalie glowed with happiness, but Makela felt otherwise. She feared her daddy because she still remembered.

The day it happened, Makela was sitting on the sofa with a storybook in her hands. When her daddy came into the room and stood near her, she looked up. He smiled at her. He was wearing a gray suit, a pink shirt her mother made, and gray suede shoes. He was what her mother called, *picture perfect.*

She loved her daddy, but at times he frightened her. When he continued to smile at her, Makela jumped from the sofa, rushed to him, and wrapped her arms around his legs. She wanted a hug. It was the biggest mistake of her brief life.

'Goddammit! Makela,' he yelled. 'Now look what you did. You stepped on my shoes.' At the same time he raised his hand, slapped her face, and she fell to the floor.

As she lay crying, he bent down. He said he was sorry, but when he tried to touch her, she moved out of his reach. She stayed in the corner until he left the room, and only when her mother came to see about her did she feel safe. If she lived to be a hundred, she would never forget his gray suede shoes.

The preacher said the devil was always at work. Makela believed it was true. She was sure the devil lived in their house, and she called him *daddy*.

# CHAPTER 29

When Shelton went to get Natalie and Makela and bring them back to the farm, Koko came too.

Natalie felt good as Shelton drove up the long tree lined driveway and their pretty white house came into view.

The next morning, as she went about her routine of preparing breakfast, Natalie hummed happily. As she put jam, butter, and a pitcher of milk on the table, Makela sat quietly and watched.

Koko slept late, and Makela wanted to wait for her to eat. But as Natalie placed a plate of sage sausages on the table Makela's mouth watered. She was hungry, and she hoped Koko would soon join her. Otherwise, Makela would eat without her. But just as that thought took hold, Koko came into the room.

"Hi, Koko," Makela beamed admiringly. She loved Koko and wished they were sisters. But her mama said they were cousins and that was close enough.

"Hi, Makela. Morning, Nat," Koko said.

"Morning, dear." Natalie hovered over the stove. "Did you sleep well?" she asked as she put fried white potato patties on the plate she held.

"I sure did," Koko replied as Natalie placed the plate on the table. "And I'm really hungry."

"Hum, I suppose you are," Natalie said as she went to the stove to cook an egg for Koko. "So sit and we'll eat."

"Nat," Koko called softly causing Natalie to turn around.

"I wish you were my mama," she blurted as she pulled the chair from the table and sat down.

"Oh, honey," Natalie said, touched by the sentiment. "It's nice that you feel that way, baby, but I'm your aunt." Taking the egg over to the table, she placed the plate in front of Koko. Then she gave the little girl a hug as Makela smiled approvingly.

She took biscuits from the oven, she put several on a plate and put them on the table, too. "Now that we've solved that problem, let's eat."

"Hey," Shelton said as he came into the house causing everyone to focus attention on him. Natalie smiled but Makela tensed, and Koko simply stared. Though it was early morning, Shelton had already worked with his daddy for hours. "Is breakfast ready? I'm hungry."

"When you wash your hands, you can join us," Natalie told him.

"Well, now. Do you think I'm gonna work in horse and cow shit all morning and not wash my hands? That's a dumb thing to say," he told her as he left the room to wash his hands.

Natalie prepared Shelton's plate and sat down. Then she studied Koko for some family resemblance. She saw nothing that shouted Dawson. But that didn't matter. Alan had claimed her as his daughter. Therefore, Koko was a Dawson and her niece.

"I wish Miss Neva hadn't chased my mama," Koko said as Shelton returned to the room.

"What's she talking about?" Shelton asked.

"You know what she's talking about. So don't you say a word," Natalie said as Shelton, looking rather sheepishly, sat down.

"Who told you Neva chased your mother?" Natalie asked.

"I hate her," Koko said ignoring Natalie's question. "And when I grow up I'm gonna get her, too."

"Whoa," Shelton said. "How you gonna do that?"

"Now, you listen to me, little girl," Natalie interjected before Koko had the chance to answer Shelton. "Don't ever let me hear you talk about *getting* anyone again."

It shocked her to know this child, no bigger than a thimble, harbored such thoughts.

"Oh, come on, Nat," Shelton said. "No need to get upset. Koko is a child. She's just talking."

"Perhaps, but even so, I don't want to hear it," Natalie replied.

Koko was a plucky little girl. Even at this young age she was smart and seemed much older than her years. In fact, darkness of night never bothered her. She could easily walk outside with only the moonlight to guide her. So some folk called her *the little old lady*. Outspoken and bossy when at play, she was without a doubt in control of games and her playmates.

"But Nat, she...she," Koko protested.

"I don't want to hear it." Natalie spoke forcefully, but surprisingly her tone did nothing to deter or scare Makela and that was unusual. Especially, since Shelton sat with them.

"Hey, Koko. You gonna beat up Miss Neva?" Makela asked with wide-eyed interest while Koko motioned her head to indicate yes.

"I want to know how you gonna do so much, Koko?" Shelton grinned.

"I see nothing funny, Shel," Natalie said.

"I know you don't. That's because you're a stiff ass," he said.

"Perhaps I am. And if you keep on talking maybe you'd like to tell me more about the situation. I never asked before, but maybe you can explain it all to me."

"What are you talking about?" Shelton asked. Then staring at Natalie he saw a look in her eyes and realize she was serious. But this was not the time to talk about what he did with Lydia. He hoped the girls would never know. So he stopped talking and put food in his mouth instead.

"Are you really gonna beat her up, Koko?" Makela asked again.

"Makela!" Natalie's patience ebbed. "Don't you ever ask such horrible question again. Do you understand?"

"I'm sorry, Mama."

Makela wasn't sure if she was sorry, but she wanted to please her mother. Then she watched Koko eat an egg so undercooked she wondered if it would take wings and fly. She could never eat such eggs. She only ate them hard-boiled.

Her mother said if she tried to eat eggs like Koko did, she could. Her mama said it was all in her head, but she knew better. Once that awful smell got in her nose, it went right to her gut. Her stomach churned, and she sometimes puked.

Suddenly, the egg on Koko's plate made her feel sick. Looking down, Makela focused on her own plate and quickly devoured the savory sausages and potato patties.

Shoot! Koko had no mother because of Miss Neva. But Koko was tough and maybe one day she would go after Miss Neva. Makela just hoped when that day came, she would be there to see it. Oops, she thought, I better listen. Mama said something.

"You should be sorry, Makela." Natalie spoke more calmly than she felt. Obviously, this child had a streak as mean as Lydia. And what Koko said frightened Natalie. Now she wondered if Koko was normal.

No one really knew why Neva chased Lydia. She, like everyone else, suspected it was jealousy, but only Neva knew the truth. Surely, if Della knew everyone else would, too. Della kept no secrets. Or so everyone thought!

"Breakfast was nice," Shelton said. Rising from his chair, he stood, looking down at Natalie. He hoped she wouldn't start asking questions because he wasn't ready for it.

"I'm glad you enjoyed it," Natalie said.

"I gotta get back to work." He went over and kissed her cheek.

"Bye, Shel," Koko said.

"Bye, Daddy," Makela said.

"I'll see you girls later," he said walking out the door.

Soon the girls forgot Neva. Whispering as though they were privy to some incredible secret, they laughed gaily. When they finished eating, Natalie cleaned the kitchen and went about her chores, while Makela and Koko followed eagerly and attempted to help as much as possible.

When Natalie went in to check the brooder, the girls were in awe. There were approximately a hundred chicks there and the electric light bulb above the chicks kept the small pen at just the right temperature.

The small, furry, yellow chicks were pretty and looked like toys. Fascinated, Makela and Koko begged Natalie to let them hold one.

"They are not toys," Natalie explained. "They are baby chicks, and you can easily hurt them."

"Please, Nat," Koko said. "We won't hurt them."

"Please, Mama. Can we hold just one?" Makela begged.

"Okay," Natalie relented. "But only for a minute. First, put both hands together and cup them like this," she demonstrated with her own hands. Then gently picking up a chick, she placed one in Makela's hands and another in Koko's."

"They're so little, Nat," Koko whispered.

"Yes, they are," Natalie said as she took the chick from Koko's hand and placed it back in the brooder.

"They're so pretty, Mama," Makela said as Natalie took the chick from her hand, and put it back in the brooder, too. The two girls stared at the chicks.

Since Makela saw only baby chicks inside, she wondered if someone had caused their mama's death, like Miss Neva caused Koko's mother to die.

"Mama?" Makela blurted. "Did someone kill their mama?"

"Of course, not Makela."

"Well, where is she?"

"Yeah, Nat. Where is she?" Koko asked.

"She's around here somewhere," Natalie said.

"But where, Nat?" Koko asked.

"Listen," Natalie sighed. "Their mama isn't here. That's why I'm taking care of them."

"Oh, did she go to Chicago?" Koko asked.

"Yes, she did. She went to Chicago just like everybody else goes there. Only she's not coming back," Natalie laughed but she was already exasperated by questions, and the day had just begun. As they left the area, the girls forgot about the brooder chicks.

When Natalie milked the cow, they looked on. As Natalie pulled on the cow teats, a stream of milk went into the bucket. The task looked easy, and Makela was the first to volunteer.

"Can I do it, Mama?"

"I don't think so. It's not as easy as you think it is."

"Oh, Nat," Koko chimed. "Let me do it, please."

"That would be a waste of time." But when they insisted she, again, relented.

When they squeezed and pulled the cow's teats, but failed to produce milk, she laughed. Later, as she nursed bruised thumbs, she explained they were too young for the task. "But with time and practice, you can do it."

Fats Hopper carried precious food commodities, which he sold from the back of his truck. Pushing steadily on the horn, he hoped to alert everyone, just in case they had not seen the trail of dust.

He had driven around the community twice a week during spring and summer with his daddy since he was a boy. But these days his daddy usually kept busy at the Kitchen, and he worked alone.

The mighty Mississippi was rich with fish, and he went there twice a week. Nobody around here was real fussy and whatever he brought back they eagerly accepted.

At the sound of the horn, Natalie took the large pan from the wall hook in the kitchen. Then she and the girls went out and waited for the red truck to arrive.

"I got fish, ice, and hot tamales today," he shouted pulling the truck into the yard. "Hey Nat, how's it going?"

"Just fine, Cash. How about yourself?" she asked approaching the truck.

"Ain't complaining 'bout a thing," he smiled and swung his legs to the ground. Grunting, he struggled to push his too heavy body off the seat. "You sure you okay?" he asked.

Natalie studied him. He needed to lose quite a few pounds. She was certain he weighed closer to three hundred pounds than the two hundred odd pounds he claimed.

"Believe me, Cash, I'm okay," she answered hoping to satisfy his curiosity. She knew his concerns were sincere. He cared for her since they were children. He would kiss her feet if she gave him the chance.

She was fond of him too. But Shel stole her heart. Now, she naughtily wondered what it might be like to have a romp in the hay with a man his size. She chuckled. "What kind of fish you got?"

"It makes no difference." He laughed. Going to the back of the truck, he opened the box cover. "You know you gonna take whatever I got."

"You got that right." She gazed down into the truck bed. "Looks like catfish and perch. Give me a couple of each."

"You mean you want four of them?"

"That's exactly what I mean. I got some pretty hearty eaters here."

"You betcha. How 'bout hot tamales?"

"Okay, I'll take eight."

"And ice?"

"Fifty pounds."

"Lawdy, Nat. What you do with so much ice all the time?"

"How many times must I tell you? I make ice cream during summer."

"Oh, yeah. I forgot."

"I make an even bigger batch now that Koko is with us. She likes it as much as Makela and Shel. And you know how Makela is. Each time she tastes it, she acts like it's her first."

"Sounds like Makela's as hooked as a river fish." He gazed down at the tiny girl and wondered where she put so much of the cold treat.

"That she is. Of course, I love it too." In fact, Natalie thought, there were times when the dish was so satisfying it brought her to the brink of ecstatic pleasure. Chuckling, she wondered what he'd say if she told him just how much she liked it. Of course, she didn't dare express her feelings. After all, it wasn't something he would expect her to say. So she kept her secret.

"Seems you got yourself a regular little visitor now." He pointed to Koko.

"She's no visitor. She's family, and she's really something." What would he say, she wondered, if she told him the pint-size child had plans *to get* Neva? She decided to keep that to herself, too.

"You might not believe this, but she's a wise little girl."

"Is that a fact?" He glanced over at Koko. "Humm, I guess that's a part of Lydia in her."

"I didn't say *wild*, Cash. I said *wise*," Natalie laughed.

"Oh, got ya," he said. After a moment of silence, he asked, "Did you ever stop to think about what you're doing, Nat? I mean maybe she's..." But he couldn't say it.

"Maybe she's what?" She laughed and cocked her head to the side. She knew exactly what he wanted to ask. But it wasn't a subject for discussion with him or anyone else. Koko was Alan's child, and that was that.

"Oh, it's nothing. I'm happy for her," he said. "And there's one more thing."

"What's that?"

"She couldn't be in better hands."

"Why, Cash. That's quite a compliment."

"You're quite a lady."

"Thank you." She gave him her best and brightest smile.

"I didn't see Shel for a couple of days. Is he behaving himself? I mean is he treating you right?" He liked Shel, but there was room for improvement.

"Things couldn't be better," she told him.

Although she heard rumors about Shel and Melanie, she thought, Shel denied them. So she had no reason to complain. Not only did she love Shel, she actually liked him too for the time being.

"I'm glad." Surprisingly, Fats climbed onto the back of the truck with ease. He hooked each fish by the gill, and put them in her pan. Then he put on gloves, picked up an ice pick, and chipped at the big block of ice until it split. He grabbed it with the steel tongs then stepped down to the ground. Lifting the ice, he carried it onto the back porch where he put it inside the small icebox.

He turned and saw the girls playing under the pear tree. But Natalie was beside him, and he took the liberty of letting her know one more time how he felt. Drinking in her beauty, he said, "You know you should've been my wife."

"Perhaps," she said looking into his gentle face as both laughed loudly. "But I think you've found your mate."

"What you mean by that?" he laughed.

"Zenna. I hear she's quite pretty, and you think a lot of her. I'd like to meet her sometime."

"Okay. I'll bring her next time I come out here. Well, it's always good to see you, Nat. But I gotta get going."

"You bet. You take care now." She walked back outside with him and waited while he got back into the truck. As he slowly drove away, she waved, and burst into uncontrollable laughter as the thought of having a romp with him persisted.

Later, that evening, after she put the ice cream custard in the small hand freezer, the girls took turns rotating the handle. When the ice cream became frozen, Shelton finished the job.

While he went into the yard to start a smolder to keep the mosquitoes at bay, she helped the girls get their baths. Then she dusted their small bodies liberally with talcum powder.

They sat on the front porch, and she served them the yummy treat. Within moments of tasting it, both girls asked for more.

Natalie sat beside Shelton. Sniffing the night air, she smelled jasmine and other scents too numerous to name as she too savored what she thought was the most delicious ice cream she ever made.

When they could hold no more, the girls went into the moonlit yard, explored the star-filled sky, and marveled at what they saw.

"Look, Makela. There's a falling star," Koko shrieked relishing her discovery.

"I see it. I see it. Look, I found the Big Dipper!" Makela yelled just as Koko pointed to the man in the moon. Then they gazed silently at the billions of stars and wondered if God was among them.

Soon they tired of their adventure and returned to the porch. They then attempted to count the innumerable fireflies that flashed in the night like stars in the sky. However, finding it an impossible task, they sat quietly and listened to the night noises until their eyelids grew heavy.

"Okay girls. It's time to call it a day," Natalie announced. Then she ushered them into the house where they climbed into bed.

The very next week when Fats took a run into the countryside, he took Zenna with him.

As soon as Natalie heard his horn, she went to the front porch. She realized immediately he was not alone. Both he and the young lady got out of the truck, and he introduced her.

"Hey, Nat. I want you to meet Zenna."

"Hi, Zenna. I've heard things about you," Nat said as she left the porch and came into the yard.

"You have?"

"Yes, I have, and they're all good."

"I like your house, and the tree-lined driveway is lovely," Zenna said.

"Thank you. I like it, too. Would you like to come in for a glass of lemonade?"

"No thanks," Zenna said.

"We appreciate the offer, Nat, but we got work to do," Fats told her. "I got all kinds of stuff today. So what would you like? By the way, I'm gonna marry Zenna."

"Good for you. I guess congratulations are in order."

# CHAPTER 30

On a tranquil Sunday afternoon, Natalie sat quietly in the swing on the porch with family and her friend Elizabeth in the stifling heat, and hoped the rains would soon come.

They had eaten some time ago, but the piquant aroma of the meal still lingered. The air was permeated with a mixture of cigar smoke and wine, which her daddy, Marcus, and her uncle, Percy drank liberally.

Natalie tried hard to think of things other than the heat. So she focused on the plants in the yard, which provided a kaleidoscope of color and fragrances in spring and summer. The trees her mother planted years before now circled the property and helped keep the house cool most days. However, today the heat was overwhelming.

The magnolia tree still stood majestically in the front yard. But it was the scent of the honeysuckle vine that gingerly scaled the wall, some jasmine, and the glass of wine she consumed earlier that made her heady. She longed for Shelton, but he was elsewhere.

Elizabeth looked at Natalie and from the look on her face, Natalie was in love with that no good Shelton, and it broke Elizabeth's heart. "I think you need to get away for a while, Nat."

"I'll think about it," Natalie said.

Suddenly, the children who were playing games in the yard, raised their voices.

Feeling somewhat faint, Natalie left the swing, went to the living room, and peeked inside. It was opened only on weekends and for special occasions. She stepped inside and glanced about.

Shear, frilly, white curtains hung at the windows. The burgundy sofa and chairs were beautiful and looked inviting, but looks deceived. In actuality, the furniture was as hard as rocks. Even so, she sat in the middle of the sofa. Her little cousins, Queenie and Sophia, came into the room and started a minor dispute.

"This is the same furniture Aunt Odessa had when Nat was a little girl," Sophia declared as she sat on one side of Natalie and Queenie sat on the other.

"That's not so, Sophia. Is it, Nat?" Queenie asked.

"Of course not, Queenie. Mama bought this set only a short time ago."

"See. I told you so, Sophia." Queenie smiled triumphantly, but Sophia was not ready to let her off the hook and found some other subject to dispute.

"Stop that bickering," Helene yelled.

"I think they're discussing, rather than bickering, auntie," Natalie told Helene. While the girls debated some other trivial matter, Natalie studied the tapestry that covered one wall and a picture that hung on the other.

Looking down, she ran her fingers over the dainty, white, crocheted doilies on the arms of the chairs and sofa. These were things her mother made. Yellow stained and cracked photos of dead relatives stood on the end tables. Studying the memorabilia made her feel lonely.

In one corner of the room was an old gramophone, which was cranked up and played only on request. It was a piece of history that she speculated her mother planned to keep forever and pass it on. The records were very old. When played, the singers' voices trembled. Smiling, she thought of Makela who once asked if the people were singing underneath water.

Soon her buttocks grew tired of the unforgiving sofa. Standing up, she rubbed her hips. When Queenie and Sophia stood up and did the same, she laughed. She returned to the swing and sat beside Elizabeth.

"Are you feeling okay, Nat?" Elizabeth looked concerned.

"No need to worry. I'm okay."

As Queenie and Sophia rushed from the porch into the yard to join several other youngsters who were playing games with Makela and Koko, Tamara came through the gate.

"Hey, Tam. Come on in here," Odessa said.

"What's up, young lady?" Percy asked.

"It's hot as hades is about all I can say."

"It sure is," Elizabeth said.

"You want something to eat, Tam?" Odessa asked.

"No thanks. Can't eat too much in this heat."

"Want a glass of wine?" Odessa asked.

"No thanks, Mrs. Dawson. Too hot for that too, but I will take a cold lemonade." Tamara walked over to the small table and filled a glass. "How's life treating you, Helene?"

"I got a good husband, the store is doing great, and I got a loving family. I can't ask for more."

"Guess you're right about that," Tamara said. Turning and walking over to the swing, she sat beside Natalie and Elizabeth, as the children began to chant.

"Opossum in the persimmon tree,

Rabbit on the ground,

Rabbit told that dirty scoundrel,

You better shake them persimmons down," they chanted.

Then Koko yelled. "No, no. Don't do it that way."

"I don't care what's going on. Koko's the loudest kid in the group. And she's always giving orders," Marcus said.

"That's our Koko," Odessa agreed.

"Even so, they should have their heads in books, Nat," Marcus said irritably.

"For heaven sakes, Daddy," Natalie retorted testily. "They're just children. They need some play time."

"She's right, Marcus." Helene chimed in agreement.

"Games are a waste of time," he said. "They need a good education. And the sooner they get it, the better. I still believe in it."

"I know you do, Daddy. Even though Alan didn't become a doctor he's doing something he likes. Military life seems to suit him."

"You're right about that," Odessa said. Natalie respected her daddy, but there were times he was fanatical and got on her nerves. He read any printed material within his reach. And had difficulty understanding why others were not as passionate about it as he was.

"You of all people should know I'll see that the girls spend time with their books," Natalie assured.

She understood he wanted the best for the children, and it wasn't just family either. He often tested youngsters' knowledge, and he was often surprised when they proved more knowledgeable than he imagined they were. But others disappointed when they were unable to give him specifics about the area in which they lived. They were the ones he sent to her for help.

❦ ❦ ❦

Two individuals were entwined on the bed. The room was hot. Though the window near the bed was open, it did little to relieve their overheated bodies. But they were so engrossed the weather bothered neither of them.

"Do you really love me, Shel?" Melanie asked.

"Of course, I do baby," he said pulling her close as she melted in his arms.

When his hand brushed lightly against her breast, she gasped and pressed closer to him. His warm breath caressed her ear briefly before he kissed her face and neck.

Then bringing his head up slowly, he repositioned himself downward and took her nipple into his mouth. He caressed one, then the other, while his fingers expertly manipulated that sacred spot between her legs.

Raising his head, he kissed her eyes then rammed his tongue deep into her mouth. Hovering over her, he spread her legs with his knee, but did not enter her. Instead, he teased her with his rock hard prick. She moaned and urged him on, but he pulled back making her want him more.

When she could stand it no longer, she reached down, and took his throbbing cock in her hand. Shivering with desire she guided him into her.

Now it was just the two of them. He was hers completely, and she planned to keep it that way.

Though he was unable to see the love in her eyes or the passion on her face, Shelton knew it was there. As he thrust deep and pumped into her hot wetness, Melanie moved rhythmically, matching his every move as her moans grew louder with each stroke.

"Is it good?" he whispered breathlessly, nestling his face deep into her neck.

"Oh, yes," she answered hoping the exquisite moment would last forever.

"Is it good?" he asked again.

"Yes, yes, yes," she said assuring him that this particular performance surpassed any other. Feeling in total control, he smiled confidently. Then as they started to twitch and bounce about frenetically, Melanie's moans grew even louder. Grabbing the corner of the sheet, he stuffed it into her mouth to muffle the scream which could be loud enough to wake the dead.

As they lay panting like two spent racehorses, Melanie felt deliriously happy and held him tightly for some time before he rolled over onto his back.

"When are we gettin' *married*, Shel?" she asked.

"Well, now, honey. Let's not rush things. You know I love you, but I'm already married. Of course, you never know what's in the future.

"By the way, don't ever tell anybody about us. It could cause me a lot of problems. I don't like problems. Do you understand me, Melanie? Now you just hang in there," he said and kissed her briefly. Melanie smiled, thinking she could hardly wait until he divorced Natalie and married her.

🍁   🍁   🍁

Dark, ominous clouds gathered overhead, and Natalie once again sniffed the air. A breeze caressed her body, and she was relieved that rain would soon come.

"Hey, you tykes," Marcus called out. "The rain's coming soon." The youngsters seemed oblivious to the weather and drew themselves into a circle.

While her sister, Bonnie, had meat on her bones, Birdie was skinny as a rail. Holding a handkerchief in hand Birdie was ready to play. As the wind increased, Marcus wondered if the breeze wouldn't blow Birdie away. The two girls intrigued everybody, and every child in town loved them. Few understood anything they said including their parents. After agonizing over the problem for some time, they gave up, and learned to live with it.

He continued watching as they launched into still another silly game. As Birdie chanted, the others chimed in. Otherwise, no one would understand what she said.

"I lost my hanky yesterday, I found it again today. I filled it full of butter milk,

"I b'lieve I'll throw it away, away,

"Milk in the pitcher, butter in the bowl,

"Can't find my sweetheart, to save my soul," they chanted.

"Are those girls still tongue-tied?" Tamara asked.

"If that's what you call it, I guess so. It's still difficult to understand them. I wish I could help them in some way. But I don't have the answers," Natalie replied.

As the chants grew louder, Natalie watched the youngsters plead for Birdie to drop the hanky. But Birdie ignored them and skipped around the group once more before dropping it behind Rabbit. Rabbit quickly picked it up and began to skip and chant as Birdie stepped into his vacated spot.

"I swear," Elizabeth said. "That boy, Rabbit, should've been a girl. Don't you think so, Nat?"

"The answer to that one is yes," Percy said before Natalie could respond. "He's as giddy as they are about those games."

Percy laughed as the young boy dropped the hanky at Makela's heels who held it and skipped around the circle teasing her playmates as long as she could without a fight.

Finally, she dropped the coveted cloth behind Koko. As it glided to the ground Koko shrieked excitedly. Picking it up, she too skipped and chanted.

"Looking at those tykes brings back so many memories. You girls played the same games." Odessa felt misty.

"I know, Mama. And they're having such a good time," Natalie said as Shelton came into the yard.

Leaving the swing, Natalie went to the door and waited. He greeted everybody and kissed her cheek. Taking his hand in hers she led him over to the swing.

"Hey, Tam, Liz," he said, cheerfully.

"Hey, Shel," Tamara and Elizabeth spoke in unison as they gave one another the eye because both suspected he was cheating on Natalie again.

"Hey, you tykes," Marcus called out again. "The rain's coming. It's time to come inside.

The girls came onto the porch, and their playmates went home.

"I'd better go, too," Tamara said. "No need to wait for the rain to start. "I'll see you later."

"You bet," Natalie said.

"That goes for me too," Elizabeth said. "I gotta find Dominic."

"Oh, nothing to worry about," Marcus assured. "He's out there somewhere with Brick and Goose." Marcus looked at Natalie. As she grimaced, he and Percy laughed.

"I hope you're right," Elizabeth replied. "Wait for me, Tam."

While Koko and Sophia quarreled over the old rocking chair, Makela went to the bathroom. As she entered the small room, she remembered something her Gramma Odessa once told her.

As a child, her Gramma used a dark and dank outhouse. The only light came through small cracks in the wall. It was horrible. The stench was awful. Flies and insects swarmed about her. Her stomach often hurt because she was so afraid of being bitten by things she couldn't see. She was often unable to relieve herself.

"What kind of *things* Gramma? You mean spiders and snakes?" she had asked.

"Yes, baby. I was afraid of anything and everything that crawled," her Gramma replied. Thinking about her Gramma's suffering saddened Makela. Even though she sat on an inside toilet, she suddenly looked around for crawly creepers. Satisfied there were none, she relaxed and expelled her little guts.

# CHAPTER 31

After leaving the Dawson's home, Elizabeth walked up the street with Tamara. Then they went their separate ways. Tamara went home, and Elizabeth went to the canal and got Dominic.

"Can I stay a little longer, Mama?" he asked.

"No, you can't. A storm is coming, and it's dangerous to stand under trees when lightning strikes. I've explained that before."

"Oh, all right. I'll see you guys later," he told his friends, Brick and Goose.

Not long after they reached home, the storm arrived with fury. Rain fell in sheets and thunder rolled. Lightning crackled noisily and flashed beautifully across the horizon. However, it was a beauty few appreciated, and Elizabeth knew such a display often brought death and destruction.

When such storms arrived, it was customary for everyone to turn off the radio, go to bed, or find some corner and hope to keep safe until it ended.

While the wind roared like a lion in the night, everyone in the house either sat quietly or took a nap. Elizabeth lay quietly on her bed and thought about her life, past and present.

She loved Meadowsbrook, her family and friends, and she hated the thought of parting with them again. But she aspired to more than Meadowsbrook offered.

Though men asked her out, she had no interest. Her interest was her son. She simply wanted to raise him without conflict, so he would grow into a good wholesome man, with a promising future. There was nothing promising in Meadowsbrook.

Her thoughts turned to Natalie and she felt sad that Natalie's marriage had turned into a fiasco. Yet, Natalie refused to give up and continued to try to make it work.

Tamara said she was thinking of leaving Meadowsbrook, and Elizabeth wondered if it wasn't time for Natalie to leave, too. She would talk to Natalie about it later.

As the wind rattled windows, she recalled her first meeting with Vince after she came back to Meadowsbrook, and emotions stirred within her.

❦ ❦ ❦

She was dancing with Fats that night at her homecoming celebration, when she saw Vince come through the door. When they were close to him, he spoke and the sound of his voice took her back years. He and Fats spoke briefly. Then Fats walked away.

"Hey, Lizzy," he said.

"Hey, Vince."

"It's been a long time," he said. "How you doing?"

"I'm okay," she said thinking he was just as handsome as the last time she saw him. However, she noticed a few strands of gray hair mixed in with the black. His eyes were still a pretty green, but several crows feet were at the corner of his eyes.

"It's good to see you, Lizzy. And you look good, too," he said.

"So do you. And you haven't changed much either."

"Is that good or bad?" he chuckled.

"It's good," she replied.

"Thanks, Lizzy. Listen, when can I see you? I'd like to talk with you."

"Tomorrow is good," she told him.

The next day, Vince stopped by Elizabeth's house. "Come on in," she said when he knocked on the door then walked in as easily as if it were his own home.

"How are you, Lizzy?"

"I'm just fine. Would you like to sit a while?" she asked.

"Don't mind if I do." He sat in the arm chair near the door, and she sat across from him on the sofa.

"I'm glad you came back. Maybe we can pick up where we left off."

"Please. Don't start that now."

"Why not? I want to get acquainted with the boy. And at the same time we can get to know one another again."

"But if you were that interested in us it seems you would've done something long ago."

"That's not true, Lizzy."

"That's got to be it, Vince. You married, didn't you? And the only reason you're not married now is because your wife died."

"What can I say?" He shrugged his shoulders.

"Nothing," she spoke softly. "We know how it is. You live in your world and I in mine."

"So what? We still got Dominic to think about. Maybe we could be…"

"We can't do a damn thing more than what we're already doing. You go your way and I go mine."

"Hold on now, Lizzy. There's no need to get all riled up about this. We were both young and these things happen. I think we should at least try to be on good terms since I'm Domnic's daddy. Whatta you say?"

"I say when I first left here, I thought of nothing but you. You were on my mind day in and day out. I say I loved you so much I couldn't see straight, and it took years to get over you. And all I got from you was a check in the mail. You didn't even say you cared or anything else."

"Well, I said I'd take care of the boy. I did that. You never had to worry, did you?"

"No, I had no money worries, but I was young and I guess I expected more. Then you didn't even tell me when you got married. Nat told me."

"I'm sorry, Lizzy. But what was I to do? Back then things were a son-of-a-bitch and they still are. I knew I should've stayed away from you, but I loved you so much just looking at you drove me crazy." Vince shook his head and smiled. "Do you ever think about the time we had back then, Lizzy?"

"How can I forget?" she whispered. "It was a special time, and it's tucked away in a corner of my heart forever."

"I have a place in my heart for you, too. It's something no one can ever take from me, Lizzy."

"I'm glad to hear that."

"If you remember, I always told you I'd do anything for you. I still feel that way. I haven't changed. You have. But I understand that. I should have taken you away from here then, but I was too goddamn set in my ways. In fact, I should have followed you. I know it's too late for this kind of talk now, but I should have married you, Lizzy. But it was such taboo."

"It still is, Vince," Elizabeth said walking over to him. She leaned down and kissed his lips lightly.

Instantly, he stood up, took her in his arms, and kissed her warmly. Looking at each other, both realized they would always be bonded because of Dominic, but they had no future together. He had his life, and she had hers. He was simply Vince the meat man. He was no more to her than her son's daddy, and the sadness she felt for what they once shared and lost was more painful than anything she ever knew.

"I still care for you, Lizzy. There's no need for us to live like strangers. I'd like to see you again."

"I don't know, Vince. Let me think about it," she said deciding to use caution before treading too far into his territory again.

🍁 🍁 🍁

On Sunday, before the storm, the Pearson brothers had been invited to perform at a church several miles from town. The roads were rutty and water puddles from the last rainfall still stood in trenches. Afraid such conditions might wreak havoc on their car, they rode horses instead.

At the church, they sang beautifully. The heartfelt songs stirred emotions in some folk, emotions which they never knew they possessed.

Women shouted, dresses rose above their knees, eyeglasses and hats fell to the floor, and men of the congregation praised the brothers loudly.

The clouds grew darker, and after services, several members offered the brothers shelter from the approaching storm. They declined all offers, and mounting their horses, they rode towards home.

The morning after the storm folk found the wind had uprooted trees, ripped off rooftops, shattered windows, and completely obliterated the house where Georgia Mae once lived. But the Pastures no longer lived there because Deacon and other family members returned days before the storm and took Sadie and Caleb north. The house was empty.

By noon the next day folk learned the brothers had not come home, and everyone in town searched for them. Several hours later, they found them holed up in an old shack for shelter.

They were only several miles from town, but it was obvious lightning had struck quite close. All three were dazed, and their horses were dead.

Everyone was saddened to hear such news, but Doc Peterson assured them the brothers would live.

❦   ❦   ❦

It was a hot afternoon and just about every boy in town was already frolicking in the cool canal water. When Brick, Goose, and Melanie arrived, they sat near the water's edge under the drooping willow and watched others enjoying the water. But they were there only minutes before the boys in the water began taunting Brick and Goose.

"Hey! When you jackasses gonna jump in?" shouted one boy as he floated about.

"You know they can't swim," Melanie said. "So just leave 'em alone?"

"Whatta you mean they can't swim? They can do everything else," the boy sneered.

"If they don't try it, they ain't gonna ever learn," another shouted.

"Admit it, Brick. You got no balls," yelled still another boy evoking laughter from those within earshot.

Neither he nor his brother Goose could swim. That was the reason they sat with their cousin Melanie, instead of jumping into the water. But the teasing raised the hairs on Brick's neck.

Tiring of the taunts, he decided the only way to stop them was to get into the water. Standing, he pulled off his pants and Goose, following his lead, did the same.

"Don't be stupid, Brick," Melanie pleaded. "You'll drown out there."

He knew Melanie was scared. So was he, but he couldn't let anyone know.

"Hey, Mel," he said. "If we don't jump into the water, they'll never stop the razz. We gotta do it."

Fats Hopper stood at his truck talking with Shelton Lamont while the two little girls, Koko and Makela, stood nearby. When he saw Brick and Goose start towards the water he shouted. "Hey boys, you sure you know what you doing?"

"No, they can't swim," Melanie screamed as Brick and Goose jumped into the water.

Within seconds Brick was struggling to stay afloat. He tried to call for help, but water filled his nose and mouth. Throwing his arms wildly, he thrashed about, but the boys kept on laughing.

"Hey, Brick. Wake up. Wake up." He opened his eyes. Goose stood over him trying to hold his flaying arms. Relieved it was just another bad dream and he was home in bed, Brick breathed deeply and stretched like a purring kitten.

❦ ❦ ❦

Marcus admired Natalie's work so much, he renovated the little barbershop and gave the space to her as a dress shop. She was elated, and spent much of her time there sewing when not on the farm or in the classroom.

She had quite a clientele, and they weren't all women. Some were men who were reluctant in the past, but came to her now because they wanted to wear shirts or trousers like those Shelton wore. She even took some finished items to Helene's store and hung them in the window to be sold.

As Natalie walked the short distance from the big house to the shop, Makela and Koko followed on her heels. Looking up, she saw the two Joyride boys amble towards them.

Two lost souls, she thought, because there was no structure in their lives. They knew nothing of discipline, and she wondered if Jenny and Spuds Joyride gave them any serious attention. The boys seldom attended school. When they did, they showed little interest in their schoolwork, but they did cause disturbances.

In fact, they caused so much unrest, Delano Phillips asked them not to return unless they became serious about school.

Though Dominic spent time with the boys, he studied and completed his homework assignments. But if he stayed in Meadowsbrook, Natalie wondered what the future held for him.

Suddenly, she looked down at Makela and Koko and pondered their futures, too. Since the storm, there was lots of work to do, but the two boys showed no interest. They were very close and you never saw one without the other. Because of their strong bond, both had almost drowned together earlier in the year.

Rumor was other boys teased them, and they foolishly jumped into the canal to prove their manhood. Almost too late, they found themselves in more trouble than they could handle. Lucky for them, Natalie thought. Shel and Cash jumped in the water and rescued them.

"Daddy talked to a pretty girl, Mama," Makela told her later. Shelton had taken her and Koko with him to the popular spot that day.

"It was Melanie, Nat. He kissed her too," Koko blabbed as Shelton explained the kiss was simply Melanie's way to thank him for saving the boys.

Of course, she worried there was more to it. Melanie was very pretty and much to her chagrin, Shelton had a hard time passing a pretty woman without dropping his pants. She hoped that had not happened.

"How you doing, Miz Lamont?" The boys spoke in unison treating her with respect they seldom showed others.

"Morning, Wesley. Morning Sebastian," she said.

"Hi, Brick. Hi, Goose," Makela and Koko yelled. Nat cringed. The girls chuckled at her visible annoyance. As she opened the shop door, the boys sauntered up the street.

🍁 🍁 🍁

It was Della's day off. She was sitting on the porch with Carrie and her dog Lockjaw, when she looked up and saw Brick and Goose coming up the street.

"Lawdy, here comes the worst boys in town. I guess you heard. They stole a boy's bike, broke it, and left it on the roadside," she explained to Carrie.

"Now how do you know that?" Carrie asked.

"Because the boy beat the hell out of them, and they confessed. Somebody should've drowned them two when they were born."

"Jesus! That's an awful thing to say, Della."

"It might be, but that's how I feel."

"Well, they ain't exactly cats, you know," Carrie said. "They're boys."

"I know that. But it's just a little past noon. There's lots of work to do around here, and they could make a few dollars. Instead of working, they would rather walk the street," Della explained.

"I know. They might be better off with their daddy, Slick," Carrie said.

"Hey, boys. How come you ain't working?" Della yelled, ignoring Carrie and turning her attention to Brick and Goose who were rocking and humping their way closer to the house.

"Cause we don't wanna," Goose shouted.

"What you mean you don't wanna? Don't you know you can't be empty-headed moochers the rest of your life? Don't you know you gotta work to live? What is it you boys want out of life anyhow?"

As usual, it was obvious to the boys Della wanted to get nosy. So Brick decided they should stop.

"You can bet it ain't you," Brick bellowed as Goose joined him in laughter.

"Why, you little water brain rascal. Just you keep it up and you'll get yours." Della slowly patted Lockjaw's head.

"Yeah, we know. But we won't get it from you 'cause you ain't got nothing we want." Goose stuck his thumb on the tip of his nose and gestured obscenely.

"Say what you want, but Jenny oughtta put your asses out in the field. Let you find out what real hard work is like," she said.

"Yeah? Well we ain't working in the fields in the hot sun," Brick shouted.

"Hard work might make men outta ya," Della said.

"We already men," Brick yelled. "And you can just kiss me where the sun don't shine." Brick turned his backside in her direction and shook his hips.

"Why, you little jelly brain bugger. You just better mind your manners. Otherwise, somebody's gonna *kick* you where the sun don't shine." Della yelled.

"That's for sure," Carrie agreed. "Somebody will box their ears or put a boot in their black asses."

"I'd like to see my dog chew the pants off their unruly asses," Della laughed.

"Oh, come on, Della. You don't really mean that do you?"

"Hell, yes. I mean it."

"But the dog might hurt them," Carrie said.

"So what? They got no respect for anybody. I'd chase them myself if I thought I could catch them."

"Forget it, Della. They'll get theirs."

"Damn right, they will," Della said getting up and opening the screen door.

"Come on, boy," she called. The dog walked out the door and stood on the top step until she gave the command. "Go get'em, boy."

Leaping into action, Lockjaw chased the boys like they were rabbits as Della whooped with laughter. She only returned to her chair after the dog and the boys were out of sight.

"Why you never got married, Carrie?" she queried as she sat down.

"Why do you want to know?" Carrie asked wondering if Della already forgot she sent her mad dog on an errand. "Why do you ask so many questions?"

"I don't ask that many. Do I?"

"Yes, you do," Carrie said as the crazy dog ran back into the yard as fast as he ran out. He was winded. Della got up to let him onto the porch just as Melanie Joyride came up the street.

"Hey, Melanie," Della shouted. "Where you going all dolled up this time of day?"

"To church," Melanie answered pointedly.

"What church? In case you don't know it, this ain't Sunday. Anyway, if something was going on at one of them churches, I'd know."

"Just goes to show you don't know everything, Della. You just think you do," Melanie shouted, then disappeared around the corner.

"Now, you know as well as I Melanie never goes out looking like a ragamuffin. And you had no right prying into her business," Carrie said.

"Shoot! The only business she's got is monkey business. Mark my word. She's up to no good. She's got it all, but something is wrong 'cause she's never satisfied. And she thinks she's slick as boiled okra."

"I like Melanie," Carrie said.

"Well if she was doing with your husband what she's doing with Nat's husband, you wouldn't like her."

"I declare," Carrie said. "I never heard that, and you don't know if it's true. Just because you're devious, don't mean everybody in town is. You're lucky you never been backed into a corner. You'd better be careful or someone might chase you down the tracks like Neva chased Lydia. And you should be especially careful now that Neva's coming back."

"Why would someone want to do something like that to me?" Della was indignant. "I..."

"You ought to know the answer to that," Carrie interrupted.

"What did I do?" Della pondered momentarily. "Tell me, Carrie. What did I do?"

"You mean lately, don't you?" Suddenly, Carrie wondered if Della played the part, or if she really was dumb. Surely she knew people suspected she was involved in Lydia's death.

"You gonna answer my question or not?" Della asked hoping to change the subject that made her nervous.

"Which one you want answered?"

"I want to know why you never married."

"Because somebody killed the only man I ever cared about in a Saturday night brawl. Cut him everywhere but on his tongue. I never knew the reason. Seems no one else did, either.

"Some say it was about a gambling debt. Others said a woman was involved. You know how that goes. The man suspected of doing it was never punished. Some say he's up north somewhere.

"It took time for me to get over it though, and I never met anyone else. I'm glad about that. Loving someone other than self is a burden.

"I mean, who needs it? Look at Nat. I don't know what Shel's got, but she's so in love with him she's almost crazy.

"Just look what happened to poor Lydia. I got no proof. But I'm sure it all boils down to some man.

"I guarantee it wasn't about Billy either. You can go to the bank on that. No way. As a matter of fact, look at your own situation."

"What do you mean my situation?"

"I mean you're not happy. You care more for that dog, Lockjaw, than you do Warren. And you worry so much 'bout everybody else's affairs, you never stop to think about your own.

"You don't know where Warren hangs his hat half the time." She glanced sideways. Della's mouth hung open. "Shut your mouth before a fly blows your tongue."

"Well, as I live and breathe!" Della gasped.

"I hope I satisfied your curiosity."

"Lawdy, Carrie. I can't believe you."

"I know. But you wanted to know so I told you. Since I'm your friend I spoke my mind."

"Lawdy, I hope you are my friend. I guess I should mind my own business." Della spoke faintly.

"That would be best," Carrie said. But even as she spoke, she knew that it was impossible for Della to zip her lips.

# CHAPTER 32

❀

"Queenie, Sophia!" Percy Dawson called out as he walked into his house. When he got no answer, he called out for his wife, Helene. After walking into the back yard, he realized no one was home.

He supposed they were at the store or the big house. Now he wondered why he hadn't built more rooms onto his brother's house and moved his family there.

After surveying the storm damage, he made a list of things needed for repairs. In order to get materials, he had to make a trip to Baysville lumberyard, but he needed help to do it. Even though most folk were already hard at work, he got into his truck and drove to Michael's Market where he hoped to find a spare hand.

"Hey, Percy," Virgil yelled from the steps just as Percy drove up and parked. "What's up, man?"

"Not much, Virg." He got out of the truck and walked over to where Virgil stood. Seb and Candyman sat motionless as if glued to the bench.

"The storm damaged my roof, and I gotta go to Baysville and pick up a few things. I'd like to hire someone to help me, but seems everybody's tied up."

"That's not so," said Seb. "I'll help you out."

"Thanks, old…" Percy started then caught himself. Looking down at the old men, he marveled that they endured so much, but survived in spite of hardships.

"Thanks for the offer, Mr. Pardeau," he said giving the older man due respect. "I appreciate it, but the work is a little heavy for you. Don't worry, I'll find someone."

Just as he spoke, he saw Dominic approach them.

"Hey, Dominic," Percy said. "How would you like to make some money?"

"Doing what?" Dominic asked.

"My house was damaged in the storm, and I got to go to Baysville for materials. I could use someone like you to help me load the truck."

"Okay," Dominic said. "But I gotta ask my mama if I can go."

"Sure thing. You go ask her, and if she agrees, we'll leave when you get back."

"Okay, Mr. Dawson," Dominic said rushing back up the street to his grandma Ernestine's house.

At that very moment, Percy saw those two moronic terrors, Brick and Goose Joyride, striding towards them like two high-spirited horses. When one of these characters appeared, so did the other.

He imagined, like most young boys, they awoke in the morning holding onto rock hard cocks, which led them to believe they were full-grown men.

Percy felt he was an authority on just about anything and everything. He scrutinized the boys critically. Their reputation preceded them, he thought. They were only about twelve and thirteen years old, but were known as the worst boys in town. He considered them gangsters without Tommy guns. He didn't like either. It was just that pure and simple.

Had it been left to him, they both would be in jail. Of course, he had to admit there was no evidence of their committing any specific criminal act, but he was convinced they warranted punishment.

They were the reason he was so strict with his girls, Queenie and Sophia. He wanted the best for them. So he was careful about who they called friends.

After all, the proof was in the pudding. These boys were no more than riffraff. Nat and others had tried to tame them. But the boys proved they would never amount to more than what they already were. And that was two little brainless wonders.

The way he figured it, they had only one objective in life and that was to get their hard cocks off. He knew they eyed his girls. But in order to get to those girls they had to first walk over his dead body.

His girls deserved better, and he intended to see they got it. If either boy ever set foot on his property, his gun was ready. He planned to shoot them both.

They thought only of themselves. Actually, they reminded him of Shel who seemed to sometimes forget he was married and reacted to women like a church mouse to cheese in winter.

"Nat, too," he whispered to himself, "was lost in a way." He still smarted because even after he offered his advice she married Shel, but he never spoke about her situation afterwards. He often wondered what she found so appealing about the man. He was black as a berry and Nat, obviously, thought he was just as sweet.

But rumors of Shel's shenanigans were rampant. He knew Shel was a skirt chaser, and so did everyone else in town. He was sure Nat knew and had regrets, too. But she was tough as nails, and would never discuss it with family. "Especially me," he whispered.

In the meantime, Dominic returned, and Percy turned his attention to the boy.

"What did Liz say?" he asked.

"She said I could go with you. But she said I should be careful because some folk in Baysville aren't friendly."

"Don't worry, Dominic," Virgil said. "I think you'll be okay."

"Yeah," Pardeau said. "Just stick close to Percy."

"I'll do that, Mr. Pardeau."

"Hey, Brick, Goose," Dominic said happily.

"Hey, Dom," they chorused.

"What's the hurry, boys? Somebody shoot at you?" Virgil asked.

"Nope. Miz Della's dog chased us," Goose said.

"You mean Lockjaw scared the breeches off you?" Virgil grinned broadly when he saw Brick's torn pants.

"Nope, he tore 'em. He almost bit me." Brick pulled at the tear in his pants.

"What you mean he almost bit you? You bad ain't you? You should'a bit him back," Candyman snickered.

"You boys ought to be workin' anyhow." Seb Pardeau picked up his guitar and strummed lightly.

"You boys want to work?" Percy hated himself. These boys were his last choice for anything, but he desperately needed help. They were clearly the only two able bodied souls who had time on their hands.

"Why? You got somethin'?" Brick sneered.

"Now, look'a here boy," Virgil said. "No need to get antsy. You ain't jumping anybody here. You should've used all that energy on that dog back there. Now just you take it easy."

"It's all right, Virg," Percy threw up his hand in mild protest. Percy spoke confidently, but wasn't sure what to expect. Both boys were known as crafty, but he wanted neither boy to think he was a pushover.

He hoped the little bastards would jump him. Hell, he had a few tricks up his own sleeve. He would teach both a little *refinement*.

"Yeah, I got something," he answered. "I'll pay you a good wage, too. Now, do you boys want the work?" Percy folded his arms and waited.

"You need the money, boys," Virgil coaxed as Brick stepped back and whispered to Goose.

"No need for discussion. You better take yo' po' asses on and do the decent thing," Seb Pardeau advised.

"He's right, boys," Virgil interjected. Dominic is gonna help him. Of course, Dominic likes money, don't you Dom?"

"That's for sure," he answered. Dominic, who stood by all this time, was taken aback by the banter. He knew better than talk to Mr. Dawson that way. If his mother ever heard he'd done such sassy talk, she would tan his hide good. If she didn't, his grandma or great grand, Bessie Mae Wanker, would. And that wasn't something he could get ready for.

"See you later, Virg," Percy said. Feeling a little deflated by the two young boys' actions, he walked back to his truck with Dominic.

It wasn't until he opened the truck door that he realized Brick and Goose followed them. As he and Dominic climbed inside so did they.

As Percy drove along, the boys observed the flourishing fields. No one spoke a word. So they drove in silence all the way to Baysville. When they arrived, Percy instructed the boys to stay inside the truck and wait there until he called them.

Just as Percy entered the store, a little blond, white girl named Peggy McLaren who lived nearby came around the corner bouncing her ball against the wooden fence.

When the ball bounced out of reach to the other side of the fence, she stared at the ball for a while. Looking around, she hoped to find someone to help her get it back.

Noticing the parked truck on the opposite side of the road, she crossed the street and stared at the three boys.

Though she was only six years old, little Peggy was well aware of the rules. She was taught never to talk to boys who looked like Dominic, Brick or Goose. However, she wanted her ball. So she boldly walked closer to the truck and yelled, "Hey, boy! Can you get my ball?"

All the boys saw her, but none of them moved a muscle as their unblinking eyes focused on something in the distance they couldn't see. They knew so much as a glance in little Peggy's direction could mean certain death. Theirs!

"Get outta here, little girl," Goose hissed hoping she disappeared as quickly as she appeared. When she stood her ground, the three boys slid down in the seat and stayed there until Percy came back. Then she became his problem.

"Come on, boys. I'm ready to load the truck," Percy said. While he glanced at the little girl, the boys climbed from the truck.

"Hey, mister," she said. "Can you get my ball?"

Percy said nothing. As the boys walked towards the store, he considered fetching the ball. But then a red-faced man came out of the store, and stared at Peggy and them.

Suddenly, Percy knew the man didn't like what he saw. Percy imagined the sight of the boys, breathing the same air as the little girl, upset the man.

"Hey! Get back in the truck, boys." Percy spoke more calmly than he felt as the red-faced man went back inside the store.

As the three boys started back towards the truck, little Peggy continued to scream for her ball, but Percy felt she was the least of his worries. Just as the boys reached the truck, the red-faced man came back into the yard carrying a rifle.

Goose and Dominic frantically jumped into the back of the truck and lay down on their stomachs. But before Brick could join them, the red-faced man raised the gun and fired, grazing Brick's leg. Suddenly, Brick screamed.

Percy was still some distance from the truck. But at the sound of the shot, turned around, and stared at the red-faced man as he laughed uproariously. Unable to move, Percy's mouth dropped open. He felt sick to his stomach and wanted to throw up. His tongue felt thick and swollen. When he realized what was happening, he too turned. He hurried back to the truck and climbed inside. As he, nervously, turned the key in the ignition and erratically drove away with the three frightened boys, he was unable to speak. His temperature rose, his body shook, and for the first time in his life Percy knew. He knew what so many other black men knew. Even though his skin was white, his eyes were blue, and his brown hair was as straight as a pin, it made no difference to the red-faced man. Percy knew he had looked the devil in the eye, and lived to tell about it.

# CHAPTER 33

Della felt hungry. Deciding to treat herself, she went to Michael's Market to splurge. As she approached the store, she saw Candyman Cates and Seb Pardeau sitting on the bench.

"I hear Neva is back in town and staying with you," Candyman said when she was closer.

"That's right. She is."

"Seems to me, you living dangerously," Seb Pardeau said.

"Why you say that?" Della asked.

"Because some folk are mad at Neva and you, too, for what happened to Lydia," Candyman said.

"Don't tell me these folk still holding a grudge?"

"That's right," Seb Pardeau said. "And from what I hear, they plan to do something about it too. I think you oughtta be careful," Pardeau warned.

"Jesus," Della said, wondering if she made a mistake by letting Neva stay at her house. Della had gone to the store to get garlic sausage, a loaf of bread, and a soda pop, but she instantly lost her appetite and went back to the house.

The next morning Warren Gilliam, a dark brown skinned man who wore his black wavy hair cut short, sat at the breakfast table and watched as Della hand-fed her dog and talked about what happened to the three boys.

"I hear Brick got shot, but Goose, Dominic, and Percy are okay," Della said. "Percy ain't talking, but seems some red-faced man shot off his gun as if it was a cannon all because some little white girl wanted them boys to get her ball."

"What...what's that?" Warren asked.

"Lawdy, Warren. What's wrong with you? I was talking about the Baysville incident. I think it did something to Percy. Don't you?" Della bit into a piece of meat then pushed the remainder at her dog. He snatched it ferociously while staring at Warren.

"Yeah...yeah. He's...he's a little quieter now," Warren replied.

"You bet he is. His head's no longer stuck up his butt. Yes, indeed. I think he realizes even though he's sheriff in Meadowsbrook he got no authority once he leaves this town. That badge is no good in Baysville, and he's no better than anyone else around here." Della laughed.

"It's...it's no laugh...laughing matter, Della," Warren stuttered. "The whole thing's too ugly for any man to swallow. Now you...you listen to...to me," Warren said. "I got no love for Brick or Goose, and Percy's a bit uppity, but I feel sorry for all of them." Warren paused and chuckled. For the first time in his life, he spoke without stuttering. Della was so busy with her dog she never paid attention.

"There was no reason for the man to shoot off his gun. I'm sorry it happened, and I'm glad they came out alive."

Warren knew things could be worse. The red-faced man could have killed them. No one would have spoken out about it again, and that would have been the end of it. They would just be four dead niggers, but they were lucky. They lived to tell about it.

"I don't want to hear anymore about it." Warren spoke softly about the matter, but he was actually mad as hell that Della treated her dog better than she treated him. He felt mad enough to jump across the table and choke her.

Della never cooked anymore, and he was no garlic sausage sandwich man. He wanted a real meal. But she always had some excuse as to why she didn't prepare a good home cooked meal. It was either too hot or she was too tired when in fact she was really too drunk.

So, he ate most evening meals at the Kitchen with Fats, the Joint, or at Brandy's. He worked hard six days a week. Still, he came home to an empty table, an indifferent wife, and a crazy dog that took over his house. He heard the rumors. Everybody said Della had the balls in the house. But he knew better and would soon prove it.

He didn't know where the dog came from, but he arrived home one day and Della said she found it. They waited for someone to claim the dog, but when nobody did, he suspected the dog belonged to her all along.

It wasn't long before Della pledged her allegiance, not to him, but to the goddamn dog. The dog was in. He was out, he thought as he poked his food with his fork.

"What's wrong, Warren?" Della asked pleasantly. "How come you're not eating your breakfast?"

"I don't feel like eating," he said. As he watched her stroke the dog's head he got so mad he wanted to kill the damn dog.

But he did nothing now just like he did nothing when Della put the dog in the bed with them. He wanted to kill her and the dog back then, but he made a mistake. He killed neither and things just got out of control. Soon the dog dared him to get in his own bed. So he slept on the sofa while Della slept with the dog.

"Dammit!" he hissed.

"What's wrong, Warren?"

"Nothing," he muttered while thinking the shit stinks. There was only one thing to do. He had to get rid of the dog. The urge to jump Della was so strong he gripped the table edge with both hands to keep them off her throat.

He still remembered one evening when Lockjaw caught another dog in a deadly grip and thrashed the dog about like a rabbit. Then Della justly named the son-of-a-bitch *Lockjaw*, and the dog was as crazy about Della as she was about him. Now the damn dog beat him to the table every morning.

He suspected Della cooked the dog's evening meal, too. Then the two of them ate dinner before he came home, and no doubt from the same plate. When she wasn't feeding the dog, she was hugging the dog. Warren felt it was years since she hugged him.

Suddenly, he wanted to give Della a piece of his mind. But he decided she might have a right to act the way she did since he spent much of his time across the tracks at Brandy's house.

Brandy Flowers was midnight black with skin as smooth as velvet. Thanks to Ernestine Farrell and Madam Walker's products, Brandy wore her thin, fine hair in a bob, and looked good every day. Brandy was Warren's girl and treated him like a king.

He supposed Della didn't hug him 'cause he spent his time hugging Brandy. But he was a man, and like most men, he had needs. Della turned him loose a long time ago. That's the reason Brandy came into his life. Hell, it was time he made some changes. He had to make up his mind about where he wanted to hang his hat.

A horn sounded interrupting Warren's thoughts and the dog, a ready warrior, stared at the front of the house. Marcus had arrived to pick him up for work. Pushing back his chair, Warren stood up and looked down at Della and her dog.

Jeez, he wanted to jump them both. He had to watch his step and be careful because the dog was a killer. He knew damn well if he touched Della, the dog would go for his throat, and he, not the dog, would be the loser. If he choked the dog, it was a guarantee Della would kill him.

Snatching his cap from the wall peg and plopping it on his head, he said, "See you later."

"Sure thing, Warren," Della said rubbing Lockjaw's head.

As he rushed from the kitchen, he collided with Neva who was just released from Whitman.

"Morning, friend," she laughed.

"Morning, Neva," he said thinking she looked crazier now than when they put her away. Billy wanted nothing to do with her, but she and Della were still friends. Della worked for the Beetleman family in Baysville and got Neva a job there, too. Now they worked together, and he wondered how the family could stand the two of them.

Upon reaching the door he looked back, and decided the three of them plus the dog were a deadly mix.

"Shoot!" he mumbled once he walked outside. "If I don't make a move now, I'll spend the rest of my life on the sofa while that frigging dog sleeps in my bed."

"I'm gonna *kill...kill...*that fuckin' dog," he said as he got in the truck causing Marcus to roar with laughter.

# CHAPTER 34

Reverend McCord was so in love with Tamara, he found it hard to concentrate. He decided he would ask her one more time to marry him. If she turned him down, he would have to forget her and move on. But he hoped she would say yes.

If she agreed to marry him, he would give her time to adjust to his way of thinking, and would let her know she had to leave her way of life behind. There would be no more singing at the Lounge or in nightclubs. She had to conform to his way of living.

However, if she didn't, and he still wanted her to be a part of his life, he knew the congregation would give him the boot. He loved his church too much for that. Therefore, there was only one thing to do. He had to make Tamara change her mind and her ways.

When he reached Tamara's house, he sat in the car a moment. After taking a deep breath, he got out, walked calmly to Tamara's door, and knocked. When she sleepily opened the door, he found waiting impossible."

"Hey, baby," he gushed. "Will you marry me?"

She looked as sweet as a piece of candy, and he was ready to treat her as such by licking her from head to toe.

"Hmmm," she said with eyes half closed. "I guess so, since it's the only way I can stop you from coming to my house so early in the morning and disturbing my sleep."

At that moment, he grabbed her, put his arms around her waist, lifted her, and swung her around. He kissed her face. Then he put her down. As her feet touched the floor, he kissed her lips.

Taking her hand, he led her to the bedroom, took off her gown, and gently laid her on the bed. He hurriedly removed his clothes and looked down at her. Her body was beautiful and caused his mouth to water as much as delicious food on a dinner table.

He caught her by her legs and pulled her to the edge of the bed. Getting down on his knees, he put his head between Tamara's legs. As he licked her like an ice cream cone, she screamed so loudly, he was certain the fruit fell from nearby trees. The Reverend Buddy McCord felt he was the happiest man in the world.

🍁 🍁 🍁

Odessa invited Elizabeth and her family to dinner for the last time before they boarded the train. It saddened Odessa that Elizabeth was leaving, but she understood. Unlike her daughter Natalie, Elizabeth had experienced life in the city. It was another world, and she was ready to return to that world.

Though Natalie vowed never to leave Meadowsbrook, Odessa wondered just how much longer her daughter would feel that way after spending so much time with Elizabeth. Then there was Tamara who went north often and returned with stories of the big cities and bright lights. And she always brought back a book of some kind for Natalie to read.

For that reason Odessa knew in her heart Natalie would one day take off to see what the rest of the world was about.

"What will I do when Nat leaves?" Odessa whispered as she busied herself about the kitchen.

On that Sunday afternoon, the house became crowded fast. Guests lolled about the porch. As Odessa made her way through the crowd, she noticed Zenna who was usually a quiet young lady, was quite talkative today.

"How are you, Zenna?"

"Oh, I'm fine Mrs. Dawson? I'm also happy."

"Good for you. Now tell me. What's made you so happy?"

"Fats asked me to marry him."

"That's wonderful, Zenna," Odessa said. "And what did you say?"

"I said yes, of course."

"I'm happy for you, honey. I wish you well."

"Thank you, Mrs. Dawson."

Tamara was happy about the promise she made to the Reverend McCord. That is until she talked to Elizabeth and Natalie, and they broke her gleeful spell.

"What do you plan to do about the career you always wanted?" Elizabeth asked.

"That's right. You must decide whether you want that career or you want to go into the church," Natalie reminded her.

"I agree with Nat. Remember what we were taught?" Elizabeth asked.

"What's that?" Tamara asked.

"You can't serve two masters, Tam. If you marry Buddy, you got to go into the church," Elizabeth said.

"She's right, Tam. You must make certain you're ready to give it up and reform," Natalie said.

"I know you're both right. But I've tried to put it out of my mind until now. We haven't set a date for the wedding yet, and I think I know why we haven't discussed it."

"Why?" Elizabeth asked.

"I think he's hoping I'll reform."

"Do you think you can do it?" Natalie asked.

"I don't know. I really don't know." Tamara shook her head as she glanced over at Buddy who talked to several folk. As if she commanded it, Buddy looked at her and winked. Tamara's heart felt heavy.

Though the gregarious Reverend Buddy McCord held several folk spellbound, his mind was elsewhere: specifically, on Tamara. He would do something special for her, he thought. After all, she would soon be his wife.

Marcus and Percy joined several guests under the big elm in the back yard and talked about the latest events when Dominic joined them. "Well, son," Marcus said. "I hear you're leaving us?"

"Yes sir. But only because my mother thinks it's best. I really like it here," Dominic said leaning against the big tree. "I have friends here now."

"Sure you do," Percy said sarcastically. "Believe me. I think your mama's doing the right thing after what happened in Baysville."

"Yeah," Marcus said. "I got a feeling your friends won't be around here much longer either. Times are changing, and most young folk are leaving the area. Your mama wants a better life for you, son."

"I know she does," Dominic said.

"Did you talk to your daddy lately?" Percy asked.

"Yes, sir. I talked with him, my uncle, and granddad. We visit them, but mostly at night," Dominic said.

"That's for your protection, son. If some folk around here knew what that family was up to all hell might break loose. But there's one thing for sure. They're good people. Otherwise, they wouldn't give a hill of beans about you or Tam," Marcus told him.

"I understand that, sir," Dominic said. Just as he looked around, Brick and Goose ran into the yard trying to escape several aggressive geese outside the gate.

At that very moment, Sophia, who stood on the porch, saw the boys. "Hey, Brick," she yelled. "They won't hurt you."

"We know that," Goose said.

"Well, if you know that, why are you running?" Sophia laughed as the boys rolled their eyes.

"It's okay, son," Marcus told Dominic who was anxious to join Brick and Goose. "It was nice talking with you. Now go on with your friends."

As Warren Gilliam came into the yard, Marcus chuckled and elbowed Percy. "Hey, Warren, what's up?" Marcus inquired. "How's Della?"

"Nothing's happening, man. And Della's sick," he said when he wanted to tell him she was drunk. Though Neva was Della's friend, Della knew she made a mistake by allowing Neva to stay with her because some folk still wanted revenge. And that scared Della.

Warren was a good man, Marcus thought, but Della didn't treat him right. Personally, he wondered why Warren stayed with her. Of course, that wasn't something he would ever voice to anyone, when he constantly told his own family marriage was a lifetime commitment. As far as he was concerned, Della was a real dragon lady who breathed fire every time she opened her damn mouth.

Shelton, who had left earlier, returned to the big house along with Greyland and Jozell to join the festivities. As they came onto the porch, Greyland and Jozell moved on, but Shelton searched the crowd for Delano Phillips. Realizing the sickly looking son-of-a-bitch was nowhere to be seen, Shelton's disposition changed. He geared up to enjoy himself.

Shelton hoped Delano was too sick to come, or, better yet, Shelton hoped he was dead. But just as Shelton joined Natalie who stood talking with Tamara and Elizabeth, Delano came onto the porch, and Shelton wished he had spent more time with Melanie.

"We're sorry you're leaving, Liz," Jozell said. "But we understand. "Don't we, Grey?"

"We sure do," Greyland replied.

"Thanks. I've enjoyed the stay. But it's time to move on," Elizabeth replied. Then as an afterthought, she said, "Maybe you'll come to California one day. If you do, I hope you'll come to see me."

"Of course, we will. We wouldn't dare come there and not visit you," Jozell said.

"Hey, Liz," Fats said as he and Zenna approached them. "You know I'm really gonna miss you. We go way back."

"You better believe it," Elizabeth said. "By the way, I want to wish you and Zenna a long happy life together. I wish I could stay for the wedding, but I gotta get back now and get Dominic ready for school."

"I know you do. When you gonna get married, Liz?" Fats asked.

"When and if the right man ever comes my way," Elizabeth laughed.

"I'll talk with you later. I've got to help Mama and Auntie Helene." Natalie excused herself. Leaving Tamara and Elizabeth, she joined Odessa and Helene in the kitchen, and helped them prepare the tables. The two small tables on the back porch were set up. It was where the youngsters would sit and eat.

Odessa had already put the white linen cloth on the big table, and the white linen napkins lay beside each plate. Across the room near the window was a smaller table set up for four additional guests.

As Odessa dished up the food, Natalie and Helene placed each dish on the table.

Today they would dine on roasted golden brown chicken and roasted pigeon glazed with sweet wine, sugar, and blackberry sauce.

A platter of smoked beef steaks, a bowl of brown gravy, and a large bowl of green beans graced the table, along with bacon bit cornbread.

The rice was cooked with finely chopped nuts, a hint of dried apricots, and fresh celery from the garden.

The cucumber and tomato salad was garnished with chopped green onions, a bit of sugar, homemade wine, and vinegar dressing. Then Odessa placed a bowl of the spicy chowchow in the middle of the table.

They would later enjoy peach cobbler, pound cake, and Odessa's delicious handmade ice cream, all washed down with milk, lemonade, and homemade wine.

But it wasn't until Helene placed the hot yeast rolls on the table that the succulent dishes caused Natalie's mouth to water.

"Looking at this table makes me hungry, auntie," Natalie said.

"I know what you mean. I'm hungry too," Helene chuckled. "When it comes to putting a meal on the table, no one can outdo Odessa."

"Amen to that." Natalie smiled.

When Odessa called, "Come and get it," Elizabeth's grandma, Bessie Mae Wanker, was the first to arrive in the dining room.

"Gracious, Odessa. It's been a long time since I sat at your table. But you didn't change one bit. You still cooking big, delicious meals. Seems you outdid yourself today. And I can't wait to taste it."

"Why thank you, Mrs. Wanker. I'm glad you came. Have a seat."

Seated at the big table were Elizabeth, her mother Ernestine, her grandma Bessie Mae Wanker, Aunt Violet and Uncle Joe; Natalie sat across from Shelton, Tamara sat across from the Reverend McCord, Helene across from Percy, and Delano across from Warren. Odessa sat at one end of the table while Marcus sat at the other.

Paige Peterson, who Odessa still expected to marry Alan and become a part of her family, was invited. However, she had to work late, and would come later. So one chair was left vacant for her arrival.

Fats, Zenna, Greyland, and Jozell sat at the small table near the window, still close enough to converse with everyone else.

"Whatta you think about that Neva coming back here?" Bessie Mae Wanker asked. "I say she better watch her back."

"Oh, come on, Mama," Violet said. "No one wants to talk about that."

"I do," Uncle Joe said. "I don't know the woman, but I heard a lot about her. Now what I can't understand is why she chased the other girl, Lydia, onto the tracks. Did she ever tell anyone?"

"Not that I heard," Marcus said. "And it's bothered me ever since. Just doesn't make any sense to me."

"You were there, Fats," Percy said. "What happened?"

"I don't know what happened," Fats said. "Everything happened so fast. I just know Neva came home in a snit and starting shooting. I was scared so I ran. And I think about it every day. I wish I could've helped Lydia in some way. But at the time, I was thinking only of dodging a bullet."

"I don't know why she came back," Odessa said.

"I don't either," Fats said. "I just wished she stayed away. Too many folk are still pushed out of shape for what she did. But she and Della are still friends. Ain't that right, Warren?"

"That's right, Fats."

As the conversation continued, Natalie watched Shelton. He still seemed uncomfortable after all these years when someone spoke of Lydia.

"You were there weren't you, Shel?" Tamara smiled slyly.

"No, I wasn't. I was home with my family just as you were home when Tobias came up missing," Shelton retorted.

"Now, now," Helene intervened. "Let's not get ugly here."

"Please," Natalie said. "I'd like to enjoy this time with my friends.

"Yes, indeedy. Let's keep it pleasant," Odessa said. "We can do nothing to change things. So no need hashing over plowed ground at this time."

"That's right. It's all dead and stinking," Ernestine said.

"So what kind of work you do, Joe?" Marcus asked changing the subject.

"I work at the shipyard," Uncle Joe said.

"You like it?" Marcus asked.

"Like it?" Uncle Joe repeated. "Jesus, man! Show me a man who's doing something he really likes."

"I do," Marcus said. "I always wanted to build things. Even though I own farmland, I enjoy erecting buildings."

"Yeah, I hear you've built lots of homes in this area and beyond."

"That's right. I have."

"That's great," Uncle Joe said. "But everybody's not so lucky; especially, during these times. You're the only man I ever heard speak that way. But it's the money that keeps most of us going."

"It's the money that keeps me going, too. Perhaps I wouldn't love it as much if there was no money to be made," Marcus said.

"And money is what makes me love working in the store. It takes money to live, and it sure takes money to die," Helene said as she glanced briefly at Elizabeth. "We sure gonna miss you, Liz. After all, you're like family."

"I know, auntie," Elizabeth said. Although they weren't related, Elizabeth felt as close to the family as they did to her. "I'll miss you too. By the way, I love those shoes I bought from you last week."

"Good. I'm glad I got products that satisfy my customers."

"I need a new pair of shoes for winter, Helene," Bessie Mae Wanker said. "I'll be coming over there next week."

"And I'll look forward to seeing you."

"I just want to take this time to tell Tam and Nat I expect them to come visit me soon," Elizabeth said. "In fact, I want them to promise me right now. You know, just like we did when we were kids."

"I promise," Tamara laughed looking at Natalie. "Come on Nat, promise Liz."

"I promise," Natalie said meekly while staring at Shelton.

Suddenly, Bessie Mae Wanker looked down at the empty chair. "I guess that empty chair is for Georgia Mae," she said.

"Oh, for heavens sake, Mama, don't you start on that," Ernestine said.

"*Shut up*, Ernestine," Bessie Mae shouted. "You know and I know if that Sadie had sent for me instead of some butcher, Georgia Mae would be sitting right there in that chair. I was a good midwife. I would've treated that girl right. It just makes me mad after all these years that instead of giving that girl a good tea she let someone…"

"For heavens sake, Mama," Violet interrupted. "We don't want to hear it. That kind of talk gives me the chills."

"I'm sorry 'bout that Vi. But I'm just mad."

"I wish you would let it go, Mama," Ernestine said.

"Lawdy," Bessie Mae shook her head from side to side. "She was a smart girl. What a waste. I still miss that little Georgia Mae."

"So do we, Mrs. Wanker," Natalie said sadly. "I miss her every day."

"We all do," Elizabeth whispered.

"And how." Tamara spoke softly.

"The last time Georgia Mae was in my car, she told me she would never ride with me again because I drove too fast," Shelton said.

"Well, that's the truth, Shel," Elizabeth said. "You do drive too fast."

"Yeah, I miss Georgia Mae, too," Fats said. "We talked every day when she left the drugstore."

"Who is Georgia Mae?" Zenna asked. "And what was she doing at the drugstore?"

"She was our friend, and she worked at the drugstore," Fats answered. "We'll talk about it later, Zenna." Then there was silence.

The next day, Monday, Natalie and Tamara stood with family and friends as Elizabeth and Dominic boarded the train along with Aunt Vi and Uncle Joe.

"We gonna miss you," Tamara shouted as tears formed in her eyes.

"We love you, Liz," Natalie said as indescribable loneliness clutched her heart. For the second time their friend Elizabeth was leaving them.

When the train pulled from the station, they waved, and everyone stayed there until the train disappeared.

🍁 🍁 🍁

On Saturday, the following weekend, the Reverend McCord joined Fats and Zenna in Holy Matrimony. Fats had never been so happy, and Zenna was even happier.

Later, everyone went to the Lounge where Tamara, Seb Pardeau, and Candyman Cates performed.

"Now that I have a real family," Zenna said. "I'm happier than ever."

"I'm glad Zenna, because you make me happy too," Fats told her while his mother, Sissy, beamed as she approached the bar.

"Hey, Eva," Sissy said. "How you doing?"

"I'm doing just fine, Mrs. Hopper. What can I get for you, milk, tea, or lemonade?"

"Are you kidding me?" Sissy asked laughing as her husband Tex joined them. "Today is special, Eva. We want a real drink."

"Right," Tex said smiling down at Sissy. "Our son finally found someone who loves him, and he loves her just as much. Give us your best scotch. This is a day to celebrate." Sissy smiled up at Tex.

🍁 🍁 🍁

When Elizabeth reached San Francisco, she called. "Hey, Nat. Just want you to know we arrived safely."

"I'm glad," Natalie said.

"I expect to see you and Tam soon," Elizabeth chuckled.

"You bet," Natalie said as she wondered why she responded in such a positive way when she wasn't sure if she would ever leave Meadowsbrook.

"By the way," Nat said. "I wish you had stayed a few more days because they finally finished the swimming pool."

"Oh, Nat! That's wonderful. I know everyone will make use of it."

"I'm sure they will," Nat said.

"Well, I gotta go now," Elizabeth said. "I'll talk with you later."

"Okay, goodbye, Liz."

❦   ❦   ❦

"Wait, wait, Daddy. Don't go yet. You might hurt Mama," Makela pleaded excitedly as Shelton let the car roll slightly while Natalie attempted to get inside.

"Shut up, girl," he yelled as they prepared to leave their house. "Good grief, I'm not gonna hurt your mama."

"Don't scream at her, Shel." Natalie scowled as she got into the car. Her body tensed, and she sat silently as he drove like a madman down the road. She hated speed, but she dared not speak for fear she might hit a raw nerve which could spoil her day. So, she gazed across the fields and wondered if there was any truth to rumors about him and Melanie.

"What you think about the red-faced man with the gun, Nat?"

"It's not something I want to talk about, Shel."

"Well, I think your uncle knows that *tin badge* he wears means nothing except here in town. I mean he wasn't so tough he could stop that man from shooting off his gun," Shelton laughed. "He knocked ole Percy down a size or two."

"Okay, Shel. We both know uncle wasn't always the nicest person. "He…" she hesitated. Rumor was the red-faced man shot, not at Percy, but the boys. The incident worried her uncle, but he moved on.

"I know he never liked me. He thinks I'm *too black* for you."

"Obviously I love your color since I married you."

Though color differences weren't discussed openly among her people, Natalie learned early on that skin color did make a difference with many, even those in her community. Those with lighter skin and pretty hair got more attention than others.

Worse yet, she'd heard youngsters who were hardly out of diapers recite that old, ugly adage, "If you're white, you're right. If you're brown, stick around. If you're black, get back." Nat hated to hear such sickness repeated by the youngsters, and she made it a point to scold any child who dared voice it. Then she explained they should never allow the color of a man's skin to cloud their judgment. No one should ever suffer at the hands of others simply because of the color of his skin.

"So look around you before you voice such ugliness," she told them.'Though our colors vary, we're all in the same boat, and if others have their way, they will sink that boat.

"Therefore, you must love yourself regardless of your skin color, and let no one make you feel less than a man."

Of course, she knew she was often showered with unwanted attention simply because of her hair and her skin color.

She suddenly returned to the present and, disgusted with Shelton's ridicule of her uncle, spoke up in his defense.

"I want you to stop being so harsh, Shel. I've forgiven him for his narrow mindedness. Furthermore, Uncle Percy has changed. You know that."

"Damn right, he changed. That redneck with the gun let him know he was just another dirty nigger." Shelton shook with laughter.

"Oh, Shel," she said. "I hate that word."

"Okay." He glanced over at her. "You're right. It's no laughing matter."

"It's over. And it's something I try not to think about." She sighed. Frowning, she looked at Shelton, then stared out the window again.

"You know he never liked me. He never thought I was good enough for you."

"Shoot, Shel. That's a dead horse. Obviously, his opinion meant little to me. I married you, didn't I? I don't want to discuss it anymore. Uncle is a different man now."

"All right, all right." Shelton had the final word just as they arrived at the school. Jamming his foot on the brake caused the car to swerve slightly. Makela screamed, and Natalie held her breath and grimaced. When the car stopped, they both instantly jumped out of the car.

"Hey, Nat, I'll see you this evening, baby," he called as she and Makela hurried across the school yard without looking back. Shelton laughed as he put the car in gear. Then he pushed his foot to the floor. The car accelerated, and the tires squealed loudly as he drove away.

That same day, Natalie was surprised to see Brick and Goose return to school. Though Brick still carried the scar on his leg and was still sore from the shotgun wound he got from the red-faced man, both boys seemed more mature now.

In fact, they showed qualities few knew they possessed. Showing genuine interest in their schoolwork, they no longer acted insolent. Natalie suspected the terrible incident scared them so their attitude changed.

She saw a change in her uncle, too. He was quieter. The arrogance he once displayed was gone. He seemed preoccupied now. When the two boys stopped by the house to talk with his girls, Sophia and Queenie, he made no objections.

If he still considered them brainless wonders, only he knew, since he no longer openly expressed his opinion about them. He treated Shel with respect, too, and she appreciated that.

# CHAPTER 35

Della was a domestic who worked for the Beetleman family in Baysville. She went out of her way and asked them to give Neva a job, and they did. Now she and Neva worked side by side. But Neva had a problem. She guzzled more of Mr. Beetleman's booze than he did.

Things were so bad Della worried both would get fired. So Della had a talk with Neva. Neva promised she would do nothing to jeopardize their jobs. Neva was gonna straighten up and fly right. She did for a while.

But just when Della thought things were working, Neva did the unthinkable. Only the two of them were at the Beetleman home the day it happened. Neva got drunk as a skunk, climbed into Mr. Beetleman's bed and fell asleep.

"Did you lose your mind, woman?" Della screamed down into Neva's face.

"I don't shink sho," Neva slurred.

"Of course, you did," Della said. "Otherwise, you wouldn't be in Mr. Beetleman's bed."

"What you shay?" Neva squinted trying to focus her bleary eyes.

"I said you're in Mr. Beetleman's bed."

"Ya sho?" Neva asked as innocently as a child, but made no attempt to move.

"Hell, yes, I'm sure. Now get your ass outta of that bed before Mrs. Beetleman gets home and boots us both outta here."

Della pulled Neva out of the bed and helped her down the stairs. She got a pan of cold water and washed Neva's face. Then returning to the room, Della changed the linen.

"You know something, Della. Things ain't what they used to be," Neva mumbled when she later sobered up. "I don't think anybody likes me anymore and that includes Billy. I think my luck might change if I go north."

"You could be right. Maybe nobody wants you around. And as for going north, you gotta make up your own mind. I'm your friend, but I can't do that for you.

"But I got news for you, Neva. Unless you stop drinking so much, your luck ain't gonna be no better up north than it is here."

"I don't drink any more than you do," Neva said heatedly.

"That may be, but I never slept in Mr. Beetleman's bed, did I?"

That incident occurred around the same time someone tried to torch Della's house while they slept. The fire died out, but now Della was too scared to close her eyes. She spent half the night staring out into the dark waiting for what she hoped never came.

🍁 🍁 🍁

As soon as Handsome Jim reached the crowded, dimly lit bar, he saw Neva and Della. He had learned a lot since he came to town. Della kept the town abuzz about something she said or did, and her friend, Neva had chased Lydia onto the railroad tracks to her death.

He decided it was time he met Neva and Della, but before he approached the two barracudas he needed a drink.

"Hey, Zeke," he shouted. "Give me a drink, will ya?"

As soon as Zeke poured the drink, Handsome Jim grabbed the glass and quickly gulped it down. "Hit me again, and give the ladies whatever they want, too." Handsome Jim waved his hand towards Della and Neva.

Zeke, looking down the bar asked, "What ladies? You mean them two?"

"Yep. You got it right. Them two." As the rotgut burned his belly, Handsome Jim locked eyes with Neva.

Sitting at the bar, Della looked at the faces around her and wondered which one of her neighbors tried to burn down her house. Of course, Carrie warned that folk planned to avenge Lydia's death. Della never really believed it, but now she did.

"Hey, Zeke," Della said. "Give me a rum and coke." She hoped the drink would help shake off the gloom she felt hanging over her.

When Zeke placed the drink on the bar, she pushed money at him, but he waved her off. "Put it away, Della. It's paid for."

"What do you mean it's paid for? Who paid for it?" Zeke humped his shoulders and gestured with upturned palms as he busied himself with other customers. He later brought them more drinks, but refused to take their money.

"I want to know who bought these drinks, Zeke," Della demanded later.

"Good grief, Della. Does it really matter?"

"I want to thank them," Della said.

"Well, if that's the case," Zeke chuckled. "I'll tell you. Handsome Jim bought them."

"Handsome?"

"Yes, you heard me," he grinned. "Now, what you got to say about that?"

"Just who the hell is Handsome Jim anyway? I been trying to find out for a long time, but nobody around here will tell me anything."

"From what I hear he's a friend of Tilly's. If you want to know more, you'll have to ask him or Tilly."

"Tell Handsome Jim I appreciate the drinks," Della said.

Sometime later, Handsome Jim knew he was drunk when Della, who had her hair piled high on her head with cheeks rouged as red as a tomato, looked good to him. But he wasn't completely out of it. His head was still clear enough to know if she was the only woman on earth and he the only man, he wouldn't fuck her with another man's cock.

As far as he was concerned, she was nosy, talked too much, and kept no secrets. She had tried to find out about him since he arrived, but Tilly seldom talked to anyone and Virgil knew not to say a word about him. So keeping his secret was easy. Feeling no pain, he maneuvered through the crowd and made his way to Della and Neva.

"Hey, Della," he shouted. "You wanna dance?"

To his amazement, she kept her mouth shut and followed him silently onto the floor.

"How you know my name when I barely know yours?" Della asked.

"Honey, everybody knows your name. And my name's Handsome Jim. How're thing's going?"

"Everything's fine," she replied. Of course, he knew that was a lie because someone had just tried to burn down her house.

"Can I ask you a question?" Della pried.

"You already did."

"What's your relationship with Tilly?"

"She's just a friend," he said. "But I'm sure you already know that."

They danced to several tunes and, to his surprise, Della never got tired. But he did. He thanked her and took her back to the bar, then walked away.

"How was it out there, Della?" Neva asked.

"He threw me everywhere but upside the walls, girl. By the way, he says he's just a friend to Tilly. But as far as I'm concerned he's a skin flint."

"Why would you say that?" Neva asked.

"He didn't offer me a drink."

"Jeez, Della. Zeke just told you he bought your first drinks."

"So what? He should've offered me one personally. I'll tell you one thing. If he asks me to dance again, I'll tell him to stick it in his ear."

"You think it's long enough to do all that?" Neva elbowed her, and both whooped with laughter.

When Handsome returned to the bar, Della introduced him. "Neva, this is Handsome Jim. Jim, this is Neva."

"Hey, Neva," Handsome Jim said. "What's goin' on?"

"Just death and taxes," she replied, but immediately regretted the words, as Lydia's frightened face, which constantly haunted her, flashed before her eyes. For that reason, death was not a topic she wanted to dwell upon.

"Hey, Zeke, did you forget about us?" Handsome asked when he saw Neva's empty glass. Handsome Jim's big eyes bore down on Neva. His top teeth somewhat protruded, his ears were too big for his small head, and his feet reminded Neva of long, thin, boat paddles.

"Are you married?" Neva asked.

"Nope and never was," he answered. His name was misleading to say the least. Handsome, he was not, which she was certain played some part in his never getting married. Who, she wondered, played such a cruel joke on him? At first, she felt sorry for him. But then he started to talk to her and made her laugh.

"Would you like to cut a rug?" he asked.

"Yeah, I would." She stood and reached for his hand. It was warm and strong and she suddenly felt good. As they glided across the floor, she wondered if this chance meeting hadn't already changed her luck.

She realized there was no need to feel sorry for him. He was so sure of himself he needed no sympathy from her. Suddenly, she didn't care if he had three horns on his head and walked like a duck. She needed a friend, and for some reason, she felt she found one.

❦   ❦   ❦

Late one night while the whole town slept someone finally succeeded in burning down Della's house. At the time, only Della and Neva were in the house, and had it not been for the dog, Lockjaw, they might have perished. Della screamed so loud she woke everyone in town, but there was little anyone could do. The house burned to the ground.

Even though she was afraid to do so, Carrie offered Della and Neva a place to stay. They accepted, but Neva stayed only a couple of nights, and on the last night Neva spoke to Carrie about the arrangements.

"I want to thank you for your hospitality, Carrie."

"You're welcome, Neva. I'm sorry it happened, but glad I could help you in some small way."

"I realize now my life will never be the same here again. I can't change things. So it's time for me to move on and leave Meadowsbrook behind."

"Well, then. If that's the way you feel, I wish you all the best," Carrie told her.

Then Neva went to see Handsome Jim. After expressing her fears to him about the people of Meadowsbrook, he agreed to take her away.

Several days later, they packed up, said their goodbyes, and left town. Della and Carrie were relieved.

❦   ❦   ❦

"I'm glad," Koko told the family when she learned Della's house had burned.

Hearing her granddaughter speak in such an angry tone made Odessa wonder about the child's sanity. She supposed children went crazy, too. Though she never spoke about it, there was something wrong with Lydia. From what she heard and saw of Tilly, Odessa believed insanity did run in that family. And there were times Koko said things that worried her.

"That's an awful thing to say, Koko. And I don't ever want to hear you say that again," Odessa said.

"She has a bad streak, Mama," Natalie said. "I don't know what you can do about it."

"Don't you worry about it, hon. If she keeps it up," Odessa replied, "perhaps, we'll send her back to Tilly." Koko hated Tilly as much as Tilly hated

Koko. Odessa knew sending her back to Tilly would be a punishment worst than death for both of them.

❧   ❧   ❧

When the last school bell rang one afternoon, Koko and Makela ran from the classroom with several playmates at their heels. Once outside, they hurried up the street to Michael's Market where they found Seb Pardeau and Candyman Cates huddled near the old potbelly stove.

"Evening Mr. Pardeau, Mr. Cates," the children greeted acknowledging Pardeau first out of respect because he was oldest.

"What you learn in school today?" Seb asked.

"We learned the world really is round," Rabbit giggled.

"Laugh if you want, boy," Cates said. "But you better learn all you can. You gonna need your education even if the world is square." His remarks evoked laughter from the youngsters.

"We know that, Mr. Cates." Birdie spoke, surprisingly, clear enough to be understood.

While the other youngsters talked with the elderly men, Koko paid little attention because her mind was elsewhere. Long ago, she promised to give sweet treats to her friends, but she never made good on the promise. Now she decided, this would be the day to do so. After all, her mama was part owner of the store.

"Hi, Uncle Virg," she said cheerfully while glancing across the room at the large jar of candy canes on the other counter.

"Hey, Koko. It's good to see you, baby. Come on over and give your uncle a kiss." He pointed to his cheek and leaned over the counter. She brushed her lips against his face then looked around for Tilly.

"She's in back," Virgil winked. "You really want to see her?"

"Nope," Koko smiled.

"Didn't think so," he said. While studying Koko fleetingly, he spoke to Makela. "How you doin' Miz Makela?"

"I'm fine, thank you, Mr. Henderson." Makela flashed her best smile and hoped it might entice him to offer them goodies. Much to her disappointment, he did no such thing.

But at that very moment, Koko went over to the other counter and stuck her hand in the candy jar. Just as she pulled several pieces of candy from the jar, Tilly entered the room. Her hand still in the jar, Koko froze and stared at Tilly.

Rushing over to Koko, Tilly slapped Koko's hand. The candy jar fell to the floor. As candy spilled, Makela and the other children scrambled to pick up the candy from the floor. Tilly looked down menacingly at Koko. Koko felt anger like she never felt before. Staring up at Tilly, she dared Tilly to touch her. Tilly smacked her face. "You can't just come in here and give away the store, girl," Tilly yelled. Koko never uttered a sound.

"Hold on, Tilly. No need for all that," Virgil spoke softly. It was a cold, blustery day, when folk wrapped scarves around their necks, stuffed their hands in gloves, and every youngster in town wore brogans on their feet. Virgil could feel the anger between the two. He rushed forward. But before he reached them, Koko raised her right foot and brought it down hard on Tilly's. It was the same foot Lydia threw the brick on years ago.

As Tilly screamed painfully, Koko kicked her hard on the shin. Tilly crumpled to the floor. "Oh, my God," she screamed. "Get her away from me. She's just like Lydia. She's crazy."

Virgil grabbed Koko's arm and pulled her back. Then he helped Tilly hobble to her stool behind her counter. "Now, see what you did," Virgil said. "You made Koko mad. And you got yourself all scarred up because of a few sticks of peppermint candy."

"Forget you, Virg. I know where your loyalty is," Tilly whined as Koko and the other children hurried out the door. While a grinning Virgil went back to his side of the store, Candyman Cates and Seb Pardeau who usually had something to say about everything were speechless, and neither moved a muscle.

❦ ❦ ❦

"How did this happen, Tilly? Did Virg do this to you?" Doc Peterson asked as he dabbed at the gash on Tilly's leg.

"No, Virg didn't do it. That wild ass niece Koko did it," she hissed.

"Nah, I can't believe it. What she use on you, a sledge hammer?" Doc laughed. His laughter was nothing personal since he chuckled at everything. It was simply a reflex that kept him from crying for all the poor suckers he treated every day. They fought each other with knives, guns, and anything else they could put their hands on. And it was their reactions to one another that kept him in action.

"No, she didn't use a sledge hammer. She did it with them hell buckle shoes she was wearing." Tilly spat out the words angrily.

"Oh, I suppose you mean brogans. Lawdy! There's a wonder your shinbone isn't cracked." He inspected the leg and the foot.

"You'll be sore for a few days. But you'll live," he explained as he bandaged her leg.

"You know, if Koko's anything like her mother, we won't have many dull moments around here. I mean she did promise to kick ass when she grew up. Didn't she?" Doc Peterson chuckled again.

"She's only eight and already causing damage." He looked at Tilly. Her expression let him know she was none too pleased about what he said. But he didn't give a damn. There was no love lost between him and Tilly, and Tilly needed him more than he needed her.

Though he knew further comment would enrage Tilly even more, he spoke his mind anyway.

"Yes, siree. I don't think Koko can wait to kick ass," he chortled.

Tilly was more upset with herself than with Doc. He had been the same as long as she could remember. But to think her leg might carry scars because she refused to give that wild banshee niece candy canes made her see red. That shoe felt like a hammer hitting her leg.

Carrie, who worked the night shift, saw the bandage on Tilly's leg as Tilly left the examining room. "Hey, Tilly," she called out. "What happened to you? You look like a horse kicked you."

"I'm in no mood to talk right now, Carrie. I'm sure Doc Peterson will tell you the whole damn story." Tilly continued down the hall and out the door.

🍁 🍁 🍁

When Marcus's mother Maude became gravely ill, he decided to move his parents to Meadowsbrook. They protested, but he ignored their protests. They were getting older, and he knew that time had come when they needed family. Now they were living with him and Odessa in the big house. Natalie was elated by their arrival.

When time allowed, she and Helene helped Odessa take care of Maude. Before long, Maude improved, got out of bed, and started to live again.

Conrad was a pharmacist, and not yet ready to die in a rocking chair on the porch. So he worked alongside Spuds in the only drugstore in town.

Spuds and Jenny Joyride were thinking about selling the drugstore, and Conrad planned to buy the store whenever they made that decision.

🍁  🍁  🍁

On the day Koko tangled with Tilly, Maude helped Odessa and Natalie prepare the evening meal. While Makela and Koko sat at the dining table and studied, Conrad and Marcus read the newspaper.

In the meantime, Shelton came to the house. Since it was time for dinner, he knew the family were in the dining area and entered the house by the back door.

"Evening," he greeted upon entering the room.

"Evening, Shel. How you doing?" Conrad looked up briefly then turned his attention back to the newspaper.

"I'm okay, Granddad. But it's as cold as a bear's booty out there."

"Yeah, it is," Conrad replied. At the same time, Marcus lowered his newspaper and scrutinized Shelton, and wondered if his son-in-law had just gotten out of some woman's warm bed.

Feeling like a bug under a microscope, Shelton became nervous. When someone knocked on the front door, he rushed to answer it, which gave him the chance to breathe.

"Hey, Shel," Doc Peterson said when he opened the door.

"Hey, Doc," he said as Doc entered the house. "What brings you this way?"

"Well, I just thought since Doctor Flack's in town it was a perfect time to visit and eat some of Odessa's cooking," he said. Of course, he had another reason too. He wanted to look at the little girl who busted Tilly's chops.

"Hey, Doc," everyone greeted when he entered the dining room.

"Lawdy, Doc," Odessa said as she came from the kitchen. "What brings you here this time of evening? Nothing drastic I hope." She'd just seen him several days ago, and she hoped he was not the bearer of bad news.

"No bad news, Odessa. Doc Flack's here, you know. So I thought it might be a good time to socialize with friends." Turning, he looked at Maude. "How you feeling these days, Grandy?" he asked using the endearing term Natalie and the younger children in the family used when addressing the older woman.

"I'm well, Doc. In fact, I feel like a new woman these days," Maude responded.

"Good to hear that. You certainly look the picture of health," Doc told her.

"I'm glad you came," Odessa said. Then she did what Doc expected her to do. She invited him to eat.

"You should've brought Ellie and Paige," Odessa offered.

"Hey," Doc said. "Somebody in this family's got to work."

Everyone sat down to eat and Natalie listened as Koko announced she wanted to work at the horsepital.

"The word is hospital, Koko," Natalie corrected and spelled the word.

"By the way, Tilly came to the hospital this evening." Doc Peterson winked at Koko who looked as if she wanted to jump out of her chair. "Somebody beat her to a bloody pulp." He exaggerated.

"What happened, Doc?" Natalie voiced concern.

"Why don't you tell Nat what happened, Koko?" Doc Peterson laughed. When Koko refused to speak, Natalie asked him to explain.

Laughing hysterically, he told them about Tilly's visit. "That's what spurred me to come over here. I just wanted to get a good look at Koko."

"Now, now, Doc. This is no laughing matter." Odessa seemed visibly upset.

"I know. I know." Doc raised his hands in defense. "But it's nothing to cry about either. Who knows? Tilly probably deserved it."

"Don't talk like that Doc. It'll only encourage her. The child has enough problems already." Then, looking at Koko, Natalie asked, "Why did you do it?"

"She hit me first," Koko remarked. "So I hit her back."

"Had you girls waited for me, this would not have happened," Natalie explained. Then she remembered *she* was trying to dodge Delano who was becoming a pest.

"She deserved it anyway." Koko assured her.

"She didn't deserve anything," Odessa snapped. "And I don't want to hear you talk that way either."

"I only wanted some candy," Koko muttered.

"I don't care what you wanted," Natalie said. "You had no right to attack Tilly."

"And Tilly had no right to attack her," Shelton said defending Koko's actions. "All Tilly had to do was to give her a few pieces of candy. Tilly's got problems. She never treated Koko right. You and everybody else know that. Koko just defended herself. So that's that."

"Shel, please don't encourage her. We don't want Koko running around town acting wild," Natalie retorted.

"Tilly's not dead, is she? If she's in such bad shape Virg would've told me. And Doc would've kept her in the hospital," Shelton said.

"You mean you knew and never mentioned this?" Natalie was indignant.

"I was gonna tell you, but Doc beat me to it." Shelton looked at Doc then both laughed.

"If she ever hits me again, I'm gonna get her when I grow up."

"Don't you ever let me hear you talk that way again, little girl." Natalie had heard enough.

Speaking more calmly, Odessa said, "I want you to learn to control your temper, child."

"That's enough!" Conrad spoke for the first time. "I've heard enough. I'd like to eat my meal in peace." Glancing over at Koko, he smiled. "No need to make a mountain out of a molehill. So let's forget it."

"I think I want to be a doctor just like you when I grow up," she said. Doc studied her briefly and wondered if she knew what she wanted. But any way the cookie crumbled, she was a smart one. She knew the run-in with Tilly left a bad taste in the family's mouth. Now, to appease them, she pulled a rabbit out of the hat and got the attention she desired.

"That's great, Koko. Come see me when you're ready to start learning." Hell, if she really wanted to study medicine, he would be the first to help her.

"That's great, Doc. That's mighty nice of you," Marcus exclaimed, overjoyed his granddaughter might study medicine. Then directing his attention to her, he said, "I can't think of a better profession, honey."

"You're right about that, Marcus." Conrad knew the thought of her studying medicine would make Marcus happy.

"How about that, Doc? Seems you've inspired our little Koko," Conrad said while he wondered if it would come to pass. If she did hold on to that idea, he would help her every step of the way.

"I think it's great, Conrad. Marcus tried so hard to push Alan into medicine. But he never sold Alan on the idea. But Koko just might be the one to do it," Doc said.

"It would make us proud if you became a doctor. We'll do all we can to help you get there," Conrad expounded.

"Okay, Granddaddy," she smiled charmingly.

"If you're gonna be a doctor, I'm gonna be a nurse," Makela chimed in.

Natalie smiled. Her daughter knew a good thing when she saw it and right now she wanted to share in the attention, too.

"You can't be a nurse, Makela." Koko spoke authoritatively.

"Why can't I?" Makela pouted.

"Because there'll be lots of blood. You don't like to see blood," Koko reminded her.

"It's okay, Makela," Natalie comforted. "If you work hard, you can overcome your fears. I'm confident you will become a nurse."

It was true Makela shied from blood. When time came to slaughter livestock, she stuck her fingers in her ears to block out the animal cries. Eventually she went to the front of the house and stayed there. But Koko was different. She went into the back yard where the men worked so she could see everything.

The girl never flinched nor did she allow her eyes to waiver. When one of the men plunged the knife into the struggling animal's throat, she stood her ground. Then she stared intently as the substance, which sustained the animal drained and soaked into the ground.

Later, when they cooked livers, hearts, and kidneys, Koko never thought twice about what she saw. In fact, she was the first at the table and acted like she hadn't eaten in days. But the mere smell of fresh meat offended Makela. She was unable to eat and excused herself from the table.

It was days later after the cleanup and the fresh smell dissipated that Makela attempted to help make sausages. Failing that, she stood by and watched while others made easy what she found so difficult.

"But, Nat," Koko started.

"We know, Koko." Natalie held up her hand. "However, I'm confident Makela will change, and she too will be ready to study medicine when she grows up." Natalie smiled at her daughter.

"Well, then. Whenever you're ready young lady, come see me," Doc said. "And I'll put you to work, too."

"Okay, Doc." Makela's mouth stretched into a wide grin.

# CHAPTER 36

Only months after Handsome Jim and Neva left town, Marcus sat down at the dining table, and picked up the newspaper. He was shocked by the article he read.

> A well dressed man calmly walked into a Kansas City nightclub several nights ago and put a bag on the bar. After ordering drinks, he laughed and talked with other patrons.
> When he later walked out leaving the bag, another patron grabbed the bag and hurried after him. However, in the process of doing so, he dropped the bag and a woman's head fell out onto the floor. A gruesome sight.
> Even so, the man who brought the bag into the bar made no attempt to run. Instead, he picked up the head and put it back in the bag. To the astonishment of everyone, he put the bag back on the bar. Then, he casually walked to the washroom.
> When he returned to the bar, he sat down, ordered another drink, and waited for the bartender to call the police. When the police arrived, he told them the head in the bag belonged to his wife, and her name was Neva.
> "I did it. But I made sure she was *happy* first," he told them. "You see, she chased my sister to her death several years ago."
> "What's your name," the policeman asked.
> "Junior," he said. "Jake Wade Junior, but you can call me Handsome Jim."

Some folk swore the news was so powerful it woke Lydia from the dead, and they heard her cry the same night Handsome Jim did it.

When Neva's Cousin Joe heard of her death, it was so painful, he howled like a wounded animal, and the echo was heard for miles.

"Lord have mercy!" Della yelled before Carrie reached the steps. "As I live and breathe. I can't believe it. Did you hear what Handsome Jim did?"

"Yes, I heard," Carrie said shaking her head in disbelief.

"Lawdy, I never knew Tilly had a brother 'cause she never whispered a word. Can you believe it? I can't even sleep," Della cried.

"Lawdy, Della. I'm so sorry. It's so awful to know one human being can do such a horrible thing to another. And just to think Neva thought Handsome Jim loved her." Carrie rushed over to Della, held her and both women cried.

"She was my friend, Carrie. It's real scary you know. I'm scared Handsome Jim might come back for me. All that time he lurked around here I had no idea who he was.

"Just goes to show some folk can keep a secret," Carrie said.

"I hope he never gets out of jail," Della said.

"You better keep on hoping, 'cause you gotta remember one thing. Neva was a black woman. Hell, they might not keep him locked up for more than a week. If he gets out, he might come after you since you and Neva were friends," Carrie said.

Shocked senseless, Della went to bed and was so quiet she didn't even talk to Lockjaw.

❈ ❈ ❈

Billy, at one time, thought he wanted revenge, but he came to terms with Lydia's death and decided to let it be.

Rumor was Billy cried several days, not because he loved Neva, but because he never imagined she would meet the devil and die such a horrible death.

❈ ❈ ❈

On Saturday afternoon when Harry went to Billy's to party, Thea was so sickened by the event she refused to go with him. She stayed home.

❦ ❦ ❦

"Damn, Jozell. Can you believe the man worked alongside me? I thought he was normal, but this just goes to show you never know folk. Who would've thought such a nice man could do something like that?"

"I know what you mean, Grey. I can't believe it either."

"You want to go visit Billy for a while?" Greyland asked.

"I don't think so. Why don't you go," she replied.

When Greyland arrived at Billy's, Shelton, Warren, Fats, and Harry were already there. All were saddened by such horrible turn of events, events which were unimaginable to them.

❦ ❦ ❦

Makela was afraid of the dead and was certain Neva's ghost would pay her a visit. She insisted Natalie let the light burn in her room. Natalie gave in, but when Makela fell asleep, Natalie went in the room and turned off the light.

When Makela awoke later engulfed in darkness, she crawled under the covers. Unable to sleep any longer for fear of ghosts floating about her bed, she wished for the dawn to come.

Natalie, like her daughter Makela, had a hard time sleeping for she kept seeing the torture Neva endured, and she couldn't get the picture out of her head.

"Isn't it awful, Nat?" Tamara asked days later when she visited the Dawson home.

"Yes, it is, Tam. How gruesome," Natalie said shaking her head.

"I agree. You know you look at the folk around here and you think they're normal and this is simply a little peaceful, shady niche. But all you got to do is look under the covers," Tamara said.

"You're right about that. It just goes to show looks are quite deceiving."

❦ ❦ ❦

The sadness Odessa felt showed on her face as once again she wondered about Tilly's family and sanity. When Odessa told Koko Neva was dead, the little girl's expression didn't change.

Fearing Koko might say something she was not ready to hear, Odessa decided to let Neva rest. But then Koko spoke. "I guess she can talk with my mama now."

※ ※ ※

A few days after everyone had read the shocking article, Helene kept her store open later than usual because Bessie Mae Wanker came in and tried on every pair of shoes she thought would fit her feet.

Just moments later, Zenna came too. "I came to buy winter shoes," she said.

"Honey, I got all kinds of shoes here. Just take your pick," Helene told her, as Thea came in, too.

"Hey, Thea," Bessie Mae Wanker called out while trying on still another pair of shoes.

"I can't believe what happened to Neva. Can you?" Thea said. "I heard Neva planned to get rid of Lydia all along. All that time I thought Neva had lost her marbles. But that's not so. Can you believe that?"

"Well, I didn't hear anything like…" Helene said.

"I got reason to believe what I heard is true, Helene. You know why?"

"No, but I'm sure you'll…" Helene said as Bessie Mae Wanker sat with one foot stuck halfway into another shoe.

Then Thea told the story of what happened between Lydia and another woman some years earlier in Sugar Hill when Lydia got too friendly with a man.

"Some tough chick threatened Lydia and she shot at the woman. From what we heard, that bullet hit the girl and almost ripped off her ear. She lost her hearing after that. Can you believe that?"

"My God!" Helene said.

"Wait," Thea said. "I ain't through yet. Can you guess who that tough chick was?"

"Neva," Bessie Mae Wanker shouted from among the shoe boxes.

"No, it wasn't Neva. It was Neva's cousin," Thea said shaking her head. "And Neva waited all them years to get even with Lydia."

"Lawdy, that's awful," Bessie Mae muttered.

"Yes it is. And all because of some man Lydia didn't even know. Just the thought of it makes me sick," Helene said.

"Wait a minute, Thea. How come you know so much about it and Della was Neva's friend and Neva never told her anything. That's unusual ain't it?"

"Yeah," Thea said. "But who's to say she don't know. I got a feeling Della just kept her mouth shut for once."

"Well, if she knows and kept quiet, it's a first. Shoot, I got a feeling Della's lips are flapping when she sleeps," Bessie Mae Wanker said causing everyone to laugh.

"Helene," Zenna called. "Could you come over here? I think I found a pair I like."

"Hold on a minute, Zenna. It's getting late. Guess I better lock the door."

"Now just you wait a minute, Helene. Don't you dare lock up this store before I find me some shoes," Thea said.

Gossip continued about town as to the reason Neva chased Lydia onto the tracks that fateful day. But there were few who really knew the truth.

After all her customers left the store, Helene closed up and went home.

"You won't believe this, Percy," Helene said as she walked through the door. "Everybody came into the store just before closing time and Bessie Mae Wanker tried on every shoe in the store. And she only bought a pair of house slippers."

"You got to be kidding," Percy laughed.

"No, honey. I'm not kidding. Thea came in and held us all captive."

"What she talking about?" he asked.

"Neva, of course. That's the most interesting subject we got right now."

"It's real sad about Neva. You know, if I had been sheriff when she chased Lydia, I would've put her in jail. She would still be there, and she would be alive today," Percy said.

"You know, I never thought of it that way, honey," Helene said as she sat on the sofa, took off her shoes, and put her feet on the hassock.

When Virgil heard the news about what Handsome did, he was shocked. The Handsome Jim he knew was soft spoken and mild mannered. He never thought the man had a deceitful bone in his body. Virgil grieved for two more lost souls.

❦ ❦ ❦

When LuLa Hanks read the article about the unspeakable thing her nephew had done, she was devastated. What, she wondered, would happen next? Was her whole family insane?

Though she expected compassion from no one, she wondered if poor Tilly needed her. She immediately called her niece.

"Oh, Tilly. What an awful thing to happen," Lula said.

"Yes, it is. I couldn't believe it, auntie."

"Would you mind if I came to see you, Tilly?"

"No, I wouldn't mind at all," Tilly said. "In fact, I was just thinking about you. It seems our family is getting smaller by the day. I was wondering if...if you... How would you like to live in Meadowsbrook?" Tilly asked surprising Lula.

"What're you talking about, Tilly?"

"I mean I think it's time we got to know one another better," auntie. "I think I need you here with me," Tilly said as a tear rolled down her cheek.

"Oh, honey. I don't know. I can't give you an answer right now. But I would like to come see you."

"I'd like that, auntie. I'll see you in a few days," Tilly said.

Lula put the receiver back in the cradle and wondered what happened to her niece. Tilly actually talked like she was sane, and that made Lula feel good.

❦ ❦ ❦

Once again Tilly felt a dreadful pain in her heart. First, she hurt for the death of her sister, Lydia, and now for this tragedy with Handsome Jim. She never knew her daddy had other children until Handsome Jim showed up on her doorstep. When he told her who he was, she was taken by surprise. But she believed he was her half brother because her daddy had relatives in Kansas City and went there to visit often.

She liked Handsome instantly. Even though she wanted Neva severely punished, she never wanted something so awful to happen. Now she wondered if Handsome Jim planned it or if he had snapped. Tilly mourned as did everyone else in town.

# CHAPTER 37

Though Warren spent lots of time with his cousin, Shelton, they were quite different. Shelton threw caution to the wind, while Warren a quiet, personable, and unassuming man, kept secrets. Whatever he did behind closed doors, stayed there. But his life with Della was in shambles.

After the house burned down, Della stayed with Carrie while Warren stayed elsewhere. In spite of the fact that Warren wasn't staying with Della she believed he would come back when the house was rebuilt because he was helping Marcus rebuild it.

She also thought he was staying with Shelton, Greyland, or one of his friends. She really didn't think it was important about where he stayed. She took him for granted. Underneath it all she was afraid to show love. Afraid it would never be returned, she didn't offer it. That's why she loved her dog Lockjaw who loved her unconditionally.

But Della was in for a rude awakening. The last day Warren and Marcus worked on the house, Warren walked away from the house and Della in the same act.

After walking through the house, she came back onto the porch prepared to tell Warren how pretty it was and how much she appreciated the work he and Marcus had done. But just as she was about to speak, Warren was already walking up the street.

"Where the hell you think you going, Warren?" Della yelled threateningly.

"Where you can't find me," he yelled.

"Why, you heartless bastard," Della shouted. "I know where you going."

"Forget you, Della. We know where your heart is. Don't we?" he yelled.

As he disappeared around the corner, Della realized she was alone except for her dog, Lockjaw. Suddenly, loneliness engulfed her, and she cried.

Warren suffered from asthma, and the realization that he actually had the guts to walk away from Della was almost too much for him to take. He started to wheeze. He expected asthma would one day kill him. Slowing his pace, he hoped it would not be now.

"Hey, Brandy," he said when she opened the door. "I'm gonna stay this time."

"Are you sure?" Brandy studied his face. "Are you sure you're ready?"

"I'm sure. Della loves her dog. Not me."

"Well, I got news for you, honey. I love you more than Della loves that dog," Brandy told him. Then speaking softly, she said, "Our son will be glad to have his daddy home." The son she spoke of was Theodore who everyone called Rabbit.

"That goes two ways," he said feeling he had found a real home at last.

🍁 🍁 🍁

Only days later, early in the morning, Tamara's phone rang. She smiled. Thinking it was the 'good' Reverend McCord, she reached for it. "Good morning," she said passionately with closed eyes. But to her surprise, on the other end was some woman ranting and raving. Though sleepy, Tamara immediately became alert. Opening her eyes, she sat up.

"Who is this?"

"Never mind who this is, you lousy bitch," the woman said. Then the phone went dead. Tamara held the phone for some time before she called the Reverend McCord.

"Have you any idea who it could be?" she asked.

"No, I don't, honey. I'm sure it's just some nut giving you a hard time."

"I hope you're right."

"I know I'm right. I love you, Tam."

"And I love you." Tamara hung up the phone, but unable to sleep, she got out of bed.

🍁 🍁 🍁

In the meantime, the Reverend McCord got on the phone and talked to the Reverend Sylvester Paxton in Chicago.

"I don't want my life ruined, Syl," McCord told him.

"Don't worry, Buddy. Since you know who made the call, we'll take care of it."

The woman who made the call was one of Slick's girls and a member of Reverend Paxton's church. Her name was Bonita Hernandez. Her mother was black and her daddy was Puerto Rican. She had a pretty face and a beautiful body. However, Bonita had one flaw. She was jealous beyond belief.

She fell in love with the Reverend McCord the first time he made love to her. She believed that intimate evening was a prelude to marriage. When he said he loved her she actually believed it. She wanted to marry him, and she was sure it would happen, but when he returned to Chicago, he surprised her.

"I've met someone," the Reverend McCord told her.

"Whatta you mean you met someone?" Bonita asked.

"Just what I said. I met a woman. I love her, and I plan to marry her."

"In other words, you're leaving me?" Bonita felt sick.

"That's exactly what I'm telling you. It's time I got married. I really love this woman."

"You mean to tell me you been *fucking* me and this other woman all along?"

"That's right, my dear," said the Reverend McCord.

"Why, you lousy son-of-a-bitch! You're no better than a street nigger. All this time, I thought you were a true Man of the Cloth, when all you wanted was to get your dick off." Bonita was devastated. "Well, I'll tell you something, Reverend. If I can't have you, no other woman can either."

"Ah, come on Bonita," the Reverend said brushing her off. "You don't really mean that."

"Don't you love me just a little bit?" she asked sweetly.

"Of course, I do, Bonita," he said.

"Then I see no reason why we can't be friends," Bonita said trying to calm down and think about the situation.

"I agree. We can be friends, but I love Tam and I'm gonna marry her," he said hoping the message registered somewhere in Bonita's pretty little head. When he left Chicago, he thought Bonita understood his position.

But, the message never registered, and Bonita had not understood anything he said. So now he had a problem on his hands and wondered how he would explain this woman to Tam. Perhaps, if Syl could to talk to Bonita and calm her down, he thought, Tam would never know he and the woman were ever involved.

❦   ❦   ❦

It was a Friday when Bonita arrived in Meadowsbrook. And she went straight to Jenny Joyride's house because Slick Joyride sent her there.

"My name is Bonita Hernandez," she said when she walked into the post office. "Slick Joyride told me I could stay here a few days."

"Oh yeah?" Melanie said looking Bonita up and down.

"That's right," Bonita said.

"Well, I guess that's settled then. Come on in. My name is Melanie. Slick is my uncle." Melanie came from behind the counter, then the two women shook hands, and Melanie picked up Bonita's bag and led her down the hallway to the living quarters.

"Umhum, Melanie," Bonita said. "You sure got a nice house."

"Thanks, but it's not mine. It belongs to my parents. I'm just staying here until I get married."

"Oh?" Bonita exclaimed.

"Yeah. I expect my man to pop the question any day now," Melanie said.

"Well, good for you. I expected my man to pop the question any day, too. But then this Tam popped into his life. So I came to get things squared away."

Melanie paused a moment and gave Bonita some thought. She had to admire her coming down here to get things squared away. She was sure Bonita came to square it away with the Reverend McCord, but just to be sure she wasn't squaring it away with Shelton, Melanie asked, "Just who is this man you gonna square things away with?"

"His name's Reverend Buddy McCord," Bonita replied.

"Good for you, Bonita," Melanie said breathing a sigh of relief. "You go get him. Tell him like it is, girl. Let him know you ain't no door mat," Melanie egged her on.

"Don't worry. That's exactly what I plan to do. Shoot, I'm in trouble, and I don't intend to have this baby without marrying his daddy first."

"Wow!" Melanie was surprised and impressed with Bonita at the same time. "I tell you what, Bonita. We're going to the Joint tonight, girl."

"What's the Joint?"

"That's where Tam hangs out. Some folk call it the Lounge. But me, I call it the Joint. Tam sings there, and you can get a good look at her when she's on that stage."

So, on her first night in Meadowsbrook Bonita and her new found-friend Melanie stepped out together. When they entered the Lounge as if they owned it, every head turned. Tam was already on stage at the mike.

"Hey, pretty," a man called out while someone else whistled.

"Where you find that pretty little thing beside you, Melanie? How about introducing us?" someone else asked.

But Melanie simply laughed, waved her hand, and led Bonita to the bar.

"That's her," Melanie whispered as they took seats at the bar.

"Well, he didn't tell me she was white. Why, she looks like alabaster."

"Well, from what I see, you kinda white yourself," Melanie said looking Bonita straight in the eye.

"My mother is colored, and my dad is Puerto Rican," Bonita told her.

"Well then. You and Tam's got a lot in common. Tam ain't white. She's just almost," Melanie said. "Girl, her mama was as black as the ace of spades. You see that old man sitting back there?"

"Yeah."

"Well, that's her daddy. Them other two with him are his sons, Frank and Vince. They're Tam's brothers. Folk call that one Vince the meat man," Melanie pointed to Vince. He delivers meat to Michael's Market. They own the meat packing company in Baysville.

"They ain't even supposed to be here. Shoot, we live by rules down here. But them three do whatever they want. You'd think they lived right here in town.

"They come in here ever so often to see her." Melanie pointed at Tamara.

"I see," Bonita said as the jealousy she felt for Tamara became overwhelming.

"Hey, Zeke," Melanie called. "Can we have a couple of drinks down here?"

"You sure can, beautiful. What you drinking?" he asked.

"Rum and coke's good," Melanie said.

"I'll have a gin and tonic," Bonita said.

"Whatever your little hearts desire." Zeke poured the two shots. As Melanie put money on the bar, Frank Baraldi came to the bar and gave both women the once over.

"Give'em whatever they want, Zeke," Frank said as he put several bills on the bar. As Zeke poured Frank a shot, Bonita glanced up at him and he winked. Bonita smiled, but turned back to her concern. Tamara.

While Tamara crooned, Bonita tried to listen, but it was hard to do. The more she looked at Tamara, the angrier she got. This was the woman the Reverend McCord dumped her for. Bonita was so furious she couldn't even taste her drink. She felt hot all over, and her heart almost jumped out of her chest.

As Tamara left the stage and approached the bar, Bonita, unable to contain herself any longer, threw her drink in Tamara's face.

"Hey," Zeke yelled. "That's not allowed here." But before he spoke another word or Tamara realized what happened, Bonita scratched Tamara's face. Tamara put up her hands in defense, but Bonita proceeded to punch her and pull her hair. Throwing Tamara to the floor, Bonita tore Tamara's dress clean off.

"Get her off me," Tamara yelled as Frank along with Zeke and Billy Hardwood, rushed to her aid and pulled Bonita away.

"What's wrong with you and who are you?" Tamara cried.

"I'm Bonita Hernandez. And I was gonna marry Reverend McCord before you got your hooks into him."

"I got news for you, Bonita. You can still marry him. I don't need you or Reverend McCord in my life. You can put your money on that."

Eva brought a wrap to cover Tamara. "I want you out of here, Bonita, or whoever you are. And don't come back," Eva yelled.

"That's fine by me, baby," Bonita said as she sashayed out the door with Melanie at her heels.

"Now looka here Bonita, you never told me you were gonna kick her ass."

"Hell, I didn't know it myself, girl. But I just got mad," Bonita told her. "Now I got to go see you-know-who."

"Well, my friend. I think you better go see you-know-who alone."

"I can do that. Just point me in the right direction," Bonita told her.

Frank was quite disappointed. What he had seen of Bonita he liked. But now that she attacked Tamara, she was definitely off limits. "You gonna be all right, Tam?" Frank asked as Pete and Vince joined him.

"I'm gonna be okay," Tamara said taking a seat at the bar. "Don't worry. And thanks for your help."

"You want us to do anything else?" Frank asked.

"No, no. Please leave it alone," she said. "I'll take care of it."

"Okay, okay," he said.

"You want us to take you home, Tam?" Vince asked.

"No, I'll be okay."

"Come on boys," Pete said. Then turning to Tamara, he said, "We're leaving now, but we'll see you again soon."

"Okay, Papa," a quite shaken Tamara whispered as Zeke poured a drink and handed it to her.

"Thanks, Zeke," she said trembling.

"Are you all right?" Zeke asked after she gulped down the shot.

"Yeah, I'm okay."

"Take her home, will you, Billy?"

"Okay, Zeke." Then Billy led her out to the car and drove her home.

"Thanks, Billy," Tamara said once he stopped the car in front of her house.

"Hold on. I'll walk you to the door."

"I'm okay. You don't have to."

"I know. But I want to see you inside the house first." They got out of the car and Billy helped a rattled Tamara to her front door.

"Can I do something for you?" he asked.

"No thank you, Billy. I'll be just fine."

"Oh, well. I guess your Reverend McCord's got a lotta questions to answer."

"Not necessarily. As far as I'm concerned, Bonita answered them all."

"What you gonna do now?" Billy asked.

"I'm gonna tell Reverend McCord the well's gone dry."

"You mean you gonna let him go?"

"That's exactly what I mean," Tamara said.

🍁    🍁    🍁

The Reverend McCord was fast asleep when rapid knocking on the door awoke him. Jumping out of bed, he rushed to open it. To his surprise, Bonita Hernandez from Chicago stood staring at him. He was speechless.

"Well, aren't you gonna invite me in?" she asked sarcastically.

"Ah, ah," he stammered.

"What's the problem? Cat got your tongue?"

Actually, he felt something had more than his tongue, and he wondered how he was gonna get out of this mess. Syl was supposed to take care of Bonita. Syl was supposed to solve his problem, but obviously Syl hadn't done a damn thing. Otherwise, Bonita would be in Chicago and not on his doorstep.

"Yeah, yeah. Ah, come on in. It's good to see you, Bonita."

"Don't give me that good-to-see-you bullshit, you lousy son-of-a-bitch. How could you do this to me?" she cried.

"I explained things when I last saw you. I thought you understood."

"I came to tell you, I just kicked your woman's ass."

"You what?" he screamed.

"That's right. I kicked her ass right there in front of everybody in that goddamn lounge," Bonita shouted. "Now what the hell you gonna do about that?"

"I'm gonna do what I should've done a long time ago. I'm gonna kick your ass if you don't get on the next train and get the hell out of here."

Bonita was so enraged she pulled her switchblade from her pocket, snapped it open and slashed the Reverend's cheek. Blood gushed down his face and dripped onto his robe.

As she swung at him again, he grabbed her arm and twisted it. The blade fell to the floor. She dropped to her knees. He slapped her face, hard. Looking up at him, she said, "I love you and I'm gonna have your baby. How could you do this to me?" She hurt so bad.

"Get out," he screamed. "Get out of my house and out of my life." Then he pulled her by the arm, dragged her to the door, and threw her out. "Make sure you're on the next train north."

As soon as the Reverend McCord pushed Bonita outside and shut the door, Bonita cried so hard she could hardly see. She hadn't meant to lose her temper. She was sorry. She felt weak. Her head spun. Thinking she'd made a mess of things, her stomach started to churn. Stopping and leaning against a tree, she emptied her stomach contents on the roadside with only the man in the moon to see. She had no idea what the future held for her.

"What happened with you and the Reverend? Did he hurt you?" Melanie asked a haggard looking Bonita as she came into the house.

"No. We had a fight, and I hurt him," Bonita said explaining the latest events.

"You mean to tell me, you cut him! Girl, you're something else," a wide-eyed Melanie said. "What you think he's gonna do?"

"I don't know, and I don't really care," Bonita said.

"What you gonna do now?" Melanie asked.

Certain she'd never see the Reverend again, Bonita's shoulders sagged, and hot tears ran down her face. "I'm going home tomorrow and talk to my mama. This news will break her heart."

"I'm sorry, Bonita. I hope things turn out okay for you. And if you ever want to come back down here, I'll be glad to see you. You're something else," a misty eyed Melanie said shaking her head. "I hope you'll write me when you get home."

"I'll do that, Melanie," Bonita said. "And I thank you for your hospitality."

"Girl, the pleasure is all mine. I like you a lot. Come on," Melanie said. "Let's get you cleaned up so you can go to bed."

🍁 🍁 🍁

The Reverend rushed to the bathroom where he grabbed a towel and held it to his face. Looking in the mirror, he saw he needed stitches. He grabbed his keys, jumped in his car and went to the hospital to see Doc Peterson.

At the hospital, the Reverend McCord jumped from his car and rushed inside.

"Hey, Doc," he yelled distressfully. "Help me, will you? I've been cut."

"Lawdy," Carrie shouted. "What happened, Reverend?" But before he could respond, Carrie called for help. "Hey, Doc, come quick," she said while leading the Reverend McCord to an examining room. Then, waving her hand, she indicated that the Reverend McCord climb onto the table.

Doc Peterson entered the room, followed by Doc Flack the surgeon, who was in town that week and Doc Peterson's wife, Nurse Ellie. When they saw the blood flowing from Reverend McCord's face, they all began to speak at once.

"What happened?" they asked. "Who did this to you?"

"Lawdy, I wonder what's gonna happen next. Can't understand why someone would cut a good man like you, Reverend," Ellie said.

The hospital staff bombarded the Reverend McCord with questions, but his only reply was a painful groan.

"Okay, Ellie. I want you and Carrie to quiet down and make yourselves useful." Then, both nurses went to work as Doc Peterson looked down at Reverend McCord.

"Okay, Reverend. Let's take a look at your face," Doc Peterson said pulling the towel from the wound.

"Damn, man," Doc Peterson said. "Seems you made somebody real mad. By the way, this is Doc Flack. You probably never met him, but I'm sure you've heard of him." Doc Peterson chuckled. "He's gonna take care of you."

"Umhum," was all the Reverend McCord said.

"Goodness, man. Guess somebody didn't like that pretty face of yours. You want to tell us about it?" Doc Flack asked.

"Not now," the Reverend McCord said. "All I want now is to get my face sewed up and go home."

"Well, now Rev. We gonna definitely sew up your face. Then we'll give you something to sleep," Doc Flack said taking the needle from Ellie's hand and jabbing it in the Reverend McCord's arm. "But you won't be going home tonight."

"Okay, Ellie. Doc Flack will stitch him up and Carrie can assist," Doc Peterson said. "We have other work to do."

"Okay, Doc. Fine by me," Ellie said. Then they both left the room, and the Reverend McCord spent a painful night in the hospital.

Early the next morning, Bonita said good-bye to Melanie. As Bonita climbed aboard the train and headed north, Melanie felt sad, and wished she was getting on the train with her new friend. The thought of leaving Meadowsbrook had never entered her head before, and it surprised her.

About the same time Bonita was boarding the train, Carrie's shift ended, and she went to Della's and told her about the Reverend McCord's ordeal. Though Carrie couldn't say exactly how the Reverend McCord got his face whacked, Della seemed to know everything about Tamara, Bonita, and the Reverend.

"I swear, Della. You get more news than the Chicago Defender," Carrie told her.

"Nothing to it, Carrie. Billy was there when this Bonita jumped Tam. So the way I see it, Bonita probably jumped the Reverend, too."

"I suppose you're right," Carrie murmured.

Later that morning, the Reverend left the hospital and not long after he arrived home, Tamara knocked on the door.

"Oh, my God," the Reverend said raising his hands, "I was just getting ready to come see you. Come on in and have a seat."

"I don't want to sit down." Tamara studied his bandaged face before speaking again. "Did Bonita attack you, too?"

"Well, yes, she did."

Feeling Buddy played her for a fool, she asked, "I'd just like to know one thing. Are Bonita and I the only women in your life?"

"Wait now. I can explain. I can explain it all." He was desperate.

"I bet you can," Tamara said calmly. "But there's no need to bother. Bonita explained it all."

"Listen, there's nothing going on between Bonita and me. The woman is out of her mind."

"Oh, Buddy." Tamara shook her head sadly. "It's not just Bonita. Though I must admit she's part of it since I don't appreciate your wild ass women jumping me in public. But the other thing is I can never be the woman you desire. I'll never give up my way of life for yours. You see, I like living free on the edge."

Crushed, the Reverend McCord looked at Tamara. He liked living the edge too. He simply approached it differently. Otherwise, he wouldn't be in this awful mess.

The Reverend McCord had given Tamara his mother's ring, a family heirloom. The ring once belonged to his great-grandmother. When Tamara took it off her finger and gave it back to him he felt empty.

"Oh, Tam," he sighed. "Won't you at least sleep on it one more night? Won't you even reconsider what we have?"

"I don't think so, Buddy. It was good while it lasted. And I did love you, but I never cared enough to give up my dreams."

Just as the realization of what happened hit him, the Reverend McCord was devastated. When Tamara turned and started for the door, he opened it.

As she walked away and out of his life, he stood at the door until she disappeared around the corner. Then closing the door, he fell to his knees and cried. He cried not only for the loss of Tamara, but because he realized Bonita was going to have his baby. And he knew if he asked God what path to take, God would say, "You already know the answer, son. Marry her. Marry Bonita."

❦    ❦    ❦

The news of Tamara and Buddy's breakup saddened Natalie and her whole family. They wanted Tamara to find someone who truly cared for her.

"It's nothing to cry about," Tamara told them. "I'm not changing my life for any man. I don't care who he is or what he's got."

"Oh, don't you worry, honey," Helene told Tamara. "You'll find the right man one day, and he'll not want you to change one thing."

❦ ❦ ❦

After praying and thinking about what transpired between Tamara and Bonita, the Reverend McCord made a decision.

He knew he had lost Tamara forever, but Bonita still cared for him, and to be truthful he cared for Bonita, too. He knew it was time he did the right thing. So he went to see Marcus Dawson a man he considered a friend.

"I'm sure you heard it's over between Tam and me," the Reverend said.

"So I heard," Marcus said.

"Since Bonita came here, I'm too embarrassed to return to the church," the Reverend told Marcus.

"Well, these things happen, Reverend. But you just pick up the pieces and move on," Marcus explained.

"I know. But I need to get away. Bonita needs me. So I'm going to see her, and I don't know if I'm coming back."

"Well, Reverend, you seem to be on the right track. So go on and do what you have to do. We'll make do here. We'll talk to Reverend Brown. You know him. He's a young preacher over in Sugar Hill. Perhaps he'll fill the spot."

"Thank you, Brother Dawson," the Reverend said. "I got things to do. So I'd better get going."

"You do that, Reverend and good luck with Bonita," Marcus chuckled.

# CHAPTER 38

It was almost Christmas, and Alan returned home for the holidays. And as soon as he arrived, he went to visit Paige. Afterwards, he returned to the big house, where Marcus met him at the door.

"It's so good to have you home again, son," Marcus said. "It's good to be back, Daddy," he said as they made their way down the hall to the dining room.

"Hey, Alan," Maude said as they came into the room.

"Hi, Grandy. How you feeling?" he asked.

"I'm just fine, now that you came home in one piece."

"Thanks, Grandy. But the war's over, you know," he explained as he pulled a chair out from the table and sat down beside her.

"I know that, but you still flying them planes, ain't ya?"

"Yes, I am. But no one's shooting at me now," Alan laughed.

"So what's up, son?" Marcus asked as he too sat down.

"I went to see Paige."

"Oh?" Marcus said.

"Do I hear wedding bells?" Maude asked.

"I guess you can say that, Grandy. We decided we'd get married while I'm home instead of waiting."

"You sure you ready this time?" Marcus asked.

"I'm positive, Daddy."

"I'm glad to hear that. Paige is a wonderful young woman," Marcus said.

"I agree," Conrad remarked as he put the newspaper aside. "I think she'll make you happy."

"I think so too," Alan grinned.

"My word, I'm so glad to hear the news," Odessa said cheerfully as she came into the room from the kitchen. "We just finished dinner. I'll get you something to eat."

"No, don't bother, Mama. I ate with Paige and her family."

"Oh, all right," Odessa said. "Then I suppose I'd better make some kind of plans for your wedding."

"Hold on, Mama. The Petersons will take care of everything. All you need do is cook one of your outstanding meals, which we can enjoy afterwards.

"If you say so, son," Odessa replied happily. Though she told no one, her prayers had been answered. Paige would soon become family.

"I'll talk to Reverend McCord and ask him to come to the house and perform the ceremony."

"I don't know if he'll do that," Marcus remarked.

"How's that?"

"Well, first of all Tam broke off the engagement, and some woman cut him."

"Good grief, what happened?"

"The Reverend came to see me," Marcus said shaking his head. "It seems this pretty young woman came down from Chicago, New York or somewhere up there. Seems she had her clutches into Reverend McCord long before Tam did. She went to the Lounge one night and jumped Tam. Then she went to Reverend McCord's and cut his face.

"He's too embarrassed to come out of hiding, and even though Reverend Stringer still sits in the pulpit, he's too feeble to carry on. Right now we got Reverend Brown from Sugar Hill filling in for Buddy until things are clear and decisions are made."

"Good Lord. Is Tam okay?"

"Yeah, Tam's okay. But this strange young woman scratched her up a bit."

"Well, where is Reverend McCord now? Is he in town?" Alan asked.

"Don't know for sure, but you can always call him."

🍁 🍁 🍁

Not only did Alan call the Reverend McCord, he went to his home, but the Reverend McCord was not there. Alan soon learned the Reverend was out of town for an unspecified number of days.

In Reverend McCord's absence, the Reverend Brown from Sugar Hill agreed to officiate. Three days later, Alan and Paige took their vows in the front room of the big house before family and friends, and Tamara sang to music provided by Seb Pardeau and Candyman Cates who never missed a beat.

Later, Natalie expressed her innermost feelings, "Oh, Paige," she gushed. "I love weddings and I'm so happy for you. I just hope you're as happy with Alan as I am with Shel."

"Thanks Nat. I'm very happy," Paige said. Of course, she thought to herself, she had no plans to go through the kind of hell with Alan that Nat went through with Shel. It just wasn't gonna happen. As Alan approached them, she turned and smiled.

"Congratulations, Alan," Natalie said happily.

"Thanks, sis."

"That goes for me, too. I'm happy for you," Tamara said.

"I know you are, Tam," he said giving her a hug. Then looking down at Paige and putting his arm around her waist, he asked. "Are you happy, baby?"

"If I was any happier, sweetheart, it would be a crime, and Uncle Percy would put me in jail," she giggled.

"Well, Marcus," Doc Peterson said. "I always wondered what it felt like to be a member of this family."

"So how does it feel Doc?"

"Great, my friend; it feels great."

"And that goes for me, too," Ellie laughed.

Then they all sat down and enjoyed a meal tasty enough for royalty.

🍁 🍁 🍁

Christmas was just a week away when Shelton decided to drive with Percy to Baysville to shop. As he pulled the car alongside the curb, Percy looked at the sign above the store window and read aloud, "Ross's Furs and Finery." Turning to Shelton he asked, "You ever shopped here before?"

Shelton studied him and decided the man who sat beside him now had changed. When Percy first asked if he could tag along, Shelton was hesitant, but finally agreed. He had expected criticism, but was surprised that their conversation was light and pleasant.

"Can't say that I have," Shelton replied turning off the motor and taking the key from the ignition. Then both got out of the car and went inside.

The store was empty except for a man and a woman whose perfume caught his immediate attention. He secretly inhaled and wondered about the name of the intoxicating fragrance. Since it was taboo to question her, he hoped to find a similar bouquet for Natalie.

The woman turned and looked at him as if he called her name. Her lips parted in a slight smile. She was as pretty as she smelled, but she was white and to return the smile could be a deadly mistake. He instantly turned his head just as the razor-faced clerk approached him.

There was quite a contrast between the clerk and the pretty customer. The customer looked perfect, while the clerk's clothes hung sloppily about her body. One stocking was snagged, and her shoes needed a shine. What she needed, he thought, was to soak herself in that very same sweet water the customer used. But that was no business of his. He had come in to make a purchase.

"Can I help you," the clerk asked.

"I'd like to buy a fur coat," he told the clerk while Percy browsed nearby. The clerk looked stunned. Lifting her head, she turned up her beaklike nose as if he were offensive. He understood her attitude. Though it left a lot to be desired, this was the nature of the beast. He expected her to demand, idiotically, like so many whites did. "Don't you know how to say ma'am?" But she smiled, nervously, instead and asked, "Don't you know these are fur coats, and they cost lots of money?"

"I got lots of money," he answered.

"Hey, Shel," Percy said coming over and standing next to him. "Why don't you try another store?"

"Why should I try another store? They all act about the same. Hell, one store is as good as the other."

The clerk was nervous and shifted her weight from one foot to the other. Turning, she went to the back of the store. When she returned, she brought back old man Ross, the owner, who gave them the once over.

"These furs cost lots of money, you know." The old man spoke patronizingly.

"I know that. I'm Shelton Lamont. I live in Meadowsbrook. I got money."

"Oh, yeah. You're Thad Lamont's boy." The old man chuckled.

At that moment Shelton hated the old man. Shelton knew if he lived to be a hundred years old, he would always be a 'boy' in this old man's eyes. His anger surged. He wanted to shove his fist down the old man's throat and his foot up his ass. But he knew to do so could mean certain death. So he rammed his fists, not down the old man's throat, but deep into his pockets.

He knew it was time for him to leave just as Percy said, but he didn't. He and the old man continued to stare at each other. The old man rubbed his chin thoughtfully. Then he yelled to the clerk, "Okay, Joanie. Come on over here. Give the nigga whatever he wants."

Turning swiftly with Percy at his heels, Shelton rushed out the door, got into the car, and drove away.

"We should've left before that happened, Shel."

"I know. Now you can say you told me so."

After asking around, they went to the other side of town to Max Feldman's store. Folk said he had a good reputation and treated everyone with respect. He was in business to make money. Since money never changed color, there was no way to indicate the color of the hand that passed it across the counter. Both Shelton and Percy laughed at the description of the man.

"Here we go again," Shelton said looking at Percy.

"No. There you go again. I didn't promise Helene any fur," Percy laughed. "So I'm not buying her one."

"I didn't promise Nat one either. But I'm gonna surprise her." After agreeing to meet back at the car in an hour, Percy walked up the street and Shelton went into Feldman's store.

Upon reaching the door, Shelton hesitated before entering. But once inside, he was surprised when the clerk, though white, spoke to him in a civil tone. When he realized he was treated with quiet dignity, his spirits lifted. He pushed aside the earlier ugly incident and bought Natalie a coat.

Then went up the street and purchased additional items. Afterwards, returning to the car, he put his packages inside and waited for Percy who didn't show up at the time they planned. Then he got this great idea. He went back into the store.

Christmas was a special time for Natalie. Holiday festivities actually put her in a trance. She became as giddy and as excited as her daughter, Makela, who felt sugarplums really did dance in her head as she waited for Santa to arrive.

Several days before Christmas, Natalie joined her mother, Odessa, her grandy, Maude, and her aunt, Helene, in the kitchen where they sipped home-made wine while baking cakes and pies for the holiday meal. The wine made Natalie heady. So she left the kitchen, went into the dining room, and stood at the window.

"You all right, Nat?" Helene asked as she entered the room, pulled a chair from the table, and sat down.

"Yes, I'm fine, auntie," Natalie said as she opened the window and let the crisp, cold air caress her face.

Natalie was in love, and like a child who looked forward to Santa's arrival, she could hardly wait to lie in Shelton's arms again. Life was good. Shelton had turned a new leaf. As of late, he treated them swell. She had no complaints.

"I just need some air," she answered. Gazing upward, she studied the gray clouds and wondered if they signaled a white Christmas. Of course, it made little difference to her whether it did or didn't snow. What mattered to her was family.

The season brought back good memories, and she often drifted into a world where only she and Shelton existed, and she became captive to some alluring, magical, spell.

Alan was home which meant the family would be together for the holidays with the exception of her Uncle Russell who never came.

He left home long ago on a quest for freedom, and never returned. The family understood to some extent. However, they were disappointed and disgusted when he decided to pass for white and deny his heritage, thereby severing his family ties.

When her mother and grandy came into the room, Natalie closed the window, and pushed her Uncle Russell to a corner in her heart where he could exist without pain. Then she walked to the table to join the women with whom she shared a strong bond.

Koko spent Christmas Eve with Makela at the farm. After enjoying the peppermint candy, pecans, and candied popcorn, all of which Shelton prepared, the girls lay in bed and talked excitedly about their expectations.

"I'm gonna stay awake all night so I can see Santa," Makela announced.

"Uh, uh," Koko mumbled. "Sorry, Makela, but you'll never see Santa."

"Oh, yes I will."

"Oh, no you won't because there *is* no Santa," Koko wisely informed her.

"There is so," Makela yelled.

"No, there isn't. Shel bought presents, and he and Nat will put them under the tree for us. If you don't believe me, ask Nat."

"I don't want to hear it." And for the first time in her life, Makela hated Koko. "I don't want to ask Mama anything," she said feeling so sick her stomach hurt. Hot tears stung her eyes, and she cried not because she didn't believe Koko, but because she did. She was hurt and angry because the *magic* of Christmas was gone.

Realizing it would never return, she wept as she took a leap towards another world, which she was not ready to enter.

Koko took Makela's hand in hers. "I'm sorry," she said. "I cried too when I learned Santa didn't really exist."

So on the very night when Makela should have been happiest, she was sad. Her imaginary world shattered, she felt strange.

On Christmas morning, the world seemed different because she accepted the fact that there was no Santa. Sighing, she closed that special door to Santa's world and followed Koko to the Christmas tree where they found, among other things, a bicycle for each of them.

Early Christmas morning, Shelton awoke Natalie with warm kisses and probing fingers. Their lovemaking was intense, and Natalie was swept away on a magic carpet that glided into a world only she knew.

Looking down, Shelton saw desire in her face. Natalie, like all the others, forgot the time of day at his slightest touch. She often called him savage. He smiled. He was good at what he did and, now, like always, she joined him in his savagery.

Natalie cried out. He covered her mouth with his to muffle her earth-shaking screams of pleasure. They exploded like some volcano, which had lain dormant for eons then suddenly erupted pushing forth its lava and ash. Together they reached the outer limit of pleasure—complete ecstacy.

Later that morning when Natalie and Shelton joined the girls, Koko ran to Natalie and threw her arms around her neck. "I love you, Nat." Not sure about Shelton's mood, she stood motionless, momentarily. Then he held out his arms. Rushing to him Koko thanked him with all her heart. "I love you too, Shel," she gushed causing Shelton to smile.

"Aren't you going to give your daddy a hug?" Natalie asked when Makela hugged her and kissed her cheek. Ignoring Natalie, she walked away and sat near the Christmas tree. Makela looked at Shelton and suddenly, it all came rushing back.

She glanced down at his feet and remembered the grey suede shoes he once wore. But he wore leather house slippers now. Sure, she wanted to throw her arms around his neck, but she couldn't.

"Why don't you kiss him for me, Mama?" she said.

"No, Makela. I think you should do that yourself," Natalie answered.

When Makela made no attempt to approach him, Shelton went over and sat on the floor beside her. He put his arm around her and kissed her cheek. She looked up and smiled.

"Oh, Daddy," she cried with mixed emotions. "This is my best Christmas ever."

Natalie was thrilled with her gifts, too. When she opened the big box she almost fainted. Inside was a beautiful, black, ankle length, fur coat. She caressed it gently. As she took it from the box, Shelton came over and helped her slip into it.

It felt warm and the satiny smooth material soothed her. Smiling, she turned and looked at him. As she pulled the lapel around her cheeks and buried her face in its softness, she wondered if she was dreaming, or if she had died and gone to heaven. She couldn't believe Shelton had given her such an expensive gift, and tears clouded her eyes.

Feeling content, Shelton grinned broadly as Natalie threw her arms around his neck. "I love you, Shelton Lamont," she shrieked convinced he loved her too.

"I love you, too, Nat," he said.

They later had breakfast with Shelton's family at Thaddeus Lamont's home. Afterwards, he, Natalie and the girls went into town where they spent the remainder of the day with Natalie's family.

That evening, Shelton took Natalie to the Lounge to listen to Tamara sing. And like Makela, it the happiest Christmas Natalie ever had.

🍁　　🍁　　🍁

"I wish you would stay for the coming holiday, son," Odessa said to Alan.

"I know you do, Mama. But I'm stationed on the west coast now and I gotta get back on time. We'll celebrate on the Base," Alan told her. "By the way, once I get settled, I'll send for Koko."

"Oh," Odessa was surprised. She would miss Koko, but she was pleased that Alan finally decided to take the child. "You just let me know when you're ready, and I'll send her your way."

"I'll do that, Mama," Alan said. And just two days after Christmas, he and Paige caught the train and left town.

🍁 🍁 🍁

A week later, Natalie wore her beautiful coat to church. After services ended, she stood outside and talked with several members of the congregation while they admired her coat.

"Oh, my," Carrie Lucas exclaimed touching the sleeve. "That is the prettiest coat I ever saw."

"I agree. It is pretty," Della commented.

"Thank you, ladies," Natalie said graciously.

"I wish I had one like it," Della said.

"Well, who do you think's gonna buy you anything?" Thea asked. "You never treated Warren right, He's gone forever. So stop your wishing,"

Della was so stumped by the comment, she had nothing to say. Her silence surprised everyone within earshot.

🍁 🍁 🍁

It was New Year's Eve, and a very pleased Shelton beamed that he put a smile on Natalie's face and made her feel like the happiest woman in the world.

To make sure he did everything right, Shelton spent the day with Natalie and her family. Later that evening, a short time after dinner, he took Natalie to the Lounge to celebrate.

When they stepped inside, Shelton smiled and waved to everyone as Natalie once again told him how happy she was to be his wife. Looking around, he made sure Melanie was not there. Satisfied that she went to Sugar Hill as planned, Shelton took Natalie in his arms, proceeded to dance, and have a good time just like they had before they married.

"Oh, Shel, I feel like a princess," Natalie confessed.

"You look like one too, baby," he told her and Natalie walked on air. She had everything she ever hoped for. Her world was perfect, she thought as Orchid Fountaine came to the table.

"Hey, Shel, how you doing?"

"I'm fine, Mrs. Fountaine."

"And how's your mama feeling?" Orchid asked.

"She was too sick to get out of bed today," he said.

"I'm sorry to here that. Tell her I'll try come out to see her soon," Orchid said.

"I'll do that," he said.

"And how are things going with you, young lady? You look quite happy," Orchid said.

"I am very happy," Natalie smiled.

"I'm glad to hear that. My, my," Orchid said. "What a pretty coat. Umhum, made especially for such a pretty lady," Orchid complimented.

"Why, thank you, Mrs. Fountaine." Natalie glowed.

"You're welcome, darling. Now I got to get back to work. This is one of the busiest nights of the year. It's good to see you out and about. Hope you have a good time tonight, honey," Orchid told her.

"I intend to do just that," Natalie said lighting up like a Christmas tree ornament.

Moments later, Tamara joined Natalie and Shelton at the table. They talked for a while then Shelton left them to talk with other friends.

"What's going on, Nat?" Tamara asked as she watched Shelton work his way through the crowd.

"Things couldn't be better. I'm very happy."

"That's great. You look lovely, and that coat is absolutely stunning," Tamara said.

"Thanks, Tam. You look rather stunning yourself," Natalie said speaking of the beautiful blue gown Tamara wore, which she made.

"I look good because of your talent, my friend," Tamara said. "You know that. You know, I often wonder what I would've done through the years without you and Liz. Your friendship sustained me."

"That goes for me, too. I just wish Liz was here now. I'd love to share this time with her, too. Shel has changed for the better and these are my best holidays."

"It's about time he did something right. I'm really happy for you," Tamara said. Turning her head towards the bar, she called for Zeke to send over a couple of drinks.

Zeke waved acknowledging the order just as Shelton returned to the table.

The night was clear and beautiful, and the stars were out. Midnight arrived, and as firecrackers burst loudly in the air and folk shot off their guns, Shelton slowly turned to Natalie. Raising his glass, he looked into her eyes.

"To my true love and the most wonderful woman in the world," he said. Then he kissed her. As Tamara led them in Auld Lang Syne, Natalie beamed.

# CHAPTER 39

The weekend following the New Year, the loud, pulsating music invited folk to enter the Lounge and have a good time. Just as Melanie reached the door, a group of people rudely pushed past her.

Stepping aside, she allowed them to forge ahead. She was in no hurry. Upon entering the door, she stood momentarily until her eyes became accustomed to the dimly lit atmosphere. Then she slowly slunk across the floor as gracefully as a leopard stalking prey. As heads turned, she smiled.

"Hubba, hubba, you looking good and sweet as candy tonight," Bull Jackson yelled. "How about a lick, baby?" he whispered when she was closer to him.

"No, thank you." She laughed when she really wanted to smack his face and tell him to get back in the kitchen where he belonged. Bull worked with Eva in the café, which was further back past the bar and known as the Bayou Bowl.

As far as she was concerned, Bull was a good name for him. He was a dark-skinned, short man, with an unusually thick body and thick neck, and he had the biggest eyes she had ever seen.

She still smarted about that day at the canal when he taunted Brick and Goose until they foolishly jumped into the water. Bull was much older and should've known better. Both boys almost drowned.

No. She didn't need the likes of him. She already had her man who not only made her feel like a million-dollar baby, he kept her looking like one, too.

Tamara was on stage singing a torch song when Natalie and Helene entered the door. Her long, red hair hung down her back, and she wore one of Natalie's latest designs, a long, emerald green satin gown with a long sash. The gown fit her like a glove.

The dance floor was crowded, but Natalie and Helene finally made their way to the bandstand where they waved to Tamara until she saw them and returned the wave.

The music taunted them to dance, and because Natalie's feet tingled she hoped Shelton was there because she was ready to enjoy the evening.

"This was a good idea, Nat. The music is great, and I'm glad I came," Helene said.

"So am I, auntie. The music makes my feet itch," Natalie said just as Percy came up and grabbed Helene's hand.

"Fancy seeing you here," he grinned and danced Helene across the floor.

Natalie watched them briefly. Looking around, she saw Billy rock across the floor with Carrie Lucas. Natalie started to push her way through the crowd, but someone caught her hand.

"How you doing, beautiful?" Fats teased.

"Oh, it's you, Cash," Natalie said.

"The one and only," he said. Then grabbing her hand, he swung her about smoothly. He was a big man, but his weight posed no problem for his feet. He was still a good dancer. They danced to two tunes.

"Thanks, Nat. I enjoyed that."

"You're welcome, my friend. I enjoyed it too. By the way, are you happy with Zenna?"

"I'm happier than ever," he said, "How about another dance?"

"I don't think so," Natalie said. "Why not get Zenna out on the floor?"

"Guess I'll do that," Fats grinned. "See you later."

"Sure thing," she replied as she started towards the bar. But before she got there Delano Phillips pulled her back onto the dance floor. He too was a smooth dancer, and she glided with him.

"Can I have just one more dance, Nat?" he begged thinking how good she felt in his arms.

"Not now, Delano. Perhaps some other time," she said.

"Okay, okay." Delano threw his hands up defensively. "See you later."

"Sure thing," she answered as Tamara came from the stage to where she stood. Then the two women snaked their way through the crowd to the bar.

"If you're looking for Shel, he's not here," Della informed Natalie.

"Thanks, Della. But I'm not looking for anyone," Natalie lied as Carrie came over. "It's good to see you out and about, Nat."

"Thanks, Carrie. It's nice to be out."

"Hey, Tam," Carrie called. "Girl, you sure can sing."

"Thanks. Glad you enjoy it."

"Lawdy, Nat. Do you know Mel…" Della started, but Carrie's elbow connected with her ribs signaling her to keep her mouth shut.

Natalie looked up. Zeke, whose round pleasant face reminded her of a beautiful ripe peach, reached across the bar and took her hand in his.

"How you doing, beautiful?" he inquired as his wife, Eva, came from the kitchen to the bar and waved.

"Hey, Nat," Eva said as she took money from the counter and put it into the register. "It's good to see you."

"Thanks, Eva."

"You sure looking good," Zeke said. "Hope you have as good a time tonight as you did last time."

"I hope so too," Natalie leaned over the bar and whispered as the music started to play again. "By the way, have you seen Shel?"

"Sure. He and Grey came by earlier, but they left just before you came in. Now, what would you like? Name your drink. It's on the house. You can have anything your little heart desires."

"Oh, my God!" Tamara exclaimed. Natalie turned. "Do you see what I see?"

"What is it?" Zeke asked. "You two look like you saw a ghost." Turning his head, he stared.

"I don't know how you do it, Nat. If I was Shelton's wife, I'd poison him," Tamara said.

"Good grief, Tam, don't talk that way. You'll just get Nat all riled up. And as for you Nat, you should forget it," Zeke said.

"How can I, Zeke?" Natalie felt faint and grabbed the edge of the bar as her happiness slowly ebbed. For standing just a few feet from her was an undeniably happy Melanie Joyride wearing a coat identical to hers.

As Melanie raised her arm to wave to someone across the room, Natalie caught a glimpse of the wide, gold bracelet. She couldn't be sure, but it was her guess everything Melanie wore was exactly like hers.

Shelton lied again, and she wanted to scream. But she didn't. She wanted to rip Melanie's face to shreds. But she didn't do that either. She was glad the band played loudly so no one could hear the loud pumping of her heart.

"I'm so sorry about this shit, Nat. I gotta get back to work, but we'll talk later," Tamara said. "Okay?"

"Okay," Natalie said as tears stung her eyes.

🍁   🍁   🍁

Just as Melanie threw back her head and laughed, she saw Natalie. Her laughter died as she stared into the face of the one woman she wished never existed. She longed for the floor to open up and swallow her.

Now, she knew why that bastard told her to wear the coat only when she went out of town.

But what good is it to have a pretty coat like this and never wear it, she thought. I want folk to see me. I want folk to know how much I mean to my man. I want everyone to know Shel's gonna leave Nat soon and marry me.

Even though she tried to convince herself that this was true, she didn't believe it. Suddenly, she felt sick. She knew Shel, and there was only one thing she could do now. She prayed he wouldn't kill her.

🍁   🍁   🍁

Helene was stunned to see Melanie wearing the same coat as Natalie.

"Oh, no," she exclaimed. "Look Percy."

"What is it?" he asked.

"Can't you see? Melanie has the same damn coat as Nat."

"So what?"

"So what? It means Shel gave it to her," Helene said.

"Maybe he did and maybe he didn't," Percy said hoping it wasn't so.

"We'll find out soon enough," Helene said as she walked away and elbowed her way through the crowd.

"I can't believe this. I knew Shel had gall, but I never expected the bastard to do something like this," Helene said when she reached Natalie and Zeke. "I'm so sorry, Nat."

"Here, Nat. Take this. Drink it." Eva handed her a shot of liquor. Natalie accepted and took a sip.

"I wouldn't blame you if you jumped Melanie. She's no kid. She knows exactly what she's doing. I got no pity for her or Shel," Eva said.

"I suppose that little minx is wearing the same perfume, too." Natalie spoke softly though she seethed.

"What's that?" Zeke asked.

"The perfume," she muttered. "I'll bet Melanie's wearing my perfume, too."

"Come on, Nat. Let's get out of here," Helene coaxed.

"You want someone to drive you home?" Zeke asked.

"No need to drive us. The crisp air will be good for us." Helene took Natalie's arm and guided her through the crowd and outside into the cold night air.

"I'm so sorry this happened, Nat," Helene said once they were outside.

"So am I," she cried. Remember the day Sebastian and Wesley almost drowned?" Natalie asked speaking of Brick and Goose.

"Of course, I remember. I guess if Shel and Fats hadn't pulled them from the water they wouldn't be around now," said Helene.

"Well, according to Makela and Koko, Melanie was there and Shel kissed her. I wish she had jumped in the water and drowned."

"Oh, stop it, Nat. You don't mean that," Helene reprimanded. "You're just upset."

"Shel said Melanie meant nothing to him, but he lied."

"I know. So you gotta talk to him," Helene told her. Then they walked home in silence.

❦   ❦   ❦

As Natalie and Helene came onto the porch, the radio was playing softly and a bright light from the room shimmered onto the porch.

Several weeks earlier Odessa removed the uncomfortable sofa and chairs from the living room and replaced them with much softer furniture. This was where her daddy and granddaddy spent their evenings now.

"Listen, Nat. I'm curious. Can you tell me what Shel's got that makes you go through so much with him?"

"I love him, auntie," Natalie whispered as they tipped down the hallway to the back of the house where family members sat around the dining table.

"I don't know why I asked," Helene sighed. "But you gotta use your head instead of your heart, honey. You can't go on like this. It's time you did something about your situation."

"What's wrong, Mama?" Makela asked as Natalie and Helene came into the room. "Why are you crying?" Makela went over and stood near Natalie.

"It's nothing, Makela. Don't worry. She'll be okay." Helene pulled out a chair and motioned Natalie to sit.

"What is it, Nat?" Odessa looked concerned. "Looks like you saw a ghost."

"She did," Helene retorted. "We saw Melanie Joyride."

"Queenie, Sophia. Take the girls and go up front," Odessa said at the mention of Melanie's name.

"I don't want to go to the front," Koko protested.

"Unless you want your behind warmed, you'll get out of here," Odessa threatened. "Now," she said once the girls left the room. "What did Melanie say to upset you so?"

"It's not what she said, Odessa. It's what the little minx wore," Helene said.

"Mercy, Helene. What's all the suspense? Tell us what you're talking about," Maude demanded.

"Melanie was wearing a coat exactly like mine." Natalie spoke for the first time since they entered the room.

"What's wrong with that?" Odessa asked.

"Shel bought it. That's what's wrong with it."

"Oh, Nat, don't go jumping the gun now," Odessa chided though she suspected Natalie was right.

"For heaven's sake, Mama, how can you say that? I know Shelton. He's been sweet on Melanie for a long time. He's also the only man in town who can afford that coat."

"Or fool enough to buy it," Maude muttered.

"I agree. It's no coincidence." Natalie suddenly hated the coat. Standing, she let it slide to the floor. Odessa picked it up. Holding it to her cheek, she wondered how something so beautiful could cause so much ugliness.

"Now you listen, Nat. First you talk to Shel. Listen to what he says before you accuse him. Things might not be as bad as they seem." Even as she spoke, Odessa's gut told her Shelton was as guilty as sin.

"Oh, come on, Odessa. Nat's no fool. Shel lied. He's sleeping with Melanie and it's time Nat faced it. Shel is a heartless bastard," Helene rationalized.

"My Lord, Helene," Maude said. "I never heard you speak your mind before.

"I know, but I'm mad. I just wish Nat would wake up."

"If Shel gave Melanie that coat," Odessa said. "He's the biggest rat in town."

"Sure he is, and Nat deserves better, but Nat's got to work it out. We can't do it for her," Helene clarified. "Of course, I'd like to see her happy."

"So would I," Odessa sighed.

"Yeah, but we don't want to accuse Shel before we know the facts," Maude reminded. "Now, if he did buy the coat, I'd like to kick that hot-blooded devil where it hurts."

"So would I, Mother," Helene looked at Odessa who still held the coat. "That coat just might be the straw that breaks the camel's back."

"You could be right, Helene." Odessa caressed the coat as she thought about her son-in-law. He was, in her opinion, as slick as boiled okra. Usually, he was able to talk his way out of a clamshell, but she wondered if he could get out of this one.

"I'm so sorry, Nat. I've been through a lot with your daddy. I've stuck with him over the years. But he never bought anyone a coat like this. Not even me. I can't tell you what to do, hon. Only you can make that decision. All I can say is think about it first. Things just might blow over."

"Shame on you, Odessa," Helene shook her head.

"What would you do, Helene?" Odessa queried.

"I'd send Shel packing, and I don't mean tomorrow, either." Helene looked serious.

"Don't worry, auntie." Natalie realized Helene showed a part of herself she usually kept hidden. "I'll talk with him tonight. And for your information, Mama, things can't get much worse. Shel treats Melanie better than other women he's known."

"Well, just remember. I'm here for you." Odessa left the room to put the coat away.

"So am I, honey," Helene informed her. "You're not alone."

"I appreciate that, auntie. Life's funny, you know."

"Yeah, it is." Maude agreed as Odessa came back into the room.

"Men have approached me for years, but I never gave them a chance because I loved Shel."

"We know that," Odessa said.

Vince Baraldi's brother, Frank, was sweet on me, but I didn't want that kind of relationship. So, I never gave him the time of day. And there were others, too. Cash was crazy about me, but I loved Shel." Natalie grimaced as anguish squeezed her gut. Moments later she went to the bedroom and got the coat.

"Why don't you take it, auntie?" She laid it on Helene's lap.

"I can't do that. You know as well as I if you don't wear the coat home you and Shel might do battle right here. That's not what you want. You want to talk to him in the privacy of your home. So wear the coat home."

"She's right." Maude pushed her chair back and stood up. "I'm so sorry. I hope things work out for you, Nat." Maude kissed Natalie's cheek. "I'm off to bed. Good night, dear."

"Good night, Grandy."

"I hope things work out, too," Odessa said as Maude left the room.

"I know you do. But it's over, Mama." Natalie took the coat back to the bedroom and laid it on the bed. She would wear the coat home, but it would be the last time it touched her body.

❦ ❦ ❦

"What's wrong, Nat?" Shelton asked once they were in the car and on their way home.

"We'll talk about it when we get home," she snapped. As they drove in silence, she still saw Melanie in the same coat, and it made her skin crawl.

When they arrived home, the house was cold, but she took the coat off anyway and threw it on the sofa. While Shelton lit the gas heater, she helped Makela prepare for bed

"Can we just leave Daddy and go away, Mama?" Makela asked when they were alone. Natalie put her finger to her lips signaling Makela to keep quiet.

Natalie now accepted the fact that her husband could never be faithful. She was tired, and it was time she started thinking with her head instead of her heart. She returned to the bedroom, sat on the bed, and waited for him to come into the room.

"I went to the Lavender Lounge this evening," she said as soon as he entered the room.

"So, did you enjoy yourself?" There were times when he hated Nat's uppity ways. Everybody else called it the Joint, but it was the *Lavender Lounge* for her.

"No. I didn't exactly enjoy it. Melanie Joyride was there," she said.

"So what?" He spoke nonchalantly, but he fumbled nervously with his shirt buttons. "It's not the first time you saw Melanie. I told you she means nothing to me."

Shelton thought about how he gave Natalie everything she needed. He even gave her special Christmas gifts. Here he was being offered more pussy than a reigning king, and instead of taking advantage of the opportunities, lately, he stayed home just to make her happy. Any other woman would let things be, but Natalie wanted his soul.

"Melanie lives in this town too, you know," he told her. "So it won't be the last time you see her. Now what's the big deal?"

"You should know what the big deal is," she snapped. Then she got up and went into the bathroom where she stayed longer than necessary. She wanted him to squirm before she gave him a piece of her mind. Of course, under the circumstances, she was amazed she had a mind or that it even worked.

Wearing a long nightgown, she returned to the room ready for bed.

"That's a pretty gown," Shelton said hoping she already forgot about Melanie.

"As I said earlier…"

"I hope you don't start on that Melanie thing again. 'Cause I don't want to hear it."

"I saw Melanie this evening and…"

"You already told me that," he interrupted her in mid-sentence. "Tell me something I don't know. What's got you so unnerved?" He spoke more confidently than he felt. "I asked you a question," he yelled as Natalie turned back the covers on the bed.

"I heard you." She went to the dresser and sat down. Picking up the brush, she ran it through her hair. Then staring into the mirror she was taken aback. What she saw scared her. Her hair was sprinkled with gray. Life was passing her by. Death would soon claim her, and she had not yet lived. It was time she did something. She turned and faced him.

He obviously took her for a complete fool. Otherwise, he would have known she would learn about him and Melanie. But, like most men, he was an egotist.

"Melanie wore a coat exactly like mine." She spoke softly but sternly.

Looking smug, he stood in the middle of the floor. His hands fell limply to his side, and his shoulders slumped. Then he sat heavily in the chair and stared at her.

Now he understood why she was rankled. He was rankled too. Natalie had done the unusual and went to the Joint without him.

He wasn't sure what he felt about Melanie. He told her never to wear that damn coat in town. But she had done exactly that, proving she was as brainless as her two cousins. He couldn't wait to see her 'cause he was gonna trounce her ass like elderberries for wine. But first he had to settle things with Nat.

"So? When they made one of them coats they didn't stop, you know. They made lots of them."

"I'm no idiot, Shel. So don't play me for one. We both know how Melanie got the coat. She also wore jewelry like mine, and I suppose you gave her the same perfume, too. So don't lie about it." Her voice trembled, but she held back the tears.

"Now you listen to me, Natalie Dawson Lamont. I want you to stop talking crazy."

"You *bastard*," she hissed as she lost control. "You were man enough to give Melanie those things. Why aren't you man enough to admit it?"

"Why should I? I told you I didn't give her anything, Nat."

Suddenly, his composure returned. He was as cool as a springtime breeze and believed his own devious bull.

"My God, Shel. I've always loved you. I thought you loved me, too. But I was wrong."

"I do love you, Nat." He bent down and pulled off his shoes. "Whatever you might think about me, I do care for you. Now, let's end this talk," he said feeling in total control.

"You couldn't possibly care," she said ignoring his request. "Otherwise, you wouldn't have done it."

She had done so much to hold him. She wasn't sure, but she suspected Koko was not her brother's child, but perhaps his. So she kept Koko close to Makela.

She thought when they knew for sure who the child was they would explain it to the girls. These things happened every day in their neck of the woods. And most folk, handled them in a civil fashion just as she did.

She wanted to talk to Shelton about it, but it was never necessary because Alan accepted full responsibility for Koko and that put an end to it. She loved Shelton so much, but he couldn't see it or accept it.

"Goddammit, Nat," he screamed suddenly. "So what if I gave her the coat? I never been a pussy-whipped wimp and I ain't about to become one now."

He was as much pissed with himself as he was with Natalie and Melanie. Sure he acted like a fool, but he gave Natalie everything. Still, in his mind she was a vixen and wouldn't be satisfied until she held his balls in her hands and blew on them. The more he thought about the situation, the madder he got.

He remembered the humiliation he suffered to buy that damn coat. The only difference between him and Percy was nobody fired a shot.

If Percy had just come back to the car on time, he never would have gone back into that store.

Of course, he wanted to blame Percy, but it was his own fault. He knew it was the wrong thing to do. But he thought he could get away with it.

Returning to the present and the situation with Natalie, Shelton asked, "What you intend to do about it, Nat?" Then rushing to the dresser where Natalie sat, he opened one drawer after the other. He would show her. She'd only read books about the river Nile, but she actually thought she was as important as one of them goddamn queens everybody talked about.

"What's wrong with you, Shel? What're you looking for?" she asked timidly.

"The scissors," he yelled as he pick up the shears and gripped them in his hand. "I'm gonna cut off yo' goddamn hair."

"No, no," she screamed. "Please. Don't cut my hair." She tried to stand, but he wrapped her hair around his hand, pulled her to the floor and held her firmly.

"I'm tired of your whining, you little tight-ass bitch," he screamed. While jerking back her head, he put his knee on her thigh, and stared down into her face.

"It's time for you to understand one thing. I'm the man of this house. You do as I say, woman. I tell you when to breathe," he hissed. "You got a good life. Now I'm gonna teach you a lesson once and for all. I'm gonna cut off every fucking strand of your crown and glory."

"Please don't," she pleaded as the shears touched the nape of her neck and she heard the click of them. She sobbed as he sheared her long beautiful hair from her head as though she were a sheep. Throwing it aside, he let her go. Standing over her, he looked down at her.

"Come on, get up. Take a look in the mirror. See what you look like now."

She did as she was told and got up from the floor. Walking over to the dresser, she sat down. Looking in the mirror, she cried.

"That's right, baby. Cry your eyes out. 'Cause you're bald now." He laughed. "You little sidity half-breed bitch. You're just like your Uncle Percy. You think your shit don't stink.

"Now, I wanna know what you gonna do about this Melanie thing? Talk to me. Come on, tell me. What the *fuck* you intend to do?"

"I'm leaving you," she screamed causing him to step back and stare at her. The words shocked him.

Trembling, Natalie said, "I don't need this, and I'm not taking it anymore. You don't seem to understand. I can live without you."

"Oh, yeah? And who told you that?" he bellowed.

"No one told me. I just know what I want."

"And what is it you want?"

"All I ever wanted was the simple life, Shel. That's all. I've always tried to walk that extra mile for you. I wanted your fidelity and your respect, but you weren't capable of giving it."

"I suppose you think you'll get that love and respect from Delano?" It was then he actually felt the hairs rise on his neck. "Talk to me, Nat. I bet he's been honing his pencil on you all along."

Feeling nauseous, Natalie sat quietly and studied his face. It was over. She was tired.

The vein that snaked down his forehead seemed ready to burst. He looked venomous. Instinct told her he was about to strike her. He did, and the force of the blow knocked her to the floor.

She tried to stand. But he held her down and slapped her several times. Then he pummeled her with his fists. She tried to crawl away, but her long nightgown hugged her knees. As she fought to free them, he kicked her in the behind. The force pushed her into the iron bed frame. Blood spewed down her chin.

"Please, don't hit me again," she whimpered. She turned and looked up into the handsome face she loved so much, now ugly with rage.

"You're never satisfied, you lousy little minx. I'm tired of your whining. I'm gonna kick your ass 'til the sun comes up," he shouted. Then raising his foot, he maniacally, kicked her backside again.

She was certain he had lost his mind. This time he would kill her.

❦ ❦ ❦

While lying in bed, her parents' ugly voices startled Makela. She covered her head and stuck her fingers in her ears. She knew why her mother was so upset. She and Koko overheard her mama cry and the family talk earlier. Her daddy had given her mama and Melanie the same gifts for Christmas.

There were three ways to get to the dining room, but her Gramma Odessa had closed all the doors. Even so, she and Koko sneaked onto the porch and listened. By the time Queenie had found them and threatened to tell, they were almost frozen.

❦ ❦ ❦

Ignoring the excruciating pain he inflicted on her, Natalie stuck her hand under the bed and inside the shoe box. Gripping the cold steel handle, she rolled over and pointed the gun at Shelton. He jumped back. His eyes widened and mouth dropped open. "I'm sorry, Nat," he screamed. "I didn't mean it."

"You meant it," she yelled. "You meant it every time you did it. Now I want to make sure you never hit me or my child again." Then she aimed carefully, pulled the trigger, and looked dumbfounded when Shelton fell to the floor.

❦ ❦ ❦

Suddenly, Makela jumped from the bed and ran to their bedroom. She was certain her daddy had hurt her mother. But when she reached the room, she was surprised to see, not her daddy, but her mother holding the gun.

"Mama, Mama," she screamed soulfully, pulling at Natalie's nightgown. "Did you shoot my daddy?"

She didn't always like her daddy, but something tugged at her heart. When she got no response from Natalie, she knelt beside her daddy. Crying painfully, she attempted to lift his head. Unable to do so, she lowered her little head and asked, agonizingly, "Oh, Mama, Mama. Did you *kill* my daddy?"

# CHAPTER 40

As the sound of the shot still resonated in her ears, Natalie suddenly realized what she'd done. Rushing to the phone, she picked up the receiver and dialed.

"Grey," she cried hysterically. "Can you come? I just shot Shel."

"You what?" Greyland screamed.

"I just shot Shel," she repeated.

"Goddammit, I expected this for a long time."

"I'm sorry, Grey, but I thought he was going to kill me. I didn't want to hurt him."

"Is he dead?"

"I don't know."

"Okay, I'll be there shortly." Then he hung up the phone.

"What is it, Grey?" Jozell asked as she entered the room. "You look sick."

"Nat just shot Shel."

"What?" Jozell screamed. "Is he dead?"

"She doesn't know. I'm going out there, but first I'm gonna call daddy." Picking up the phone, he called Thaddeus. After speaking with his daddy, Greyland said, "I gotta call Doc Peterson.

"What'll we do if Doc's in surgery or patching up someone else?" Jozell asked.

"If he was doing all that, we'd know wouldn't we? This is Meadowsbrook and bad news travels faster here than a telegram."

"Hey, doc? This is Greyland. Nat's shot Shel. Can you meet us at their house?"

"Doc says he'll meet us there and daddy and mama will, too," Greyland said hanging up the phone.

"Which car are you driving, Grey?" Jozell asked because she never rode in the wagon.

"The Ford."

"The Ford? You mean you're not taking the wagon?" she asked.

"No, I'm not, Jozell. I don't want to even think that Shel's messed around and got himself killed."

"I'm going with you then."

"Okay, let's go." Then they both rushed out the house and got into the car.

Greyland put the car in gear and pulled onto the road. Not long after he saw the lights of other cars behind him. He was certain one belonged to Doc Peterson.

It was then Greyland realized he hadn't taken the time to call the Dawsons, but he knew they'd heard the news and a couple of those cars behind him belonged to the family.

🍁   🍁   🍁

The Dawsons knew what happened because as soon as Doc Peterson hung up the phone he told Ellie, and Ellie wasted no time calling Odessa.

The first to arrive at the farmhouse were Thaddeus and Esther, where a hysterical Natalie waited at the door and a tearful Makela stood beside her.

"Where is he?" Thaddeus asked.

"In the bedroom," Natalie replied as he and Esther hurried to the room.

When Doc Peterson entered the house he never asked where Shelton was because he already knew, and so did Greyland. They went straight to the bedroom.

Feeling despondent, Odessa hurried into the neat little farm house.

"Oh, my God. What's that monster done to my daughter?" she asked. Staring, she realized Natalie's eyes were almost swollen shut, her chin was cut open, and her long beautiful hair was cut off up to her ears.

"What have you done, Nat?" Odessa asked as the gravity of what Natalie did hit home. Natalie still stood near the front door until Odessa took her hand and led her to the sofa. She sat down beside her daughter and put her arm around her shoulder.

"I shot him, Mama," Natalie sniffled.

"I know you did, hon, and the whole thing sickens me."

"I didn't want to, but I thought he had gone crazy. I thought he was going to kill me," Natalie cried as Makela put her head in her lap and whimpered.

While the families stood by, Doc Peterson put the stethoscope to Shelton's chest and announced, "He's still breathing."

"Thank God," was the cry from everyone in the bedroom. They all started to breathe again.

"He's alive," Helene announced as she and Percy came from the bedroom to the front room.

"Thank God," Odessa sighed. "I'm so glad. I don't want my daughter going to jail for defending herself."

"Jail," Percy screamed. "Hell, if anyone deserves jail time, it's Shel. He's the cause of Nat going off the deep end."

"Shel almost killed me, uncle. I hurt all over."

With the help of Percy and Marcus, Greyland and Doc Peterson put Shelton in Greyland's car and took him to the hospital.

"I'm sorry it's come to this Nat, but it's not unexpected," Thaddeus said as he and Esther prepared to leave the house and go to the hospital.

"We know Shel brought this on himself. We've talked to him over the years, but he never listened. You know that. We'll talk at length later. I just want you to know I speak for the whole family. We still love you."

"Thank you, Papa. I'm so sorry, but I thought you'd be taking me to the morgue instead of taking Shel to the hospital."

"Let's be thankful it's no worse, and what Papa said goes for Grey and me, too. We love you. I got to go now," Jozell told her. Then she got in the truck with Thaddeus and Esther and drove off.

"Pack a bag, Nat. There's no need to stay here. You might as well come home," Marcus told her. "I'm so sorry I told you to stick with the marriage. Nothing is worth the beating Shel gave you. I never want to hear his name spoken again."

"I'd like to *shoot* Shel myself," Helene said, as they locked the farmhouse door. "I ought to throw away this goddamn key."

"No need doing all that, Helene. Just put the key under that big flower pot over there and get in the car," Percy said.

🍁 🍁 🍁

Only hours after Natalie shot Shelton, the news was all over town. Jenny Joyride immediately sat a tearful Melanie down and called Spuds.

"Now look'a here, Melanie Shel ain't your husband," Jenny said.

"I know that, Mama. But Nat didn't have to shoot him," Melanie whimpered.

"Hell, you better be glad she shot *him* and not *you*," Jenny said. "Talk to your daughter, Spuds." Jenny spoke just as he came into the room.

"I heard what your mother said. She's right, you know. Nat's tired of Shel and his crap. And she ain't crazy 'bout you. So I think it's time you put Shel behind you. Time to move on before you get hurt. You see, all your wrongdoing catches up with you sooner or later. Then it's payback time."

"And who are you to talk?" Melanie yelled.

"I think it's time to mend your ways young lady," Spuds said ignoring his daughter.

Looking up at her daddy, Melanie wondered if he'd lost his mind. Shoot! She loved Shelton and she wasn't about to give him up. She was gonna *marry* him.

❦ ❦ ❦

The day after Natalie shot Shelton, he lay in bed in the hospital moaning. When his family came in to see him he moaned louder and hoped his daddy wouldn't blame him for what happened.

"Ain't no need you moaning, 'cause you brought it on yourself," Thaddeus reminded him. "I don't know if you care or not, but you lost Nat. She's never coming back, and I don't blame her. You never treated her right even though she gave you many chances."

"I'm sorry, Shel. What happened, son?" His mother Esther asked. "Did you lose your mind? I saw Nat, and she looked like she was put through a grinder."

"Stop all that moaning," Thaddeus told him. "You were man enough to do all that shit. So you should be man enough to take the pain."

"Sorry, brother, I had a feeling something like this would happen. But I never thought Nat would do it. You're lucky you ain't dead. She never shot off that gun before. Hell, she could've killed you," Greyland said.

"Hey, Shel," Jozell grinned broadly. "Are you dying?"

"Nah, he ain't dying," Thaddeus said. "But I bet you he ain't gonna buy another fur coat. Am I right, Shel?"

"Umhum," Shelton groaned. As Doc Peterson came into the room he heard Thaddeus speak about the fur coat.

"I'll agree with you on that, Thad. If Nat had shot an eigth of an inch closer, she would've shot off his cock, and he would really have reason to groan," Doc Peterson said. "Hell, she might've put him out of action for a long, long time."

"Oh my God," Shelton groaned.

🍁 🍁 🍁

"So, you finally did what you should've done long ago," Tamara laughed the very next day after it happened. "You shot Shel where it hurts. I bet that will cool him down a while."

"It wasn't something I thought I'd ever do, but Shel went crazy, Tam. It was the only way to stop him."

"Well, we can see from the beating he gave you that you did the right thing. I can't believe him. I mean he caused the problem. And don't tell me you're going back. 'Cause if you do, you're as crazy as Shel is."

"I have no plans to ever go back. It's time I moved on," Natalie said.

"Right, it's time we got on that train and visited Liz. Whatta you think about that?" Tamara asked.

"Sounds like a good idea."

Natalie stayed in bed for three days before she was able to move about normally again.

"Do we have to go back, Mama?" Makela asked a few days later.

"Not this time, baby," Natalie replied.

🍁 🍁 🍁

"Hello, Liz? This is Nat."

"I know. And I hope you're calling to say you're coming to see us."

"That's right. Tam and I will be there in the spring as soon as school is out."

"That's great. I'm sorry about what happened," Elizabeth said.

"Oh, you already know?"

"You know Mama already called me, girl. I'm just happy things are no worse than they are. It's time you gave some thought about coming out here to live."

"I think Tam's thinking that way, too. I just might do that," Natalie said.

"I hope you mean that," Elizabeth said.

"I do. I'll talk with you about it later. Give my regards to Aunt Vi and Uncle Joe, will you?"

"I sure will and you do the same. Tell Tam I'm looking forward to seeing you both. Love ya, Nat."

🍁   🍁   🍁

Shelton didn't die, but the Dawsons wished he had, and they spent endless hours trying to find some way to put him in jail and keep him there.

"Did you see Nat?" Della asked Carrie. "Shel cut off all that pretty hair."

"It's a shame," Carrie said. "And it's all because of that little minx Melanie and a damn fur coat."

"Well, you know Shel's always been wild. But I can bet you Nat's tamed him a bit. I guarantee you he won't buy another fur coat for years to come," Della whooped with laughter.

"Hey, what's going on?" Thea asked when she caught Della and Carrie in Michael's Market. "Did you hear the news?" she asked. "Shel cut off Nat's hair and Nat shot him in the nuts."

"As far as I'm concerned, Shel deserved it," Virgil said.

"I guess you're right," Tilly said surprising everyone by joining in the conversation.

"Just goes to show. You mess with fire, you'll soon get burned," said Lula Hanks who returned to Meadowsbrook and now lived peacefully with Tilly and Virgil.

"That news is old and stinking now," Seb Pardeau said. "We know all about it."

"I'm sure you do. You might be old but ain't nothing wrong with your hearing," Thea laughed.

"That's right," said Candyman Cates. "And Shel's lucky Nat didn't kill him. I doubt she ever shot a gun before."

"Ain't it the truth?" Thea said. "I hear she still loves him though."

"Yeah, she might love him, but I bet she'll never go back," Carrie said.

"You sure about that?" Thea laughed.

"I'm just going by what Nat told me," Carrie said. "She said if she went back, the next time she might kill him, and that's not something she wants to do."

"I hear she and Tam gonna leave town come spring or summer," Thea said.

"That's the latest," Della laughed. "Stay tuned."

❦ ❦ ❦

Sitting at her desk, Natalie put the last bit of sandwich in her mouth. Chewing slowly, she mulled over her situation.

Suddenly, the enormity of what happened and the burden that lay ahead frightened her. Now as doubt consumed her, she almost choked.

Pushing her chair from the desk, she rushed over and opened the window just enough to help her breathe better.

Looking down on the playground, she watched the children at play. They amazed her. The day was cold and windy, yet they braved the elements to play games. Nothing bothered them. If one fell down, he picked himself up and tried again.

They had no worries or cares. Of course, Makela was an exception to the rule. Everything worried her. Scanning the grounds, she looked for her daughter, but saw no sign of her or Koko and presumed they'd found comfort inside the building.

She thought about how much she once loved Shelton just as Delano came into the room.

"Hi, Nat," Delano said. Beaming, he joined her at the window.

"Hi, Delano. You seem happy. What's up?"

Delano gazed down at Natalie but thought of his wife, Sunny, who had run off with that smooth talking Slick Joyride. Even though he came back to town once or twice a year, he made sure their paths never crossed. He never knew what happened to Sunny, and he never expected her back.

Even if she came back, he wanted no part of her. Besides, if he played his cards right, Nat would be his wife and the next Mrs. Phillips.

Of course, Natalie puzzled him for years. He never understood how a woman of her standing wasted herself with the likes of Shelton. Well, he sighed. He hoped she might consider giving him a bit of that affection she once wasted on her low-life husband.

"I've wanted to talk to you for some time now," he stated, "but I never got the chance. He cleared his throat. "I'm sure you know how I feel about you. And I'd like to ask a question." When she didn't respond, he continued. "I'm glad it's over between you and Shel. He was never good enough for you. Now I'm wondering if you'd consider spending some time with me."

"You what?" She was annoyed that he felt he could push his way into her life. Shel had been right, she thought. It seemed Delano did have plans for her, but he was nowhere in *her* future plans. Their closest contact was in the classroom, and she hoped to keep it that way.

She studied him. He was almost seven feet tall with skin as yellow as a squash. For the most part he was clean. But his clothes hung too loose on his bony body, and he wore the same necktie day after day around his scrawny neck.

She noticed a greasy spot on the tie and wondered if it was a remnant from Sunday's meal. He was nice and a very good friend, but that was it.

"I said I'm glad you're no longer with Shel. If you give me a chance, I'll do anything for you."

"Forget it, Delano. This is not the right time for such foolishness." She spoke pleasantly. "Even though Shel and I are no longer together, he's too crazy for me to chance such a thing. Therefore, getting close to you or anyone else would not be smart at this time.

"You and I've been friends a long time, and I think it's best to keep it that way. Friendship is all I need right now." She smiled sweetly as he grimaced, and his thin shoulders sagged.

"Think about it. You don't want me to have more problems than I already have. Do you?"

"You're right. I'm aware of Shel's temper," Delano said as he struggled to regain his composure. "I'm sorry. I didn't mean to rush you, but you know I'm crazy about you. I'd be nice to you. I'd…"

"I know all that, Delano, but I can't." She spoke softly.

"Oh, come on, Nat. You don't mean *never*, do you? Please don't shut the door on me yet," he pleaded.

"I've said all I have to say." She turned her back and looked out the window again.

Delano felt as if she had slapped his face. He was not stupid. He was just crazy about her, but she'd just told him it was never to be.

"Well, lunch is about over." He fidgeted for a moment. "I suppose I'd better get back to my classroom."

"Yes, I suppose you better," she turned around and gave him her sweetest smile.

"I'll see you later then?"

"Of course, you will," she told him. He turned and walked away, leaving her to ponder her future. Though the thought of leaving her family even for a short time frightened her, she decided it was time she spread her wings. She planned to take that trip with Tam to visit Liz as soon as school closed for summer.

The clanging bell signaled the end of the lunch hour and interrupted her thoughts. Leaving the window, she returned to her desk. As the students filed into the room, she sat down and opened a book.

Today they would read and discuss the Agricultral Chemist George Washington Carver who discovered a hundred uses for the peanut, soybean, pecan, and sweet potato. In fact, she planned to tell her students how Mr. Carver made it possible for them to enjoy that peanut butter sandwich some had just eaten during the noon hour.

# CHAPTER 41

In late spring, school ended, and those children who were destined to work in the fields did so. However, Makela and Koko were two very fortunate and happy little girls.

Weekends were especially fun because the youngsters gathered at the big house and played games in the yard. They had no cares or worries. This was their world, and they never expected it to change. But change did come at a time when the girls were happiest.

Late one evening the family was sitting on the porch when Tamara came to the house and she and Natalie began talking about their plans to visit Elizabeth.

Makela, who was sitting in the swing between Natalie and Koko, instantly protested.

"But I don't want to go, Mama," she whined.

"It's only a visit, Makela, and I'm sure you'll enjoy it."

"Sounds like a good idea," Marcus said. "It will be educational for you."

"I don't care, Grandpa. I want to stay with Gramma and Koko," Makela said looking to Odessa for help, but Odessa simply smiled. "Tell her not to go, Gramma."

"Now, now, Makela, it's not that bad. It's just a visit, hon. You'll be back in no time. So stop making a fuss."

"Geez, Makela. You're lucky. You'll ride the trains for several days, and see things you never saw before. Why, you'll even see the Pacific Ocean," Sophia shrieked. "I wish I could go."

"I don't care about the Pacific Ocean."

"Don't act ugly, Makela. You're an intelligent little girl. So act it," Marcus said. "You're about to embark on an adventure. You'll have something to tell me when you come back."

"He's right," Percy jumped in. "Take it in stride, my dear. Enjoy life. Everything's gonna be just fine."

"But everything is already fine, Uncle Percy, I'm happy here."

"We know that, Makela, but Nat needs to get away for a while," Helene told her.

"Can Koko come too, Mama?" Makela asked accepting the fact that she would take a trip she didn't want. But she hoped Natalie would say Koko could come with them. Then her stomach would feel much better.

"I'm afraid not, Makela."

"Oh, Mama," she said suddenly feeling like she would throw up her dinner.

"You know what that means, Koko?" Queenie asked. "That means you'll have Gramma and Grandy all to yourself until Makela and Nat come back."

"But what if they don't come back?" Koko asked.

"Oh, but they will," Sophia chimed.

"I don't believe you. Nothing will ever be the same again," Koko whimpered. As tears rolled down her face, her whole body ached. She never felt this way before. Makela was like a sister to her. She didn't want Makela to leave, not even for two weeks.

"I never thought I'd live to see you cry," Marcus teased. "Guess you're not so tough after all."

"Don't josh her, Marcus. The tyke's heartbroken," Odessa said.

"Of course, she is. But she's usually as tough as leather," Marcus replied.

"Don't worry, Koko. Makela is leaving, but Queenie and Sophia will be right here. You still have family here," Helene told her.

"Please, let Koko come with us, Mama," Makela pleaded.

"I can't," Natalie said making Makela feel even worse. In addition to her stomach ache, her head started to pound, too. She began to cry.

"I want to go, Nat," Koko cried. "Please don't leave me. Take me with you."

"Stop it, Koko," Conrad spoke sternly. "She can't take you. And, as for you Makela, you're going with your mama. So stop your whining."

Soon after he spoke the two girls left the porch, went into the house, and prepared for bed. Though Natalie had made ice cream, neither girl had an appetite for the delicious treat that night.

"Where do you think you're going?" Helene asked as Queenie and Sophia walked into the yard.

"Up the street," Sophia replied without hesitation.

"I think it's best if you go straight home," Helene said. "We'll be there shortly."

"Okay, Mama," Queenie said as they neared the gate. "We'll do that."

"Those girls are growing up, Helene. You can't keep them in jail, you know," Maude said.

"I know that, Mother. But I sure can try," Helene laughed.

"We just want the best for them, Mother," Percy said. "Don't want them to get into any kind of trouble."

"I know that, son," Maude said.

"In fact, I think I'll get out of here. I need to see what's happening around town anyway," Percy said as he walked to the door.

"Ain't a damn thing happening," Conrad said. "You know how fast news travel around here. Doc Peterson didn't even get a new patient today."

"You got that right," Marcus chuckled.

"I hate to see Makela and Koko take the separation so hard," Tamara said changing the subject. "Perhaps we should take Koko with us. I'm sure Liz wouldn't mind."

"You know me, Tam. I'd never do that without first discussing it with Liz."

"I know, Nat. I just hate to see them cry so much. I still remember how much it hurt when Georgia Mae died. And when Liz left us it felt like she died, too. Shoot, we were teens and you know how we carried on. Remember?"

"Yes, I do," Natalie said as she once again felt Georgia Mae's presence.

"Now Tam, don't you start, too," Conrad said. "Makela and Koko will get over it. They're children. Anyway, you'll be away for only two weeks. Believe me. They'll live."

"I guess you're right," Tamara said.

"From what I hear," Maude interjected. "Alan plans to come later in the summer and take Koko back with him."

"That's wonderful," Tamara said.

"I never heard that before," Natalie said looking at Odessa. "You never told me, Mama."

"I know. I didn't want to get Koko's hopes up for something that may never happen. You see how the girls reacted to this two-week trip. If Makela knew Koko might leave for good there's no telling how it might affect her," Odessa explained.

"I see," Natalie said as the wheels in her head began to spin.

"You're right about Makela. That child feels everything deep in her little soul," Maude said.

"That's for sure. Well, I'd better get going. I gotta go to work," Tamara said. "Hey, why don't you come over tonight, Nat?"

"Thanks, but I think I better stay with the girls."

"Okay, I'll see you later then."

"Night Tam, see you tomorrow," the family said in unison.

"Wait up, Tam, I'll walk with you. It's time I got going, too," said Helene.

"As you know, Liz, Tam and I were very close when we were young," Natalie later explained to the girls as she sat on the edge of the bed. "Then Liz went away."

"Did you hurt when she left, Mama?"

"Yes, I did. I was sick for days. I felt so lonely I thought I would die. It took time to get over it, but I did. Then I got on with my life. Now, I want you to understand this, Koko. Tam and I plan to visit Liz, but should we decide to stay, I'll send for you. How would you like that?"

"Oh Nat, you promise?" Koko asked excitedly.

"I promise."

Youngsters knew Makela would be taking a trip, so they came to spend time with her and Koko.

As they played about the yard, Shelton sat on the bench beside Natalie under the elm and studied her face. "I don't want you to go away," he scowled.

"I don't know why. You don't need me. You have Melanie. Anyway, I promised Liz I'd visit, and I plan to keep my word. Perhaps we can talk when I come back."

"I don't believe you're coming back."

"What makes you think that?"

"I got my reasons," he said thinking he had really screwed up this time and Nat might never forgive him. "But if you come back home, I promise to be a better person."

"You've made promises in the past. As of now, I'm in no mood to discuss it. I never expected you would ever do what you did to me. You hurt me terribly. I simply can't trust you anymore."

"Jesus! What do you want me to do, Nat?"

"Nothing," she answered softly without a quaver. "It's over, Shel. Now, leave me alone and go on back to Melanie."

She stood and strolled across the yard. It wasn't until she went into the house that Shelton realized Natalie, who once had it bad for him, didn't want him anymore. No woman had ever left him before, and for the first time in his life he felt the pain of rejection, the sense of feeling unworthy.

He stood, but his legs felt like rubber. Afraid he would fall if he tried to walk, he sat down again.

While the other children played noisily, Makela came and sat beside him. Her eyes were sad, and he quickly put his arm around her shoulders. They sat like that for some time and listened to the rustle of the leaves in the evening breeze.

After a few moments passed, she left him to join the other youngsters again, but he stayed under the tree. Only when he was sure his legs would carry him, did he get up and slowly walk from the yard.

🍁   🍁   🍁

A week later, Natalie, Tamara, and Makela said goodbye to family and friends. Makela and Koko cried. As the train pulled from the station, Makela stood at the window and waved until she could no longer see family or the town she loved.

"Come on, Makela," Tamara coaxed. "Sit beside me and look out the window."

"I don't want to. I want to stay with Koko and Gramma."

"I know you do," Natalie said. Then Natalie pulled Makela from the window onto the seat beside her, and wiped Makela's eyes.

"I don't know why we couldn't bring Koko," she lamented. "I don't want to live without her, Mama."

"I don't think you'll have to, Makela. We'll return home in two weeks," Natalie said as she wondered if that was true. Her mother said Alan was making plans to send for Koko. That wasn't something she wanted to tell Makela now. After all, Natalie wasn't sure what she might do.

Soon Makela became quiet, curled up, and fell asleep. Looking over at Tamara, Natalie smiled. Tamara actually wore a pair of sandals on her feet, and slept as soundly as Makela.

As Natalie stared out the window into the darkness, the clickety-clack of the steel wheels was calming. She thought of Elizabeth and how wonderful it would be to see her again.

At the same time, she thought of her friend Georgia Mae and shivered. She quickly pushed Georgia Mae back to that special place in her heart. Looking down at Makela, she pulled the small blanket around her shoulders and thought about the family she left behind.

Though she tried not to show it, she already missed everyone. Even though the trip would be short, leaving her family affected her as deeply as it did Makela.

Resting her head on the back of the seat, Natalie closed her eyes and remembered the past years and the life she lived with Shelton.

She often criticized others for resolving their problems by resorting to violent acts. She never thought it would happen to her. Now, she realized there are times when one has no choice but to defend one's self.

The night she and Shelton fought, she was so afraid he'd lost his mind and would kill her. Therefore, she did the only thing she could. She pulled the trigger.

What was so sad about the whole situation was she still loved Shelton. But Shelton had a problem which only Shelton could solve. So she would never go back to him.

As of now she looked to the future and would always protect not only herself, but also her child from unhealthy elements. Then pondering, she wondered how long it would take to heal.

# CHAPTER 42

When the Reverend McCord left Meadowsbrook, he went to Chicago in search of Bonita Hernandez. Bonita, however, had returned to her home—Harlem, New York.

In the meantime, the Reverend Sylvester Paxton's church was in turmoil. After some sincere deacons and sisters heard rumors about prostitution, they investigated. Finding the rumors to be true, they immediately gave the boot to the Reverend Paxton, and his friend, Brother Slick Joyride. Then the brothers and sisters told Sylvester and Slick to get out of town.

"Where you going, Syl?" Slick asked.

"Think I'll try California," Sylvester replied. Winking, he said, "Might be good pickings out that way. What about you?"

"That sounds like a winner. Think I'll give it a try, too," Slick shot back and both hopped in their respective cars and drove across country.

The congregation then invited the Reverend McCord to take over the pulpit, and he did so gladly. But realized something was missing. He needed a woman at his side. He had thought Tamara was that woman. She was not, and he hadn't treated Bonita right. When Tamara walked out of his life, he knew he got what he deserved.

Bonita was going to have his baby, but he'd treated her despicably. Now, he regretted it. Even though Bonita had cut his face, he knew she'd lost her temper because he'd pushed her to the edge. He wanted to talk to her. He wanted to tell her he was sorry.

He called, shocking Bonita. They talked. Taking a train to Harlem, he paid Bonita a surprise visit.

As she opened the door, he took her in his arms and held her for a while. "Oh, Bonita," he said. "I'm so sorry for my actions. Please let me make it up to you."

"I thought I'd never see you again," Bonita said. Bewildered, her arms hung limp at her sides.

"I know. But I've done a lot of thinking, and I want to marry you."

Bonita was stunned. Was this a dream, she wondered? These were the words she'd wanted to hear him say when she went to Meadowsbrook.

"What about that woman, Tamara?" she asked.

"That's over, Bonita. Will you marry me?" he asked.

"Yes. Of course, I'll marry you," she said. Deciding this was not the time to be coy, she threw her arms around his neck, and laid her head on his chest. "Would you like to come inside?" she asked. Then they walked hand in hand down the hallway to the living room.

The Reverend McCord met Bonita's mother and the three of them talked for hours. Several days later, The Reverend did exactly what he was supposed to do. He married Bonita right there in her living room. They both were happy.

❦ ❦ ❦

Back in Meadowsbrook, Virgil came from behind the counter and stood in the doorway. One of the old men said something to him, but he paid little attention, as he was in deep thought. He not only missed Koko, he missed that little Makela, too.

He still remembered the day Nat came into the store and took Koko away. He had planned to talk to Nat about Koko, but he never got the chance.

It was close to a hundred degrees in the shade that day, but Nat came in smelling like a rose and as unruffled as a daisy in the morning dew. Virgil had to admit he dreamed about climbing in her bed. But so did every man in town. He was sure Nat was aware of it. But she loved that no good son-of-a-bitch, Shelton.

Nat talked with Koko and there was something in Nat's eyes that day. He couldn't explain it. She never came to see Koko before, but there she was wrapped up in the child. He wondered if Nat had read his mind. She came through the door with one little girl and breezed out with two.

She was in a class all by herself. He had to respect her. After all, Shel had been sweet on Lydia, and Koko was Lydia's child. Family life had always been a mixed bag in their town.

No one knew for sure who Koko's daddy was, but obviously Alan Dawson didn't care. One could only respect a man like that.

Nat and Tam went to visit Liz for two weeks and stayed. Alan and Paige later returned for a visit. They took the car he'd left with his family some time ago and took Koko, too. Now they were all living out in California. But what could he say? He wasn't Koko's daddy. She was a Dawson.

Returning to the present, Virgil sighed. As he turned to leave the doorway, one of the old men interrupted his thoughts and asked what he presumed was a senseless question. He wasn't sure. He simply nodded by reflex, and hoped he hadn't given away the store.

Pulling on the horse's reins, Thaddeus Lamont sat in the saddle, and looked at the lonely house for some time before guiding his horse over to the rail under the pear tree. Dismounting, he hobbled to the back of the house and onto the porch. Then he sat down in the old rocking chair where he'd sat so many times in the past. He reminisced. Makela was his only grandchild. Visiting with her and Nat had been an enjoyment he'd always looked forward to. He hoped Nat would come back soon. He was still mad with Shel for his actions. Suddenly, Thaddeus felt lonely and sad. He wanted to cry. And he did.

Sitting on the bench under the big elm tree in her back yard, Odessa enjoyed the late spring breeze rippling through the leaves as she thought of Natalie. She missed her daughter, but it wasn't something she often discussed with family. She missed Koko and Makela, too. Though Natalie called and wrote often, Odessa's heart was heavy.

"Hey, Odessa," Helene yelled as she came into the yard.

"Hey, Helene. Come on in and sit a while," Odessa said tapping a spot on the bench beside her.

"Where's Mother?" Helene asked referring to Maude as she sat down.

"She just went inside. She wanted to rest a while."

"I suppose getting that letter from Russell after all these years, knocked the wind out of her," Helene said speaking of Marcus and Percy's older brother who left home long ago and was passing for white.

"Ah, come on, Helene. Who you razzing? It knocked the wind out of all of us. Now you tell me something different."

"Yeah, you're right. Do you believe he's coming home?" Helene asked as both women looked at one another.

"I don't know. Did you ever think about doing it, Helene? You could, you know." Odessa waited for an answer. "I know, but that kind of freedom isn't worth the sacrifice. I love the closeness we share as family too much. Do you think he's really coming home?" Helene asked again.

"I don't know. But Marcus and Percy hope so."

"Yeah, I know they're *hoping*," Helene said. "Heard from Nat lately?"

"Talked with her this morning. She sends her love, you know."

"And I send her mine. How're they doing out there?"

"Just fine it seems. She's doing what she likes best. She's working in a tailor's shop. And Tam's finally signed some sort of contract to make records."

"That sounds great. But I still want them to come back here. Did you tell Nat about Russell?"

"I did," Odessa said.

"What did she say? Is she coming home?" Helene asked.

"She was surprised to know we heard from him. Said they're coming home. Don't want to miss her Uncle Russell's homecoming.

"Did you tell Alan, yet?"

"Not yet. Nat said she'd call him. And Paige called last week. They're coming back to visit this summer, too."

"Well, that's enough news to perk us all up," Helene chuckled. "I hope Nat keeps her word. Lordy, I really miss them. It's too quiet around here without Koko and Makela. It would be good to see all of them. I wish they'd *all* come home to stay."

"I know you do. So do I," Odessa said. Though Natalie had not promised to stay in Meadowsbrook, Odessa hoped she would.

"How're the girls doing in the store?" Odessa asked referring to Queenie and Sophia.

"Well, let's just say they're in there. And I must be out of my mind to leave them alone."

"Umhum. Guess that means you won't be staying here very long."

"You got that right," Helene laughed. Then after a pause, she said, "You know my girls are growing up so fast it makes my head spin."

"I know. And Meadowsbrook is changing. Streets are being paved and given names. They're putting in sidewalks, we're getting numbers on our houses, and the bank building will soon be finished."

"That's for sure. Kind of exciting, isn't it?" Helene spoke as she stood.

"It sure is. Town's growing by leaps and bounds. Leaving so soon?" Odessa asked.

"I guess I better if I don't want Sophia to give away the store. You want to come with me?"

"Thanks for asking, but I think I'll sit here a while longer. Then I'll go in and cook my dinner."

"Good. You do that and we'll come by later and help you eat it."

"Okay, I'll look forward to that," Odessa said smilingly.

"By the way, have you seen Shel since Nat left?" Helene asked.

"No, I haven't. Don't think the menfolk want him around here just yet," Odessa replied.

"I know what you mean. I sometimes wonder if he's sorry for what he did. You know Nat, Odessa. Regardless what happened between them, she never lost her civility. I don't know if I could be so strong. Shel broke her heart many times before she pulled that trigger."

"Yes, indeedy, he sure did," Odessa said. "I never had that kind of love for anybody."

"I never did, and I never will," Helene said. The two women stared at one another in silence until Helene cleared her throat and spoke. "You know how Percy is. He talks about what happened as if it were yesterday. He still wishes he could put Shel in jail."

"I know, but I hope we'll soon heal and move on."

"Me, too," Helene said as she neared the gate. "I'll see you later." Turning, she waved. Then she walked out the gate and onto the street.

Closing her eyes, Odessa remembered the first time she came to Meadowsbrook. At the time she saw very little beauty about the place. But now she had grown to love it, and beauty was everywhere because improvements were being made and everything was in bloom.

Sniffing the air, a mixture of fragrances tickled her nose, and she felt blessed that she enjoyed so much of life.

🍁   🍁   🍁

Shelton parked the car in the front yard and went into his house. For a moment, he stood in the center of the floor as the silence engulfed him. He missed his family.

Natalie had done what he suspected she might do. She and Tamara went to San Francisco to see Elizabeth. They never came back. Alan lived on the west coast too, and now that he had come and taken Koko back with him, Shelton didn't expect Natalie to ever come back.

She wrote her mother often, but she didn't send him so much as a note.

Suddenly, Shelton did what he was compelled to do every day since Natalie left. He went to the closet and peeked inside and stared at the coat which caused so much trouble.

He first offered the coat to his mother, Esther, but she refused it. "What can I do with it?" she asked. "I seldom leave the house."

"It's beautiful, Shel," Jozell said when he offered it to her. But she did nothing to spare his feelings.

"I don't want it. It would only remind me how much you hurt Nat. I can't accept it. Now you take that coat and do what Nat told you to do."

After that, he got the bright idea that someone in the Dawson family might want it. But he quickly abandoned that thought since he didn't want another bullet.

He read the note Natalie pinned to the coat again, and it infuriated him. He suddenly wanted to strike out at somebody, but he was alone. So he kicked the wall. Full of fury, he snatched the coat off the hanger, got back in the car, and drove into town.

When he arrived at Melanie's house, he was still pissed off. Mindful that Melanie still lived at home with her parents, Jenny and Spuds, Shelton knocked lightly on the door. When Melanie opened it, she was all smiles.

"Hi, Shel," she greeted "It's good to see you."

Looking around, Shelton hesitated before stepping cautiously into the front room. "You alone?" he asked.

"Yes, I am," she said confident he had come to pop the question she'd waited so long to hear. "Why do you ask?"

"I'm asking because I came to give you another coat."

"I don't want it," Melanie shrieked when he thrust the coat at her. "It belongs to Nat."

"Not anymore. Read the note. Nat wants you to have it," he yelled causing Melanie to whimper. "So don't tell me you don't want it. And stop that sniffling 'cause it's all your fault. You fucked up. None of this shit would've happened if you had done what I told you to. But you're too goddamn thick to follow instructions. You had to wear that coat," he said even though he knew the real blame lay at his feet.

"I said I don't want it," Melanie said again just as his hand connected with her face. Reeling from the blow, she was shocked. Shelton said he loved her and had never hit her. As he slapped the other side of her face, she stumbled back and cried out. He caught her and put his hand over her mouth. She tried to speak, but found it impossible.

"Shut up," he hissed. "If you open your mouth again I'll push my fist in it. Do you hear me?"

Melanie moved her head to indicate she understood. And at the same time, in a flash, she wondered if the time had come for her to pack her bags, take the northbound train, and look for her friend, Bonita.

He let her go and walked to the door. Just as he reached for the doorknob, he turned and spoke. "I'm sorry I ever laid eyes on them fucking furs." He wanted to punch Melanie again, but he realized he'd done enough. His temper had already caused too much damage. He'd lost his family.

Instead, he clenched his fist tightly and just before he opened the door to leave the house, he punched the wall. Once in the car, he stared at his bleeding knuckles, and wondered if the day would soon come when he hated Melanie as much as he hated them goddamn coats.

There were only two people in town who knew the reason Neva chased Lydia. One was Shelton Lamont who *couldn't* talk about it. The other was Della Gilliam who knew she *wouldn't* talk about it for fear of Shelton.

It happened one day soon after Billy and Neva got married. Shelton stopped by to see Billy, but Billy had gone to Baysville on business.

Standing at the screen door, Shelton knocked. Neva came to the door.

"Where's Billy?" he asked.

"He's in Baysville on business. Why don't you come in and have a drink?" she asked.

"Thanks, but I'll come back later," Shelton said.

"What's the hurry?" Neva asked. "Come on in and have a drink with me."

"I got no time to have a drink with you, Neva," he said.

"Ah, come on in, Shel. I won't bite you," She laughed.

The sensible part of himself told him to go home while the whorish part accepted her invitation. He went inside, she poured the drinks, and they sat on the sofa. She on one end and he on the other. After only a couple of rounds, Neva moved closer to him. Rubbing him lightly between his legs, and gazing into his eyes, she let him know what she wanted.

A little voice warned he was treading in dangerous waters. Remember, this is your best friend's wife. But he didn't listen to the warnings. He was aroused. His brains were in his pants.

"What time's Billy coming back?" he asked.

"He just left," Neva grinned slyly. "So he'll be gone a while." Leaving the sofa, she went over, closed the front door, and locked it. As she approached the sofa again, he stood up, grabbed her hand, and led her to the bedroom.

"Hurry up. Pull off them drawers," he said as he unbuttoned his pants and pulled down his own drawers around his ankles. Then pushing her back on the bed, he quickly plunged into her.

"Is this what you want?" he asked as he pumped deep into her. "Is this what you been waiting for?"

"Oh, yes, Shel. It's what I want," she whispered. "Lawdy," she cried.

"Good. Cause I'm gonna give you every inch of it, baby."

"I love you, Shel," she told him as she cried out in ecstacy.

"You can't do that baby. I'm married, and you're married to Billy," he told her. As she lay still panting, the realization of what he had done hit him. He'd fucked his best friend's wife in his best friend's bed. "I need to clean up. I gotta get home," he said standing and looking down at his drawers and pants still at his feet.

It was something he tried to forget. He even told Neva he never wanted it to happen again, but Neva never forgot, and because she couldn't have him, she went over the edge.

There was a gnawing ache in his gut he couldn't get rid of. Spiritually, he knew he'd done something wrong. It was his secret. It was his burden.

Suddenly, he was overwhelmed, and for the first time he was in sheer pain for his past actions and for the loss of his family. He wanted Natalie and he missed Makela. He tried to hold back the tears, but could not. Lowering his head, he wept.

There are choices in life, and one must decide which path to take. Many inhabitants of Meadowsbrook took the low road and never learned to live differently, which caused much tragedy along the way.

Life is like a well full of water. It can be cool and refreshing. If we drink slowly, we can enjoy each drop. Love of family and friends is a gift which comes from the heart, but all too often that gift is abused by loved ones.

When we learn that love which was once so abundant is forever lost, we yearn for it like we thirst for water after the well has gone dry.

## The End

978-0-595-36079-6
0-595-36079-3

Printed in the United States
50152LVS00003B/70-165